Dear Reader,

FalconClaw – The Sleep Room is a crime drama, psychological/paranormal thriller that will keep you up at night and have you guessing what's going to happen next.

With the rugged North Philadelphia area as the backdrop, you get to walk in the footsteps of Philadelphia Police Detectives Frank Collazo and Penelope Bristow as they track down the most notorious serial killer in the history of the City of Philadelphia.

This story incorporates both real-life and fictional situations and people whose stories must be told. While the ending to some real-life characters and situations has been fictionalized for dramatic effect.

I hope you fall in love with these characters and are thrilled with all of the twists and turns that this fast-paced drama brings you. It will keep you turning the pages and questioning everything. Enjoy!

Happy Reading,

Praise for the FalconClaw Detective Series

Sequel to Old Man Winter but a stand-alone mystery in itself – Couldn't put it down

This is a stand-alone book that is an excellent and breathtaking mystery that was hard to put down. The last part of the book is a non-stop page-turner. I had read the prior book, which was also excellent, and though some earlier things are resolved, it is not absolutely required to read the prior book though I would recommend it. The book is set in actual locations in Philadelphia and there are even pictures included. The story revolves around two police detectives who encounter a serial killer who focuses his evil intent on his pursuers, and it becomes a life-and-death struggle to the bitter end. This is one book you won't regret reading.

Rose

Wow!

I just finished book two of the FalconClaw detective series and trust me, this one could be a stand-alone. As good as Old Man Winter but different. The modern day Frank and Penny are as powerful of characters as the originals. Set in North Philly 2016-17 the drama is real! The Schuylkiller is dastardly and cunning and Frank, and Penny are having a hard time figuring it all out. The end is traumatic but satisfying. I cannot wait for the next installment. Wow! Just Wow!

Joshila B.

Incredible follow-up to Old Man Winter

In this book you follow the modern day frank and penny as they hunt down a serial killer that is terrorizing north Philly. Along the way, you get pulled into the investigation which results in a very satisfying ending. The author states this is a series, I cannot wait to see what the third installment has to hold! Suspenseful, thrilling and satisfying, I have been a fan of every book from Michael Cook, and I cannot wait to see what else he has in store for us!

Lane

Outstanding – Couldn't put it down.

I thought the author's first three books were exceptional efforts, but this new book surpasses them. I'm incredibly impressed with how he first wrote two excellent sci-fi books, then followed them up with murder mystery books. If you are looking for a book that will give you the creeps, then look no further, this is in. Chapter twelve left me stunned with the realism brought to the words. This guy can write in a way that makes you feel the story. Give his books a chance, and I assure you that you will have found a new author to add to your favorites list.

Amazon Customer

Murder/Mystery with a Spiritual Epiphany

Time waits for no one. FalconClaw however takes you thru a roller coaster ride of who done it and who did it historical, somewhat fact based fiction. Credits at the end of the book speak volumes to the authors dedication to articulating a story with reverence and authentic vision. This reader looks forward to more adventures of Frank & Penny.

Doug

Amazing Read 10/10

What a fantastic read! Putting the book down was impossible and I was kept on the edge of my seat the entire time. I love the way that the characters are haunted by their pasts and familial relationships. The book was very emotional and heart wrenching. Loved it.

Katie Foodman

Really Good Book!!!

This book was just as good as, OMW!!! The characters were people I would hang out with!!! Except for the killer!!! I loved the way Old Man Winter made a visit to Falcon Claw again!!! I also loved the part of the story about the problems women have in the work place!!!

Sunset6339

Acknowledgments:

Thank you for letting me share this work of fiction that ties in some actual historical events and places. The story of FalconClaw – The Sleep Room is the sequel to Old Man Winter – Heavenly Gates

I'd like to thank my wife and children: Kristin, Aubrey Carin, Lola Kristine, Maggie Mae, and Carrick Michael, for helping me to breathe life into the characters that you're about to meet. I'd also like to thank my beta-readers and editors, Maribeth Pickens, Vern Preston, Karen Cook, and Bob Nielsen, and Andy Kastelik. All of these wonderful friends and family members were all so supportive in my journey, and without them, this book doesn't get written.

To my best friend and business partner, Piyush Bhula, thanks for always being there at every turn. And finally, to Jeremy Ledbetter, for always being there and for his wonderful cover design work.

I'd like to make a special shout out to my new friend, Bonnie Ross. Bonnie was there from the literal beginning of the Old Man Winter series as she hung out with the woman who inspired the powerful female lead in book one, Penelope Brace. Thanks for showing me around the mean streets of Philly and thanks for always making women's rights top of mind and fighting the good fight.

Fine Print:

www.OldManWinterNovel.com

"Walls covered with tear-filled cracks
What stories could they tell?
The pain that lies within this room
Could make sick a man who's well"

Michael Cook is a published poet, author, and accomplished business professional and entrepreneur. Michael is also the owner of the #7 Escape Room experience in the World, Odyssey Escape Game, located in Alpharetta, GA, and Schaumburg, IL.

A resident of Suwanee, GA. Michael is a father of four children, a husband, a brother, and a friend.

FalconClaw
THE SLEEP ROOM

A novel by Michael Cook

© 2021

Prologue – Monsters Create Monsters

North Philadelphia – Friday, January 20, 2017, 8:03 pm.

The smell of winter was thick in North Philly as Frank Collazo took it in through flared nostrils, nostrils that looked more angry than curious. His window was cracked open a little, and he leaned in toward it. He was looking for the precious air that might tame his anxiety but was unable to find it. Not in that moment, that day, or that week. Frank's psyche was ravaged by his circumstances, and his face showed it.

"It's a little chilly in here, Frank. You want to roll up that window there, buddy?"

"Monsters create monsters, Penny. I keep telling you that." Frank exhaled fully. "But you keep giving people the benefit of the doubt," he said as his partner sat quietly in the passenger seat.

"Yeah, yeah," said Penny, staring out of her window.

Moments later, the city-issued, unmarked Dodge Charger pulled over on a dark corner, and Penny got out. Frank rolled down the window for parting words when Penny leaned in and said, "Let me tell you something, Frankie. I choose to keep on believing, and you should, too. That hate's gonna eat you up, boy."

"Sure, whatever, Penny," Frank was dismissive.

Before the window went back up, Penny said, "Anyways, get home safe, Partner. Wherever home is these days?" she smirked.

"Oh, yeah? Well, you need to get you and your mom out of that tinder box!" Frank yelled back. "That place is one match away from going up in smoke!"

"Frank, this place has been here since I was a little girl," yelled Penny, "and it ain't going nowhere. And neither is my mom! See you Monday, Frankie boy!"

Penny gave Frank one last look and smiled before disappearing into a stairwell that led up to a one-bedroom apartment. The place she shared with her mother sat benignly above an old fabric store. The store had been owned and operated by a woman who'd lived just behind it and had been in business since 1988.

As Frank drove off, he'd reasoned that Penny thought most people were good and kind but knew very well what the City of Philadelphia's dark side had to offer. "How could she not," he said aloud, "with the scum we deal with every day?"

Frank had just dropped off his partner, fellow Homicide Detective Penny Bristow, at her mother's apartment above Fabrics linen store. The tiny store sat on the less than modest corner of West Coulter and Germantown Avenue in Penn-Knox, Germantown's Northside. To its left sat the historic St. Luke's Episcopal Church, built in 1811.

Since her divorce from her abusive ex-husband, Dan, Penny had been staying with her mom, Bonnie. It'd been a little more than six months since Penny's separation.

Bonnie Ross, a long-retired nurse with Philadelphia's American Red Cross, was a vital part of the effort to pass the Equal Rights Amendment back in the early seventies. Penny's father was a cop who died in the line of duty back in 1996 when she was just fourteen years old. He was shot and killed in a shootout with bank robbers who'd been cornered on a dead-end street in Rhawnhurst. Her mother never remarried, and Frank was sure that Penny wouldn't either. *"Not after what her ex had put her through"*, he thought.

"That guy's lucky I never got involved. He wouldn't have lasted thirty seconds with me," Frank mumbled to himself as he revved his engine and turned onto E. Chelten, heading west over to Manayunk.

The road was slick but without curves, allowing Frank to negotiate the North Philly grid in the dead of another miserable winter. The clapping of the wiper blades on the Dodge Charger helped to drown out the noise in his head. Like Penny, Frank, too, was working through the remnants of a failed marriage. He didn't miss his soon-to-be ex-wife but was having trouble only seeing his son on the weekends. The custody battle was raging, but Frank knew he had no chance of winning custody of his little man, Conner. In Frank's line of work, no judge in his right mind would allow a little boy to be put in harm's way.

Detectives had enemies, people they'd put away or were trying to. Frank knew the game and knew that being a cop in the big city had consequences. Consequences of which his wife, Joanne, wanted none of. Consequences that included a bullet through the back of his Dodge Charger while stopped at a gas station at the intersection of Fox Street and West Abbotsford six months earlier. They never caught the person who fired the shot, and It was never determined if the bullet was meant for Frank, or not. For Joanne, though, it was the final straw. A Judge agreed, awarding custody to Joanne pending a jury trial.

Frank had been a detective for the Philly P.D. since 2010, working out of the 39th District in East Falls. He and Penny had been partners for the last three years, and some in the station house whispered that it was their partnership that put an end to each of their marriages, but they were wrong. Frank, a seventeen-year veteran of the department, took on Penny as his partner just after she'd been promoted to the rank of detective. In her thirteenth year on the force, Penny had grown close with her partner.

Sexual tension crept into their relationship from time to time, but Frank never seriously entertained the notion of compromising their working relationship. Working long hours together brought them close. Tip-toeing near it, as recently as Christmas, neither had ever stepped over the line. Even if they had, it'd be hard to blame them. Both were lonely, newly single, and desperately trying to fill a void that could never be filled.

Frank also lost his father, Sal, who was on the job back in 1992 when a serial killer named Vincent Charmaine Walker set a trap for the unsuspecting Salvatore Collazo, a twenty-year man with the Philadelphia P.D.

Like Penny, Frank was just a kid, fourteen, and had no siblings and a mother who'd refused to remarry. Frank, like his partner, had to become a cop. It was the only way he could get revenge on his father's now-deceased killer. 'Get all the other bad guys off the street,' a mantra that he and Penny shared.

Frank Collazo knew that for every monster taken off the streets, two more were waiting in the wings, practicing their craft on rabbits, kittens, and puppies. Waiting until they'd built up their confidence and graduated to killing their ultimate prey, unsuspecting human beings. Regular people, just trying to make sense of the hand that life had dealt them, thinking that things couldn't get any worse, until they did.

Frank and Penny were still trying to figure out what happened to retired detective Frank Bruno in the early morning hours of Christmas Day, 2016, when a well-known socialite and philanthropist, and the daughter of a famous Philadelphia lawyer went missing after attending a New Year's Eve party. Belinda Mereby was last seen getting into a limousine outside of the historic Strawberry Mansion after attending a private, black-tie affair in the early morning hours of New Year's Day.

Just hours after Mereby went missing, the limousine was found partially submerged in the Schuylkill River, a favorite dumping ground for murdered victims and vehicles involved in criminal activity on Philly's northside.

No less than ten bodies a year had been found on the north banks of the Schuylkill since the 1980s. Its polluted water and savage undercurrents seemed to go hand and hand with Philadelphia's dirty underbelly.

Who picked up Belinda Mereby that night, and where was she now? Detectives in the 39th were all brought in on the high-profile case as the city's Mayor, Donovan Taylor, and Mereby's father, Clinton Mereby, were once close associates in a notorious and long-defunct law firm in the 1970s. In the early seventies, the firm was famous for representing the plaintiffs in FalconClaw's MK-Ultra mind-control experiments case. The press and local politicians all had their eyes on the investigation, and anything less than a quick capture and prosecution of the perpetrator would have been unacceptable.

Frank drove around for a while before parking his car down the street from his third-floor, one-bedroom flat above The Mad River Bar & Grill, on the intersection of Main Street & Shurs Lane in Manayunk. He tried hard not to be there, sometimes even sleeping in his car overnight. The tiny apartment reminded Frank of a patient who was in a coma. He knew he was alive but not really living when he was there. When Frank saw his son on the weekends, he never took him there. He didn't want his only child to see what'd become of him. Instead, Frank's wife, Joanne, let him stay with her, not trusting their son to be with Frank outside the house since the shooting incident six months prior. Frank would sleep on the floor next to his son's bed. He'd hold his son's hand until he fell asleep, and most mornings when he awoke, his son would be curled up next to him on the floor.

Frank was a regular guy, just trying to make sense of the hand that life had dealt him, thinking that things couldn't get any worse, until they did.

Chapter 1 – Frank Bruno

Nazareth Catholic Hospital – Christmas Morning 2016, 3:17 am.

Frank Collazo pulled into the parking lot of Nazareth Hospital to find his partner Penny Bristow already there. She was pacing near her car, waiting for her partner's arrival. Three squad cars were parked haphazardly nearby, idling in the blizzard conditions, flashers off.

Frank stepped out of his car as Penny approached and said, "This better be good! It's freezing out tonight, and oh, yeah, it's Christmas!"

Pulling her clenched fists away from her mouth, Penny said, "The call said a possible kidnapping. Some old guy went missing."

Frank looked over Penny's shoulder as a uniformed officer approached.

"Ash, whatta we got?" asked Frank.

"Hey, Frank. Hey Penny. Why'd they send Homicide?" asked Officer Ali Ashfaq, rubbing his hands together, trying to stay warm.

"Because we were on-call when it came in."

"Well, glad to see us uniformed boys aren't the only ones working on Christmas morning."

"So, Ash," Frank rubbed his hands together. "I heard you were on-scene on West Pacific where that ten-year-old little boy accidentally shot himself. Is that right? That had to be rough, huh?"

"Yeah, it was an all-around messed up situation. The kid was home alone with his sister and found the gun in a kitchen cabinet," Ash explained. "It was a real mess."

"Yeah, that is tough." Penny looked over at her partner, knowing that his son was also ten years old.

"All right. So, whatta we looking at here?" asked Frank.

"Yeah, so this one's a little strange. The nurse on duty, last name O'Connell, states that a patient went missing out of the window of his room about ninety minutes ago."

"The window?!" Penny was surprised.

"Yeah, you got it, Detective Bristow, the window."

"What floor?" asked Frank.

"The second," said Ashfaq. "Come on. I'll walk you guys in."

As the trio walked toward the front entrance, Frank surveyed the landscape and remarked, "What's up with all the snow, anyway?"

Now inside, Frank and Penny exited the elevators on the second floor and took a left. Passing the Nurse's Station, they saw a shaken O'Connell being consoled by two other nurses as two uniformed officers questioned her. Just down the hall, outside room thirty-eight, a hospital security guard stood watch.

The two Philadelphia police detectives entered the dark, freezing cold room, their frozen breath preceding them. Inside, they saw an empty bed and robe lying on the floor. The room's only window was hung open. Snowflakes fell peacefully through the window and onto the floor, melting into a puddle that reflected the night sky and the falling snow. The bedside heart rate monitor continued to pulse at a relaxed forty beats per minute as its cord dangled to the floor. In the corner of the room, now floating free, a red balloon hung in the air.

Penny pulled back the curtain next to the bed and said, "Well, whatta we have here?"

An old empty bassinette box was on the floor with faded red letters running down the side that read J.C. Penny's. At that moment, both detectives heard the sound of a little boy laughing just outside the window.

Frank, standing closest, looked out the window to investigate. Looking down at the snow, he said, "Hey, Penny, come and take a look at this."

Detective Penny Bristow walked over to where her partner was standing. The two detectives looked out the window and then down at the snow. Both witnessed what appeared to be several sets of footprints leading away from the hospital.

"You see that?" asked Frank.

"See what? The footprints?" asked a sarcastic Penny. "Yeah, I see them. What am I, hard of seeing over here?"

"Ha-ha, wise ass." I count six sets," said Frank.

"Yep, that's what I see."

"Well, we've got a problem," said Frank.

Penny interrupted her partner, "Yeah, the snow's starting to come down again. Those footprints will be gone in a few minutes."

"Whattaya think, three coming, three going?" asked Penny, as she took several pictures using her cell phone.

"That wouldn't make any sense," said Frank. "It'd have to be an odd number if the old man went out this window. Right?"

Penny agreed with a nod.

"It looks to me like they're all leading away from the hospital. Whoever took the old man entered the room through that door and not this window," Frank reasoned.

"Huh," Penny shrugged while looking back at the door. "Let's see what Nurse O'Connell has to say."

Detective Room – 39th District Headquarters – later that morning, 10:37 am.

Frank and Penny were the only two detectives scheduled for the Christmas holiday and were sitting at their desks, writing up their report. Both were in shock after discovering who the missing person was. Seconds later, the door to the second-floor Detective Room flew open, and in walked their District Captain.

"Captain, surprised to see you here." Frank was startled. Jumping from his chair, he was apprehensive with the news he was about to share with his Captain, Rosalyn Sumner, as he hadn't finished writing his report yet.

Sumner, a twenty-three-year veteran of the department, had recently been promoted to Captain of the 39th District after serving as a Captain in the 24th District. Sumner was a hard-nosed Philadelphia cop who was North Philly born and raised and had been with the department since 1989. Her father, Carl D. Sumner II, served 35 years in the department before retiring.

A former First Lieutenant in the United States Army, Sumner was first promoted to the rank of Detective in 1998. She made headlines in 2003 by becoming the department's first black female Lieutenant and then by becoming the first black female Captain in 2008, taking over as the Commanding Officer of the 24th District.

"Surprised?" said Sumner. "So you thought Doug wasn't going to tell me what happened after you texted him earlier this morning? He told me you were coming in to write up the report. Do you have any idea who your missing person is?"

"Yeah," Frank nodded. "It's retired Detective Frank Bruno. We contacted his next of kin, and they filled us in." Frank looked a little pale. "The nurse on duty states that she went to check on him around 1:30 am after she felt a draft in the hallway just outside his room."

"So what else do we know?"

Penny spoke up. "Captain, we entered the room to find his bed empty and the window wide open. Inspecting the ground outside below, we observed six sets of footprints leading away from his second-floor window but none leading up to it. The nurse swears no one entered the room. It's like he was carried away or something."

"What do you make of it, Frank?"

"I'd say we got a mystery on our hands, Captain." Frank's eyes went wide. "The nurse said he wasn't even able to walk. Apparently, he was on his death bed. My question then is, how did he get from the bed to the window? And, the latch locking the window is tough to lock and unlock. I'm not sure former Detective Bruno could have done it alone."

"Do you guys have any idea what that man accomplished in his career?" Sumner asked.

Frank replied, "I know that he's a legend of the department, and that he solved a bunch of cold cases back in the day."

Penny added, "He worked the 39th and solved the 'Boy in the Box' case, right?"

"Yeah, and a bunch of other ones, too," said Sumner. "He worked with my father back in the seventies and eighties."

Sumner looked down and shook her head side to side in confusion. "Who in the hell breaks a dying man out of a hospital in the driving snow on Christmas Day?"

"I never even heard of such a thing," said Frank.

"Do either of you know what happened up at FalconClaw back in 1974?" asked Sumner, looking at Frank and then over to Penny.

Frank was uncomfortable with the question, and Penny noticed.

"I do," said Penny, swallowing hard. "I was named after his partner who went missing that night."

Frank looked at his partner, then to his Captain, then back at Penny, and asked, "Named after who?" He wore a look that conveyed he was left out of the conversation, but not for long. "One of you gonna tell me? Or what?"

Captain Rosalyn Sumner smiled, winked at Penny, and said, "Penny, tell Frank what the 'B' in your middle name stands for?" Sumner already knew the answer to her question and was surprised that Penny hadn't told her partner.

Penny was stoic as she looked over to Frank and said, "Bryce."

Frank looked puzzled for a moment as his brain struggled to make the connection. "Holy shit!" his jaw sagged.

Looking at the half-written report in his hand, he tried to speak before Sumner spoke back up.

"Find out what happened to the old man. We don't need another cold case filling up what used to be called the Penelope Bryce Cold Case Unit storage room," said Sumner. "Don't wait for your Sergeant to get back. I want daily updates. I once met Frank Bruno back in the day. This whole department owes him a debt of gratitude."

"Yeah, sure, Cap. We're meeting with his two daughters tomorrow morning. We'll keep you posted."

"Frank, don't you have a son that needs tending to on Christmas?"

Frank shrugged. "Yeah, but I thought we needed to get on this one right away, seeing who he was and all."

"Well, go see your kid, then," directed Sumner.

"I'm good, Cap. I got him on Christmas Eve and the wife on Christmas Day this year. We've agreed to alternate holidays."

"So, you saw him last night, then, I hope?"

"Yeah, I stayed there until I got the call. Since the shooting, I haven't taken him out much. Luckily, he was sleeping and didn't see me go." Frank was saddened.

"That stuff's tough during the holidays," Sumner was empathetic. "I want that report as soon as it's written up." As Sumner turned to leave, she added, "You two have a good holiday, and thanks for coming in on Christmas."

"Will do, Cap," Frank nodded in affirmation.

"Merry Christmas, Captain," said Penny.

As Sumner began to walk away, Penny added, "Captain, I didn't know that you knew my middle name. Impressive making the connection."

"What can I say? I used to be a detective." Sumner smiled. "Merry Christmas, Penny."

As Captain Rosalyn Sumner turned to leave, she mumbled under her breath, "Frank Bruno, missing on Christmas Day. What in the hell is this world coming to?"

Two hours later, Frank smiled and busted his partner's chops while sitting at a window table at Billy Murphy's Irish Saloon. "So, it's Penelope Bryce, then?"

"Yeah, yeah, yeah. Go ahead, make some jokes, why don't you?"

"No, not sayin it's funny, I just can't believe you never told me, that's all. So what gives?" asked Frank. "We've been partners for three years, and you never told me you were named after Philly's first-ever female detective?"

"Yeah, well. Let's just say I'm not fond of the name Penelope." Penny looked flustered. "My mom is the only person on earth that calls me that."

"So, what's the big deal? I kinda like it."

Penny shook her head. "Well, don't get used to it, Frankie Boy. I won't respond to you if you call me by that name."

"I still don't get it. I like the name. I think it's cute," Frank razzed his partner.

"Yeah, right. Just what a thirty-something, divorced woman wants to be called, cute." Penny rolled her eyes. "My mom always said she thought the name sounded like candy and that I was 'sweet.' Never liked it. Plus, there were like five other girls with the name 'Penelope' in my grade school when I was little."

"Well, you're named after someone famous," said Frank. "That's gotta mean something."

"My mom actually knew her before she went missing," Penny revealed.

"No shit!" Frank reached for his beer. "So she knew her back in the day, huh?"

"The seventies. They were a part of the Philadelphia Political Women's Caucus and would go to women's meetings together before the Equal Rights Amendment went in front of Congress. My mom was a lot younger than her, but Bryce took her under her wing. After their Thursday night meetings, she would take my mom to a 'cops only' bar over by Wayne Junction. Penny Bryce actually introduced my mom to my father," said Penny. "I guess being a cop was what I was supposed to be."

"How old is your mom, anyway?"

"I know, right? She looks great! For that time, she started late. She didn't plan on having any kids until she met my dad. She was thirty-one when she had me in 1982."

Frank did the math in his head. "So that makes her what, sixty-six?"

"So, you can spell, and do math?" Penny smirked. "Now I see what Joanne used to see in you."

"Funny girl, Penelope." Frank shot back. "Don't you have a birthday coming up, too?"

"I'm gonna be thirty-four on April 11. I'm not a 'girl' anymore, sorry to say," Penny sighed. "My mom actually turns sixty-six two days before my birthday on April 9."

"You're still a kid, Penelope. Sweet as candy, too," Frank chuckled, reaching for his Bud Light.

"Like you're an old man, or something? Whattaya forty now?"

"Easy, girlfriend. Those are fighting words. I'll be thirty-eight in June."

Penny sighed again. "We're both still so young. "Me? I'm feeling old as hell, to be honest with you," she said. "I mean, both coming out of failed marriages, you got a ten-year-old kid, and I'll never have one at this rate. I'm washed up, Frank. A real has-been." Penny's jab at herself couldn't hide her truth. She was feeling worthless.

After a few minutes of silence, Mike Murphy walked over with two cheesesteaks and fries. "This one's on me, fellas," he said. "Oops, sorry, Penny. It's Christmas, and you're on the clock keeping the neighborhood safe."

Mike Murphy was the pub's owner and had been since his father Billy died just before New Year's day back in 2011. "Whattaya two doing working on Christmas Day, anyway?"

"Thanks, Murph! Mighty nice of you," said Penny. "But we can ask the same of you."

"I wanted to give Karen the holiday off cuz her mom's not feeling too well, and it's Christmas, you know."

Frank said, "Send her our love, would ya?"

"Will do," said Murph. "So, whatta youse guys doing working today?"

"We're working a case, a kidnapping over at Nazareth Hospital last night."

"Geez, a kidnapping on Christmas Day?! Who was it, a newborn, or something?" Murph shook his head. "The whole place is going to hell!"

"No, an old man, believe it or not," said Frank. "And, yeah, Murph, it's all going to hell." Frank looked out the window and thought of his son, Conner.

"Well, I'll let you two get to eatin, then," said Murph. "Give me a yell if you need a refill on those brews."

After more silence and rearranging her fries, Penny said, "I also hate being named after someone else. It's like you have to live up to what that person did or accomplished. It makes you feel like you're a loser, a failure. You know what I mean, Frank?"

"Penny, my name is Frank. Do you have any idea how many 'Franks' are in my family? In this city?"

Penny arched a brow. "So, you were named after someone?"

"Can't say for sure, but it's likely." Frank wiped the beer foam from his three-day-old, unshaven scruff under his nose. "That's why I named my son Conner. I didn't want another Frank Collazo walking around with a stereotypical Italian name."

Penny shook her head in agreement. "I like it. He's a cute kid."

She paused and asked, "Why do parents do that to a kid, anyway? I want my own identity. I want to write my own story, not be the continuation of somebody else's."

"I'll toast to that!" Frank raised his bottle and tapped Penny's.

Two hours and four beers later, it was time to go. "Listen, Penny, I'll wrap up the report and get it to Sarge and the captain," offered Frank. "I'll take you back to your mom's. It is Christmas, after all. You have somewhere to go, but I don't. I'll just call you with questions."

"You sure, Frankie?" Penny's face showed her appreciation. "You trying to steal my heart, or something?"

"Call it a Christmas gift. And, I ain't no rebound if that's what you're asking!" Frank shook his head and sighed. "The alcohol must be gettin' to you, plus, you ain't my type," Frank chuckled. Now standing, he threw two twenties on the table and reached for his coat.

"Yeah, yeah, I seen you're type, Frankie Boy. Joanne's got nothin' on me." Penny's feelings were mildly hurt as she shrugged off Frank's insult.

"I didn't mean nothin' by it," Frank caught himself. "Just sayin, we make better partners in crime than in the sack."

Penny smiled and flirted, "Well, you clearly ain't never seen me in the sack!"

"Easy partner, don't let the beer get you into trouble, now."

"Yeah, you're right, Frankie. Partners in crime is definitely the way to go for us washed-up Philly cops."

After an uncomfortable, conversation-free ten-minute ride to Penny's, Frank parked the unmarked car in front of the fabric store and said, "Okay, I'll call you if I have any questions."

Penny nodded, and without a word, got out of the car. As she was about to shut the door, she leaned back in. "Hey, Frankie, it's Christmas, and my mom's got a ham in the oven," said Penny. "Why don't you finish the report and come back here for dinner? My mom would love to see you again."

Frank purposely paused before responding, "Yeah? You think that would be all right with her?"

"Yeah, Frankie. It'd be okay with me, too." Penny flashed a modest smile. "Dinner's at seven! Don't be late!" Penny slammed the car door and walked toward the stairwell entrance next to the door to Fabrics.

Frank rolled down the window and yelled, "Wait! What's the apartment number?"

"2C," Penny yelled back, smiling. "See you later!"

A smiling Frank waited a second before pulling away. He wanted to see if Penny looked back. She didn't.

After his smile subsided, Frank strangely felt sad and lonely. He liked Penny but needed to step back from the line he'd drawn between him and his partner. He lied to Penny earlier when he said she wasn't his type. She was, but his life's goal was to get the bad guys, and being a good cop without scandal or conflict on the job was the only way he planned to do it. He'd honor his father by only having dinner with Penny, and nothing more.

What Frank didn't tell Penny earlier was that his father was lured to FalconClaw by his killer, Vincent Charmaine Walker. Tonight was the night he'd finally tell her the story of what happened on Halloween back in 1992.

Chapter 2 – Trick or Treat

Bonnie Ross insisted that she'd clean the dinner mess so that Frank and her daughter could just put their feet up and relax after the long day. A day that'd begun nineteen hours earlier when they'd received the call to go to Nazareth Catholic Hospital.

"Thank you, Bonnie. Dinner was awesome, and the company was even better."

"You see, Penny. I told you that you should've married a cop instead of a fireman." Bonnie Ross blushed as she waved off Frank's compliment.

Blushing like her mother, Penny responded, "Okay, Mom, the dishes are calling. Bye!" Penny waved her off.

Seconds after walking into the kitchen, Bonnie peeked her head back into the tiny living room and said, "You know, Frank, you're more than welcome to stay the night. You can have the couch, and I can sleep with Penny."

"Mom! The dishes are waiting!" Penny shooed her mother away.

"Sorry, Frank, she likes to embarrass me."

"Don't worry about it. She's sweet, just like candy," Frank winked as he teased his partner.

"So, on a serious note, I sent the report to the sarge and the captain. Pretty straightforward since we don't have much to go on."

"Maybe we'll learn something more tomorrow morning when we meet his daughters," said Penny.

"Yeah, I spoke to them today. They're both sick about it, " said Frank. "The older daughter, Jessica, is worried her father might have wandered off, but the younger daughter, Madeline, was saying that it was just like what happened to his partner back in '74." Frank's tone changed. "Penny, do you know what happened at FalconClaw back then?"

"My mom told me that Penny went missing the night of Christmas Eve and that Frank Bruno was the last one to see her alive," explained Penny. "It was a mystery for a long time because they never found her body. By the time I was born, though, it was old news. My mom only told me about it once when I was around ten. Every time she talks about Penny these days, she never talks about that night."

"Did somebody call me?" Bonnie poked her head back into the living room.

"No, Mom. We're just talking business over here." Penny again shooed her mother away.

"Bonnie, hold on," Frank looked at Penny and then back to Bonnie. "Would you mind if I asked you what you knew about the disappearance of Penelope Bryce back in 1974?"

"Oh, dear..." Bonnie walked in, set her dishtowel on the table, and then sat down.

"It's okay, Mom." Penny noticed that her mom's face had gone white.

"No, no, Penny, I'm fine," said Bonnie.

"Go on, Bonnie. Tell me what you know." Frank was genuinely curious after skimming through the cold case file prior to coming to Penny's apartment.

"Well, it's been forty-two years since that night." Bonnie folded her hands together in a way that revealed her discomfort. "It happened early Christmas morning over at Heavenly Gates when they actually called it that."

"As a nurse, I went there many times to draw blood and to provide free check-ups for the elderly, but not until after it re-opened in 1978," explained Bonnie. "I hated going there. It was terrifying, that place. Just knowing that my friend had disappeared into the woods behind the estate had always haunted me. It was worse than going to old Byberry Mental Hospital up near Trevose."

"Penny had gone to Heavenly Gates that night to interview a suspect or something, and her partner, Frank Bruno, went looking for her, but she was gone by the time he got there," she explained. "I had heard that they found two sets of footprints leading away from the main entrance as if she was led away by someone," she revealed.

Frank and Penny immediately looked at each other when they heard 'footprints leading away' from the scene.

Frank looked back at Bonnie and echoed her words, "Footprints, you say?"

"Yes, two sets. They never mentioned that in the papers, but your father told me about it later." Bonnie looked at her daughter. "They think she was kidnapped, or something." Bonnie looked white as a ghost. "I don't understand. She was such a wonderful person. Many thought it had something to do with the lawsuit against the city. I suppose she had enemies, but to kidnap her and, well, she's never been found. Where could they have taken her?"

Penny asked her mom, "Did dad ever say if Frank Bruno was suspected in the disappearance?"

"Oh, I don't know about that," Bonnie's brow rose. "If they did, he never told me. He was well-respected in the department. That Frank Bruno was an important man." Bonnie nodded and exhaled fully. "Did you know that he solved the Boy in the Box case? And the case of that little Fox girl that went missing up in Burlington."

"Frank, is that who went missing last night?" Bonnie looked sick. "Was it him, then?"

Penny noticed her mom becoming emotional and said, "That's all, Mom. You should go finish the dishes now."

"Yes," said Frank. "It was him."

Penny spun her head around in Frank's direction to scold him. She shook her head no, hoping that Frank didn't share too much information. "That's enough, Frank." Penny ground her teeth.

"Yes, Bonnie, it was Frank Bruno who went missing."

Penny was pissed.

"Oh, dear," Bonnie stared blankly across the room. "I bet he went looking for her?"

Penny looked confused, "What? Mom, what do you mean, 'he went looking for her?'"

Frank slid to the edge of the couch, hanging on Bonnie's next words.

"I bet he felt guilty for her being kidnapped. Maybe he was ready to die, and he wanted to look for her one last time," thought Bonnie aloud. "Maybe he just wandered away in the snow like my friend did all those years ago."

"Bonnie, how did you know it was Frank Bruno that went missing last night?" asked Frank.

With tears welling in her eyes, Bonnie said, "I heard Penny on the phone with you last night. Something about a man being kidnapped early Christmas morning, and my mind went right to Penny Bryce, 1974," she explained. "I thought, wouldn't that be strange if on the forty-second anniversary of her disappearance that the last man to see her alive would go missing, too. Frank, you know the sign of the angels is eight, right?"

"Eight?" Frank looked puzzled. "The sign of the angels?"

"Yes, eight. Four times two is eight. Forty-two years to the day?"

"Oh, Mom. Come on," Penny rolled her eyes.

"No, Penny, let her talk."

"No, I'm just being silly," said Bonnie. "I was just lying in bed last night wondering about things. It is a strange coincidence that it was Frank Bruno, though. Don't you think? I mean, on the anniversary of Penny going missing, he goes missing, too?"

"Mom, listen, you can't say anything about this. Let people find out through the media. Don't say anything as this is an active investigation," cautioned Penny.

"Oh, I won't, Penny." Bonnie put her finger to her lips. "Your secret is safe with me. And besides, who am I going to tell?"

As Bonnie rose and turned to leave the room, she turned to her daughter and Frank and said, "I think that the two of you were supposed to be the ones looking into his disappearance. Forty-two years to the date, and Frank Collazo and Penny Bristow are searching for Frank Bruno as he searches for Penny Bryce." Bonnie looked convinced with her next words. "I certainly don't think that that's a coincidence. Do either of you?"

Bonnie Ross buttoned her lips, rose to her feet, and left the room, leaving her daughter and her guest stunned.

Penny, a little embarrassed, looked at Frank and apologized. "I'm so sorry about that. My mom's pretty superstitious."

Frank shook his head. "No, it's okay." Pondering his words for a second, he added, "It sounds crazy, but what if the old man, not of sound mind, actually did jump out of that window and went looking for his old friend?"

"You don't really believe that, do you?" Penny was surprised. "The footprints came from somewhere."

"Just saying, the whole thing is crazy, and any explanation is a good place to start."

"Well, we meet the daughters tomorrow," said Penny. "Let's see what they have to say."

"Penny, why did we get the call?" Frank looked off, staring at nothing as he pondered his question.

"It's my fault, probably," said Penny. "I'm the only detective without kids."

"Maybe." Frank wasn't convinced.

Frank got up and moved from beside Penny on the couch to the old, brown, dusty recliner Bonnie vacated moments earlier. Reclining it, he unwittingly revealed a hole in the heel of his right sock. "Is this okay?" he asked.

Penny smiled and said nothing about the hole. "Of course. My mom won't come back in here tonight. She usually goes to bed around nine-thirty, and now it's ten." Penny didn't know if Frank was sending her a message by switching seats.

"Man, this old chair is comfortable. I could fall asleep right here."

"Go for it. My mom already invited you to stay. If she saw you laying there, she'd find a shawl and throw it over you."

Frank abruptly folded the recliner back into position and leaned heavily toward Penny. "Penny, listen, I need to tell you something just in case our investigation of Frank Bruno takes us up to FalconClaw."

"Sure, what's up?" Penny could tell something was bothering her partner.

"I know we've been partners for three years, but I never shared the details of my father's death with you before."

"Okay?" Penny was both eager and apprehensive to finally hear the story.

"Okay, here we go," Frank exhaled. He was nervous and relieved to finally tell the story. A story he'd never told anyone before.

"So, have you ever heard of the serial killer, Vincent Charmaine Walker?"

"Yeah, but I never wrapped my head around that middle name, though. Charmaine?" Penny shook her head. "I don't get it."

Frank looked perturbed, "Penny, focus for a minute. This is important to me."

"Oh, yeah," Penny caught herself. "Sorry, Frank. Continue."

Frank exhaled fully one more time and then continued. "For two years, my father and his partner were after this guy who had killed eight people in the Philly area and a young couple over in Camden." In telling the story, his eyes got big. "The eight in Philly included a family of four. A mother, father, and two kids under the age of five."

"Yeah, I remember reading an article about him during police academy training back in 2003. Do you remember the class they had on serial killers?" asked Penny.

"Of course. I had to sit through it, surrounded by thirty other cadets. You could imagine how uncomfortable that was for me," said Frank. "What they didn't cover in the class was who his last victim was."

Penny winced and uttered, "Your father?"

"Yes, my father. He was the eleventh and final victim of Walker." Frank looked solemn. After collecting himself, he continued.

"It was a Saturday night, Halloween, 1992, when my dad and his partner, Diego Ramirez, followed a lead to FalconClaw. They'd heard from a source that the man they were looking for once worked at FalconClaw as a night-time janitor from 1988 until 1991. Their source suggested the former employee still had keys to the exterior basement door located in the back of the mansion. The week before, they'd received a letter from Walker saying, 'another soul be damned,' at midnight on Halloween. The note was anonymous but addressed to my father and titled, 'Trick or Treat?'"

Penny hung on Frank's words. "Did they have the name of their suspect yet?" Penny asked.

"No, the identity of Walker wasn't known yet. But law enforcement knew who it was from. The letter ended with the phrase, 'Go Falcons!' That was the name of my baseball team, but my dad thought Walker was trying to divert him away from FalconClaw that night. His partner thought the opposite. Ramirez thought it was a trap and that Walker was trying to lure them to the mansion instead. A total of eight districts were on the hunt for Walker, but back then FalconClaw resided in the 14th where my father worked."

Frank took another deep breath and continued. "Ramirez thought they should go up there with backup, but my father didn't want to spook Walker with a big police presence if he was, in fact, there. He told my mom that he wouldn't make it home for dinner and told me that he wouldn't make it to my baseball game," revealed Frank. "But he sent a unit up to Hunting Park and had them stay the entirety of the game to make sure I was safe. I remember that night, we lost the game, but I got to ride home in a police car. My friends thought I was cool."

"Anyway, my dad had Ramirez ring the bell in the front while he went around to the back of the building to snoop around. He wanted Ramirez to divert any Saturday night staff resources to the front of FalconClaw while he looked for access to the basement in the back," explained Frank while Penny sat silent. "They didn't have a search warrant and didn't want to make a big fuss at the front door. My dad just needed a little time to investigate around back."

"The source specifically said that Walker might still have keys to the basement, so that's where my dad went." Frank sighed.

"My dad found the door to the basement unlocked. It was on the southwest corner of the estate and was like one of those old-fashioned farmhouse basement doors. There were two doors that you'd lift up and walk down a set of stairs to enter. The padlock was off, just sitting on the ground. Almost like an invitation. They had their radios turned off, so Ramirez didn't immediately know that my father was entering the basement."

"Ramirez had told him to wait, but my dad was a hero, and he liked being the hero." Frank got teary-eyed. "I was fourteen, Penny."

"I know how you feel, Frankie." Penny reached for her partner's hand. "I was also fourteen when my dad was killed in 1996. It was the week before my birthday."

"Thanks, Penny. We had it tough as kids, huh?"

"You never forget," said Penny. "Get all the bad guys off the street, right?"

"Right, Penny. Damn right!" Frank's eyes went tight.

"So, what happened after he went in?" asked Penny. She paused before adding, "Unless, of course, you're too uncomfortable talking about what went down in there."

"No, I'm good," said Frank. "It feels good to get this out there."

Frank continued. "He entered the basement alone. That was a mistake that heroes make. Only Walker knows what happened next, and he took that to the grave, but minutes later, muffled shots were heard by a cook in the kitchen just above the area where he was found bleeding out. There was little Ramirez could do by the time he got to him. My father took three bullets in the back. One hit his liver, one severed his spinal cord, and the other one entered his lung."

Frank appeared pale to Penny. "Did he ever get a shot off?"

Frank said, "That's just it. He'd been issued a Glock just a week before but never actually fired it. He hated it. He said he preferred his service revolver. The first shots that that gun ever fired were into my father's back. Only three shots were heard, and they all hit my dad at close range. The gun was nowhere to be found when they processed the scene. The following January, though, it was finally recovered when Walker was eventually apprehended after a shootout with police in East Germantown. One of the bullets that my father loaded into that very gun ended up lodged against the spine of one of the responding detectives that helped to collar him that day back in '93. That detective? It was Ramirez. That son of a bitch killed my father and almost got his partner, too."

"No shit!" said Penny. "Is Ramirez still alive?"

"Nah. He died two years ago. My mom and I kept up with him over the years."

"That's crazy!"

"My mom saw him once at a grocery store, and she told me she felt strangely connected to the man, seeing how a bullet my father once held in his hand lived inside of him. Ramirez was the last person to see my father before Walker took his life. My mom said that when he died in 2014, it was like my father dying all over again."

"Jesus, Frank. I'm so sorry."

"She said that she never got remarried because it would've had to be another cop, and she didn't want to lose another husband that way. She's still angry that he died a hero," said Frank.

"When she died last year, she mumbled Ramirez's name on her death bed," revealed Frank.

"That's heartbreaking. My mom feels the same. She'd never remarry," said Penny. "Before the shootout that killed my father, he had never discharged his gun in the line of duty. They say he died a hero, but I'd rather have a coward for a father if it meant he'd still be alive."

Frank thought about what Penny had said and wasn't sure that he agreed with her or his mother.

After a few moments of silence, Frank looked away and said, "It was a set-up, Penny. A note was found in my father's pocket, and it read, 'Death to the Damned.' The soul to be 'damned' from the anonymous letter was my father."

Penny was floored. "You're kidding me?!"

"Nope. Walker finally admitted it before his execution in 2002. He said my dad was good at his job and was getting too close. The anonymous source that told police Vincent Charmaine Walker used to work at FalconClaw was Walker himself," revealed Frank.

Penny gasped.

"If my father would've only looked into who worked as a janitor at FalconClaw during those years," Frank paused, "then he would've discovered that every janitor that worked there in 1992 had all been there since 1985. There were no janitors that came and went from FalconClaw between 88 and 91."

"Penny, it was shoddy police work that got my father killed," said Frank. "That's hard to live with."

"My God, Frank. That's unbelievable." Penny sat shocked.

The reason I'm telling you all of this is because if we have to go to FalconClaw as part of this investigation," Frank paused, "I'm not sure how I'm going to react."

"Of course, Frank. I get it."

Frank rose to his feet and shook off his emotions, and said, "I gotta get home. Big day tomorrow, we interview Bruno's daughters."

"You're leaving?" Penny was caught off guard. She felt a connection with her partner, and she didn't want the night to end just yet.

"Yeah, it's getting late." Frank reached for his coat after slipping his shoes back on.

Penny struggled with her words. "Um. Ah. You could always stay here tonight. I know you hate your place." Almost stuttering, she added, "I mean, my mom said it was okay. You could crash on the couch if you want to."

Frank zipped up his coat and half-smiled. He'd like nothing more than not to have to go home but knew that sleeping at Penny's was a bad idea.

"Penny, half of the 39th already thinks we're sleeping together. It wouldn't look too good if my car was seen parked out on the street overnight."

"Well," said Penny, flirtatiously batting her light brown eyes, "if they already think we're sleeping together, then who cares if they see your car?" Penny smiled, adding, "The car is city-issued, and we could say that I took it home for the night."

Frank found it hard to argue with Penny's rationale. He looked his partner dead in the eye and said, "Penny, you look sexier right now than I've ever seen you before." His eyes got wide. "And I think you look sexy all of the time."

Penny blushed.

"If I stay here tonight, we both know I won't be sleeping on that couch."

"Well, if you're gonna fuck me tonight, it'll have to be on that couch because this is a one-bedroom apartment, and my mom's sleeping in it right now." Penny shot Frank a sly grin and closed the distance between her and her partner. Her slender, five-foot-four frame was dwarfed by his.

Frank backed up and turned toward the door. "Well, in that case, I'll wait because the first time we have sex will be at the Ritz Carlton downtown."

Penny was flustered as she approached her partner standing at the door. "Frank, umm." Penny hesitated in a moment of vulnerability. "I need to kiss you right now."

"The Ritz Carlton, Penny." Frank reached for the handle, opened the door, and walked out.

A frustrated Penny stood at the top of the stairs as Frank walked down to the street. "What time you picking me up in the morning?" she yelled down to him.

"Nine o'clock sharp. Be downstairs, Partner?"

"Yeah, whatever, Frankie Boy!"

"Oh, and Penny!" Frank yelled up the narrow stairwell.

"Get you and your mom out of this tinder box."

"Whatever, Frank!" Penny was frustrated.

She closed the door behind her and tried to catch her breath. She'd never been so turned on by Frank before. She wasn't sure how she'd get to sleep lying next to her mother, so she'd settle for the couch instead.

As Frank closed the stairwell door down on the street, his back fell against it, and he, too, had to catch his breath. He wanted Penny bad but was not about to cross the line he'd laid down at the beginning of their partnership.

Driving home, the snow fell heavily in North Philly, and Frank Collazo thought of Frank Bruno and his partner, Penelope Bryce, and what had become of the two. He then thought of Penny Bristow and what the future held for each of them.

Chapter 3 – Strawberry Mansion

East Fairmount Park, Philadelphia – December 31, 2016, 10:16 pm.

Originally named *Summerville* in 1789 by its owner, prominent Abolitionist, and Judge William Lewis, Strawberry Mansion resides in East Fairmount Park, Philadelphia's largest municipal park. Lewis played an important role in the 1780 'Act for the Gradual Abolition of Slavery.' The mansion's name was later changed sometime between 1846 and 1867 when farmers used to rent the mansion for the summer and sold their strawberries and cream to the public. In 1927, the house was restored and classified as a Historic House Museum and hospitality house. By the early 1990s, the house could be rented for private affairs such as weddings, banquets, receptions, or parties.

On New Year's Eve 2016, Strawberry Mansion was rented out by Warren Jacks, a prominent defense attorney and former U.S. Attorney for Philadelphia's Eastern District. Jacks was also a former Professor at his alma mater, Temple University's Beasley School of Law.

Jacks was hosting a party for the upper echelon of Philly's societal elite. His guests included politicians, corporate CEOs, friends, family, and his lover, Belinda Mereby. Jacks' wife and three grown children were not in attendance that evening.

Belinda Mereby grew impatient in the back of her limousine while waiting in a long queue of black cars, dropping off their VIP guests in front of the historic house. She could see no less than a dozen cars in front of hers wrapping around the circular drive in front of the white, Federal-style mansion. Bored, she counted twenty-seven windows on the mansion's front but only one tiny door where its guests were received.

This is ridiculous! It's taking forever! She texted Jacks. *If I weren't wearing these heels, I'd get out and walk!* Her fingers feverously stabbed at her iPhone.

I told you not to text me on this phone! No more! Jacks texted back. *I'll see you when you get in. I'm just inside the main entrance greeting guests, don't make a scene when you come in.*

"Fuck him! Don't make a scene?" Mereby uttered aloud in anger, getting the attention of her driver, who glanced at her through the rearview mirror.

"What in the hell are you looking at?" she snapped at the man.

The heavy-set black man in a black suit and chauffeur hat looked away, choosing to say nothing. He was now convinced there'd be no tip forthcoming from his agitated fare.

"You better look away!" she growled.

Mereby wore a dark blue, strapless gown and matching shoulder shrug, shamelessly covered by an outdated fur shoulder wrap that Jacks had gifted her several years earlier.

Belinda Mereby and Warren Jacks first met while each attended Temple University in the late eighties and early nineties. Jacks studied law while Mereby studied political science. In the years following their time at Temple, Mereby was a regular on the social circuit, always attending high-end functions, but she never had a job as far as anyone knew. She was best known for her philanthropy efforts, volunteering only sparingly while giving away large sums of her father's vast wealth. Though her family's pedigree matched that of Jacks,' his parents were not fond of the young Mereby's appearance and forbade him from seeing her. They weren't a fan of her bright orange hair and pale complexion.

Jacks went on to get his law degree and found success as a prosecutor and law professor. After college, he married the daughter of another prominent attorney and two-term Congressperson for Philadelphia's 2nd Congressional District.

Jacks fancied his wife of twenty-five years in public, but it was Belinda Mereby that he'd always fancied in the bedroom. For more than twenty-five years, he had cheated on his wife with Mereby, but rumors persisted that a younger version of Belinda, a former student of Jacks at Temple, was waiting in the wings, ready to replace the aging socialite. Jacks was hoping Mereby would move on but had, in recent years, begun to believe that she never would. He wanted their relationship over with but feared his lover wouldn't go away quietly.

Belinda Mereby always assumed Jacks would live up to his twenty-five-year-old promise that he'd leave his wife one day and marry her. But now, the twenty-five-year-old lie wore on Mereby like the wrinkles on her face, an unwelcomed and stark reality. A reality that she was ready to confront one last time.

Though her father, Clinton Mereby, was also a famous attorney, he never favored the notion of silver spoon-feeding his only child well into adulthood. When Belinda turned thirty-five, he cut her off the family payroll and insisted she find her own way. Since that time, she'd been quite the financial burden to her lover, Jacks, and like Mereby's father, he now, too, was ready to move on.

Ten minutes later, Belinda Mereby stepped out of the door of the limousine opened by her driver. She nodded politely to the chauffeur and feigned appreciation with a phony smile. After the door was closed behind her, she whispered, "Go fuck yourself," to the man and then walked off.

Now inside, Mereby stood impatiently in a reception line, waiting to shake hands with the man she felt she deserved. Her flaming red hair and pale complexion caused her to stand out in the crowd. The look on her face revealed her contempt for the man playing host. After twenty-five years as Jacks' mistress, lying on her back waiting for the cheating prick to finish, she felt like she deserved more than a handshake.

Moments later, as the two shook hands and exchanged kisses on each cheek, Mereby whispered to her lover in one ear, "You're a prick!"

While Jacks whispered to her, "You look like shit!"

An hour later, Jacks had Mereby bent over a wine rack in the basement's wine cellar. Several kitchen staff witnessed the affair, but neither Jacks nor Mereby seemed to notice.

After Jacks pulled his pants up and Mereby lowered her dress, Jacks said, "You look ridiculous in that dress! And what was with that fur wrap you wore in? For the love of God, fur wraps went out fifteen years ago. I told you to donate that thing."

"Fuck you, Warren!" Mereby snapped back. "You bought me that fur, remember?"

"Yeah, like seventeen years ago!"

"Warren, we need to talk."

"No, we don't. We're through. Tonight was it for us."

Using the glass door of a wine refrigerator as a mirror, Jacks adjusted the bow-tie on his tuxedo and ran his hand clumsily through his slicked-back salt and pepper hair. "You go upstairs, walk out that door and get into the first black car you see, and never contact me again. We're done. Rachel and I are going to make it work. Things are different now that the boys have moved on."

"Oh, fuck you! You get to fuck twenty-five years of youth out of me and decide you're going to move on with a twenty-five-year-old whore!" Mereby pulled the shrug around her shoulders. "You think I don't know about that little bitch in your office?!"

"She's an advisor to my firm, and she's not a whore. She's a professional, and I consider her an asset."

"You mean ASS-et, don't you?! How many times have you had her bent over your desk? Does Rachel know about her, too?" Belinda Mereby was seething. "Perhaps I'll make a call to her after I leave here tonight."

Jacks lunged at Belinda with contempt, grabbing both of her shoulders and pushing her up against the wine rack, causing several bottles to crash to the floor. "If you decide to make that call, then you'll pay an awful price."

"Oh, whattaya gonna do, big bad prosecutor? Hit me on redirect?" Mereby spit in her lover's face. "Fuck you and get your filthy hands off of me, you son of a bitch!" Mereby adjusted her torn shrug. "I don't need your filthy dick or your dirty money. I'm through with you, too!"

As Jacks and Mereby collected themselves, they noticed two kitchen staff standing in the hallway looking in at them. Warren Jacks raced from the tiny room and mumbled, "Put in on my tab," while wiping Mereby's saliva from his chin.

Belinda Mereby ignored the house staff, fixed her make-up and dress, and exited the basement.

For three hours, Belinda Mereby tormented her former lover by throwing herself at every single man at the party. When it was time to leave, Mereby exited through the side door of the historic home, making eye contact, and blowing a kiss to Jacks just before leaving, humiliating the party's host. It was after 2 am, and several black cars awaited departing guests outside.

As Mereby approached the cars, only one driver exited his vehicle to accommodate her, saying only, "Ma'am," as he tipped his cap and opened the rear passenger door.

Mereby looked the large, middle-aged white male up and down and uttered, "I guess you'll have to do."

Now inside the limo, Mereby removed a compact mirror from her bag and checked her make-up one more time.

As the car wrapped around the circular drive in front of Strawberry Mansion and onto Greenland Drive, Mereby looked up and said, "Aren't you going to ask me for an address?"

"Oh, I know where you're going. It's all been arranged." After the sinister response, the driver closed the glass window between the front and rear cabins.

A slightly nervous Mereby said, "Wait a minute," as the tinted window went up, but no response came back. As the car headed west onto Strawberry Mansion Drive Bridge, Belinda Mereby felt a sense of foreboding. When it turned right onto West Strawberry Mansion Drive North and then merged onto MLK Jr. North, panic set in. Mereby lived west of the Schuylkill, and now she was heading north.

Desperately scratching at the bottom of her handbag, the intoxicated Mereby realized that her cell phone was missing. Breathing heavily, she cried, "The wine cellar."

"Stop the car!" she screamed while banging on the glass partition. Mereby screamed again, frantically reaching for door handles that had been forcibly removed earlier. Through the tint, she could see the driver's dark eyes in the rearview mirror glancing at her and then back to the road.

At that exact moment, while cleaning up broken glass and spilled wine in the basement of Strawberry Mansion, a female staff member heard the muffled sound of a vibrating cellphone. Following the sound to the floor, the woman discovered it lying under a cabinet door. Reading the phone screen, the ominous message read, *You've threatened me for the last time!* The name of the person displayed on the text? W.J.

Chapter 4 – Missing

Second Floor Detective Room – 39th District – New Year's Day, 2017.

"All right guys, let's gather round. Looks like it's just the three of us on this disgusting holiday," said Detective Sergeant Doug Riley, who'd just returned from Christmas vacation. "The roads were a mess coming in!"

Penny sat at her desk facing Riley, who stood at the rear of the room, his back to the Schuyler Street windows. Frank stood to the side of Penny's desk with notes in hand.

Outside, the snow was mostly melted, leaving slushy roads covered with salt, slag, and sand, revealing potholes the size of manhole covers. It hadn't snowed since Christmas morning but still took nearly a week of unseasonably warm temperatures to melt off the ten inches of snow that fell on Christmas Eve.

"Happy New Year, guys! Looks like we drew the short straws, huh? At least we had off for New Year's Eve." Riley's failed attempt at enthusiasm didn't seem to energize either Frank or Penny.

The two detectives hadn't spoken much since Christmas night. Since interviewing Frank Bruno's middle-aged daughters, Jessica and Madeline, the day after Christmas, Frank had barely said a word to Penny. Penny felt shunned and didn't know how to break through the wall between her and Frank.

"So whatta you two got on the Bruno disappearance, anyway? It's been almost a week, and the Captain wants to hear something other than 'nothing.'"

Penny, wanting desperately to hear Frank say anything, deferred to him by looking up and lifting her chin, giving him the go-ahead.

Frank looked over his notes and then back to Riley. "Okay, well, I'm not allowed to give you nothing, so I'll give you something." Frank looked at his notes again.

"At approximately 1:30 am on Christmas morning...."

Sergeant Riley threw up his hands, interrupted his detective, and said, "Frank! Tell me what I don't know already, would ya?"

"That's just it, Sarge, we got nothing. Frank Bruno disappeared into thin air. He's a ghost." Frank Collazo was purposely brief, not trying to hide his frustration.

"Sarge," Penny added. "The daughters have different opinions on what might've happened. The older one thinks he just wandered off as his mental state had deteriorated greatly in the last two years. Her words, not mine," said Penny. "But the younger one, Madeline, thinks her father walked out of that hospital on his own and with a purpose."

"Whattaya mean, 'purpose?'" Riley's curiosity was aroused.

"This is gonna sound a little crazy, but Madeline thinks he went looking for his old partner, Penelope Bryce."

"You mean, his old partner that went missing up at FalconClaw back in the 70s?" Riley smirked. "You're right. That is crazy."

Frank spoke up. "Both daughters stated that he never really recovered from that loss. They said that that loss overshadowed the loss of his wife just four months prior that same year."

"We also studied every closed-circuit camera viewing that area, both city-owned and from private businesses," said Penny.

"And?" Riley prodded.

"Nothin, Sarge," Frank shook his head. "We got six sets of footprints in the snow leading away from his hospital room, and they end at precisely where the first camera should have picked up anybody out there walking in the snow."

"Whattaya mean, 'end?'" Riley wasn't content with Frank's reporting. "You mean like they stopped at a road, or parking lot, or something?"

"No. No road. No parking lot. They just stopped in the courtyard," Frank added.

"So, there was no camera viewing the courtyard near his window?"

"There was one facing that side of the hospital, but it conveniently wasn't working that night," Penny looked perturbed.

At that moment, a call came from downstairs. Riley answered the phone. A uniformed supervisor called up to the Detective Room to inform the three detectives that another person had been reported missing.

"Okay, what's the name?" Riley asked the supervisor. "Really? How long has she been missing?"

Penny and Frank looked curious, both standing now.

"But that's less than seven hours. Do you know what today is? It's New Year's Day. She's probably sleeping one off."

"No, shit?!" Riley blurted out. "All right, McLaughlin, bring him on up!"

Doug Riley hung up the phone and turned toward his two detectives. "We got company, fellas." Riley began to straighten his tie. "Criminal Defense Attorney Clinton Mereby is on his way up. His daughter's gone missing."

"No shit?!" exclaimed Penny.

Frank said, "I hate that prick! He made all of his money getting the bad guys off. This should be interesting."

Just minutes after 9 am, the Operations Room Supervisor, or ORS, Sergeant McLaughlin, walked through the door escorting Mereby. Clinton Mereby wore a brown leather jacket, a green polo, and khakis. The white-haired, heavy-set man appeared to the three detectives to be holding a plastic bag. The only time they'd ever seen the elder Mereby was in court, wearing two-thousand dollar French suits and thousand dollar shoes while helping white-collar criminals get their charges dismissed.

The detectives witnessed a haggard, impatient, frightened old man. Mereby had to be in his mid-seventies, thought the detectives.

"Mr. Mereby, Sir," said Riley, as Frank and Penny let their sergeant do the talking. "Sorry to hear about your daughter. What can you tell us, Sir?"

Mereby was trembling. "My daughter went missing last night sometime after 2 am. Please don't tell me I have to wait twenty-four hours before reporting her missing. She's in trouble, and time is of the essence."

Riley turned to Frank. "Frank, get Mr. Mereby here a bottle of water."

Penny was closest to the breakroom, so she went instead.

"You can go, Sarge," Riley motioned to McLaughlin by lifting his chin.

McLaughlin turned toward the door and disappeared into the stairwell without a word.

Frank seemed to snap out of his funk. Observing the old man, he could see that whatever circumstances surrounded his daughter's disappearance clearly had Mereby terrified.

Penny returned and handed the elder Mereby the water. When reaching for the bottle, the man's hands shook so violently that Penny had to help it into his hand.

"Mr. Mereby, what leads you to believe that your daughter's in trouble?" Frank beat his Sergeant to the obvious question.

Riley cut Frank off, taking a half step forward to position himself between Frank and Mereby.

"Yes, Mr. Mereby, what can you tell us, Sir?" echoed Riley.

At that moment, Mereby revealed what was in the plastic Cousin's Supermarket bag. Trembling still, Mereby's shaking hand pulled out a tiny purse that was in poor condition and appeared to Riley and Frank to be wet.

After setting it on Penny's desk, which was nearest to the stairwell door, Mereby said, "It belongs to my daughter, and she's missing."

Riley, recognizing that the purse could potentially be evidence, used a pencil from Penny's desk to tip it over to examine both sides. "Where was this found, Mr. Mereby? It looks as if it's been outside."

"A twenty-year-old kid was out with his friends drinking last night when at around 4:15 am they witnessed a limousine in front of them toss it from its window."

"Hmm, I see. Did they get a plate number and description of the car? I can understand now why you're so worried," said Riley.

"I don't know, other than the fact it was a limo! Just find my daughter!"

Penny entered the conversation and asked, "How did you come into contact with the purse, Mr. Mereby?"

"Evidently, the juvenile that found it took it home and showed his parents this morning because he thought the name and picture on the driver's license looked familiar," said Mereby. "As you know, my daughter is well-known in the City of Philadelphia and is on the news from time to time. The parents determined it to be my daughter and drove it to Belinda's address found on the driver's license and left it with the person at the front desk, who in turn called me immediately."

"And what is that address?" asked Frank, reaching for a pencil as he shuffled some papers on his desk.

"She lives in the penthouse at the Chamounix Condominiums on West Ford Road, just east of the Schuylkill."

"Mr. Mereby, Sir. That's the 16th District's jurisdiction. What brings you to the 39th?"

A beleaguered Mereby responded, "When I got the call from the concierge in her building, I immediately called her cellphone."

"And?" asked Riley.

"Her phone was answered by an employee at Strawberry Mansion in East Fairmount Park, the historic house, not the neighborhood. Belinda attended a party there last night, which was hosted by Warren Jacks," offered Mereby. "Historic Strawberry Mansion is the last place she was seen, and if I'm not mistaken, that's in your jurisdiction." Mereby looked away and hesitated before mumbling, "And...."

"And, what?" asked Frank.

Mereby cleared his throat and hesitated before speaking. "My daughter has been romantically involved with Warren Jacks on-again, off-again for the last two decades."

"I thought Jacks was married with grown children," said Penny.

Riley broke back in, "Okay, Mr. Mereby, perhaps your daughter is with Jacks right now. Have you contacted him yet?"

"No, but I know that he's at home right now."

"And how exactly do you know that, Mr. Mereby?" asked Frank as Penny and Riley looked on with curiosity.

"I know a lot of things and a lot of people. I've never been a fan of Warren Jacks. That's all I'll say for now regarding the man," said Mereby. "Now, my daughter is missing, and she's not with her lover or at her home. She's not in possession of her cell phone, and her purse was found off of Route One up in Germantown."

"Germantown?" Penny questioned aloud while Frank jotted it down.

"Eastbound, or Westbound side?" asked Frank.

"I have no idea," Mereby sighed and looked each detective in the eye. "If you don't think she's in trouble, then you're not very good at your jobs. I have her purse right here, and I've already reached out to Strawberry Mansion. They are in possession of her phone, as I have stated already."

"Mr. Mereby, Sir," Riley paused, "on its face, your daughter attended a New Year's Eve function at Historic Strawberry Mansion, dropped her cellphone, and or lost her purse. Or perhaps somebody five-fingered it," offered Detective Sergeant Riley."

"Detectives, what woman leaves a party and doesn't take inventory of her cell phone and purse?" Mereby was condescending.

Riley and Frank looked at Penny, and she shrugged and said, "He's got a point."

"Either way, she's a grown woman and has the expectation of her privacy," said Riley. "Just because we think she's missing doesn't mean that she's in trouble. We can write up a report but can't start a missing person's investigation until twenty-four hours have passed."

Mereby's face went red, and he screamed, "To hell with department policy! My daughter is in trouble, and the clock is ticking, Detectives!"

The three detectives were at a loss as Clinton Mereby angrily walked over to the Schuyler Street window and made a call on his cellphone. The three detectives half-smiled with Frank whispering, "Who does this guy think he is?"

Less than sixty seconds later, Mereby walked over to Riley, who he suspected was the highest-ranking detective in the room, and said, "Here, it's for you," handing his phone over to him.

Riley looked perplexed and glanced over at Frank and Penny before taking possession of Mereby's cellphone. Raising it to his ear, he said, "Hello."

The voice on the other end was deep and throaty as if just awakened. "Is this the Detective in Charge?"

The voice sounded somewhat familiar to Riley. "Yes, this is Detective Sergeant Douglas Riley. To whom am I speaking with?"

"Detective Sergeant, this is Mayor Donovan Taylor. My friend is clearly upset about his daughter being missing. I ask that you set aside protocol and get two detectives over to the old mansion without further delay. Can you do that for me as a favor to the City of Philadelphia?"

Riley's face went white as he stuttered, "Ah, of course, Mayor Taylor. I'm sure we can accommodate Mr. Mereby, Sir."

Shocked by who the caller was, Frank and Penny looked at each other and immediately knew they'd be heading over to Historic Strawberry Mansion.

Mereby grabbed the phone out of Riley's hand and said, "Thanks Don," to the caller, then hung up. He then pointedly said to the three detectives standing at attention before him, "Find my daughter, now!" Handing his business card to each of the three detectives, he said, "I want hourly updates!"

"And," Mereby paused, "you need to look into Jacks."

Entering the stairwell, he looked back and shouted, "Hourly, Detectives!" before disappearing down into the stairwell.

"Holy shit!" Riley looked stunned. "What in the hell just happened?"

"Sarge, you call the Captain. Penny and I will get right over to Strawberry Mansion."

Moments later, Frank pulled out of the parking lot behind headquarters and onto Schuyler Street. "Whattaya think is the fastest way over there at this time of day?"

Penny said, "Right down 13 and then left on Ridge, then a right on Huntingdon."

"Yeah, yeah. I remember now. It's been a minute since I was there."

"Me, too," said Penny. "I had my wedding reception there back in 2012."

"No shit?"

"Yep, July 14, to be exact." Penny looked exasperated. "I celebrated my fourth anniversary by packing up my stuff and moving in with my mom."

"Man, I remember that day. So that was your actual anniversary, huh?"

"A day of celebration," nodded Penny. "Me and my mom got drunk that night," she remembered fondly. Smiling, she added, "I jammed to Kelly Clarkson's *Since you been gone* that whole night."

"Hilarious!" Frank laughed.

Penny looked over at her partner and asked, "Frank, are we gonna talk about that night, or what?"

"What night?" Frank was bobbing his head and singing, "*Since you been gone*," under his breath.

"Frank, gimme a break! You know what night."

"Oh, yeah." Frank's smile ran away from his face as he merged onto Ridge. "Not much to say," he shrugged. "We were both drunk."

"I wasn't drunk, asshole!" Penny looked miffed.

"Penny, I like you. And I do think you're sexy as hell, but as far as us ever being more than partners," he paused, "it's never gonna happen."

"Well, that's fine. I was thinking the same thing, anyways." Penny lied. "I just wanted to clear the air, that's all."

Frank inhaled deeply through his nose and let out an exaggerated exhaust saying, "Whew!" then chuckled. "The air smells pretty clear to me."

His expression put off Penny.

"So, no sex to save the relationship, then?" he asked his partner in jest.

"What?" Penny was baffled.

"I'm joking," Frank smiled at his partner. "It's a line from Seinfeld."

Penny smiled half-heartedly. "Yeah, well, at least Jerry knew what he was missing out on."

"Whattaya mean?" Frank stopped smiling.

"Jerry and Elaine were a couple before they became just friends. They'd had sex before."

"Bullshit! Jerry and Elaine were never boyfriend and girlfriend. I'll bet you fifty bucks you're wrong."

"Deal, come over to my place tonight, and we'll binge watch it."

"Mmm-hmm. I see what you're up to, Penelope Bryce Bristow." Frank shook his head.

"Oh well. It was worth a try." Penny turned to look out her window.

"No kidding, Penny. I'm serious. We're partners, and I'm not messing with that shit. We work too well together. Plus," Frank paused.

"Plus, what?" asked Penny.

"Plus, I'm a professional." Frank smiled and looked over at Penny. "I never mix business with pleasure."

"Oh. Okay, Mr. Ritz Carlton," Penny busted her partner's chops.

Frank smiled and said, "I tell that to all the girls." He lied.

Turning onto Cumberland Drive, then Greenland, Frank said, "All right, let's get in there and see what we can come up with."

Chapter 5 – The Schuylkill

The Schuylkill River (pronounced scook-aule) runs northwest to southeast through Eastern Pennsylvania. From Pottsville to Philadelphia, it winds and curves 135 miles and drains into the Delaware River. The waterway brought millions of tons of coal into Philadelphia during the nineteenth and twentieth centuries, feeding the booming city's thirst for iron and steel.

Previously called The Manayunk by the Danes and The Tulpehocken by the English, the river was finally called Schuylkill by the Dutch. *Kil* meaning creek; *Schuylen*, meaning to hide or skulk.

The river, polluted over many decades with highly acidic waters draining from dozens of coal mines upriver, is filled with heavy metals, irons, and other deposits, giving it an orangish hue.

Neither its color nor its current were able to hide the Schuylkill's secrets, though.

Historic Strawberry Mansion – January 1, 2017, 9:42 am.

Standing outside their vehicle, Frank said to Penny, "Penny, look around. This whole place could be a crime scene. We don't know that Belinda Mereby ever left this place last night. Keep your eyes open."

Entering through the tiny front door, Frank looked to his left and saw a large living room that had been stanchioned off. The room was adorned with paisley, old English armchairs, a circular couch, a mahogany grand piano, and a harp that sat to the left of a tiny fireplace. A large sitting room with a red velvet couch and two matching armchairs were to his immediate right. The fireplace on the back wall was much larger than the one in the living room.

"Jesus! How much did you pay to have the reception here?" Frank's brows stood at attention. "This place is really extravagant."

As Frank turned to look at Penny, he'd noticed that she'd continued walking down the large foyer, peeking into a small room at the end of the hall. Frank then continued down the long white runner, which partially covered what he perceived as the original hardwood floors from the 1700s.

Frank could see Penny flash her badge to a woman who'd emerged from a tiny reception office. The woman seemed surprised by the appearance of Philly Detectives, displaying to Penny a look of concern.

As Frank approached, he could see Penny put her badge away and say, "We're here to speak to anyone who might've been working last night."

"What is this all about?" asked the middle-aged woman who introduced herself as the mansion's curator.

"We're investigating the disappearance of a woman who may have attended a party here last evening," explained Penny.

"Oh, you must be referring to the New Year's affair last evening hosted by Warren Jacks," said the woman.

"That's the one," said Frank, now joining the conversation.

"Is this about Belinda Mereby?" asked the woman.

"Yes," said Penny. "How did you know that?" Penny looked at her partner and then back to the woman.

"Well, her cellphone turned up last night and was ringing all morning," explained Jacqueline Jefferson, the curator of Strawberry Mansion. "I had to turn it off as it became quite the annoyance to my staff and me."

"Did anyone else come here looking for Ms. Mereby or her phone?" asked Penny.

"No, but her father, Clinton Mereby, called earlier this morning regarding the lost phone," explained Jefferson. "It was placed in our lost and found last evening."

"And what time did you arrive this morning, Mrs.....?" asked Frank.

"It's Jefferson. Miss Jefferson," said the woman. "I arrived at 8 am, sharp."

"Is the mansion open for business today?" asked Penny.

"Yes, we open at 12 pm for tour groups," explained the curator.

Frank looked at Penny and then at Jefferson. "Well, this entire place may very well be a crime scene. It'd be best if you canceled any tour groups coming through today."

"I beg your pardon?" Jefferson was aghast. "We have a women's group coming through today that planned the event several months ago. I doubt very much that we will cancel that tour." Jefferson was defiant. "I can assure both of you that Miss Mereby is neither in this home nor is she on the grounds."

"Ma'am," Penny interjected. "The woman that went missing last night might very well still be here on the premises. Until we say otherwise, Historic Strawberry Mansion is a crime scene until all staff have been questioned. So I'd suggest you pick up the phone and call whoever you need to call."

Frank was impressed with Penny's tone. "Miss Jefferson, before you get on the phone, I have more questions for you."

Jefferson was reluctant, but the situation's gravity began to sink in as a look of resignation befell the woman's face.

"Do you know who found the phone? An employee, or a party guest?" asked Frank, flashing his credentials for the first time.

"That, I'm not sure of, but it shouldn't be too hard to ascertain that information, Detective Collazo," said Jefferson, looking over his badge and I.D.

"We only had sixteen staff on duty last night. I can contact each one if you'd like. Several of them are working today."

"Yes, we will need you to do that for us," said Penny. "In the meantime, we'll need to speak to each staff member working today that worked last night. And we'll need a quiet place to sit down and speak to them."

"Detectives, what are you suggesting happened here last night? I mean...." Jefferson hesitated. "I, I, mean, from a lost phone to a crime scene? Well, I...."

"Mrs. Jefferson," replied Frank.

"It's Miss." Jefferson corrected Frank.

"Miss Jefferson," Frank addressed the woman. "Belinda Mereby went missing early this morning, and as far as we can tell, this is the last place she was seen."

Jefferson looked worried. "So, are you suggesting....?"

"We're not suggesting anything," Penny cut the woman off. "Now, please, round up those employees that were working last night. We'll wait here."

"Along with those working last night but not on duty today," Frank paused. "You'll need to ask them to come in ASAP. This is an urgent matter, and time is of the essence."

"Yes, of course, Detectives." Jefferson feigned cooperation. "I'll need a few minutes to get those involved up here to meet with you. After that, I will begin making calls." The woman nervously nodded and said, "Now, if you'll excuse me, the two of you can wait in the front room without the stanchions."

"Oh, and Miss Jefferson," said Frank. "The camera here in the corner...." Frank pointed to a single camera in the corner above and to the left of the reception office that appeared to be viewing the foyer and front door of the mansion. "And the two in the corners flanking the front door. How long do you keep the footage from those cameras?"

"It depends on how much activity is going on in the camera's field of view," said Jefferson. "They are motion activated. The DVR can keep the footage for up to a month or more."

"Well, we'll need to take a look at that footage from last night," requested Frank.

"Do you have a warrant, Detectives?" Jefferson flashed an insincere smile as she looked at both Frank and Penny.

"Ma'am, as both my partner and I have communicated to you, we have probable cause to suspect a guest of this home may be in grave danger." Penny was forceful. "If you'd prefer, we can have you and your employees come down to the 39th District Headquarters for questioning. Additionally, we can request a warrant and have our cyber-forensics unit take possession of all the cameras and DVRs on-premises if that would be better for you. Your choice, but make it fast. As my partner told you moments ago, time is of the essence."

Frank looked on as Penny continued to impress him.

"No, that won't be necessary. I will pull up the camera footage for you." Jefferson, realizing the detectives had called her bluff, acquiesced.

"Thank you, Miss Jefferson," Frank was conciliatory. "We'll wait up front. Take your time."

As Frank and Penny walked back toward the front of the house, Frank's cellphone rang. "This is Collazo," he said into his phone.

"Frank, it's Riley."

"Hey Sarge, whattaya got?"

"Frank, we got a limo being pulled out of the Schuylkill River as we speak. Just north of you off of MLK, under the Twin Bridge's overpass where Route 1 merges onto 76 West. It's just East of the Falls Bridge and just feet from the train trestle," explained Riley. "Some cyclists spotted the top of the car sticking out of the water."

Frank mouthed, "Holy shit," to Penny as she saw his chin drop.

"State Troopers are on scene along with uniformed officers from the 5th. There's a Marine Unit just south of Laurel Hill Cemetery. They're loading up now and will be en route shortly. Get on J Band for an ETA on their arrival," said Riley. "Divers will go into the water on your command. Get over there and put Strawberry Mansion on hold for now. I'm sending Wade and McCurdy over there, too." Riley's voice was loud enough for Penny to hear the update.

"Roger that, Sarge. Penny and I will get over there ASAP," Frank told his supervisor. "I'll give you an update in an hour or so."

"That's good, Frank. Listen, you don't call Mereby with any updates. The Captain said he'll call him when we have something to report. Got it?"

"Roger that, Sarge. I got it," said Frank.

Frank hung up and turned to Penny.

"I heard everything," said Penny. "I'll let Jefferson know to get all the eyewitnesses here by 3 pm."

"Whattaya wanna bet that's the limo?" asked Frank.

"I have no doubt that's the car," said Penny. "I just pray to God Belinda Mereby isn't in it."

Frank shook his head, acknowledging Penny. "Me, too," he sighed. "I'll pull the car around. Meet you outside in five."

The skies were overcast, and rain was in the forecast as the Dodge Charger rolled across the Strawberry Mansion Bridge.

Penny looked over at her partner and said, "What in the hell is going on, Frank?" Shaking her head, she added, "I mean nothing much has happened since Halloween, and now we've got two missing persons and a floating crime scene in the Schuylkill River."

"Well, this is what we signed up for," Frank said as he turned right onto MLK.

"What I want to know is where that car entered the river?" said Penny.

"That's probably why some guys from the 5th are on scene," reasoned Frank. "I don't know what the currents were like since last night, but it likely went in upriver."

"Whattaya think, Iron Works? City Avenue? Falls Bridge?" asked Penny.

"There's no telling. Maybe the boys in the 5th can shed some light on it," said Frank. "It's possible it went in right on the Schuylkill River Trail."

"Yeah, upriver makes no sense if the purse was found off of Route 1 coming south down from Germantown. Why go over there to dump it?" Penny was thinking aloud.

"I'm still wondering what took the limo up toward Germantown just to come back south again." Frank's questions were mounting in his head. "I mean, why come back south? Why not dump the car upstate?"

"The whole thing stinks," said Penny. "It's like breadcrumbs. I mean, Strawberry Mansion, up to Germantown, back down Route 1 to MLK, and almost back to the mansion." Penny shook her head. "It's like this guy's a rookie at kidnapping or...."

"He wants us to follow the breadcrumbs," Frank finished Penny's thought.

"There you go, Frankie Boy. You're smarter than you look." Penny poked her partner.

"Well, if I was as smart as I looked, I'd be Detective Sergeant by now." Frank launched a smile as he approached the Twin Bridges.

As the Dodge slowed down, Frank and Penny counted multiple units on scene. There were two gray State Police Interceptors: a Ford Taurus and a Ford Explorer. In addition to the Staties, there were three Philly Police cars, two wreckers, and a fire truck. Flashers were on, and local traffic was being diverted both north and southbound on MLK.

As Frank and Penny exited the car, Frank popped the trunk, and the two put on their police-issued rain jackets and blue surgical gloves before approaching.

Officer Carl Fitzpatrick approached Frank and Penny as they got closer to the scene. "Hey, Fitz. Whatta we got?" Frank recognized Fitzpatrick from his time working in the 39th.

"We got a black stretch Lincoln Town Car, almost fully submerged," said Fitzpatrick. "We think it went in early this morning at this location."

"Why's that?" asked Penny.

Fitzpatrick lifted his chin to point. "Fresh tire tracks are leading right off the River Trail into the water. The car appears to be hung up on something just below the water line. Probably a submerged tree stump, or something," said Fitzpatrick.

"Is the Marine Unit on scene yet?" asked Penny.

"Not yet," said Fitz.

Frank grabbed his walkie and asked the dispatcher to transfer him over to J Band.

Frank placed the walkie-talkie to his mouth and barked, "Yeah, this is Detective Frank Collazo from the 39th. We're here on scene at the Twin Bridges. What's the ETA on the Marine Unit?"

The radio coughed, and the male dispatcher said, "About five minutes out. Be on the lookout."

"Copy, that!" said Frank.

Lowering the walkie, Frank looked at his partner and said, "Don't look now, but your ex is standing at the back of that fire rescue unit."

Penny wore a look of dread as her eyes went in the direction of the fire truck and said, "Shit!"

Frank chuckled and began walking with Fitzpatrick while Penny looked down, shaking her head in disgust.

Frank beat Penny to the scene, purposely passing closely by his partner's ex-husband, Dan.

"What's up, Asshole?" said Frank, smirking.

"Fuck off, Collazo!" Dan Bristow barked back.

Dan Bristow smiled when he looked back at the Dodge Charger and saw Penny approaching. "Hey, Penny! How ya doing?"

"Go to hell, Dan!" said Penny as she blew past her ex.

Now at the foot of the river, Frank squatted down to get a better look at the tire tracks leading into the water. He instructed a police photographer to quickly get pictures before the rain came down as it was beginning to drizzle. Frank then took out his cellphone and snapped pictures of his own.

"So, whatta we got?" asked Penny of her partner.

"Well, the ground's been soft since all the snow from Christmas," Frank pointed. "It looks like the person who tried to push the car down the embankment thought they could get enough leverage and let gravity do the work from there."

"Looks like he was wrong," said Penny.

"Look at these shoe impressions running down the middle of the tire tracks," said Frank, pointing. "That's the dumb son of a bitch pushing from the back."

"He didn't plan on the soft ground, did he?" Penny smiled.

"Yeah, if you look," pointed Frank. "The top of the car never went under the water.

"Oh, yeah. I see." Penny squinted toward the black car that was ninety percent submerged in her estimation. "What are the wreckers waiting on?"

Just then, the Marine Unit pulled up on scene. "Them," said Frank. "Those guys will survey the area around the car first to make sure no evidence is destroyed."

"You think she's in there?" asked Penny, looking at her partner.

Frank shook his head and winced. "We're gonna find out in the next twenty minutes."

Penny grimaced. "I don't want to be the one making that call."

"The sarge said Sumner will be making all the calls to Mereby," said Frank. "This is some high-level shit we stepped into," he added. "When the Mayor gets involved.....," Frank's eyes widened. "It's gonna get lots of attention. By the book, Penny!" Frank walked closer to the river to address the Marine Unit commander.

Thirty minutes later, the Staties and officers from the 5th had all left once it had been determined that the 39th had jurisdiction. Fire and rescue stood by, along with an ambulance, as the wreckers slowly pulled the Lincoln from the water. After the car was completely on shore, one Marine Unit Officer approached the rear passenger door to release the water from inside the vehicle. Everyone on the scene quietly hoped no corpse would be found inside.

Before the car door was opened, only the passing cars from Route 1 overhead, the sound of the flowing Schuylkill, and the rapid clicking of a police camera could be heard at that moment.

With the muted click of a door handle being pulled, an avalanche of muddy water rushed from the car. Frank held his breath. After nearly all the water deluged the ground around the car, the severed head of a black male rode the last wave of water onto the soaked ground. Everyone gasped while cyclists and curiosity seekers in the distance behind yellow police tape groaned in horror.

Penny's hand went to her mouth as Frank looked down and slowly shook his head. After collecting his thoughts, he said, "That ain't Belinda Mereby."

"Jesus Christ!" said Penny. "Where's the rest of the guy?"

Frank's eyes went toward the back of the stretch limo and said, "We'll let the boys from Engine 59 pry open that trunk."

Penny turned to walk away and radioed her dispatcher that a coroner would be needed. Just then, Detectives Kyle Wade and Cindy McCurdy arrived on scene.

"Here comes your twin," Frank said to Penny as he spotted Kyle Wade and Cindy McCurdy walking up on their location. Everyone, including Frank, thought Penny and Cindy were sisters because they shared the same height, hair color, and facial features.

"Holy shit!" yelled Wade. "Is that a head on the ground over there?"

"Yep," Frank's eyes went wide as he nodded. "And I got money the rest of him is in that trunk."

Engine 59 applied their hydraulic extrication tool to the vehicle's trunk, and when they opened it, a headless corpse was found floating in the coffee-colored water.

"Hey, Penny." Cindy McCurdy walked over to Penny. "What's up, Sister from another Mister?!"

Cindy always looked up to Penny, who was three years older. The two were good friends and hung out a few times a month.

"What in the hell are we looking at?" McCurdy couldn't bring herself to look away from the severed head lying just twenty-five feet away.

Penny, not in a joking mood, winced. "I'd say we got a homicide on our hands."

McCurdy's head went back as her eyes flew open in obvious agreement. "Yeah, no shit!"

The firemen on the scene looked to be wrapping up when Engine 59's Dan Bristow yelled out, "Okay, we're all done here, fellas! Let's move it out!"

As Bristow walked by his ex-wife, he mumbled, "Good luck with all that."

Penny said nothing.

"Oh, hey, Cindy!" Dan smiled and winked at Penny's lookalike, trying to make his ex-wife jealous.

McCurdy rolled her eyes and whispered, "Creep."

Penny again shook her head in disgust.

Frank turned to Wade and McCurdy and said, "You guys call in the Crime Scene Unit and stick around until they wrap up. Penny and I have to get back to Old Strawberry Mansion."

After a brief updating of the facts at the scene, Frank and Penny were back in the Charger.

After a moment of silence, a look of horror flashed in Penny's eyes, and she said, "You don't see something like that every day."

At that moment, Frank abruptly stopped the car and vomited out the partially opened driver's side door. Recoiling back into his seat and wiping his mouth, he said, "I've never seen anything like that before!"

Frank continued driving, making a U-turn onto MLK southbound. "Let's go watch some surveillance footage," he said.

As the car straightened itself, Penny heard Frank mumble to himself, "I sure as hell didn't sign up for that."

Chapter 6 – Breadcrumbs

Sitting in the Historic Strawberry Mansion parking lot, Frank called his Sergeant, Doug Riley.

"Sarge, Penny, and I are back at Strawberry Mansion. I've got Wade and McCurdy wrapping up at the Schuylkill scene. CSU should be there shortly." Frank was stoic. "We found a corpse in the trunk, Sarge."

"I heard. Kyle texted me a picture. Jesus Christ, Frank, what the hell are we lookin' at here?"

"Some serious shit, Boss!" responded Frank. "It looks like the deceased is the limo driver, based on the clothes he was wearing."

"We'll need to confirm that," said Riley.

"That's why I'm calling, Sarge. Can you have Kyle and Cindy trace the limo back to the company that owns it, and then find out who was driving it last night? We need to determine how the person who dumped the limo got out of there without a ride, or if they had an accomplice."

"Once they get back to Headquarters, have them log in and view camera footage from the Twin Bridges off-ramp to 76 North, MLK in both directions, and the River Trail itself," requested Frank. "Based on when the purse was seen being tossed from the car, the timeframe should be anywhere between 4 am until the time of the limo's discovery."

"Yeah, I've already got Cole and Brooks looking at CCTV footage now," said Riley.

"Penny and I will be here at the mansion for a few hours interviewing everyone that worked last night," said Frank.

"Frank, this shit got real in a hurry!" said Riley.

"Yeah, we thought Old Man Mereby was just overreacting!" said Frank. "You know, Sarge, if those kids don't see that purse being tossed out the window, we're not connecting Mereby to the limo."

"Yeah," said Riley. "That occurred to me, too."

"Okay, well, Penny and I will check in later."

"Okay, Frank. I'll talk to you later."

Penny looked over at her partner and said, "Frank, if we find out when that car was dumped, we're gonna see our killer on one or more of those cameras."

"Penny, this all feels too planned," said Frank, while scribbling in his notepad. "I mean, to kill the limo driver, snatch Mereby, take her up north somewhere, and come back down south to dump the car, then get away?" Frank shook his head, "I don't know, Partner. That takes a lot of time and planning."

"Not just that," Penny added. "It would also require perfect execution."

"There's got to be more than one person involved if this kidnapping was perfectly orchestrated and executed," said Frank.

"Maybe old man Mereby will get a ransom call today?" thought Penny aloud.

"My gut's telling me there won't be any ransom call." Frank flipped through the pages of his notepad. Looking back up to Penny, he added, "Kidnappers don't cut people's heads off....."

"But murderers do," Penny finished Frank's thought.

"Penny, who throws evidence out the window at four in the morning when there's a car right behind you?" Frank shook his head. "This fucker's leaving us breadcrumbs for a reason." He paused, "He's either reckless and lucky, or he's calculating and smart. Either way, there's no perfect crime, so he likely fucked up somewhere. We just need to find out where."

"The camera footage will help," said Penny.

Minutes later, Penny and Frank were greeted by Jacqueline Jefferson in the mansion's foyer.

"Detectives, I have some good news for you."

Frank and Penny looked at each other and were skeptical after what they'd just seen at the river.

"And what would that be, Miss Jefferson?" asked Frank.

"I have video evidence showing Belinda Mereby exiting the premises and getting into a car on the estate's northside," revealed Jefferson. "The car then drove away with her in it. That means that she's not here on the property." Jefferson was almost celebratory.

Penny and Frank perked up with the revelation. "Well, show us that footage now and tell the staff on duty who worked last night that they'll have to wait," said Penny.

"I have more good news to share as well," offered Jefferson.

Frank asked, "Oh, and what's that?"

"I have three staff members who saw Mrs. Mereby and someone matching the description of Mr. Jacks in our wine cellar just before midnight last night. As it turns out, that's where Mrs. Mereby's phone was found."

Jefferson looked proud of herself, thought Penny. "That's good detective work, Miss Jefferson, but it's Miss, not Mrs.," said Penny.

"I beg your pardon, Detective."

Belinda Mereby is not married," said Penny. "So it's Miss, not Mrs."

"Oh, I see." Jefferson was unimpressed with Penny's demeanor. "Why, thank you for the clarification, Detective. I stand corrected." Jefferson's gaze told Penny that the curator didn't care for her very much.

Penny looked over at Frank and half-smiled, letting him know that she had his back from when he misspoke earlier, calling the curator Mrs. instead of Miss.

Just as Frank and Penny turned toward Jefferson's office, they heard a commotion at the front door of the estate. Walking through the entrance was the women's group that was scheduled for noon.

Frank and Penny snapped their heads back to Jefferson and looked at her with contempt.

Jefferson smiled at the detectives and said, "As I mentioned to you earlier today, Miss Mereby is not on the premises and left here early this morning of her own volition. No crime scene here, Detectives." Jefferson flashed a sly grin. "Now, please, let me show you the video evidence." Jefferson lifted her hand and motioned for the two detectives to follow her.

"You better be right about that, Miss Jefferson, or you'll be charged with obstruction," warned Penny.

"Again, follow me, please," said Jefferson, looking confident.

Minutes later, viewing the CCTV footage, Frank said, "I'll be damned. There she is, walking out the door alone."

"Did you see that, Frank? It looked like she blew Jacks a kiss on the way out," said Penny, pointing at the monitor.

"I did." Frank pulled out his notepad. "Miss Jefferson, can you show us the footage of her outside getting into the limo?"

Jefferson toggled to another monitor and pushed the 'play' button.

As Frank and Penny viewed the footage, they could see the back of Mereby as she walked unsteadily away from the house and toward the limo. They witnessed the limo driver hastily exit his vehicle and welcome Mereby by opening the rear passenger side door of the car.

Jefferson said, "I also have footage of Miss Mereby and Mr. Jacks entering the stairwell to the mansion's basement, which is where the wine cellar is. After that, I only know what my employees have told me about what they saw down there."

"Which was?" asked Penny.

"Discretion is the better part of valor, Detectives," offered Jefferson. "I'll let you interview your witnesses. I'd rather not pass along second-hand information."

"Miss Jefferson," said Penny, "Detective Collazo and I will need you to leave the room for a moment."

"Very well, then. I'll attend to our arriving guests," Jefferson was facetious.

After she left the room, Penny said, "Frank, our suspect appears to be a tall, stocky, white male, though the images are grainy."

"Yes, and did you see how fast he got out to greet her? It's like he was making sure she didn't get into another limo," surmised Frank aloud. "That shows premeditation."

"Frank, that limo is a Lincoln, too. I wonder if Denny over in Manayunk can do something with the blurry license plate," Penny wondered aloud.

"Not sure about the plate, but it's definitely a Lincoln." Frank agreed. "It's a stretch Town Car like at the river. The other cars all look like Cadillacs." Frank pursed his lips. "That's it, Penny. That's the car!"

"Okay, so we have our initial description." Penny jotted some notes. "Now we have to find out how tall Belinda Mereby is so that we can determine the height of our suspect. Either she's really short, or our suspect is very tall."

"Okay, I'll call it in to the Sarge," said Frank, pulling his cellphone from his jacket pocket. "You get our witnesses prepped to be interviewed."

Penny left the room as Frank dialed his boss. "Sarge, our suspect is a white male, age undetermined. Height is roughly six inches taller than that of Mereby, though I'm sure she had on heels, so he's likely seven to eight inches taller than her."

"How do you know this, Frank? Eyewitness testimony?" asked Riley.

"No, we have our suspect on video, posing as a limo driver," said Frank. "My guess is the actual limo driver was already in the trunk of that car before Mereby ever got into it."

"Jesus Christ!" said Riley. "That's some twisted shit, right there."

Frank sighed. "Twisted shit is a severed head spilling out of the backseat of a flooded limousine onto the banks of the Schuylkill."

Riley conceded, "Yeah, you don't see that every day."

Frank didn't bother responding to his sergeant like he'd responded to Penny earlier when she'd uttered the same words.

"Sarge, once we find out where that limo driver was prior to going to the mansion, we'll likely find another crime scene," said Frank. "I'll call you later with more information. Get someone on Mereby's height, would you? It'll be on her Driver's License."

"You got it, Frank," said Riley. "Oh, and Frank....,"

"Yeah, Sarge?"

"I'm starting to feel like this isn't random," said Riley.

"Yeah, and I'm starting to think we're gonna find a lot more crime scenes," replied Frank. "I'm betting that Belinda Mereby is no longer with us."

"Yeah, me, too." Riley paused, then added, "I got the Marine Unit and divers sweeping downriver. The currents have been strong since the snowmelt from Christmas."

"That's good, Sarge. I'll call you later."

"Okay, Frank. If anything else crosses my desk, I'll let you know."

After hanging up the phone with his boss, Frank thought the world was a fucked up place. He'd secretly wished that Mereby had gone missing in any district other than the 39th.

Thirty minutes later, Frank and Penny sat across a folding table in an empty banquet room, interviewing the first of three eyewitnesses. The three mansion employees had told Jefferson they saw Mereby and Jacks together in the basement of the mansion the prior evening.

"Miss Valdez, can you tell us around what time you saw Miss Mereby and Mr. Jacks in the wine cellar?" asked Frank.

Gloria Valdez was nervous when speaking to the police. Her hands trembled, and she was hesitant about getting involved.

"My paperwork is in line, Inspector. I am legal to work in this country." Valdez spoke in broken English.

"Miss Valdez," Frank flashed a reassuring smile. "I'm a Detective, not an Inspector, and I'm not concerned with your legal status right now. I simply want to know what you witnessed last night in the wine cellar. Now again, what time did you see Miss Mereby and Mr. Jacks in the wine cellar?"

Valdez seemed more at ease with Frank's assurance. Looking more relaxed, she looked both ways and responded, "It was around 11:30, and they were doing it like monkeys," her eyes went wide.

"Monkeys?" asked Penny, leaning in while taking notes.

"You know, like monkeys in a zoo?" Valdez tapped on the table. "Sometimes people sneak downstairs during parties, and they do it like monkeys. Have you been to the zoo, Inspector?" Valdez directed her question at Frank while his partner looked on.

Penny smiled and replied," Do you mean they were having sex standing up?"

"Sì," responded Valdez.

Frank asked, "Did it appear to you that they were jointly engaged in the act, or was it forcible?"

Valdez, not understanding the question, shook her head, "I don't know what you mean?" she said, trying to interpret the question in her head.

"Were they having fun?" asked Penny. "You know, having a good time? Divertida?"

"Oh, yes, she liked it very much," said Valdez. "He looked very, how you say? Determinado? Angry!"

Frank and Penny tried not to smile at Valdez's description of the encounter.

"So, you believe it was consensual then?" asked Frank.

"Sì. Yes!" Valdez nodded.

"How long did you watch, Miss Valdez?" asked Penny.

Valdez looked embarrassed. "We took turns. We didn't want them to see us."

"Did you see the amorìo end?"

"Tu hablas espanol, Inspector?" Valdez looked pleasantly surprised.

"Un poquito," replied Frank. "Did you see it end?"

"Sì." Valdez's demeanor changed. To Frank and Penny, Valdez suddenly appeared troubled and concerned.

"What is it, Miss Valdez?" asked Penny.

"You see, that's the thing," said Valdez. "When they finished, they looked angry. Like they didn't like each other anymore. He was mean to her. He grabbed her and pushed her, and she spit in his face."

Frank and Penny were alarmed as they jotted down Valdez's description of events.

"What else can you tell us, Miss Valdez?"

"When he pushed her against the wine rack, several bottles fell onto the floor. Mucho problemo! Glass and wine were everywhere! Gran desorden!"

"Are there any cameras in the wine cellar?" Penny was curious.

"No, I don't think so. That's why people go in there to do it," said Valdez.

"Is there anything else you'd like to tell us, Miss Valdez?" asked Frank.

"Sì. I am the one who found the phone. And," Valdez paused.

"And?" Frank led his witness.

"After cleaning the desorden," she paused again, "I heard the phone vibrar. You know, buzz-buzz. That's how I found it."

"And what did you do then?" asked Penny.

"I picked it up and read the message on the front of the phone."

"And what did it say?" asked Frank.

"It was some kind of threat," said Valdez. "You will pay, or something like that."

Frank turned to see Penny already staring at him. "We need to see that phone, now!" he said.

Chapter 7 – The 39th District

Second Floor Detective Room – 39th District – New Year's Day 2017, 6:14 pm.

Penny and Frank were meeting with Sergeant Doug Riley, Captain Rosalyn Sumner, and Detectives Kyle Wade and Cindy McCurdy, who were all awaiting their arrival.

As Frank and Penny ascended the stairs to the second-floor Detective Room, they could hear the chatter of their colleagues trying to make heads or tails of the day's events. When Frank turned the handle and pushed the door open, the room got so quiet that a pin could've been heard crashing onto the floor. All eyes were on the two detectives and what information they might have to share.

Frank, first through the door, spotted Sumner and knew in his heart that this would be the biggest investigation of his career, all of their careers.

"Hey, Cap. Hey, Sarge. Guys." Frank nodded to the group. An evidence bag and a DVR with the cables still dangling from its back were in his hand. "Things just got a little more complicated for us."

"What does that mean?" asked Captain Sumner.

Frank wore his look of resignation like a war veteran wears a scar. He wasn't sure if he should be proud, or meek. He was conflicted. He knew that the news he was about to share would result in a political scandal. One that could unseat the headlines currently occupied by the upcoming Democratic National Convention in July.

In the past year, the city had been rocked by scandal. The previous June, a longtime Philadelphia Congresswoman, Chaka Fattah, was found guilty in federal court of laundering grants and non-profit funds to repay a campaign loan.

Earlier in 2015, State Treasurer, Rob McCord pled guilty to extortion while fundraising for his re-election campaign.

Before that, Attorney General Kathleen Kane was put on trial for leaking secret grand jury materials to the Philadelphia Inquirer and then lying about it while under oath.

What Frank Collazo held in his hand would again rock the city with more scandal just as it had desperately tried to clean up its act.

Frank placed the evidence on his desk and then took a seat. Needing a moment to collect his thoughts, he forgot to take off his coat. Penny removed hers, hung it on the rack outside of Riley's tiny office, and sat down at her desk. The silence was broken when the old radiators along the Schuyler Street windows rattled as the steam passed through them.

"All right, Collazo," barked Sumner, "enough with the dramatics. Whattaya got?"

Before Frank could say a word, Penny spoke up. "We believe that Warren Jacks is a person of interest in the Mereby case."

"Warren Jacks?!" Sumner wasn't happy. "How in the hell is he involved?"

Riley jumped into the conversation. "Jacks hosted the party, and Old Man Mereby told us earlier that he'd been involved in a relationship with Belinda Mereby for the last two decades."

"That ain't exactly front-page news," said Sumner. "Half the city knows about their affair."

Without another word, Frank shook the contents of a clear evidence bag out onto his desk. Slipping on a pair of black latex gloves, he lit up Belinda Mereby's cellphone and opened the text app.

Scrolling up past dozens of text messages from concerned friends and family, Frank stopped at a text from someone with the initials W.J.

"Last night, sometime after 11:30 pm, Warren Jacks was witnessed by mansion staff having sexual intercourse with Mereby in the basement's wine cellar," revealed Frank. "After they were finished, there was a verbal altercation between the two, and that resulted in Jacks pushing Mereby up against a rack of wine bottles and Mereby spitting in his face."

"Mereby ended up losing her phone during the struggle, and it was found later by one of the staff at the mansion." Frank looked down at the phone and said, "I'm about to read verbatim a text that came through on Mereby's phone at exactly 2:19 am, just minutes after she left the mansion." Frank was slightly nervous. "The message is from a W.J., and it reads: *You've threatened me for the last time!*"

"We confirmed that the cellphone number belongs to Jacks and that W.J. is, in fact, Warren Jacks," said Penny.

"So, Jacks threatens Mereby just minutes before she goes missing," said Riley. "Either he's involved and stupid, or he's not involved and damn unlucky."

"Do we know what threat she made toward him?" asked Sumner.

"No. Not yet," said Penny. "That's not in the thread, but we do know from other texts back and forth that tensions were high between the two prior to Mereby arriving at the party."

Frank sat up in his chair. "My guess is that he was breaking it off, and she threatened to go public or tell his wife."

"How do you want to move forward with Jacks, Captain?" asked Riley. "This is gonna get sticky, what with the convention coming into town and all."

Captain Sumner pondered the situation for a moment and said, "I'll put a call into the Commissioner first. He can decide when to get the Mayor involved. After that, though, only P.D. Leadership will reach out to Jacks' lawyer."

"Captain, we can't bring him in here, can we?" asked Frank with a quizzical look.

"No, of course not," snapped Sumner. "Imagine a guy with his influence being seen walking into the 39th? That's why I'm putting a call straight into the Commissioner's Office, bypassing the Inspector and Deputy Commissioner. Bill and I go way back. We came up through the Academy together and actually walked the beat back in the day. He'll appreciate me cutting everyone else out of the loop and going straight to him. After that, he can sort it all out."

Riley stood up and confidently said, "You want me to conduct the interview, Captain?"

Sumner looked Riley up and down and shook her head. "No. This one goes to Collazo and Bristow. They've done all the heavy lifting so far."

Riley nodded but looked a little deflated by Sumner's decision.

"And besides, this one's got lots of layers, and you've got four other detectives that I want on the search for Mereby and the lunatic that killed the limo driver," added Sumner.

"But I..." said Riley.

"Sergeant, get me the report on what was seen on the CCTV footage from the Twins!" barked Sumner. "Collazo, Bristow, you two follow me."

Twenty minutes later, Frank and Penny sat in Sumner's second-floor office, waiting for their Captain.

"Good job today, Penny," said Frank. "We got a lot of good info from our visit to Strawberry Mansion."

Penny shook her head. "I'm still thinking about that poor bastard we found in the limo."

Without another word, the door behind them swung open, and Sumner blew in as if they weren't there. The office was mundane, with no pictures on the walls and only a faded and cracked circular decal on the Yelland Street side of the room that read the motto of the 39th. The decal had a silhouette of a police badge in the middle of it from what looked like the 1930s. On the brown-colored badge were the large yellow numbers, 39, and the uppercase letters TH, flanked by green oak leaf clusters. Around the decal were the words, 'Philadelphia Police Department,' with the inner circle stating: 'Our Motto – Above and Beyond.' The logo looked like it was colored in crayon by a school-aged child from many decades earlier. No one had spoken the motto itself from the 39th in many years.

Sumner plopped down and exhaled fully, throwing a manila file folder onto her desk. "So, Frank, Penny, I need to know if you're ready to take the lead on this case?"

Penny began to say, "Yes," when Frank blurted out, "What about the Frank Bruno case from Nazareth Hospital? The old man's gone missing and needs to be found. His daughters need him back." Frank was disheartened.

He was worried about the time commitment the Mereby case would demand. He also didn't want his face in the news while going through a custody battle. He felt that he and Penny were somehow destined to find the legendary detective.

"Frank, it's not a homicide until they find a body," Sumner reminded her detective. "We're giving it to Wade and McCurdy starting now. You'll brief them with what you've got, and they'll run the investigation going forward. They'll also assist you with any small to-dos on the Mereby case."

Sumner continued, "So what I need to know, is can you handle this?"

"We got it, Cap!" Frank feigned confidence, and Penny could tell.

"Roger that, Cap! I'm all in!" said Penny, directing her stare at Frank.

"Listen, this one is gonna get a lot of press, and I want you two to be the face of the investigation," explained Sumner. "You'll, of course, say nothing to reporters, but your faces are going to be in the papers. You'll make no public statements, though. Do I make myself clear?"

"Yes, Ma'am." Frank agreed, but being in the newspapers would not sit well with his soon-to-be-ex, Joanne. He also knew that a high-profile case would allow him even less time with his son, Conner. "I'm on it, Captain! Whatever it takes. We've got a nut job out there, and we need to get him off the streets."

"What about you, Bristow?" Sumner stared down the junior detective. "You got as much vigor as your partner over here?"

Penny slid forward in her chair. "I'm in one-hundred percent, Captain!" She knew that this case would define her career, and she was up for the challenge.

Sumner sat back in her chair. Behind her, a window facing Schuyler Street. "Do either of you know why I took this job in the 39th?"

Frank and Penny looked at each other, then back at their Captain, shaking their heads in unison.

"My mother's maiden name is Schuyler, and this is the most historic and oldest police station in the United States," revealed Sumner. "Yeah, it's old, and it stinks, but I come from a police family, just like you two. I jumped at the chance to lead the men and women of the 39th because of the history of this place, the building, and the area around it," she paused. "I take great pride in serving the people of East Falls."

"My father worked here for twelve years back in the 1970s, and sometimes he brought me to work with him. He worked with the likes of Frank Bruno and Philly's first-ever female Detective, Penny Bryce," she said.

"Hell, Penny. You were named after her. That woman was an inspiration and kicked in the first of many gender-locked doors," said Sumner. "It's my guess that we'll have a female commissioner named within the next few years."

Sumner added, "I also want to ensure that the corruption in the 39th dating back to 1997, and as recently as 2011, is part of our past. We need leaders like the two of you to bring positive change to this district and the people working here in the 39th."

Sumner paused and reflected, "Did you guys hear that they're talking about removing Frank Rizzo's statue from the front steps of the Municipal Services Building? That guy cast a long and dark shadow over this department and city for decades. If it comes down, you can bet your ass I'll be there to see it."

"The 39th has had legends working here, and you both should aspire to be like your predecessors. Hell! The 39th even solved the Boy in the Box case."

Frank's thoughts went to the legendary detective for a moment. "Yeah, we gotta find old Frank Bruno," he mumbled under his breath.

"We will, Frank. We'll bring him home."

"Captain, is it true that Al Capone actually spent a night behind bars here?" asked Penny. "I mean, did that really happen?"

Frank looked on with heightened curiosity, as every cop in the building had heard the story, but no one had ever believed it.

"That story's been around forever." Sumner smiled proudly. "I'd first heard about it when I was a little kid back in the seventies."

"From what my father told me, Al Capone was in town on the night of February 13, 1929, the evening before the St. Valentine's Day Massacre occurred back in Chicago. It's been said that he needed an alibi so that he wouldn't be implicated in the crime. To get one, Capone needed to be arrested in another city. From what I'd heard, he was arrested for disorderly conduct and tried to rough up a couple of our boys. Anything he could do to make it public and to make sure he'd spend a night behind bars," explained Sumner. "Was it really here in the 39th? That, I don't know," she said. "Other reports suggest that he was in Florida at the time, but it might as well have been here. Listen, in the end, Capone was never linked to the murders. Who knows, maybe the 39th District had something to do with that, and maybe it didn't. It doesn't really matter, but it's cool to talk about."

"I know this, though. Every time I walked up those creepy steps to the third floor, I imagine that Capone did, too. If he did, he stayed in the corner holding cell overlooking the parking lot out back. I take pride in the history of the 39th, and you should, too." Sumner beamed.

Frank and Penny's pride began to swell as they felt their Captain's love and admiration for both her job and the history of the 39th.

"Listen, when you guys get in tomorrow, I need you to focus on a new lead." Sumner opened the manila folder in front of her. "Brooks and Cole viewed all footage from the Schuylkill crime scene...."

"And....?" Frank sat up in his chair, eager to know what they'd found."

Penny also hung on Sumner's next words.

"And," said Sumner, "we've got our guy on tape. He appears to be a white male, 25-45, large build. That matches what the two of you saw on the tape from Strawberry Mansion, right?"

"That's the guy, Cap!" said Frank, looking over at Penny. "What time was it?"

"The video was stamped 4:42 am when he first shows up on the River Trail."

"So, we can see how he got out of there, then?" Penny perked up.

"Not so fast." Sumner's enthusiasm was tempered. "Our suspect can be seen jumping out of the limo as it went down the embankment into the river. When it got stuck in the wet grass, he got out and attempted to push it from behind."

"Okay, then what?" asked Penny. "Who picked him up?"

"That's the problem." Sumner was matter of fact. "Our suspect disappears out of view once down under the southbound bridge and never reappears again,"

"Wait, what?" Frank shook his head in astonishment.

"So, we think he went in the river with the car?" asked Penny.

"Don't know," said Sumner. "What I do know is that our guy isn't on any cameras after that car went into the Schuylkill."

"That river is near freezing this time of year. And the undercurrents....," Frank shook his head. "No one would last long in there. Maybe a mile, maybe less."

"The train trestle?" Frank wondered aloud.

"What about it?" asked Penny.

"He may have gotten out of the water under the train tracks and hoofed it north," said Frank. "That puts him in the water for only seconds or minutes."

"North to where?" Penny wasn't convinced. "He would've had to plan for that?"

"That water's probably moving at five to six miles an hour. He could have made it over to Kelly Drive and been picked up or had a car waiting." Frank thought aloud again, failing to answer Penny's question.

"North to where?" Penny asked again.

"I don't know, but if he took Mereby up north," said Frank. "then North is where he'd be heading."

"Well, you both have some work to do tomorrow." Sumner stood. "For all we know, he got caught up in the river and swept downstream. The currents are brutal with the snowmelt. He could be dead. I'll have a Marine Unit out tomorrow looking for a corpse washed up around the Temple Boathouse. That's where the river makes its first turn south of the Twins. If not there, Peter's Island or the Columbia Bridge. If he's there, we'll find him. If he's not, then you two better find him before we end up needing more body bags."

"Frank, I think your instincts are good," added Sumner. "Up north is where you're gonna find Mereby."

"All right, you two get out of here and get some sleep tonight. It's gonna be a bunch of late nights between now and finding our perp and Belinda Mereby."

As the two detectives stood, Frank asked his Captain, "Hey Cap, so is Schuyler Street named after your mother's family, or what?"

"That, I don't know," smiled Sumner. "The next time I see Al Capone, I'll be sure to ask him."

Frank and Penny laughed while Sumner smiled. "I'll tell ya this, though. I love turning off of West Hunting Park onto Schuyler every morning, though. It feels like home," Sumner looked down introspectively.

Frank nodded as Penny exited the tiny office first and shouted to his Captain, "Above and Beyond! Right?"

"You got that right, Frank! Above and Beyond!" shouted Sumner back to her senior detective.

After the door closed, Penny looked at Frank and said, "That's some rah-rah bullshit, right there."

Frank appeased Penny's skepticism with a nod but deep inside, he was somewhat inspired by his Captain and the history of the 39th.

Later, as Frank drove back to his tiny flat above the Mad River Bar & Grill, he felt re-energized and confident. He'd work hard to live up to the rich history of the 39th. And he'd do whatever it took to find the man who kidnapped Belinda Mereby and killed the poor guy in the limo.

Chapter 8 – Body Bags

Second Floor Detective Room – January 5, 2017, 10:47 am.

Four days later, there was still no video evidence of Mereby's assailant leaving the river, and neither had his body washed up onshore. Frank and Penny had viewed hours of tape from cameras lining MLK and Kelly Drive and found nothing.

The rain fell heavily in North Philly as unseasonably high temperatures rose into the mid-forties. Frank Collazo stood with his hands in his pockets, looking out the Schuyler Street window of the second-floor Detective Room. His gaze fell upon the empty lot across the street between the Time Out Pub and West Hunting Park.

"I keep going back to where the train trestles meet the overpass, Penny." Frank shook his head in frustration, removing his hands from his pockets and turning to look back at his partner. "There're no cameras under the bridge or from Kelly up to Ridge. Whether he followed the tracks, North or South Ferry Roads, or kept going east on Kelly, there are no cameras around. How in the hell is that possible?" As he walked back to his desk, Frank was aggravated and studied the Google Earth map open on his computer.

"Because the killer knew what he was doing," said Penny. "He knew there were no cameras. He scoped it all out beforehand, Frankie."

"I think the guy rode the river fifty yards across and pulled himself right up onto Kelly Drive," reasoned Frank. "I mean, what if he planned the whole thing and had his car parked over somewhere off of Ridge?"

"You know, there's a parking lot under Route 1, right on the corner of South Ferry and Ridge?" Penny's facial expression told Frank that she was beginning to buy into his theory."

"I'm looking at it right now," said Frank, motioning for Penny to come around to his desk. "Think about it," he stressed. "It was a Sunday, early morning, and a holiday. No one would've been out on the streets at 5 am. God, I hope they have cameras on that lot."

"There's a daycare there on the corner that might have cameras, and The Trolley Car Café right behind them. Right here and here." Penny pointed to Frank's monitor. "But I've parked in that lot many times, and I don't think they have any cameras viewing it," she said.

"On the other side of that parking lot, on South Ferry," she pointed again, "there's an upscale pizza place called *In Riva*. I used to date the manager there. They might have cameras pointing to that lot."

"But if it's a Park & Pay, they should have cameras, right?" Frank suggested.

"Well, it is a Park & Pay lot, but on that end of East Falls, I don't think they do. It's not as sketchy over there," said Penny.

"Cameras or not, though, if he parked there overnight, he would've had to pay on his way out," said Frank.

Penny's eyes flew open. "I'll get on it. I'll see what cars left that lot between 4:45 and 6 am."

"Good!" said Frank. "Oh, and by the way, how do you know that area so well?" he asked.

"Before I got married, I used to live over there."

"No shit?! Where?" Frank looked surprised.

"In the Dobson Mills Apartments, right near the on-ramp to 1 North."

"That's right across the street from that parking lot, right?" asked Frank. "I think I see it here on the map. Across from the daycare?"

"Yep. It's just a short walk. I would have to park in the lot after a late night when there was no parking available at the apartment complex." Penny tapped the monitor again, indicating the path she had taken.

"Penny," Frank paused. "What if the guy had got an Uber to pick him up."

"An Uber? Really?" Penny was astonished by the suggestion. "Dripping wet, he called an Uber on a cellphone that had just been submerged in a polluted river?" she smirked. "Give me a break!"

"Yeah, you're right. Whatever." Frank felt stupid for suggesting it. He shrugged his shoulders and chuckled, "He would have stunk, too. I wouldn't have picked up the guy if I was driving an Uber."

A minute later, Detective Sergeant Doug Riley barged through the door and said, "Don't go anywhere, you two," after seeing Penny putting her jacket on. "We got the autopsy report in from the limo driver."

Frank looked at Penny, shrugged, and whispered, "He was decapitated!"

Penny also looked curious as to why the autopsy would've been relevant at the moment.

After momentarily entering his office and printing out documents, Riley emerged with two stapled bundles of paper. Tossing the first set of papers onto Frank's desk, he said, "Here's the autopsy report."

Frank grabbed the report and perused its contents. "Have we identified him yet?"

Penny looked on and asked her Sergeant, "Okay, so what's in the other hand?"

"Ballistics!" said Riley.

Frank sat up at attention.

"Our victim lost his head postmortem," revealed Riley. "He died from a single gunshot to the back of the head. A .22 behind his right ear."

"No shit?!" Frank asked. "Then why cut the guy's head off, for Christ's sake?"

"Doctor Lafferty thinks the killer might have been looking to retrieve the bullet?"

"Come on!" Penny thought that was a bit of a stretch.

"How'd Lafferty come to that conclusion?" asked Frank.

"Because much of the soft tissue in the stem and brain matter was removed from the skull, but the killer never retrieved the bullet," explained Riley. "But we did," he smiled. "It was lodged in the guy's skull bone, behind the forehead."

"And? What does the ballistics report say?" asked Penny.

Riley smiled and tossed the second report onto Frank's desk. "Two sets of striations!"

"Two?" Penny looked confused. "How does that happen?"

"A silencer," said Frank. "This guy's an idiot. If we find another .22 caliber round in someone else's head, it's gonna be easy to match up."

"Yep!" Riley's brows shot upward. "The guy fucked up! No doubt about that."

"Why wouldn't he just keep the head then, Just bury it somewhere?" asked Penny.

"For effect, maybe," offered Riley.

"Effect?" Penny was shocked at the notion.

"Listen, we're dealing with a guy that cut a man's head off and then went sifting through brain matter," explained Riley. "Nothing would surprise me."

Penny conceded with a nod, though the notion of it all still surprised the junior detective.

"Got a time of death on the limo driver?" asked Frank.

"Nope." Riley shook his head. "Chauffeurs eat at weird hours of the day, so there's no tellin' when his stomach's contents were ingested. On top of that, the river was freezing. Lafferty's convinced it was no more than twelve hours, and more likely only four to six hours before going into the river."

"That timeline fits if he dropped off Mereby and then ran into our killer before he could get back to the mansion to pick her up," Frank reasoned aloud.

"Well, once we find out the identity of our victim, then we just look through his bank records to see if he bought any food that night and when," reasoned Frank.

"But Sarge, you're assuming that she, or Jacks, ordered the same limo to drop her off and pick her up," said Penny.

"Well, it looks like you guys need to boot up the DVR from Strawberry Mansion and rewind it a few hours," suggested Riley. "We might be able to see our victim before he was killed. Or, if it was somebody else who dropped her off."

"Yeah, but no way our suspect had her in that car earlier in the night," said Frank. "He would've killed her earlier and not taken the chance of being seen at the mansion."

"I agree, but let's take a look anyway," said Riley.

"Unless he needed time," said Penny.

"Whatta you thinking, Penny?" asked Riley.

"The time between when he abducted her to when someone would've reported her missing. If she doesn't show up at the party, maybe that would have raised people's suspicions."

At that moment, Riley's cellphone rang. Penny and Frank looked on as their sergeant took the call.

"Riley here," the sergeant barked into his phone. "Kyle, whatta you got?"

Riley nodded his head and shot Frank and Penny a smile. "All right, that's good work. How do you spell that?" asked Riley.

Looking for a scrap of paper, Riley looked to Penny, who was closest. She looked around her desk and handed her boss a legal pad and pen.

"L-O-F-T-I-N," Riley mumbled as he scribbled the name. "That's good. Go ahead and run a background check on the guy and pull his employee files and timecards, too." Riley listened while Kyle Wade provided more details on the victim.

"Yeah, that's tough," he raised his brow. "Well, check with his employer regarding when they'd heard from him last," directed Riley. "Oh, and Kyle, pull the guy's cellphone records, too. Okay then, get to it!"

Riley hung up with Kyle Wade and said, "James Loftin is our victim. Thirty-eight years old. A wife and three teenage kids. Lived over in Glenwood, at West Lehigh and 11th. He's got a rap sheet, but he's been clean for the last ten years."

"Damn. That poor bastard was just a working stiff trying to get by like the rest of us." Frank looked solemn.

"What else did Kyle say?" asked Penny, shuffling papers looking for another notepad.

"Yeah, he said that Mereby's height was five foot eight. Other than that, that's all we got!" said Riley, getting ready to walk away.

"Wait a second," said Frank. Five-foot eight?" His eyes narrowed, and his head tilted.

Penny interjected. "That would make our suspect somewhere between six foot four and six foot six," she cringed.

Frank's eyes went wide. "Yeah, he's gonna be a scary motherfucker when we come face to face with him."

"All right, you two get with Kyle and Cindy later today and see what they got. Report to me before you guys head out for the day."

"You got it, Sarge!" said Frank.

"Listen, you guys have a big responsibility on this one," Riley reminded his detectives. "Don't fuck it up! Keep your heads down, and don't talk to the press. Shit's already hitting the fan down in the Mayor's office. Mereby's father is blowing up everybody's phone. The old man put up a million-dollar reward for anyone finding his daughter."

"A million bucks? Damn!" Frank shook his head.

"We're on it, Sarge!" said Penny, looking confident but feeling the pressure and the enormity of the situation.

Before disappearing into his office, Riley turned and said, "Oh, yeah, one more thing. "You're interviewing Warren Jacks on Monday at 9 am." Riley smiled, purposely waiting until the end of their conversation to share the news.

"Holy shit!" said Frank. "Where at?"

"Downtown, boys and girls!" Riley smiled again. "You're headed down to Race Street."

"Penny flashed an 'Oh no!' look, as her eyebrows flirted with her hairline.

"No pressure, guys, but the Captain, Commissioner Holden, and Chief Inspector Caffey will be looking on from another room."

"Put together your questions and have them to me by noon on Friday," said Riley.

Frank looked over at Penny, who was grimacing. His look conveyed to his partner that he, too, was nervous and wondering how they'd pull it off with the eyes of senior leadership staring at them. It also occurred to them that Jacks would have a high-profile lawyer with him, too.

"Take it easy, fellas. The brass will draft the questions," Riley smiled to Frank and Penny's relief. "We'll work some of yours in only after they've been approved."

Frank feigned displeasure. "But Sarge, how can they determine what questions to ask if they don't know what we know?"

Riley got serious and walked out of his office doorway. "Listen," he said. "This ain't some junkie from Kensington."

Riley then put both of his hands down on Penny's desk, which butted up to Frank's. "This is a well-respected criminal defense attorney, former Federal Prosecutor, and Law Professor. You think you're gonna get cute with this guy?" Riley stood up abruptly.

"This ain't just your case! It's the 39th's." Riley's face was deadpan. "But it is your career. Don't be a hero and fuck this up!"

Frank and Penny didn't see Riley's agitated state coming. Their boss just revealed to them that he was envious of their responsibility in the case. They now knew what they'd only suspected prior, that their boss felt he should be Lead Detective on the case.

An hour later, while Frank and Penny sat at their desks organizing the limited information they had, a pale-faced Riley walked out of his office and sat down at the desk next to them.

"What is it, Sarge?" Frank asked his boss as his eyes went to Penny.

"Warren Jacks is dead." Riley's face indicated to Frank and Penny that he thought the case was about to get even bigger than he'd anticipated.

"What the fuck!!" said Penny, her mouth agape.

Frank, too, looked awestruck. "What the hell is happening here?"

"Suicide?" asked Penny.

"That's what it looks like," but there was no note, and it's where he was found." Riley tried to formulate his words.

Frank and Penny looked at each other, then back to their Sergeant.

"The Twins. He was found dead in his car fifteen minutes ago. Gunshot to the head," said Riley. "Cyclists called it into the 5th. They're on the scene now."

"Whatta you wanna bet it was a .22 caliber," suggested Frank.

"Yep, they found a .22 in the car. You two need to get over there now!" barked Riley.

Frank headed for the coatrack and mumbled, "This ain't no suicide!"

As the Dodge Charger turned right off Schuyler onto West Hunting Park, heading south, Penny asked, "So, you don't think it's a suicide?"

The wipers clapped intermittently as the rain slowed to a drizzle. Frank was unsettled, and his senses were rattled. The sky was threatening, though, and a cold front was moving in on North Philly. Frank could feel it in his bones. He could feel the storm in his life merge with the storm brewing in his job. He knew that storm would bring a deluge of more bodies and missing persons. He'd try his best not to show it, but he was unnerved and wasn't sure he was qualified to run the investigation.

"Gimme a break, Penny!" Frank buckled his seatbelt. "It's a little too convenient, don't you think?" Exhaling heavily, he added, "Killer lover, overcome with grief and regret, commits suicide in the same exact spot we find the very limo that abducted his mistress? Come on!"

"Or, it makes perfect sense," replied Penny.

"No way that guy killed himself. Not a rich prick like that," reasoned Frank aloud. "Guys like that kill themselves after their money's all gone, and not before."

"Or, because he was asked to come in for questioning in the disappearance of his lover just days after the abduction, knowing that he killed her and the limo driver," said Penny. "Maybe he knew the jig was up," she added.

"No chance," said Frank shaking his head. "A guy like that would never go through a trial. No way he would've ever taken a seat in the defendant's chair after representing them and prosecuting them for decades. He'd never do it."

"That's what I'm saying," said Penny. "He killed himself to avoid all of that."

"If I had arranged the abduction and likely murder of Belinda Mereby, then killed the black limo driver who did the hit, then who's the white limo driver that picked her up?" asked Frank. "It wasn't Jacks dressed up as a chauffeur. That would suggest Jacks hired yet another person to be in on the hit? No way!" said Frank.

"You're right," Penny nodded in agreement. "This was to make it look like Jacks hired the driver to snatch Mereby. You're right. It's way too clean," said Penny.

"The Twins are back in the picture," said Frank, squeezing the steering wheel a little too tightly. That .22's coming back as the same weapon used on the driver. But why the River Trail under the Twin Bridges?" Frank wondered aloud.

"You might be right about the Schuylkill, Frank. That might very well be his escape vehicle," said Penny.

"Why the Twins?" Frank repeated. "And what's on the other side of the Schuylkill?" he thought to himself.

Ten minutes later, arriving at the scene just off the Schuylkill River Trail, Frank and Penny exited their vehicle and saw Officer Carl Fitzpatrick again.

"Hey guys!" yelled Fitzpatrick. "I figured you two would be on the scene soon enough."

"Fitz!" responded Frank. "What, they don't give you a day off?"

Penny said, "Hey, Carl."

Fifty feet away, an empty black body bag lay on a stretcher near a silver BMW X6 sport utility vehicle. The vanity plate read JAX 1. Nearby was a Coroner van and several police cars. The same yellow tape from three days prior still marked the scene.

Officers from the Crime Scene Unit were already processing the scene.

"Hey, Penny!" said Fitzpatrick. "What are the chances the three of us would be back here so soon?"

"Pretty damn good, actually," Frank mumbled as he walked away from Fitzpatrick and his partner.

"So, how ya been?" Carl Fitzpatrick tried to make small talk with Penny.

"Not now, Fitz." Penny brushed off Fitzpatrick and joined her partner at the BMW.

"Hey Denny, whatta we looking at?" Frank asked CSU Supervisor Daanesh Patel.

"Hey Frank, we waited until you got here before we extracted the body from the vehicle. Just wanted you to see it before we took him away," said Patel.

The clicking of two police photographer's cameras could be heard clicking away as Frank responded, "Thanks."

"So, you were just here on Sunday, huh?" asked Patel.

"Yeah, you heard about the decapitated body?"

"Oh yeah, the guys are still talking about it," said Patel. "It's been a while since we processed a scene like that one."

"Yeah, well, beef up your inventory of body bags because the guy responsible for this ain't done yet."

"You don't think this is a suicide?" Patel wondered how Frank could come to that conclusion when he hadn't even looked over the scene yet.

"My guess is, that it's supposed to look like a suicide, but this is without a doubt connected to what we found here on Sunday." Frank was certain.

"Well, it's going to start raining again here pretty soon. You might want to get a look inside that car before we clear the scene," suggested Patel.

"This tint definitely ain't legal." Frank surmised that if someone were in the car with Jacks, they likely wouldn't have been seen by surveillance cameras due to the darkened windows and overcast skies. He then did a 360° walk around and looked into the passenger side. There, he witnessed Jacks lying limp in the driver's side seat, head back against the door frame separating the front and back driver's side doors, with the back window blown out.

"Denny, have you found the bullet yet?" asked Frank. "He's got an exit wound, and the bullet is what likely shattered the back window."

"No, not yet," said Patel as he motioned to three CSU specialists searching the ground and nearby foliage. "That's what those guys over there are looking for."

"Has anyone moved any part of the body yet?" Frank didn't think that Jacks' head would come to a rest where it was.

"Denny, don't you think his head would be hanging forward with his chin draped onto his chest? I mean, if the bullet exited with enough force to cause a large exit wound, wouldn't it have blown his head forward? I mean, gravity would have done its job. Right?" Frank's gears were turning, and he could easily see the scene was staged.

"We haven't touched the body yet!" yelled Denny Patel from the other side of the vehicle. "And yes, blowback and gravity should have caused his head to fall forward."

Frank studied the condition of the back seat and floorboard of the SUV. Frank could see what looked like a .22 caliber Kel-Tech P17 pistol firmly wrapped in Jacks' right hand and a solitary shell casing lying on the seat between his legs. Slipping on his latex gloves, he opened the backseat, passenger side door and leaned in. He noticed irregular blood spatter patterns and then leaned back out and shut the door. "Make sure they photograph the backseat and floorboards, too," he yelled to Patel.

As Frank exited the vehicle, his gloved hand slipped on a smooth, silky substance found on the backseat. Now standing outside the vehicle, he rubbed his fingers together, raised his hand to his nose and smelled the Vaseline-like substance, and thought it smelled like wool or hay.

Penny, now standing at Frank's side, asked, "Whatta you thinkin'?"

"Like I said, this ain't no suicide," replied Frank. "Someone was sitting in that backseat when Jacks ate that bullet. My guess is that it was the triggerman."

"So lightning struck twice, huh? Right under the Twins." Penny shook her head.

"Our guy's using the river to escape," surmised Frank directing his comments to Patel. "We're not gonna see him on any cameras this time either."

"Well, last time, it was a holiday," said Penny. "Today, people are back at work. Lots of traffic on Kelly Drive."

"Hey, Denny," Frank yelled. "How long ago did the call come in?"

"About an hour ago!" Patel yelled back.

"Penny, it's been raining heavily all day," reasoned Frank. "The call came in only after the rain cleared up and cyclists were back on the trail. I got money this car's been here since before dawn. We'll need to find out when Jacks left his house this morning."

"Or last night," said Penny. "The cameras won't lie. I'll call Brooks and tell him to get on it," she said as she walked away.

Denny Patel walked over to Frank and said, "Listen, we're wrapping up here." Behind Patel, Frank and Penny could see Warren Jacks' body being placed into the body bag.

"Denny, so we definitely don't know how long the car's been sitting down here, right?" asked Frank.

"Hours, possibly. It would've been hard to spot passing by from MLK," said Patel. "I got my guys pulling video now."

Frank looked over his shoulder as Penny was pulling two raincoats from the trunk of the Charger. "Hey Penny, cancel that call to Brooksie. CSU's on it."

"Listen, Denny. Our perp is using that river to get away. I need all the electronic resources you have focused on the trestle, the Twins, and Kelly up to Ridge," said Frank. "This prick knows the area, and I bet he's nearby."

"Got it, Frank!" Patel nodded. "We're on it."

"Oh, and Denny," said Frank. "Test for the greasy substance on the back passenger side seat. It feels like Vaseline. It might mean nothing, but check it out anyway."

"Roger that," said Denny Patel as Penny walked up and tossed Frank a raincoat.

"Cancel the coat, Penny. We're outta here."

As Patel walked away, Frank yelled, "Denny, good work, Brother! Let me know what time this SUV showed up on camera this morning."

"10-4!" yelled Patel.

"I'm hungry," said Frank. "Let's grab some lunch!"

Penny shook her head on the way back to the car. "Hungry?" she mumbled.

Chapter 9 – Scars

By the Fall of 1992, FalconClaw was on its last leg. The mostly dilapidated mansion was on its third and final run as a retirement home. And after Halloween night in 1992, the home would be closed to residents for good.

In February of 1973, the home closed down after its lease with The Heavenly Gates Retirement Group expired. It sat vacant for nearly two years before Police Detective Penelope Bryce went missing from the property on Christmas morning in 1974.

After the bizarre disappearance, many community members called for its demolition while others wanted it classified as a Historical Landmark. In the Spring of 1975, the City Council voted six to five in favor of rezoning the mansion under the 'Historical Landmark' classification. Months later, the Historical Society of Pennsylvania, headquartered in Philadelphia, stepped in, and took ownership of the mansion and the one-hundred-sixty-seven acres of land it sat on. After a three million dollar and nearly four-year renovation, the Mansion reopened as a museum in January 1979 under its original name, FalconClaw.

After just over three years in business, however, the museum closed down in the Summer of 1982 after it had failed to generate enough revenue annually to cover the cost of being open.

By 1985, it was once again a retirement community, its third and final stint, and reverted to the name of Heavenly Gates.

Germantown – Penn Knox – 14th District Police Headquarters – Friday, October 23, 1992

"Hey, Sal! Got some mail addressed to you," shouted Ron Meyers, Desk Sergeant at the 14th District, into the Detective Room.

"Thanks, Ronnie!" Salvatore Collazo snatched the envelope from Meyers' hand, walked it back to his desk, and put his feet up. The Detective Room was tiny, housing only four detectives, and smelled like a three-day-old, half-eaten Philly Cheesesteak sandwich. No one was ever able to determine the source of the odor.

"Whattaya got there, Sal?" asked his partner, Diego Ramirez.

"Not sure. Looks like it might be from my guy. Let's rip this baby open and check it out."

Detective Salvatore Collazo tore open the envelope and found a tri-folded letter. The outside read: *Halloween*. The letter was from a source Collazo had been getting information from for the previous four months. Collazo had never met the anonymous source but had reason to trust him. The source had sent Collazo nine tips since that June, and all but one turned out to be information that led to an arrest. Salvatore Collazo always welcomed the information because it led to more collars than the other three detectives got all of that year.

"It's my guy," said Sal.

"Man, I wish I had that guy passing along information to me," said Diego. "That guy's right like nine out of ten times."

"Holy shit!" exclaimed Sal as his feet fell to the floor.

"Whattaya got, Sal?" said Diego as the other two detectives went quiet.

Only the humming sound of four oscillating fans, one in each corner of the room, could be heard as Sal finished reading the note to himself.

"This guy's saying that our 'serial killer' once worked at FalconClaw and might be back in business there," Collazo reported to the other detectives.

"What else does it say?" asked Diego, walking around to Sal's side of the desk.

"It says here that our 'serial' used to work at Heavenly Gates from 88 until 91 but might still have a key to the basement. He goes on to say that our killer has something planned for Halloween up at the FalconClaw mansion," explained Collazo.

"Diego, where's that letter we got last week from that psycho son of a bitch?"

"I don't know. You had it," said Diego.

Sal Collazo rummaged through the top drawer of his desk and found what he was looking for. A letter titled *Trick or Treat* included the line, *'Another soul, be damned.'* The serial killer had sent the letter to the 14th District the week before. The letter stated that the 'soul' to be damned would happen on Halloween night but didn't say where. The letter ended with the phrase, *Go Falcons!* Sal thought it was a threat directed at him or his family because his only son, Frank, played for the Falcons' baseball team.

Re-reading both letters, Sal was confused. He wasn't sure if the reference to Falcons was FalconClaw or his son's baseball team.

"Whatta you thinking, Sal?" asked Diego, as the other detectives gathered around.

"My source is saying something's happening at FalconClaw, but our killer is saying *Go Falcons!* I think our killer wants me to believe my son's in danger as a ruse," said Sal. "I think something's gonna happen at FalconClaw on Halloween night. But my son, Frankie, has a ballgame that same night."

"So whatta you saying, Sal?" asked Arthur Moates, another detective in the room.

"At first, I thought the psycho wanted me to believe my son was in danger. But now I'm sure he doesn't want me anywhere near FalconClaw that night," said Sal.

"Whoa!" said Diego. "I see it the other way around, Partner." Diego grabbed the letters from Sal and read through them. "I think the tip is bad. I think this guy wants you at FalconClaw and not at Frankie's game."

"I'm with Diego, Sal." Glen Watkins, the 14th District's most junior detective, weighed in. "You can't play Russian Roulette with your kid's safety."

"Guys, I can feel it," said Sal. "Something's going down at FalconClaw on Halloween, and Diego and I will be there." The look on Sal Collazo's face told his subordinates he was on to something.

"Well, we're going, too," chorused Moates and Watkins.

"No, no. You guys be at my son's game and have a squad car there, too," ordered Collazo. "Watkins, you sit in the visitor's stands, and Moates, you sit in the home team's stands. Be on the lookout for anything or anyone that looks suspicious. Additionally, let's make sure we have an officer hang back by his patrol car but be on foot," he directed. Collazo was the senior-most detective in the 14th District. "Afterward, have our officer give my kid a ride home. Hell, have him turn on the flashers if the Falcons win the game. Frankie will like that."

The other three detectives seemed apprehensive, but they'd agreed to follow their boss's instincts.

"Okay, but we bring uniformed back-up to FalconClaw with us," said Diego. "Just in case shit goes down."

"No," said Sal. "This one's undercover. A police presence might tip off our killer. He knows we're closing in. We almost had him last month over in Rhawnhurst. He knows we're getting close."

"Hang on a minute, Sal. None of this seems right," Diego worried aloud. "You don't even know who your source is."

"Diego, my guy ain't fucked me once," Collazo pushed back. "This guy's netted me eight collars in what, three months? I trust him. Our 'serial' is going down on Halloween night."

"I still think we need back-up down there," said Diego.

"Fine," Sal agreed. "Have a patrol car parked down around the corner on Bedford and Stuyvesant, but nowhere near the front gates. They gotta be out of sight."

"Okay, Sal. That's a deal!" Diego looked mildly relieved, exhaling fully.

Salvatore Francis Collazo's hubris didn't allow him to see that their un-named serial killer and his un-named anonymous source shared the same name, Vincent Charmain Walker.

The Collazo Home – Halloween Day, 1992

"Dad, you gonna be at my game tonight?" asked a fourteen-year-old Frank Collazo as he approached his father near the kitchen sink.

Frank broke in his new glove by mashing a baseball down into it. "It starts at six over at Hunting Park. You can't be late this time! We're the visitors, so make sure you sit in the right bleachers. The third base side, Pop."

Salvatore Collazo turned off the faucet and hesitated before breaking his son's heart again. Tossing a dish towel over his shoulder, he turned and said, "Yeah, Frankie, I wanted to talk to you about that."

"Come on, Dad!" Frank pleaded with his father. "You've only been to one game this entire year! We made the playoffs! This one's important to me!"

"I know, Son. It's just that we're getting close to catching a real bad guy, and I have to work tonight," Sal tried explaining to his boy.

Frank ground his teeth and tossed his glove and ball onto the nearby kitchen table. He then ran out the back door and sat on the back porch steps. Sparky, the family dog, ran up to Frank, sensing his pain, and sat beside him on the porch.

The sound of the screen door slamming reminded Sal of how many times he'd heard it before. How many times he wasn't there for his only son.

Sal walked out the back door and joined little Frank on the steps. "Listen, Frankie. I know you're upset, but one day you'll have responsibilities to provide for and protect your family, and you'll take them seriously. I love you, Son. But I have to work tonight. It's important."

"Ain't I important, too?" asked Frank.

"You are, Son. But what I'm doing tonight will make you and a lot of people safer." Sal placed his right arm around his son's shoulders and said, "I'll tell you what. How about I have a police car there, right near the dugout? Maybe it'll remind you that I'm not that far away. I'll have the officer radio me each time your team scores. How's that?"

Frank shrugged off his father's arm and said, "It's not the same."

"How about if you catch a ride home in the police car?"

"Seriously?!" Frank perked up. He'd never been in the back of a police car before. "Can the red lights be flashing?"

"Well, now you're asking a lot," Sal grinned. "How 'bout this, if you win, the flashers will be on? But no sirens, though. We don't want to scare the neighbors. Old man Willis, next door, will have a heart attack."

"Okay, that's a deal. But you have to come to my next game, or I'll never forgive you, Dad."

"I wouldn't miss it for the world," said Sal, placing his now welcomed arm around his son's shoulders.

Before Salvatore Collazo rose to his feet, his eyes went to the fence in the furthest part of the backyard. As the sun started to fall lower in the sky, its light reflected off of metal on the fence.

"Hey, Frankie, what's that on the back fence?"

Frank, still sitting, looked up at his father, afraid to answer his question. "Those are nails, Dad."

"Nails?" asked Sal. "Well, who put them there?"

"I did." Frank stood up next to his father and stared at the fence.

"That's a lot of nails. Why did you put them there?"

"I was mad at you," he said, looking meekly at the ground. "Every time you missed a game or a school event, I pounded a nail into the fence." Without looking at his father, Frank said, "I hope you catch your bad guy tonight, Dad." He then walked away without another word.

Sal stood there and just stared, tears welling in his eyes. There were dozens of nails in that fence. *"So many nails,"* he thought. He just stared, unable to fathom how many times he'd broken his son's heart.

Then, and there, Sal Collazo promised himself that he'd never miss another game or event in his son's life. And he wouldn't be satisfied until every single nail was removed from that fence. He'd pull one each time he attended a future game, or function.

"Frankie!" Sal yelled for his son, but no response came back. When he went back into the house, Frank had gone. Running out the front door, Sal could see the taillights of one of the other player's parent's cars turning onto Morton Street.

"Dammit!" Sal ground his teeth. "Never again!" he vowed.

FalconClaw – An hour later.

Salvatore Collazo and Diego Ramirez stood at the front gates of FalconClaw. Looking through the gates and up the hill at the sprawling mansion, Diego said, "Why'd they go back to the name Heavenly Gates, anyway? There's nothing heavenly about it." Ramirez stared blankly up the hill shaking his head. Squinting his eyes as the sun began to set behind the behemoth, he added, "This place gives me the creeps."

"Yeah, and what's with the name FalconClaw?" asked Collazo. "Birds don't have claws. They have talons." Pondering for a moment, he added, "I guess it doesn't matter, though. They both leave scars."

"Listen, Sal. I have a bad feeling about this place. Not just the place, but this day, this moment," said Diego. "It doesn't feel like we're supposed to be here right now."

"That's cuz we're not supposed to be here," said Sal to his partner. "Whatta you goin' all religious on me?" Sal shrugged. "The element of surprise, my friend. That's how you catch the bad guys."

Sal pushed the rusty gate open and walked through, scuffing the top of his new shoes on the bottom of one of the posts leaving a rust stain. "Dammit!" said Sal in anger.

"Easy, Partner. They're just shoes," said Diego.

It was neither the shoes nor the rust stain that Sal was mad about, though. He was still thinking about his boy, and he was conflicted.

At the top of the hill, now standing before the massive home, Diego said, "Man, it's a lot bigger than it looks from street level."

"Yeah, it's big, all right," said Sal. "*Scary, too,*" he thought to himself.

Diego walked up the pillar-flanked six steps to the front door and turned to see his partner walking toward the north side of the estate. He yelled to Sal, "Where in the hell are you going?!"

Sal walked back over to Diego and said, "I'm gonna snoop around the back. You get the staff's attention at the front of the place, so they don't see me sniffing around their back door. I just need a few minutes to investigate the basement door. If it's locked, I'll rejoin you up here."

"And if it's unlocked?" Sal was skeptical his partner would do the right thing.

"I'll come back up and get you," said Sal.

Diego wasn't so sure. He knew Sal liked being the hero.

"You damn sure better radio me if it's unlocked."

"That's a negative," said Sal shaking his head.

"Sal, what gives?" Diego flashed a look of concern.

"If anyone hears radio chatter coming from the back, they'll come to investigate. I'm not going home empty-handed. I'm missing my son's ballgame right now. This better not be for nothing."

"Yeah, well, going home empty-handed is better than going home in a box. You double-time it back up here if that door's unlocked. Do not enter the basement without me." Diego was adamant.

"Roger that, Partner!" Sal smiled and disappeared around the north side of the estate.

Once around the back, he turned off his radio and surveyed the property to ensure no staff were present. Staying low to the ground and close to the house, he crept to the southwest corner ducking every window along the way. And there it was, the basement door, and it was unlocked.

Sal noticed that the door was closed but that the hasp had no lock on it. He spotted the lock sitting just feet away in the overgrown grass when canvassing the ground around the basement door. "Well, I'll be damned!" he said under his breath. Looking both ways, he quietly lifted one door and then the other. The hinges squealed, and he momentarily panicked, thinking someone would hear.

The sun was beginning to set and reflected its light off the back window just above the basement door, momentarily blinding Sal as he took the first step down into the old relic.

With each step, Sal's excitement grew. He felt like a kid again, like a rookie cop about to make his first collar. His hands trembled, not from fear but anticipation. He knew in his heart that he was about to stumble upon the unnamed serial killer planning his next murder. *"The reign of terror over Philly and South Jersey ends tonight,"* he thought to himself. Reaching for his shoulder holster, he removed the unfamiliar Glock 9mm. At that moment, he was reminded that he hated the new gun he'd been issued the week prior. Looking at the weapon, he begrudgingly released the safety mechanism and slowly descended into the darkness.

Still trying to recover from the surprise flash of sunlight, his eyes were having trouble adjusting to the completely dark basement. The only light illuminating his pathway was behind him and fading with each step. Collazo knew that the sun would disappear over the south lawn in just moments and wasn't sure what he'd do then.

The hallway was as wide as it was dark, and Sal knew that the many doorways leading down the hall on each side were all potential death traps. As he passed one after the other, his heart raced faster. His now sweaty hand gripped the Glock tighter.

As the last bit of sunlight disappeared, Sal heard the familiar cocking of a hammer on a loaded revolver and froze in his tracks without another step. Collazo had determined that the sound came from his rear, but he hesitated to turn, not wanting to provoke the armed serial killer standing right behind him. At that moment, he thought of his little Frank and how badly he wished he'd gone to his son's game instead of FalconClaw.

"Don't move, Hero," came the high-pitched words of a madman.

"Are you the man I've been looking for?"

"You're damn right I am."

Sal could almost hear the man's smile through his proudly spoken words.

"You gonna shoot me with that gun you're holding?" Sal asked.

"Hmm, maybe, maybe not," said the man. "But I am gonna need you to set that gun in your hand down on the ground to your left. I see you make a move toward me and the next thing you're gonna see is your face flying off your head. This here's a .44 magnum, and I've seen it kill before."

"Okay, stay calm," said Salvatore Collazo. "I'm placing the gun from my right hand into my left, and then I'm going to kneel down and place the gun at my feet. Is that okay?" asked Collazo.

"That'd be just fine," said the man in the shadows. "You just remember that thing I said about your face."

Salvatore Collazo laid the gun on the ground and stood back up. His hands raised in the air. "Now what?" he asked the serial killer.

"I want you to take ten steps forward and then slowly get down on your hands and knees and lay flat, face down. No sudden moves, you understand me, Hero?"

"What happens then?" asked Collazo.

"We're gonna talk, tough guy, that's what. I'm gonna tell you what you want to know, and you're gonna solve the mystery of who I am, Detective."

With Collazo now face down on the ground, the killer picked up his Glock and said, "Well, would ya look at this. I got myself some new hardware."

Sal looked straight ahead, his eyes now adjusting to the darkness. Fear ran from his pores as he surveyed his surroundings. He could see no chance of escape, and unless his partner got worried about him, he would likely die. *"Right here, right now,"* he thought.

"So, before you kill me, you said I'd solve the mystery of who you were. Is that still true?" Sal could feel the killer getting closer, almost tasting his foul-smelling breath. The mold spores filling his nose could not disguise the stench of the man bearing down on him.

"That's right, Detective Salvatore Collazo. I know who you are, and you're gonna know who I am," said the killer, grinning again. "Looks like you're gonna solve your very last case. Some will say that you died a hero, while others will say you died a fool."

The man stuck the barrel of the .44 magnum in his belt and cradled Sal's city-issued firearm with joy. "Man, I like this gun. It's so much lighter than mine. Has more bullets, too."

"So, what's your name, then? And how do you know mine?"

"Why, Sal, we're old friends. My name is Vincent Charmain Walker, and I murdered all of those people they wrote about in the newspapers," said Walker. "And you found me, right before I killed again."

Once again, Sal could hear Walker's smile. "So, how'd you know I'd be here?"

"My anonymous informant told me," Walker giggled like a little girl after her first kiss. "You fell right into my trap, Hero. I knew you would because you're a hero. You lived like a hero, but you're gonna die like a little whimpering child. Just like those two cry-babies, I smoked up in Lawncrest."

Sal let out a deep breath and felt resigned to his fate. He'd never see his wife and son again. He knew he fucked up. *"Just keep him talking, Sal,"* Collazo said to himself. *"Follow your training."*

"I know what you're doing,' Detective. Keep me talking, huh? Yeah, I know how it goes. Trying to buy yourself a few more breaths," said Walker. "You wouldn't believe how chatty people get once they know they're about to die. It's kind of annoying, to be honest with you."

"So, why'd you do it? Why'd you kill all those people?" asked Sal.

"Woo-hoo! That's the million-dollar question right there, ain't it?" asked Walker. "Well, I got some bad news for you, cry baby. There ain't no reason. I did it just because."

"Is that why you're going to kill me?" asked Sal. "Just because?"

"Nope," replied Walker. "I'm gonna end you because you got just a little too close to figuring me out. And I'm gonna end you with your own gun. The irony tastes so sweet. This is the gun that you were planning to use on me."

Sal's sweat dripped from the tip of his nose onto the dirty ceramic tile. "Listen, before you pull that trigger, know this. I have a wife and son...."

"Blah-blah-blah!" Walker mocked his captive. "You all say the same thing right before I pull the trigger."

After a few seconds with no words, Sal was searching for what he'd say next when Walker broke the silence.

"Think about this, Detective Salvatore Collazo. You had a chance tonight to watch your only son play in a baseball game. Isn't that every father's dream?" asked Walker. "And yet you decided to be here with me instead. Ain't life funny? You chose me over your boy. That's some shit, right there."

Sal's tears began to flow, and he whispered, "I love you, Frankie."

Walker heard the quiet moan, pointed his gun down at his victim, and said, "Go Falcons!"

The sound of the three explosions woke Detective Frank Collazo from his sleep. Crying and panting, his sheets drenched in sweat, Frank screamed, "Dad!" A cry that his neighbors had heard many times before.

Thirty minutes later, Frank stood in front of his long since abandoned childhood home at 454 East Locust Avenue in East Germantown. Holding a gas can in his left hand, he looked up at the second-floor room that his parents once slept in. In his right hand, a loaded .40 caliber Smith & Wesson M & P. Tapping the gun nervously on his right thigh, he made his way through the broken front door and into the living room.

Looking around, Frank took a deep breath. Closing his eyes, he desperately searched for the scent of his father, but the smell of ammonia came back instead. He then walked to the back of the house and into the kitchen. Setting the gas can down on the floor,

Frank looked down to his right hand. In it, instead of a gun, was a baseball. In his other hand, a brand new baseball glove. Playing catch with himself, he looked over to the sink. There, he saw his father washing the dishes. He walked over and said, "Hey, Dad." But his father didn't notice him.

Frank then walked out the back door of the dilapidated house and sat on rotted-out wooden steps, and wept. Wiping his tears with a gun-clenched fist, he heard the jangling of the dog tag on Sparky's collar but looked around and saw nothing.

He was mad at his father, but he loved the man. Frank now had a son, and he finally understood why his father went to FalconClaw that night. Salvatore Collazo went to FalconClaw to get the bad guy off the street and protect his family and the world around them.

The moon was bright that night, and its light led Frank's eyes to the nails on the fence, shimmering in the distance. Again, he cried.

Just then, an unforgiving January wind blew, but the jacketless boy felt no cold. The screen door slammed behind him, and his father brushed up against him as he walked down the steps on his way to the fence. In his right hand, a hammer.

Frank stood and watched his father feverishly yanking nails out of the fence. Nail after nail, Frank watched his father try his best to repair a childhood that never was. After another few moments of anguish, Frank walked across what was left of the patchy brown grass toward the fence. Getting closer, he could hear his father crying through each grunt. Frank reached for his father's arm, wanting to pull it to tell him that all was forgiven. "Dad, it's okay!" But Frank was reaching for an arm that wasn't there.

Frank Collazo hit the ground and wailed. With a fleeting smile and a face ravaged by two decades of heartbreak, he looked closer. Studying the fence, he could see that all of the nails were gone. In place of the angry nails, all Frank could see were scars.

Frank ran his hands over the scars and whispered through his tears, "I forgive you, Dad."

Chapter 10 – Melrose Park

The Collazo Residence – Saturday, January 21, 2017, 8:59 am.

After parking on 12th Street, Frank now stood on the front steps of the house he and Joanne bought eight years earlier. He still had a key, but he rang the bell out of respect for his ex. Waiting for Joanne to answer the door, Frank rubbed his hands together and turned to look at the falling snow.

He missed his old house on the corner of Valley Road and North12th Street in the Melrose Park section of the North Philly suburbs. When they'd bought it, Frank's co-workers busted his chops thinking that he came from money, but it was Joanne's father who put down half of what the house cost. Cops didn't live in Melrose Park. Inspectors? Maybe, but not Detectives.

The house was way too big for just Frank, Joanne, and Conner, who was only one at the time. But Joanne's father, a wealthy architect, insisted they live there. Plus, Frank and Joanne had planned to have more kids. That never happened, and now, it never would.

Vance Conroy, Joanne's father, never approved of Frank or his profession and found it difficult to hide his disapproval. He thought his daughter could do better than a cop from East Falls. Frank secretly agreed with his father-in-law. He always thought Joanne could do better. He never felt good enough for anybody.

Still standing at the door, Frank heard little feet running across the living room floor, and then the door handle turned. "Daddy!" Conner yelled as he lunged for his father through the open door.

"Hey, Big Man!" Frank caught his son mid-flight, lifted him up, and squeezed. "Let's get inside, Big Boy! It's freezing out here."

"Daddy, are you staying for the whole weekend?"

"We'll see what Mommy says. How about that?"

Conner's head went down. "Oh, okay." Conner ran back into the kitchen, and Frank heard him say to his mother, "Mommy! Daddy said he's staying for the whole weekend!"

Frank slipped off his shoes and joined his son and his estranged wife in the kitchen. "I didn't say that, Conner." Frank grimaced as he made eye contact with Joanne.

"So, how's the case going?" asked Joanne. "I saw you on the news the other night. I recorded it and showed Conner the next morning. He thinks you're a superhero," she half-smiled. "You're getting a lot of press because of this case."

"It's a real mess, Jo." Frank removed his jacket and hung it in the mudroom which was located just off the kitchen.

"Still no sign of Mereby?" she asked.

"Nope. And Jacks' death wasn't a suicide, either," Frank whispered as Conner sat at the kitchen table playing on his iPad.

"No kidding?" Joanne looked surprised. "They haven't said anything about that in the news."

"Yeah, and they won't for a while," said Frank. "They're gonna hold onto that fact until we have more information on the perpetrator."

"Frank, listen, we need to talk about Conner." Joanne motioned for Frank to join her in the pantry.

"What's going on?" Frank looked concerned.

"Listen, Conner's not doing well in school. His teacher thinks he's showing signs of ADHD, and I think they're right. I made him an appointment to see a specialist on Monday."

"Well, that's quite a leap for a teacher to try and diagnose our son." Frank looked pissed. "He's had his issues, but I think he's just like any other little kid growing up in this world. He just needs to get off of his devices."

"Frank, she sees this stuff all the time. Teachers are trained to look for the signs. I trust her."

"Well, the only thing wrong with our son is that his father doesn't live here anymore."

"Oh, Frank. Give me a break!" Joanne lowered her coffee cup. "Don't blame it on us! It's been six months now, and he's adjusting to you not being here."

"Adjusting, my ass. He's scheduled to see a doctor on Monday." Frank was miffed.

"Listen, that's not what I wanted to talk to you about," said Joanne, pausing before continuing. "I want to keep things the way they are with the weekend visitation."

"Meaning what?" asked Frank with an attitude.

"I mean, I don't think he should leave the house with you." Joanne tried to go easy on her ex.

"Come on, Joanne!" Frank threw up his hands and walked into the mudroom. "You know that bullet wasn't meant for me!" Frank turned his back on Joanne, walked over to the side door in the mudroom that led to the driveway, and looked out to survey the landscape. As a cop, he was always on the lookout for something.

"No, that's not it!" said Joanne, now joining her soon-to-be ex-husband in the mudroom. She sat down on the bench beneath the coatrack in an effort to calm him down.

"It's the weather. It's the case you're working on." Joanne stepped lightly around Frank's emotions. "Just until Spring when things settle down a little. You're in the spotlight, and I don't want Conner to be with you on the street if you get recognized by someone. People are crazy, Frank."

"That's not fair, Joanne. I'm his father, and I shouldn't have to be locked up inside this house when I have legal visitation rights. I don't care what the Judge says. A jury will never agree," he said. "And that's where we're headed."

"That's the other thing...." Joanne again paused before continuing. "My father approached me with a proposition for you."

"Oh, here we go!" said Frank, throwing his arms up again. "I won't be paid off, Joanne."

"Frank, just listen. Sit down with me for a second." Joanne patted the bench next to her.

Frank begrudgingly joined her on the bench.

"My father is offering to buy you a reasonably priced house not too far from here if we can avoid a jury trial."

Frank was astonished. "Like I said, Joanne. I won't be paid off!" he repeated himself.

"Frank, my father just wants what's best for Conner. He doesn't like your line of work. It's dangerous. And he," she paused, "we don't want Conner down anywhere near East Falls, Strawberry Hill, Kensington, Temple, or anywhere around there. It's getting bad down there, and neither of us feels comfortable."

"Sounds a lot like he wants what's best for you, Joanne!" Frank turned away and took a deep breath. "So, what's the catch, then?" Frank was skeptical.

Joanne paused before saying, "That you agree to every other weekend only, and that you don't take our son down into the city or anywhere near where you work. That's why he's agreed to buy you a house," explained Joanne. "It's about Conner and his safety. He's his only grandson, Frank."

"What else?" asked Frank. "There's always something else with your father. I swear to god he wants to be both dad and granddad to Conner. He always wants to call the shots."

"No spousal support either," said Joanne. "If you agree, that is."

Frank again was astonished. "No support? And he'll buy me a house?"

"Child support, yes. But the funds will go into a trust for Conner."

Frank shook his head. "I don't know what your father is up to, but this all sounds too good to be true."

"There is one more thing." Joanne looked apprehensive.

"Here we go!" Frank rolled his eyes.

"You can't have Conner around other women until he's a little older and adjusted to his new life."

"There's the catch!" said Frank. "Your dad is just trying to control me with his money. Well, you tell him he's got a deal if it means that you can't bring anybody you're seeing into this house."

Joanne flashed a look of guilt and then looked away.

Frank's face went pale, and he stood up. "Jesus Christ, Joanne! You're seeing someone, aren't you?" Frank's frustrated hands came to rest on his hips. "Well, that didn't take long, did it?!"

"Frank, listen," Joanne stood and tried to reason with her soon-to-be ex-husband.

"Don't you 'listen' me! Who in the hell do you and your father think you are? You want me to keep Conner away from any women I might meet, but you're already seeing another man!"

"Has he been here? Has he been around my son?" Frank leaned toward the kitchen entrance as if to question Conner.

"Frank, calm down. I'm not seeing another man. And no, I haven't brought anyone around Conner. I would never do that this soon. The divorce isn't even final yet."

"Boy! The judge and jury are gonna love this one. Bribing me with a house and no spousal support, just to get your way. You make me want to puke!" Frank sat back down, and his head fell into his hands.

"Just think about it, Frank. My father's coming over tomorrow morning to speak with you," said Joanne. "Just hear him out, please."

Joanne walked back into the kitchen, and Frank could hear her say to Conner, "You ready for your pancakes, Big Boy!"

"I'm ready, Mom!"

Frank smiled, hearing the sound of his son's voice, and then winced as he looked around the house. He studied the features and décor of the Cape Cod-styled home, then looked out the front window, seeing the Norman Rockwell painting that was the Melrose Park neighborhood. Frank was sick. He'd never really felt at home there. Always the outsider. Then he'd heard his son's voice again and quickly realized that it was Conner's home. The only home his son had ever known.

Frank knew that eight years ago, when his father-in-law gifted him and Joanne three hundred thousand dollars for a down payment on the house, making the mortgage affordable, that he'd actually mortgaged off his future. Both as a husband, and as a father.

A moment later, the phone buzzed in Frank's pocket. It was a text from Penny.

Call me as soon as you can! It's urgent! She wrote.

Chapter 11 – Body Count

39th District Headquarters, Second Floor Detective Room – Saturday, January 21, 2017, 11:14 am.

The door at the top of the steps leading into the Detective Room flew open, and Frank Collazo walked through it. Out of breath, he said, "Okay, what more do we know?"

"A lot!" said Penny, standing next to Detectives John Cole and Robert Brooks.

Frank said, "Hey Brooksie! Hey John!" as he shed his coat and hung it on the back of his chair.

"Okay, so give it to me again," said Frank.

"All right," Penny referenced her notes. "Temple University Professor, Keith Carpenter, went missing while taking his dog for a walk this morning around 9 am. He was reported missing after the dog showed up back at the door, barking to get in. The leash was still on the dog, but there was no sign of Carpenter."

"Where's the guy live?" asked Frank.

"The old Kelly House on Henry Avenue and West Coulter," said Penny.

"No shit?!" Frank was impressed. "The guy's got money, huh?"

"Frank, there's more," Robert Brooks interjected. "The wife and her teenage son went looking for him. Following the footprints in the snow, they walked upon an area in McMichael Park where it looked like a scuffle had happened. They immediately called 911, and John and I went over afterward to interview the wife and son."

"So, why are Penny and I here on our day off?" asked Frank. "I was with my son this weekend up in Melrose Park. This better be good."

Penny stood up. "Frank, we think there's a connection between Carpenter and Mereby."

"What?!" Frank's jaw dropped, and his brows shot to the top of his forehead. "How?! What's the connection?!"

The throaty voice of Detective John Cole pierced through the silent shock of Frank Collazo. "Frank, a zip lock bag was found on the steps of what looks to be a raised cement structure where live music could be played. While the trees are mostly bare, some low-hanging pine trees obstruct the view from the street and nearby homes. Along with the cement stage, those branches could have shielded a violent struggle from passerby's and the Kelly House's southwest side.

The bag had a rock in it so that it didn't fly away. And,....."

"What was in it?" Frank was tortured by his curiosity. "Come on, already!"

"There was blood at the scene," added Cole. "CSU is on-site now."

Robert Brooks reached into his desk, removed a clear evidence bag, and then tossed it onto Frank's desk. When it landed, the thudding sound startled Frank.

Frank lifted the bag and turned it over to view its clear side. He was now able to examine its contents more closely. What he saw stunned him. His jaw slacked, and his eyes went wide again. Examining the bag more closely, Frank could see a lock of bright orange hair and a note that read, *More to Come!*

"Holy shit! This is Belinda Mereby's hair!" Frank looked up at the three detectives. "We've got a serial murderer on our hands, Fellas. Penny, the Kelly house is only like a mile from the Twins."

"I know," she replied. "It's 0.9 miles down Midvale."

"Penny, Why didn't you tell me this when we spoke earlier?" Frank looked confused.

"John and Brooksie just got back with the evidence a few minutes before you walked in. It's their case. I wanted them to tell you first."

Frank took a deep breath while running his left hand through his thick charcoal black hair and said, "Okay, so we have a connection," he paused. "But how? What more do we know about the victim?"

"Keith Carpenter, fifty years old, is the son of former District Attorney Nathaniel Carpenter. The elder Carpenter served as the lead prosecutor on many large cases back in the seventies and eighties," said Robert Brooks.

"Is Nathaniel Carpenter still alive?" Frank asked.

"Yes," said Brooks. "The phone's already ringing off the hook. Sarge and the Captain are both on their way in."

"So, both Clinton Mereby and Nathaniel Carpenter were big-shot lawyers back in the day," thought Frank aloud. "That might mean something. Belinda Mereby and Keith Carpenter? Hmm. Do we know if they knew each other, too?" Frank's wheels were turning. "If their fathers knew each other way back when then maybe they were introduced to each other somewhere along the way."

"Jacks was also a lawyer, and a former Professor at Temple, just like Carpenter," said Penny, reaching for her notepad.

"Jesus Christ!" A stressed-out Frank interlocked his fingers behind his neck, turned, and walked over to the Schuyler Street window. "They're all fucking connected!"

"Lover's triangle stuff, you think?" Brooks posed the question while raising a curious brow.

"No. No. This is revenge for something!" said Frank as he turned to face the others. "Our victims and their fathers either represented or put away a lot of dangerous people over the past four decades."

"Jesus!" said Penny. "We've got a lot of work to do if we're going to connect all of these dots!"

"There's going to be more dots, Penny. He's gonna kill again!" Frank was confident.

"Kill again?" John Cole looked surprised by the assumption. "Carpenter and Mereby aren't dead until we have a body."

"They're dead, all right!" said Frank. "And, by the way," he smirked. "We have a dead Jacks and a dead limo driver. Mereby and Carpenter are either dead or," he paused, "they're about to be."

Penny said, "All right. Frank and I will continue investigating Mereby and see if she crossed paths with any of our victims or their family members over the years. We provided CSU with hair samples a couple of weeks ago. When you guys get the evidence over to Forensics, have them let us know the moment they trace the hair back to Mereby. That should give them a head start."

"We'll see what we can lift off the rock and paper, too," said Cole.

"All right," said Frank. "Tell the captain and Sarge that Penny and I are going to map out the route between our crime scenes. Our killer either lives or works in those areas."

Less than thirty minutes later, Frank and Penny were on the scene at McMichael Park.

"Cole and Brooksie were right," said Frank. "These branches do obstruct the view of street traffic."

"Even the bare trees have a lot of snow piled on their branches," added Penny. "The assailant would have had lots of cover."

Frank and Penny ducked under the yellow police tape and nodded to CSU personnel at the scene. The two made sure to avoid the multiple yellow, numbered evidence tents marking shoe impressions as well as blood droplets. They then slowly made their way over to where CSU Supervisor Daanesh Patel was speaking to members of his forensics team while surveying the area with each careful step.

"Hey Denny, whatta we got so far?" asked Frank.

"Not much," he shook his head. We've got lots of footprints, tire tracks, and some blood," said Patel. "It's fucking snow!" he added. "That's both good and bad...."

"Yeah," agreed Penny. "It leaves us with good shoe and tire impressions but...."

"It's gonna melt soon." Frank finished Penny's sentence.

"Yeah, and we're trampling all over the scene, too," added Patel.

"So, how many different sets of footprints do we have?" asked Frank. "And what do they tell us so far?"

Denny Patel rubbed his hands together and speculated. "Two sets, the victim, and the assailant, once you take out the ones left by his wife and son who stumbled upon the scene. We also know that our perpetrator has a big set of balls on him."

"Why's that?" asked Frank.

"So, we taped off the street over there." Patel pointed to the street-side curb nearest to the park, between the cement stage and the Kelly House. "It appears that our perp either walked up on our victim or was already standing over on the stage. That's where the struggle happened," said Patel. "I mean, the fucking guy parks right next to the victim's house. I would've parked over on Midvale, or at least further down West Coulter."

"Balls, yes," said Penny, "but smart, too. If there's blood, then there was a struggle, and the perp likely knew there would be. He likely planned to incapacitate his victim and drag or carry him to his car," she surmised.

"Yeah, well, that's what happened, but he didn't drag him," said Patel. "There are only one set of footprints in the snow heading back to the car and no sign anyone was dragged. The shoe impressions of our perp are deeper than the ones leading into the park, indicating to us that he was carrying extra weight."

"Okay, so our guy is super strong, too," guessed Frank. "Do we have a physical description of Carpenter?"

"Yeah," said Patel. "He's about five foot ten and two-hundred and fifteen pounds."

"Christ!" exclaimed Frank. "If both guys were dressed for the cold, then they would have been even heavier. And it would've been awkward carrying someone if both had on winter clothes and jackets."

"So, then, we're looking for a guy that is both big and strong?" guessed Penny.

"Denny, how much do you weigh?" asked Frank, looking the CSU Supervisor up and down.

"Don't even think about it, Frank," Denny chuckled, putting a little distance between he and Frank.

"Fuck that!" Frank stepped forward and grabbed the back of Denny Patel's legs, positioned his back shoulders in front of Patel's waist, grunted, and hoisted him up over his shoulders in a fireman's carry position.

Penny was amused while Patel yelled out, "C'mon, Frank. Put me down, Man!"

"Hang on, Denny! This'll just take a second." Frank sounded winded.

Penny smiled and looked on, counting each puff of Frank's frozen breath as he carried the CSU Supervisor some twenty-five feet up the sidewalk between West Coulter and the park, gently setting him down feet first on the sidewalk.

Out of breath, Frank said, "Whew! I'm six foot two and weigh two hundred and thirty pounds, and that was both difficult and clumsy. Breathing heavily, he added, "Our victim was unconscious when the assailant carried him."

"Why do you think that?" asked Patel.

Penny spoke up. "Because he would have been yelling, kicking, and screaming along the way," she surmised aloud.

"Yeah, Penny's right, Denny," Frank agreed. "That would have been too much of a struggle to do if Carpenter was resisting."

"Well, if that's the case," Patel thought aloud, "then that explains why we found no blood on the way to the car."

"How's that?" asked Frank as Penny looked on. "Stomach wounds bleed profusely."

"If our victim was injured to the abdomen and bled at the scene, his stomach region would have been pressed against the back of his assailant. That would've prevented blood from dripping to the ground along the way to the kidnapper's vehicle," explained Denny Patel.

"So, you think he stabbed him?" Penny asked Patel.

"Nope," replied Patel.

"Penny," Frank looked at his partner, "a twenty-two with a silencer. Remember?"

Denny agreed with Frank. "Yeah, that's what I think, too. We found no signs of blood drip patterns coming from the right or left side of the assailant's footprints. You'd expect to see that with a knife attack."

"Fuck!" Penny shook her head. "This guy's a real prick! He either lured his victim over to the cement stage or walked up on him and put the gun to his belly then fired," thought Penny aloud.

"I agree," said Frank as Patel nodded his head, also in agreement.

"Okay, Denny, we'll catch up with you later, then," said Frank. "Sorry about the piggyback ride."

"No problem, Frank," Patel smiled. "I'll let you know when we match our blood up to the victim. I just hope there's blood from both victim and assailant."

"There won't be!" yelled Frank, walking away.

"Why is that?" Patel yelled back.

"This guy's too smart!" said Frank. "Oh, and Denny!" Frank yelled through cupped hands. "Let me know when you match the red hair back to Mereby!"

Patel said nothing. He was confused. He looked at the crime scene in the park and then off into the distance, southwest toward the Twins.

"It's the same guy!" Frank yelled and smiled from a distance while getting into his car.

Now in the car, Frank rubbed his hands together after starting the engine. "This guy either lives or works in the area, and I'll bet it's somewhere between here and the river."

"Why was Mereby's purse found north of here then?" Penny pushed back.

Frank did a quick U-turn on Henry Avenue and then right onto Midvale, heading south toward the Schuylkill River. "That, I don't know," he said. "Whattaya want to bet our victims are up in Germantown? Either dead or alive, they're up there."

"Man, Frank," Penny shook her head. "What in the hell is happening here?"

Frank shook his head as they passed over Conrad. "For all we know, the guy could work right there?" he lifted his chin and motioned with his eyes, bringing Penny's attention to the building on their left.

"The Mifflin School?" Penny looked dumbfounded. "Are you serious?"

"No, Penny. I'm just saying. That prick is close, and for all we know, he's monitoring the investigation." Frank paused. "I'm starting to think that he's educated, too." Frank's paranoia was in full effect as he took a long look in the rearview mirror, casting suspicions on the Chevy Nova following closely behind them.

"Yeah, I'm with you there," said Penny, staring up at St. Bridget's Roman Catholic Church as they passed. "I bet he's tied to Temple University somehow. Frank, I think he knew his victims. There's nothing random about this whole thing."

Frank nodded. "The question is, how?"

Frank hit the left turn signal while sitting at a red light at the south end of Midvale facing the river. "Where to, Partner? I thought we were heading over to the River Trail where Jacks and the limo were found."

"We are. But first, we're taking a little walk," said Frank.

After a quick left, the Dodge Charger passed under the Twins and took another left onto South Ferry Road. Frank immediately pulled the car over onto the snow-covered, grassy area situated between South Ferry, Kelly Drive, and the train trestle.

"What are we doing, Frank?"

"Follow me, Partner," said Frank, turning off the car and then exiting the vehicle.

Now standing outside the car, Frank donned a stocking cap while Penny pulled up her collar to shield her neck from the gusty wind coming off the river. After finding an opening in the traffic, Frank led Penny over Kelly Drive and onto the bike path up against the Schuylkill River.

Frank continued over the cement path onto the river wall and stood, looking down.

"You're gonna slip and fall in, Frankie Boy," joked Penny.

"Come up here, Penny!" Frank extended his hand to help her up.

Penny was careful when stepping up onto the stacked-stone wall.

"Look," Frank pointed down. "You can't fall in from here." Frank counted five steps on the wall leading down into the water.

"Penny, if you swam across the river from where the limo was found, you could pull yourself up and use these steps to get up to street level."

"So, hang on," Penny said. "You really believe he swam across this nasty, freezing cold river and climbed up these steps?"

Frank pursed his lips and reasoned, "CCTV tells us that he never emerged from the area after dumping the limo or after getting out of Jacks' Beamer."

"Then where?" asked Penny, buying into the theory but still skeptical.

Frank did a 180° turn and looked back up South Ferry. "Somewhere over there."

"That's vague," Penny rolled her eyes.

Looking back at the river, she said, "It's too cold out here. No way someone jumped into that water and swam over to here."

As the two stared across at the crime scene on the other side of the river, beneath where the train trestle meets the Twins, they saw someone kayaking down the river.

Frank smiled, raising his brow, and said, "Maybe he didn't swim at all."

"Well, now you're on to something," thought Penny aloud.

"Nah, I still think he swam across," Frank shook his head, following his instincts. "He would have had to ditch a kayak in the hours or days before dumping the limo, or Jacks."

"You're right," Penny shook her head in agreement. "He would've had to place a kayak there twice, once before each incident."

Holding hands, the two jumped down off the fifteen-inch wall and headed back to the car on the other side of Kelly Drive.

Back at the car, Frank opened the driver's side door and said, "If he got out of that river, kayak or dripping wet, he didn't go far. Let's go knock on some doors."

"I'll put in a request to have a Marine unit check downstream for an abandoned kayak," said Penny.

Minutes later, Frank and Penny parked their car in the alleyway between the *Creative Minds Daycare* and *The Trolley Car Café*. Before entering the restaurant, they silenced their phones. Now inside, they waited for someone to greet them.

From what Frank could see, the place bustled with customers and seemed short-staffed, with employees looking stressed and none wearing smiles.

After being greeted, they'd asked for a manager. Just minutes later, a tall, slender man with a pockmarked face approached the detectives and asked, "How many?" as he reached for two menus.

Penny flashed her badge and said, "We're not here for lunch. But we do have questions. Are you the manager?"

The man looked decidedly unimpressed by the fact that two plainclothes detectives were in his midst. "Listen, we're really busy. It's Saturday, and it's one o'clock," he said. Pulling out two menus from behind a podium, he added, "If you'd like to sit down and eat, that's fine. But I don't have time to answer any of your questions."

The manager was drab and unassuming, and Frank thought he wore his 'I don't give a shit' look with great pride. "If you have questions, you'll have to contact our corporate office on Monday," said the manager.

Frank stepped forward, studied the man's name tag, and said, "Listen here, Mr. Bender! We're with the Philadelphia Police Department, and we're investigating a murder that happened just feet from your doors. If you don't have time for us, I can make some by clearing this place out and questioning every employee here for suspicion of murder." Using his fingers to motion air quotes, Frank sarcastically asked, "How would your 'Corporate Office' feel about that?"

The manager swallowed hard and said, "I think I have a few minutes to give you."

Penny slid her badge back into the left inside pocket of her jacket, smiled inauthentically, and said, "Thank you, Mr. Bender."

After first conferring with a female associate, Bender led the detectives to a small, cramped, and cluttered back office and closed the door behind the three of them.

"Please have a seat, Detectives." Bender motioned to chairs sitting opposite his desk. "Like I said, we're very busy, and I'm not sure how I can assist you."

"We've just got several questions, and then we'll be on our way," said Frank.

Both detectives removed notepads from their pockets and opened them to take notes.

"Mr. Bender...." Penny started the interview.

"You can call me Kyle."

"All right then, Kyle." Penny looked at Frank and then back to the young man. "Was the restaurant opened on New Year's Eve?"

Bender rolled his eyes. "Of course, we're a restaurant. We serve food here."

"Fine. What time did you close?" asked Penny.

"2 am."

Frank jumped in. "If you close at 2 am, what time does the final employee leave then?"

"Around 3:30 or 4," answered Bender.

"Can you give us a list of who was closing that night and what time each person left?" asked Frank.

Kyle Bender looked nervous. "I don't know if I'm allowed to do that," he said. "I can ask my corporate office if you'd like me to."

"Yes, we'd like you to do that," said Penny.

"So, Mr. Bender," said Frank. "Were you open on New Year's Day? And before you answer, you might not want to roll your eyes again." Frank leaned forward in his chair. "Be careful, Son. People are dead, and we're looking for their killer."

"Yeah, sure," Bender seemed to understand. "We opened at noon on New Year's Day."

"And what time does the opening staff start to arrive whenever you open at noon?" asked Penny.

"9 am," said Bender.

"So, between 4 am, and 9 am, no one was here, then?"

"That's correct," said Bender. "No, wait," he caught himself. "We have a guy that comes in between closing and opening to clean the place. His name is Willard Clark. He's kinda weird, though. No one likes working with him, so we put him on the overnight shift."

"Weird? How?" Penny asked as Frank looked on with the same curiosity.

"It's hard to explain," said Bender. "He's aloof. Almost clumsy. You know, he's a half-wit."

A curious Frank said, "No, I don't know. What does that mean, a half-wit?"

"So, yeah. Well, we call him Lennie," revealed Bender. "Did you guys ever see the movie, *Of Mice and Men,* with Gary Sinise and John Malkovich?"

"Yeah, I remember that movie from when I was a kid," said Penny.

"Never saw it, but I read the book in high school," said Frank. "What about it? Why do you call him Lennie?"

"Well, he's a big guy and kind of clumsy," offered Bender. "Like, he could hurt someone without even trying. You know, like Lennie in the movie?"

Penny and Frank perked up when they'd heard the term 'big guy.'

"Are you saying this Willard guy might be dangerous?" asked Frank.

"Let's just say that I wouldn't trust him around children or kittens," joked Bender.

"Like how big?" asked Penny.

"He's like six foot five," Bender squinted his eyes, thinking hard. "Gotta be at least 270 lbs."

Frank's curiosity was piqued as he looked over to his partner.

Penny jotted the information in her notebook.

"He's athletic, too. Apparently, he was a big-time swimmer back in the 1990s before the accident...." Frank cut Bender off.

"Whoa!" said Frank, now on the edge of his seat. "Did you say 'swimmer'?"

"Yeah, but no one really believes him. Before we put him on the night shift, he would always walk around telling everyone that he was a swimmer for Temple back in the 1990s," revealed Bender. "But, umm, I don't know."

"Wait a second. How old is this guy?" Frank looked astonished.

"And what accident?" asked a shocked Penny.

"Yeah, well, he definitely went to Temple because we run background checks on people who hold keys to the building, but I can't say for sure if he was on the swim team or not."

Bender rose and turned toward a filing cabinet behind his desk. Opening the top drawer, he perused some files and pulled out a manila folder. Reading through an employee file, he said, "Born November 11, 1976."

"Forty years old," said Penny, doing the quick math in her head.

"So, to be clear," Frank asked, "this guy's a swimmer? Went to Temple? And has keys to the building overnight? Is that right?"

Bender nodded in the affirmative to each of Frank's questions.

"Wait, what accident?" asked Penny.

Bender raised his brow and said, "Listen, like I said. It's just what Lennie told us. Nobody really believes the guy, though." Bender interlocked his fingers and leaned forward onto his desk. "According to Lennie, he broke into the aquatics center one night with some frat buddies. They were going to swim after everything closed down. Well, as Lennie tells it, they didn't turn on the lights because they didn't want to get caught." Bender leaned back in his chair. "So, apparently, Lennie was the first to dive in, but the pool had been drained earlier that day."

Frank and Penny recoiled at the visual in their head.

"Splat!" Bender clapped his hands together loudly. "I know, right? That's a tough one to visualize."

Frank shook his head and asked, "So what, he knocked a screw loose, or something?"

"Broke his neck, too," said Bender. "After that, he lost his scholarship and dropped out. He said his parents could've paid for his tuition, but he said he was never the same after the accident."

"He was on scholarship for swimming?" asked Penny.

"No. That's just it," said Bender. "Lennie walked on and made the swim team. Believe it or not, he was on an academic scholarship.

The way he tells it, he was his class valedictorian for his high school. But, I don't know about all that."

"Yeah, he told us he and his family tried to sue Temple, but they lost the case. His parents were rich, but their money apparently couldn't hire lawyers good enough to beat the law firm defending Temple."

"And what law firm was that?" Penny raised a curious brow.

"I have no idea," said Bender. "I don't even know if any of it's true. Again, the guy's a little crazy."

"Where's this guy live, anyway?" asked Frank.

"Detectives, I can't give you his actual address without a warrant. I could get fired for that." Bender threw his hands in the air.

"That's fine," said Frank. "But you can at least tell us what part of town he lives in."

Bender was hesitant. "Fine, he lives up in East Falls, just north of here. Right up Midvale, near the old Kelly House."

Frank nearly fell out of his chair. "The Kelly House?!"

"Like I said, his parents are rich."

Frank looked over to his partner. Penny was slack-jawed and looked a little pale.

Bender said, "Wait a second! You guys don't think Lennie could be involved in something, do you? I don't want to get the guy in trouble. He's just a big teddy bear."

"No, we don't suspect him of anything, but we're gonna want to speak with him at some point," said Penny. "If a crime happened right outside of your establishment, and he was here, he might've seen or heard something."

Kyle Bender stood and said, "Listen, we're really busy, and I need to get back out there."

Frank and Penny rose from their chairs and handed the manager their business cards.

"We'll be in touch, Mr. Bender," said Penny.

Frank stood in the doorway before leaving and turned to Bender and said, "Listen, don't tell Mr. Clark that you spoke to us about him."

"Are you crazy?! I would never." Bender looked mortified at the notion. "Like I said, *Of Mice and Men*," his eyes widened.

Frank smiled, "Right. Lennie."

Minutes later, Frank and Penny stood in the parking lot outside of The Trolley Car Café discussing the revelations they'd just heard. Both were shocked and dumbfounded by what they'd learned.

As they stood and talked, a spray of water came over the top of the daycare bus parked just north of where their car was parked and landed on Frank's face and shoulders.

Frank was incensed. "What the fuck?!" he yelled as Penny laughed.

Frank then walked around the other side of the bus, confronted a white, middle-aged man, and said, "Get ahold of that hose, Buddy! You just got water on me!"

"Sorry about that, Detective. I was just washing the bus," the man smiled. "I didn't know anyone was over there."

"Did you not see my car parked over here?" Frank was pissed.

"I did see it, but I didn't see you," said the man in a cordial tone. "It's parked illegally, by the way. That's an actual road, not a driveway. Old Bridge Road. People live back there, you know?"

"Yeah, well, whatever! Just watch what you're doing." Frank wanted to be mad at the man, but he needed to get back up to McMichael Park and scout the neighborhood.

Frank looked at the man's attire and could see that he worked at the daycare center. "Just be careful next time," he said before returning to the car.

"You, too, Detective," the man smiled.

As Frank came around the bus, Penny laughed and said, "Everything okay there, Partner?"

"Shut up, wise guy, and get in the car!" Before getting in the car, Frank glanced down Old Bridge Road and could see a half dozen driveways leading up to the rear of several homes and businesses.

As they backed out onto South Ferry, heading North to Ridge, Penny gave the man with a hose a smile and a wave. The man returned Penny's smile and wave and continued cleaning the daycare bus. "He didn't mean anything by it, Frank," said Penny. "Just doing his job."

Turning back for one last look, Penny smiled and said, "That's a big dude! You're lucky he didn't get more water on you. You might've had to tussle with him."

Still miffed, Frank said, "Whatever," as he blew off his partner's comment.

Ten minutes later, idling on West Coulter near McMichael Park and the Kelly House, Frank and Penny reviewed their notes.

"It can't be this easy," said Frank. "It can't be!" he shook his head.

"You know, Frank," said Penny. "If your instincts hadn't pointed you across the river, we never would have looked at The Trolley Car Café." Penny was impressed with her partner.

"Penny, this is crazy!" said Frank, looking at his notes. "Big, strong swimmer? Temple? Lawsuit? Works close to two crime scenes and lives near another?" Frank shook his head again. "It's just too easy. No way this is happening right now!"

"Listen," said Penny. "We bring the guy in and ask him some questions. Don't doubt yourself, Frankie Boy! Even a blind squirrel finds a nut from time to time," she laughed.

"Penny, no joking here! There's no way it's this easy."

"We're gonna find out soon enough," said Penny. "I look forward to meeting Lennie."

As the two contemplated their next move, the radio in the Charger crackled. "Frank, you there?" said a voice over the M band frequency.

Frank grabbed the radio and said, "Roger that. Collazo here."

"Frank, Sergeant Riley's been trying to reach you and Penny on your cellphones but couldn't get either of you," said the 39th District's Operations Room Supervisor, Sergeant McLaughlin. "Listen, call him on his cell as soon as you can."

"Roger that, Sarge!" said Frank. "Over and out."

Frank hung the mouthpiece up and said, "Shit! We silenced our phones and never unsilenced them after we left the Trolley Car Café."

"Great! Riley's gonna think we were doing it back at my place," Penny laughed and shrugged it off. "Like you said, they all think we're screwing."

"All right, shut up for a second while I call the sarge."

Frank dialed the number and waited.

"Frank, where ya been? We got something," said Detective Sergeant Riley.

"Penny and I were interviewing a guy over by the Twins. Works at The Trolley Car Café."

"Yeah, sure. Whatever," said Riley. "Listen, we got another missing person. It was reported two days ago, but we're just learning about it now as it happened down in the 18th District."

"Who is it?" asked Frank. Looking at Penny, he whispered, "Another missing person."

"The guy's name is Daniel Oliver. He's a senior editor for the Philadelphia Inquirer."

"Okay, what about him?" Frank was unsure why the missing person was being brought to his attention.

"Well, on its face, it doesn't seem like it's connected to what's going on up here, but his wallet was found yesterday up in Germantown," said Riley.

"Okay? And?" Frank shot a 'what gives?' look at Penny, shaking his head.

"Well, the guy lives down on the Westside, near UPenn, and his family can't explain why his wallet might be found up in Germantown."

"I'll be damned!" said Frank. "We're on our way back to headquarters now. We might have a person of interest. Tell you all about it in fifteen minutes."

Chapter 12 – The Sleep Room

Location: Basement of FalconClaw – Saturday, January 21, 2017, 11:36 pm.

In the dark, dank, musty basement of FalconClaw, a generator could be heard humming through the bowels of the sleeping giant. The whimpers of gagged prisoners meshed with the generator to form the sound of impending doom.

The prisoners could hear a menacing voice singing a nursery rhyme as it approached. The voice was deep and rich and belonged to their captor. "The itsy bitsy spider crawled up the waterspout. Down came the rain and washed the spider out. La-la-la-la-la, la-la-la-la-la and dried up all the rain, and the itsy bitsy spider crawled up the spout again."

Two terrified souls dangled by their bound wrists from meat hooks in the basement of FalconClaw, their mouths gagged, and feet tied together. Hanging to their right, a dead woman with bright red hair. To their left, two empty hooks waiting to be filled.

Belinda Mereby, kidnapped three weeks earlier, had been dead for more than a week. Her bloated and putrefied body sagged in decay. On the ground, below her dangling feet, body fluids from her decay mingled with dried urine and feces as the stream of death found its way to a drain on the floor some six feet away from where the three victims hung.

All three victims had either been shot or drugged before being kidnapped, and then taken into FalconClaw through the basement door at the back of the long-retired mansion. Now hanging from stainless steel hooks, in a room lit only by a kerosene lantern, the two men dangling beside Mereby's corpse heard the sound of death approaching. The nursery rhyme sung by the killer tormented his captives.

The sound of footsteps and a stick dragging the floor beside them was getting closer. As gravity pulled on the two captive's shoulder joints, the anguish of knowing they'd soon die both supplanted and exacerbated their agony.

"Itsy bitsy spider," the voice rang out again. "Crawled up the waterspout...."

The five large metal hooks hung from a long metal bar in the cavernous room. On the first hook hung Mereby. The rope binding her wrists looked to be losing its grip on the decaying flesh and bones. Soon, gravity would do its job, and she'd lie in a heap on the dirty white tiles below.

To Mereby's immediate left, and one hook further from the door, dangled Daniel Oliver, a Senior Editor for the Philadelphia Inquirer. The man had been hanging or standing for two days straight and had been without food. His clothes soiled from his feces, urine, and blood from a gunshot wound to his right thigh.

To the left of Oliver hung Temple University, Professor Keith Carpenter, kidnapped earlier that day. Carpenter grimaced in pain after suffering a gunshot wound to the abdomen some fourteen hours prior.

The two men looked at each other but were unable to convey any hope of survival. While Oliver sobbed, Carpenter looked for anything that could help him escape.

Oliver had been taken captive while out for a run on Philly's Westside, while Carpenter was kidnapped walking his dog in McMichael Park in East Falls. Keith Carpenter hoped that somehow he and Oliver could possibly overcome their captor if the opportunity presented itself, but as he studied the amount of blood loss Oliver had experienced, he wasn't sure anymore. Looking down, he took inventory of his own physical condition, and his thoughts of overcoming a madman diminished.

The singing stopped, and the dragging of the stick went quiet, but both men knew the monster that had taken them stood just outside the door.

As the flame from the lantern behind them danced across the walls, the two men could see their long shadows struggling to free themselves on the wall directly in front of them. The monster who'd taken them had purposely placed their only source of light behind his victims, torturing them in what would be their final hours.

Each man witnessed their sad state in the form of a dark shadow. Both writhing in pain on the very walls that had seen hundreds of souls tortured and brain-washed decades before in the basement of the dilapidated mansion.

FalconClaw had once served as a psychiatric hospital back in the 1950s and 60s and was used to conduct illegal, government-approved, mind-control and brain-washing experiments on its unsuspecting patients.

A sinister laugh preceded the captor as he walked into what was once called The Sleep Room. The only sound that could be heard was the sound of urine releasing itself from the fearful bladder of Keith Carpenter.

As the twisted behemoth stood before the two men, now whistling the nursery rhyme, Mereby's decomposing wrists gave way to gravity and the ground beneath her, and she fell into a gruesome heap. The two men witnessed the horrific scene and shrieked with terror. Their pitiful moans echoed through the vast chamber, causing their assailant to grin. The men pleaded with their eyes for the mercy not granted to Mereby.

"There, there, now, gentlemen, calm down before you get yourself into more trouble than you already are," said the gruff-voiced lunatic.

"It stinks in here," said the monster holding a long wooden crutch. The crutch was a remnant of FalconClaw and a long-forgotten era in mid-twentieth-century healthcare.

"So, that little piggy went to a party," the man said, looking down at Mereby's dead body. "While this little piggy went for a run," he said while looking up at Oliver. Stepping to his right, he looked up and said, "While this little piggy walked his dog."

"What a life you have all led, blessed by fortune and fame, and all the money your fathers could bestow upon you. Fancy houses, high-paying jobs, and squeaky clean reputations."

The lunatic looked up at his victims, whose heads hung two feet above his. "My name is St. John," said the shadowy figure. "You are all here because of the sins of your fathers, or grandfathers."

"Revenge is a dish best served cold," said St. John. "I have brought you here to die. Perhaps not today, maybe not tomorrow, but you will all surely die right here in The Sleep Room."

St. John struck a match and lit another lantern. The lantern sat on a white, rusted metal table, just feet from the men. Hundreds of paint chips littered its base.

The smell of the flame was welcomed, as the stench of rotting flesh was the only odor the hanging men had known since waking up in the basement of FalconClaw.

St. John blew out the match and flicked it onto the floor. The hanging men could see three plastic jugs sitting on the table. Two contained a clear liquid, and one was filled with a goldenrod-colored substance that, to the two dangling captives, appeared to be urine.

"Which one of you will die first and join your friend here on the floor?" he said, smiling. "From the looks of it, Professor Carpenter will expire first. What with the gunshot wound to the gut, and all." St. John looked to Carpenter's mid-section and chuckled.

"Then, our acclaimed editor from our own Philadelphia Inquirer will die soon thereafter," said St. John, looking down at the gunshot wound to Oliver's thigh. "Unless, of course, gangrene sets in first." St. John winced and shook his head methodically, "Gangrene, belly shot. Both so painful."

"There will be more who will join you, you know. By now, I'm sure you've both seen the two remaining hooks." St. John looked up at the vacant hooks. The question now is, will you see me place my final victims on their hooks, or will they see you crumpled into a rotting mess on the floor as I drag them in?"

St. John wore an empty look and said, "You will all pay for what your families did to mine. A paternal consequence if you will. A fate shared could be another way to describe it. Your families will suffer just as I have suffered from the loss of my father, and my father's father, and his father before him." St. John now looked angry.

"What I have had to live with is the very thing that you have not," said St. John. "You both have your fathers, and I do not. Not since I was a boy."

"My grandfather and great grandfather only wanted to do good, but society shunned them. Labeled the son of 'monsters,' my father took his own life. He hung himself, like his father and grandfather before him." St. John rearranged the plastic jugs on the table. "I, too, have been shunned, and so now, you hang."

St. John walked over to a large metal hand crank connected to a nearly one-hundred-year-old winch. He turned to the men and said, "I will now lower you to the ground. When I do, you will be able to quench your dying thirst. Your hunger, I'm afraid, will fail to cease."

The madman turned the crank counterclockwise, and the bar containing five meat hooks, two occupied and three empty, lowered itself to the floor. As the feet of the two men touched down, their relief could be felt. As they each slowly collapsed to the dirty tiled floor, their eyes went to their assailant.

St. John again paced in front of his victims and said, "Now, which of the two of you is most thirsty? I'm gathering it's our esteemed newspaperman."

A pale and meek Daniel Oliver, suffering from two days of blood loss, released a blood-curdling moan.

"Ah, now there we are," said St. John, who knelt to get a closer look at Oliver's face. "Well, paperboy, you have a choice of three very special drinks over here on the table. The first jug," St. John pointed with the wooden crutch now back in his hand, "is filled with ninety-eight percent water and only two percent rat poisoning."

The two captives let out a sigh of hopelessness.

"The second jug, here," St. John again pointed with the crutch, "is filled with one hundred percent, perfectly fine drinking water, compliments of the old well out back."

His victim's eyes longed for the jug of untainted water.

"And the third jug, here," St. John pointed to the goldenrod-colored liquid and said, "Well, as you can see, I'm a bit dehydrated," he chuckled.

"Kidnapping people is a great deal of work," he sighed. "I can assure you that it's perfectly fine to drink, though. They say urine has minerals, hormones, and protein. Many people drink their own urine, though I'm not sure those same individuals would drink someone else's," he pondered.

The eyes of St. John's victims stayed locked on him.

"Oh, and one more thing," said the lunatic, "I may have mixed up the two jugs not containing my urine. Be careful when choosing."

The look of resignation again befell Carpenter and Oliver. Three weeks earlier, long before the two men were kidnapped, Mereby had been given the same choice. "Your dead friend over here was on a steady diet of my piss before she finally died of starvation."

"Gentlemen, before each of you choose how you'll die, dehydration or starvation, let me tell you a little about this grand old place." St. John pulled an old classroom-style tablet-arm desk from the back of the room and took a seat.

"This grand old building was built back in 1863 and has served as many things since then. It was originally a home for its founder Samuel Crenshaw. I read somewhere that he was a railroad man. After that, it became an old folks home named Heavenly Gates." St. John grinned and looked up at the massive structure above him, shrugged, and said, "I wonder how many have died in these hallowed halls before the two of you will?"

"Its original name was FalconClaw though, the same name as it bears today." St. John pondered and said, "Strange name, don't you think?"

His victims grunted and groaned, both dying of thirst.

"I mean," said St. John, "birds don't have claws. They have talons. No matter, it's a good name. A good place to die."

St. John continued his dissertation. "After that, the government took it over and conducted experimentation that would assist them in their efforts to defeat communism," he said. "Many clinicians from the top of their fields were brought in to do the patriotic work that their governments bestowed upon them. I mean, someone had to do it, right?"

"The project was called *MK Ultra*, and it would go on for years. It seems that patients were put into insulin-induced comas, and they would be asleep for days, weeks, and sometimes months at a time. This room?" he looked around and paused. "This room was called The Sleep Room."

"A genius from Montreal, Canada, was brought in. A doctor named Dr. Donald Ewen Cameron. He was the head of the Canadian, American, and World Psychiatric Associations. A brilliant man!" St. John seemed to beam with pride.

"During that time, patients suffering from a wide variety of mental illnesses would be given massive doses of LSD and subjected to intensive shock therapy, along with light and sound stimulation, all while unconscious. It went on twenty-four hours a day, seven days a week."

"Their objective, given by the United States and Canadian governments, was to depattern the minds of the patients, wiping their thoughts and memories clear. The patients were also subjected to subliminal messages played on a loop. As they slept, they would be exposed to rapid strobe lighting that would print new memories onto their blank minds."

"They were testing the notion that they could wipe away memories and replace them with new ones," St. John explained to the dying men.

The deranged giant abruptly stood, and the two frightened men recoiled in fear, avoiding any eye contact with their captor.

"So, who's first?" asked St. John. "Let me see. Hmmm, I pick the paperboy. He's been here the longest."

St. John walked over to his prisoner and pulled the gag from his mouth, and said, "You make a sound, and you die today. Not because anyone will actually hear you, but because I have a short temper for those who annoy me. Understood?"

Oliver nodded as a tear ran from his left eye.

"Which one do you choose, Mr. Newspaper boy?"

Oliver motioned with his chin to the jug filled with urine.

"Very well then," said St. John. "I'll have you guess what I had for breakfast this morning." St. John looked proud of his joke.

The madman lifted the jug from the table and removed its cap. He knelt beside his captor and poured the urine into his mouth. Oliver ingested a mouthful before gagging and vomiting onto the filthy white ceramic tiled floor.

St. John pulled back and said, "Would you prefer one of the other choices?"

Oliver shook his head violently and whispered, "More."

His captor smiled and said, "Good choice, Paperboy," before giving him more of his urine.

St. John then stood and looked down at Keith Carpenter and sarcastically said, "Okay, Shirley Temple, decision time, Professor."

St. John placed the container of urine back on the table and asked Carpenter, "You recognize me, don't you?"

Carpenter refused to look his captor in the eye.

"That's why you came up to me in the park," said St. John. "You walked up to a perfect stranger, alone in the park. No dog, no reason for being there. You thought that you knew me."

Carpenter struggled to make the connection, daring to take a peek at his captor.

St. John smiled and said, "Yeah, you know me. I had a different name back then, though."

"So, which is it, Professor? Jugs one, two, or three?" asked a smiling St. John."

Carpenter defiantly pointed his chin at the first jug filled with a clear liquid.

"Russian Roulette, huh? Very well, then," St. John smiled again. "Hell, I don't even remember which one has the rat poison in it. This should be fun."

The madman stood and grabbed the jug and unscrewed its cap. He then knelt, grabbed, and lifted the chin of Carpenter and poured a generous amount of liquid into his captive's mouth.

Carpenter instantly spit up the fluid. Gagging, he fought to rid his tongue of the poisonous concoction.

St. John stood and laughed. "We'll play this game again tomorrow!" After helping both of his prisoners to their feet, he placed the gags back over each of their mouths. He then casually walked over to the crank and raised the bar with the hooks as his victims both sobbed uncontrollably.

After extinguishing the flame from each lantern, St. John began whistling into the darkness. As he left the room, he flipped a switch, and a massive strobe light turned on, nearly blinding the dangling captives.

The forlorn sound of agony echoed through the wretched halls where the once shattered souls of the MK Ultra victims lay comatose.

Chapter 13 – The Schuylkiller Case

39th District Headquarters – January 23, 2017, 10:47 am.

Frank knocked on his Captain's office door. It was Monday morning, and Frank and Penny were scheduled to meet at the Manayunk Forensics Division Headquarters. Before leaving, the two detectives and their Sergeant, Doug Riley, were summoned to their Captain's office for a briefing on what the press had now dubbed *The Schuylkiller Case*.

"Come in," shouted Rosalyn Sumner from her desk to the waiting detectives outside her office.

When Frank opened the door, he was shocked to see Police Commissioner William Holden and Mayor Donovan Taylor sitting with Sumner, and Riley, who'd arrived moments earlier.

"Frank, Penny, please come in," said Sumner as the two detectives entered the spacious yet bland room.

The three men and one woman rose to meet the detectives, indicating to Frank and Penny that they were worthy of the respectful gesture.

"Penny, Frank," said Sumner. "I'd like to introduce you to Commissioner Holden and Mayor Taylor."

The four exchanged somewhat sincere pleasantries before all in attendance were seated. The Commissioner and Mayor sat down on the left side of the table. While Riley, Frank, and Penny sat down the right. Sumner sat at the head of the table and started the meeting by immediately turning things over to the Police Commissioner.

The sixty-one-year-old Commissioner looked frazzled. Appearing to Frank and Penny to be far older than his age. Images they'd seen in either the newspapers or on the wall in the 39th District's main entrance's foyer seemed to be of a much younger man. The stress of the day and new year was not wearing well on Holden.

The Police Commissioner was faced with mounting pressure from the public to catch the maniac that was thought to have abducted five individuals, killing at least two of them, so far. In addition, the department was staffing up to meet the challenges of the upcoming Democratic National Convention. The Convention was estimated to bring as many as one hundred fifty thousand visitors to the city.

The previous summer Pope Francis had visited the city, and its police department was ill-prepared for the influx of nearly one million people who'd converged on the city over a three-day period. From protests to parking issues to petty crime, the department was overwhelmed.

The two detectives understood why the Commissioner was in attendance, but why the Mayor? To their knowledge, the Mayor had never visited the 39th District Headquarters.

"Gentlemen, and ladies," said the silver-haired Holden. "We have a situation on our hands that appears to have grown exponentially in just three short weeks." Holden wore his look of concern like a soldier wore a wound, concerned but desperate not to show it.

"We have a well-known philanthropist, Belinda Mereby, missing for more than three weeks now." Holden leveled a judgmental stare at Captain Sumner. "In addition to the kidnapping, we have the murder of a former Federal Judge, Warren Jacks, and now the recent disappearances of Temple University professor Keith Carpenter, and the son of well-known newspaper magnate and owner of the famous Philadelphia Inquirer, Quentin Oliver III." Holden was red-faced.

"And speaking of the Philadelphia Inquirer," Holden stood up and threw the morning's newspaper onto the center of the table. The headline read, *The Schuylkiller Stalks East Falls*. "The damn press is trying to make this guy out to be Jack the Ripper, or something!"

"Yes, and the Tribune," Mayor Taylor joined Holden in his criticism of the press, "plans to run a story in tomorrow morning's paper with the headline, *The Strawberry Mansion Murders*. This situation is getting out of hand very quickly, and we have an image problem on our hands." Taylor's calm exterior was showing cracks. "First of all, no one was actually killed at the historic home. Second, people are confusing the Strawberry Mansion home with the Strawberry

Mansion neighborhood. The nearly eighteen thousand residents of that neighborhood think a madman is stalking them."

Frank unwisely spoke up and reminded everyone that a limo driver was murdered, too. "Let's not forget that we have five victims. Mereby's limo driver James Loftin was the limo-driver found dead under the Twins."

"Yes, Frank," Sumner quickly interjected, "We're all aware of Mr. Loftin." Captain Sumner read the faces of the brass in attendance and wanted to save her detective from any more unintended insults. "No one here is discounting the life of the limo driver, Frank."

"To all of you in attendance," Mayor Donovan Taylor spoke again. His raspy voice matched his freckled-faced, heavy-set physique and salt and pepper hair. The long-time African American Mayor of Philadelphia was less stoic in his delivery when he said, "The eyes of the world will soon descend on the City of Philadelphia. We will not have a serial killer terrorizing the city of Brotherly Love as it helps to nominate the Democratic Presidential candidate this summer."

"I can see the headlines now," said the red-faced Mayor. "Another Devil in the White City, just like the 1893 Chicago World's Fair." Taylor slammed his hand down onto the table. "There will be no H.H. Holmes running amuck in my city. I can tell you that right now!"

All in attendance were taken aback by the Mayor's loss of composure.

After collecting himself, Taylor added, "My good friend, Clinton Mereby, is missing his daughter, and I've assured him that we will discover her whereabouts in short order," said Taylor.

The four members from the 39th in attendance were put on notice and made very aware of their priorities. Solve the case and find Belinda Mereby long before the DNC hosted its convention that summer.

"With all of that being said," Taylor spoke again, "where do we stand in the investigation?"

All eyes at the table turned to Captain Rosalyn Sumner. Sumner looked to Frank and said, "Frank has an update from this weekend that seems promising. Frank, fill in these gentlemen on the facts of the case as they stand today, please."

Frank was caught off guard, expecting the questions to be directed to his Sergeant. Penny, too, looked off-guard as her eyes went to Frank.

"Um, yeah, so we have a person of interest that Penny and I will be meeting with today," revealed Frank.

Penny tried hard to conceal her astonishment of the revelation because she and Frank hadn't finalized a time or date to revisit The Trolley Car Café.

"The subject's name is Willard Clark. They call him Lennie. He works overnight shifts at The Trolley Car Café."

"I think I've been there before," said Mayor Taylor. "It's under the Twins, right?"

"Yes. Under the Northbound side of Route 1."

"Just off of Ridge, correct?" asked Donovan Taylor.

"That's correct," said Penny.

No one acknowledged Penny's words, so she sat back in her chair and stayed quiet.

"Yes, Mayor, between Kelly Drive and Ridge Avenue," said Frank.

"Daycare on the corner?" The Mayor looked for validation of his memory.

"That's it, Sir," Frank acknowledged the Mayor."

"Okay, so tell us about this person," requested Commissioner Holden.

Frank's brows went up, not knowing exactly where to begin. "Well, he works the nightshift, alone. Um, late thirties. Described by his co-workers as being aloof and a loner. He's a rather large man, six-foot-four, two hundred seventy pounds. A former college athlete at

Temple who just might be a little crazy. The employees there call him Lennie, like the character in the book, *Of Mice and Men*. Apparently, he's kinda slow on the mental capacity side of things due to a traumatic brain injury."

"Jesus Christ!" said Commissioner Holden. "Sounds like a monster."

"So why is this guy a person of interest in the case?" asked Mayor Taylor.

Frank replied, "Well, he's apparently a strong swimmer, and he worked the overnight shift the night Mereby went missing. He also worked the night before the limo driver was disposed of under the Twins, and the night before Warren Jacks was found dead in the same area of the River Trail."

"I'm confused," Holden shook his head. "What does being a strong swimmer have anything to do with your suspicion of him?" he asked.

Captain Sumner interjected. "We have no video evidence of our perp ever leaving the scene of the body dumps under the Twins, only the arrival of the two vehicles dumped there."

"Okay, and?" Mayor Taylor leaned forward, fully engaged in where the conversation was going.

"I think our suspect in the case of the limo driver swam across the Schuylkill and fled once on Kelly Drive, likely up South Ferry Road," said Frank. "If he did, he's a strong swimmer because that's about seventy-five yards across, fighting a strong current."

"Freezing cold, too," added Sumner.

"And this guy, Lennie. A collegiate swimmer, and kind of nuts?" clarified Taylor.

"Wow, so what else do we know about the guy?" asked Donovan Taylor.

"So, this guy Lennie," said Frank. "real name Willard Clark, tried to sue Temple University after an accident that cost him his academic scholarship...."

"Accident?" Mayor Taylor raised his brow.

"According to his manager at The Trolley Car Café, Willard told him and others that back in the 1990s, when he'd attended Temple," explained Frank, "that he and his frat brothers broke into the aquatics center one night to go swimming on a dare. This is all according to Willard."

"Well, apparently, they didn't turn on the lights because they feared getting caught. So, this Lennie guy, Willard Clark, was the first to dive in. But get this, the pool had been drained earlier that day."

Everyone around the table gasped.

"Broke his neck and knocked a few screws loose," said Frank. "He and his rich parents tried to sue the university but lost the civil case."

While Mayor Donovan Taylor was intrigued, Commissioner William Holden was skeptical. "How does any of this make the guy a person of interest in the kidnapping and murder of multiple victims?" Holden shook his head. "To pull it off, he would have to be a genius, not a man with mental incapacities."

Everyone turned to Frank, but only Holden and Taylor didn't know the answer.

"As it turns out, Willard Clark was the valedictorian of his high school graduating class and was on an academic scholarship at Temple. And his parents are rich and hired the Stengel, Bradbury, and Willis law firm to represent their son," Frank explained.

"So, he's a genius with a screw loose. What's his motive?" Holden was losing patience.

"The law firm representing Temple University was *Mereby, Godfrey & Faulkner*. Clinton Mereby himself led the defense," explained Frank. "The jury voted 11-1 in favor of Temple."

"Jesus fucking Christ!" Donovan Taylor gasped.

"Holy hell!" added Commissioner Holden.

Frank shook his head, acknowledging their dismay. Penny was full of pride in the fact that her partner had led the investigation right to the front door of where their person of interest worked.

"Then let's bring him in!" said Mayor Taylor.

"Hold on a second, Mayor," said Commissioner Holden. "Frank, you said you haven't questioned this guy yet. Is that right?"

"That's correct, Sir." Frank nodded in the affirmative.

"Does he know you're coming?" asked Holden.

"No, Sir." Frank smiled as Penny looked on.

Commissioner Holden stood to encourage Frank. "Well then, let's get in front of the guy and see how he responds to two detectives from the 39th District showing up at his place of work."

"I couldn't agree more, Sir!" Frank stood out of respect for his Commissioner's enthusiasm. "But I do have one question."

"What's that, Frank?"

"Well, at the beginning of this meeting, you had suggested that Warren Jacks was murdered." Frank wore a look as if the Commissioner knew something that he didn't. "To my knowledge, the coroner hasn't released his findings yet. Are you suggesting that Jacks was both abducted and killed?"

"Yes, of course, Frank," the Commissioner nodded. "You and your partner here," Holden looked over to Penny, "are scheduled to meet up with CSU Supervisor Daanesh Patel up in the Manayunk Forensics Division Headquarters later today, is that correct?"

"Yes, Sir," said Frank as Penny nodded.

"Well, Supervisor Patel has some news for the two of you," said Holden. "Jacks was murdered. It was no suicide, Detectives," Holden disclosed to Frank and Penny.

The Commissioner, followed by the Mayor, stood up, indicating that they were ready to leave. "Your Captain will fill you in on more details," added Holden.

"Good day, gentlemen and ladies," said the Commissioner. Be sure to let me know what you find out from this Lennie person."

Frank wore a look of frustration and mild contempt. While he had always felt that Jacks' death wasn't the result of a suicide, he was pissed that Patel hadn't informed him in real-time. After all, he was the one tasked with heading the investigation.

"Frank, don't look so surprised. This case is bigger than the 39th. Remember, Daniel Oliver was kidnapped in the 19th," explained Holden. Walking around to Frank's side of the table, he extended his hand to shake Frank's. "As I said, your Captain will fill you in?"

"Fine work, Detective Sergeant," the Mayor addressed Frank.

Frank looked confused but didn't correct the Mayor. The Mayor addressed him as Detective Sergeant while he only held the rank of Homicide Detective. He looked over at Penny, and she, too, looked confused.

The two detectives looked at their Sergeant and Captain to see if they'd also picked up on the mistake and noticed that both were grinning.

Frank's confusion was paused momentarily as both the Police Commissioner and Mayor, who were leaving, turned to address the group.

"Listen," said Commissioner Holden, "the 39th is about to get a make-over. Not just paint, but some new office space in the Detective Room and a remodeled first floor." Holden looked around the room and then to Sumner and said, "This office needs a little work, too, Captain."

Frank and Penny looked pleased. The 39th hadn't been given a renovation budget in decades, and they were pleased the historic building was getting attention from the brass downtown.

The liberal Mayor spoke up and said, "Penny, were you named after anyone special that you're aware of?" Taylor asked but already knew the answer.

"Yes, Sir!" Penny wore a look of pride. "Penelope Bryce, Sir. The Philly P.D.'s first-ever female detective."

"Yes, she was," said Taylor. "An inspiration to all of us. Well, as you may or may not know, the statue of Frank Rizzo is finally coming down. Long overdue, I might add," revealed Taylor. "The statue comes down next week. If City Council had timed it better, they could've removed it last week on Martin Luther King Day. Oh well, a missed opportunity."

Frank and Penny were again feeling out of the loop, hearing the news for the first time.

"A statue of Penny Bryce will fittingly replace Rizzo's in front of the Municipal Services Building downtown," revealed Mayor Taylor. "How far we've come as a city when a female, women's rights activist, would be celebrated at the same time a misogynistic and racist former Mayor be expelled from the steps opposite City Hall."

"The ceremony will happen on Easter Sunday. I'd like both you and your mother to be there. I understand she stood with Penny Bryce in the fight for women's rights back in the seventies."

"That's correct, Sir," Penny stood proud. "My mother's name is Bonnie Ross, and she's every bit the inspiration that Penelope Bryce was."

"Yes, yes, I'm sure she is. Frank, you'll be there, too," suggested Commissioner Holden. "It's a pity regarding what happened to Penny's former partner, Frank Bruno. He should be there, too. I hope we learn what happened to that remarkable man and civil servant."

After the Mayor and Commissioner left Sumner's office, the Captain had more news for Frank.

"Frank, I have more news for you." Sumner walked over to her desk and pulled out a black leather case that normally contained medals. When she opened it, Frank saw the red velvet lining surrounding a badge. The badge looked familiar to Frank as it matched the one worn by his Detective Sergeant, Riley.

"Frank, I'm promoting you to Detective Sergeant here at the 39th. You'll head up the team going forward," said Sumner. "And, you'll be Lead Detective across all Districts and report directly to the Commissioner and Deputy Commissioner on The Schuylkiller Case.

We're removing all of the Inspectors from the communication chain due to the high-profile and sensitive nature of this case. Commissioner Holden wants nothing lost in translation."

Frank smiled with pride and accepted the badge and promotion. Addressing his Captain with a quizzical look, he said, "We're not really going with that name for the case, are we?"

"Unfortunately, yes, we are," said Captain Rosalyn Sumner.

"Congrats, Frank." Doug Riley extended his hand to shake Frank's.

"But, Sarge, where are you going?"

"Manayunk," said Riley. "Simmons is retiring, and I was offered the same position over at the 5th. Plus, they have nicer facilities," Riley and Frank chuckled in agreement. Riley then added, "Don't worry, I'm not going that far."

Captain Sumner weighed in. "We had to make room for our rising star," she said, smiling at Frank.

"Congrats, Partner," smiled Penny. "Now I get to come in late because my partner is also my new boss."

"Easy now, Bristow!" Sumner laughed aloud.

"All right, I gotta run," said Doug Riley. "I'll see you guys up at the 5th later on."

"Thanks, Sarge!" said Frank.

"No, thank you, Detective Sergeant Frank Collazo!" Riley smiled. "You've been making me look good for years."

The two men hugged, and Riley left the office. Now standing in front of his Captain, Frank asked, "Captain, if I'm taking over for Riley, then who's getting promoted to the rank of Detective? Please tell me it's someone from downstairs."

"It is, Frank. Ali Ashfaq aced the Detective test last week," revealed Sumner. "I promoted him this morning and then gave him the rest of the week off. He'll join you in the Detective Room next Monday."

Frank turned to Penny and smiled. "Ash aced the test! That's impressive!" he high-fived his partner and was happy that someone was promoted from within the District. Both thought Ali 'Ash' Ashfaq was deserving.

Sumner looked on and said, "All right. You two get up to Forensics and see what else Patel has to say."

"Will do, Cap!" said Frank as he and Penny headed for the door.

"Oh, and also," added the Captain. "I want to hear all about your interview with this 'Lennie' guy."

Frank raised his brow and looked at Penny before responding, "You got it, Cap!"

Frank didn't have a scheduled meeting with Willard Clark. Not yet, anyway.

Chapter 14 – Manayunk

Billy Murphy's Irish Saloon – January 23, 2017, 12:16 pm.

Before heading up to the Manayunk Forensics Lab, Frank and Penny stopped off to grab a bite along the way. Walking through the side door of Murphy's, after parking illegally on Indian Queen Lane, Frank and Penny were greeted by Mike Murphy and Dane Mandato.

"Yo Frankie! Yo Penny!" yelled Mike Murphy as he dried a glass beer mug behind the bar.

The place was packed, and every seat at the bar was full. Overhead hung pictures of patrons from generations gone by. Athletes, politicians, and celebrities. Everybody knew about Murphy's Irish Saloon and for decades had wanted to raise a glass there.

Just above Mike Murphy's head, a picture of the Broad Street Bullies hanging out with Billy Murphy back in the seventies was on the wall. Like those legendary hockey players, Billy Murphy's Irish Saloon represented the fighting and winning spirit of the city of Philadelphia, then and now. Through toughness, it'd persevered and stood proud in the East Falls neighborhood as the community around it embraced its rugged North Philly roots.

The saloon was a favorite of locals from Cresson Street up to Henry Avenue and every street between Crawford west to Midvale. The tough cops of the 39th, one of the toughest police districts in all of Philadelphia, flocked to the bar and proudly called it their own.

"How's it hanging, Murph?" Frank joked with his friend.

"Straight up, Brother! Just like always!" said Mike Murphy.

Frank made a beeline for the corner table, the only table in the place that was near a window. Frank liked the table because the bar was small and cramped, and his claustrophobia would go from nearly imperceptible to difficulty breathing in just seconds.

Penny was close behind as the two navigated the busy lunchtime crowd. The smell of brew and cheesesteaks filled the musty air as the unemployed, local workers, cops, and everyday Joes celebrated an hour away from their mostly mundane day-to-day lives.

As Frank made it to the end of the bar, he greeted the only other Italian in the place, Dane Mandato, the weekday bartender.

"Whattaya say, Mio Fratello?" said Frank, addressing Dane in Italian.

"We gotta stick together, that's what," said Dane. "We're surrounded by Irish gangsters," he joked.

"Ti ho dato le spalle!" yelled Frank over the crowd noise."

"I got your back, too, Frankie!" Dane yelled back. "Whatta youse guys drinking today?"

"Just a Diet Pepsi for me, Dane," said Frank.

"Yo! Penny! The usual?" asked Dane.

"On the job, Danie Boy. I'll just have an iced tea today."

"We got a new one sure to warm your bones," yelled Dane. "It's called Victory Summer Love!"

"Sounds like some hippie bullshit to me!" Penny yelled back. "You can keep it!"

Dane smiled. "Yo, Penny! It's sweet, just like you," he winked.

"You're too young for me!" Penny joked back, but Dane didn't hear her through the crowd noise.

Now seated at their table, Penny said, "Maybe we should have a beer. It's a big day, after all. Your promotion deserves a toast."

"Yeah. I'm still scratching my head about that one. I mean, I'm not so sure I deserve it." Frank wore a look of confusion.

"Don't sell yourself short, Frankie Boy!" Penny yelled over the crowd. "The way you lied to the Mayor and Commissioner today was impressive," she joked.

"Whattaya mean?" Frank was confused.

"C'mon, Frankie. You know we don't have a meeting scheduled with Willard Clark today." Penny pursed her lips and raised a brow.

Frank winced. "Oh yeah. That," he said. "Well, we do now. If he ain't in later when we're done up at Forensics, we're going to pay him a visit at his house. I ran a check earlier today. I got his address."

"No shit?!" Penny looked impressed. "So you knew you were gonna lie?"

"How could I have known that, Smartass? We had no idea we were walking in to see the Mayor and Commissioner," argued Frank, busting Penny's chops.

"Good call. You had no idea." Penny smiled as if she had something to hide.

"You sack of shit! You knew?!"

"I heard McLaughlin talking to O'Connell downstairs," revealed Penny. "I only heard half of it, so I wasn't sure."

"Thanks for the heads-up, Partner!" Frank was sarcastic.

"Anyway, whattaya make of the Mayor coming to Headquarters?" asked Penny. "This shit's getting serious!"

"Penny, this guy's gonna keep killing until he's finished with whatever the fuck he's got goin' on!" Frank furrowed his brow. "Why now? And for how much longer?"

"I'm with you," agreed Penny. "If our guy is in his late thirties, then why start killing now? It's like something triggered the events."

"That's where we start when we meet Lennie," said Frank. "We find out when all the shit at Temple went down back in the day."

"Okay." Penny started to jot some notes. "So, one, we need to figure out when the pool thing happened. Two, when the lawsuit started and ended. And three, when this nut job started working at Trolley's," said Penny, scribbling in her notepad.

"You know, he either took that job to be close to the river because he planned the whole thing way out. Or, the Schuylkill was just a convenience."

"I think old Lennie is extremely smart," said Frank. "He'll play dumb when we talk to him. That'll be his ruse." Frank was certain even though he'd never met the man.

"So what about the Jacks' suicide business?" Penny looked surprised. "Why do you think Patel didn't let you know what their findings were?"

"The Mayor and Commissioner are involved now," said Frank. "From here on out, we're gonna be second to know. Not first."

Minutes later, Mike Murphy wandered over to their table. "So whatta youse guys havin' today?" said Murph.

"Liver and onions for me," said Frank, closing the table menu.

Penny looked disgusted. "That's gross!" she said. "I'll have a chili and some of that bread I smell baking in the back. Your mom's in today, isn't she, Murph?"

Mike Murphy smiled and nodded, "That's the only time you'll smell bread baking around here. My mom's the best!"

"So, Penny. I need a girl's opinion...."

Frank interjected. "I'm not sure she'll be of much help then, Murph." Frank tried keeping a straight face but was clearly impressed with his humor.

"Ha-ha, Frank!" Penny made a face. "Just pretend he's not here." Penny smiled at Mike Murphy. "I do it all the time."

"All right, Murph. Go ahead and hit me."

"Whoa! Penny! Easy! I'm at work over here!" Murph joked.

"Ha-ha!" Penny realized how her comment sounded.

"For real. Listen," said Murph. "I was thinking about getting a tattoo."

"No shit?!" Frank looked mildly impressed. "Your first one, ever?"

"Yeah, my wife and I are thinking about doin' one together," said Murph. "So, Penny, whattaya think?"

Frank jumped in and said, "You should get one on your lower back, Murph." He again laughed at his own joke.

"I see what you mean, Penny," said Murph. "I'm officially pretending Frank's not here." Mike Murphy paused and asked, "So, for real. Whattaya think?"

Penny looked Mike Murphy up and down, pretending to flirt, and said, "Mike, why would anybody put a bumper sticker on a Lamborghini?" she winked.

Frank nodded his head and smiled, impressed with Penny's clever response.

"I'll be goddamn!" Mike Murphy looked astonished by Penny's comment. "That's exactly what I told the Mrs.!" he exclaimed.

Penny smiled and said, "Don't do it, Murph! You can wash off piss and vomit, but you can't wash off a bad tattoo."

Mike Murphy's eyes narrowed as he cocked his head to the side. "Um. Okay. I'll keep that in mind," he said, shaking his head as he walked away.

Penny looked at Frank, who was staring back at her with a baffled grin.

"What?!" Penny looked confused.

"Da fuck does that mean? Piss and vomit?" Frank was at a loss, shaking his head and smiling.

"What? I just made it up!"

"Yeah. I could tell." Frank continued shaking his head. "Thought you were on a roll with that Lamborghini comeback, didn't you?"

"That was pretty good, though. Wasn't it?" Penny winked proudly.

"It was just okay." Frank didn't want to encourage his partner.

"So, what's the plan, anyway?" asked Penny, rolling her eyes.

"Manayunk, and then Trolley's," said Frank. "Then we go see our boy, Lennie."

One hour later – Frank and Penny walked into the Crime Scene Unit's North Philadelphia offices and pressed the down button on the elevator. The sophisticated facilities made the detectives feel like they were on another planet. The 39th Headquarters was the bottom of the barrel as far as the Philadelphia Police Department was concerned, and no pep talk from their Captain or small budget renovation would change that.

"How'd you like to come to work every day in this place?" asked Frank, marveling at the facilities.

"I was just thinking that." Penny's eyes were wide as she looked over at a stainless steel reception desk with a seventy-inch flatscreen behind it marketing the Philly P.D.

"I've never seen so much steel and glass," she said in amazement.

"Yeah. We're in the wrong job!" Frank mumbled, taking in the modern lobby.

"Well, let's go find the Schuylkiller and make a name for ourselves, and then we can start our own detective agency." Penny joked but, in reality, was dreaming aloud.

"Hold the door!" came a voice from the lobby as the elevator doors began to close on Frank and Penny.

Penny quickly stuck her foot out, causing the doors to rebound.

"Well, well, well. If it isn't Supervisor Daanesh Patel. Just the man I wanted to see." Frank busted Patel's chops for not telling him about the Jacks' findings.

Patel entered the elevator and was momentarily caught off guard by Frank's comment. After a second, he said, "I know. I know. I passed the results up the chain, and they said they'd tell you themselves," explained Patel. "My bad, Frank."

"Just giving you shit, Denny," said Frank. "No sweat, Man!"

"Nice digs around here," said Penny. "Got any job openings?" she joked.

"Anything you want, Penny!" Denny Patel smiled.

"So, no suicide, huh?" asked Frank.

The doors to the elevator opened on sub-level one, and the three walked out.

"Hold that thought, Frank. I've got a lot of good info for you. I also found out what that substance was on the back seat of the Jacks' Beamer."

"Oh shit! That's right!" Frank had forgotten about the oily substance he picked up on his rubber gloves back on January 5. "What was it?"

"Lanoline," said Patel, as he pushed open the door to his spacious office.

The room was a sterile white and chrome. The modern décor told both Frank and Penny that the Philadelphia Police Department had a bigger budget than they let on.

"What in the hell is lanoline?" asked Frank as Penny's eyes went big, admiring Patel's office.

"Channel Grease," said Patel. "Ever heard of it?"

"Channel Grease?" Frank shook his head. "No, never have."

"Oh, wow! You mean what swimmers use?" Penny turned to Frank, and her jaw dropped with the revelation. "Didn't people trying to swim across the English Channel use it to stay warm?"

"You know your stuff, Penny." Patel looked impressed.

"Channel Grease was some heavy-duty stuff they used back in the day. Like lard or Vaseline, but thicker," offered Patel. "It made swimming easier as you could glide through the water without your body hair causing too much drag. But mostly, it was used to keep the swimmers warm in the frigid temperatures of icy waters.

Frank was shocked. "Son of a bitch! The river! I was right, Penny."

"Yeah!" Penny shook her head in astonishment. "You called it, Frank. I'll be damned."

"When you said the guy was using the river to get away at the Jacks' crime scene, I thought you were smoking something," said

Patel. "But when the substance on the back seat came back as Lanoline, I gotta tell you, Frank...." Patel paused, raising his brows in admiration. "I said that old Frankie Boy's a real genius."

"It all makes sense," reasoned Frank. "It had to be the river. It had to be." he shook his head.

"So, what is Lanoline, exactly?" Frank asked Patel.

"Yeah, so, it's a waxy substance secreted from the glands of wool-bearing animals," explained Patel. "It's also called wool wax or wool grease."

"Lanoline is also used in cosmetics, too. Right?" asked Penny.

"I see you've been to the Macy's fragrance counter," joked Patel.

Penny balked at the notion. "Yeah! Not in a long time, brother!" she smirked.

"In nature, lanoline is used to protect the skin from the environment," explained Patel. "We found the substance in three areas inside the cabin as well as on the backseat, driver's side door handle, the key fob, and are you ready for this?" asked Patel, almost glowing. "The gun," his eyes lit up.

"Holy shit!" Frank leaned back onto a table opposite Patel's desk. "So, our suspect had the gun and the fob. He then ordered Jacks to get into the car at gunpoint. Then sat behind him on the way to the River Trail and once there....,"

"Boom!" said Penny, finishing Frank's thought. "Holy shit!"

"That theory matches ours," said Patel. And it's backed up by the physical evidence."

"Oh, yeah?" Frank's hands came up off the table. He looked eager to hear more.

"Frank, the blood splatter pattern in the backseat that you pointed out back on the 5th...." Patel leaned in.

"Yeah?" asked Frank.

Patel continued. "On the surface, it looks like a suicide, but as we looked closer, there was a void on the backseat where blood should have been. At first glance, we thought it might've been caused by the headrest of the driver's seat. Upon further testing, though, using luminol, you can see the shape of a person sitting just behind Jacks and to his right. Here, check this out."

Patel opened his laptop and pointed Penny and Frank to a seventy-inch television on the adjacent wall. Patel's computer projected the information displayed on its screen to the monitor on the wall.

Frank and Penny looked at the images in amazement. The images showed the backseat from different angles. The blood splatter pattern revealed a void where blood spray and splatter would normally be present if Warren Jacks were alone in the car when he shot himself.

"What about the front passenger seat?" asked Frank. Was there anyone else in the car?"

"No," said Patel. "Blood, brain, and skull fragments are found on the windshield, dash, and both front seat windows and passenger seat. No one was in the front seat with him when he was killed."

"Let me show you something else," said Patel as he searched through computer-generated images on his computer.

Appearing on the screen was a bullet trajectory image. The image illustrated a red line path where the bullet would have first exited the barrel, continuing into the skull between the right ear and temple of Jacks, passing through the skull and exiting behind the left ear. "The bullet blew out the back left passenger window," said Patel.

"And yes. Our guys finally retrieved it," he revealed to Frank and Penny, reaching into his desk drawer

"Let me guess," Frank rolled his eyes as he looked over at Penny, "we're the last to know, again?"

Patel shrugged off the comment and pulled an evidence bag from his desk. "Here you go," he said, handing the bag to Penny, who was nearest to him.

"Silencer striations again?" asked Penny, examining the bullet before handing it to Frank.

"Nope," said Patel. "The gun in Jacks' hand was likely his, though we haven't been able to trace it back to him yet. Jacks may have been concealing it in the SUV, and the killer found it only after accessing the vehicle."

"Or, it's a different killer," reasoned Frank, not believing his own speculation.

"My guess is that our perp wanted it to look like a suicide, but if he'd used the same gun that killed the limo driver, we'd know it was him," surmised Penny.

"Or, the killer brought a throwaway with him?" Frank introduced a different scenario.

Patel walked around from behind his desk and leaned back onto its front, now closer to Frank. "There's gun residue in the center armrest compartment and in the glovebox," revealed Patel. "That would suggest that it belonged to our victim."

"Yeah," Penny nodded in agreement. "A guy like that with his wealth and fame would want personal protection inside of his vehicle."

"Agreed." Frank nodded.

"So, whatta you thinking, Denny?"

"I think the perp sat behind Jacks, gun in his right hand, leaning forward between the two front seats." Denny clicked twice with a remote control in his hand, and a mock animation began to play on the television in slow motion. The short video illustrated a mock back seat and two front seats, where a transparent figure of a larger than average man sat behind another transparent image of a man in the driver's seat.

As the video played out, the figure sitting in the mock car interior's back seat placed his right elbow on the top left side of the passenger seat, resting it there.

"Frank, I think the guy had a handful of Jacks' hair in his left hand when he pulled the trigger. If you look again at the bullet's path on the big screen," Patel toggled to the previous slide, "you'll see that the barrel is at least five inches away from the entry wound...."

Penny finished Patel's assumption. "Nobody shoots themselves in the head holding the gun that far away from it."

Patel nodded and agreed. "Now, watch this." Patel clicked back to the video.

As the video played, the animated figure in the back grabs the front seat figure's head with his left hand, pulls it back, and fires one shot from the right-hand side of the victim.

"The blast residue confirms that the gun was positioned in a way that would be unnatural for someone holding it in their hand and pointing toward their head from that distance," said Patel."

"Denny, do we know what....?"

Patel cut Frank off and finished his sentence. "Yep, Jacks was left-handed."

Chapter 15 – Of Mice and Men

The mood was tense, and the words were few as the Dodge Charger made a left out of the CSU south parking lot. It'd been thirty days since the call came in that retired Philadelphia Police Detective Frank Bruno had mysteriously gone missing from his hospital room in the early morning hours of Christmas Day 2016. A lot had happened in just over four weeks, and the lives of Frank and Penny were about to be turned upside down.

There was still no sign of the legendary detective, and to Frank, it felt as if no one was looking for the old man. For Penny, she struggled with her feelings for her partner, unsure if her loneliness was what drew her nearer to him or if it was the overwhelming respect and admiration she had for him professionally. Either way, the two were connected. Partners at work, two failed marriages, and a similar fate and circumstance that happened when each was just fourteen years old. Both were left with an empty hole in their chest. A void that only a father could fill would never be filled for the two detectives hunting down a madman. A psychopathic killer that they'd meet very soon.

It was just after four in the afternoon, and the darkened skies opened up and dropped torrential rain on the Dodge as it made its way northeast through the narrow streets of Wissahickon. The two detectives were heading back to East Falls. Making a right on to Henry Avenue, they were headed back to West Coulter Street to meet the person they believed might be who the Press, the Philly P.D. brass, and the Mayor himself were now calling *The Schuylkiller.*

Just four houses up from The Kelly House and McMichael Park, where Keith Carpenter had been abducted in broad daylight, lived the quiet giant who worked nights alone at The Trolley Car Café. Was their killer the man whose co-workers dubbed *Lennie*, a hapless man child from John Steinbeck's literary classic, *Of Mice and Men?* Or was he just a gentle giant misunderstood by the people he worked with and society at large. Detectives Frank Collazo and Penny Bristow would soon find out.

Leaning forward in her seat and looking up, Penny said, "Jesus Christ! Was there even rain in the forecast?"

Hail now pelted the windshield of the Dodge as its wiper blades struggled to wipe away Frank's anxiety and consternation. He was leery of coming face to face with a serial killer and the person likely responsible for the killing and abduction of at least five people in just over three weeks. Frank's father weighed heavily on his mind as he battled the questions exploding in his head. What triggered the madman to start killing? Who would be next? And could he and Penny stop the next murder from occurring or the next abduction from happening? The questions kept coming, and Frank had trouble processing how fast things were moving.

What would happen with his custody battle? His failed marriage? His growing feelings for Penny? His lack of confidence in himself? And would his tightly concealed fear of finding and confronting the monster that was unleashing terror on North Philadelphia manifest itself to Penny?

Something had to give, and Frank was starting to feel it would be his psyche. As the Dodge turned left onto West Coulter, with the Kelly house to his left and McMichael Park to his right, the storm subsided in the North Philly skies but still raged in Frank's heart and head.

At that moment, Frank desperately wanted to be back at Penny's apartment on Christmas night. If he could do it again, he would've taken Penny's offer and slept on that couch. Just knowing that the only person in his life that could save him from himself was sleeping in the room next to him would've given Frank something he'd been missing for a long time. Peace of mind.

Frank looked over at Penny and half-smiled. She raised her chin in acknowledgment of the fear her partner felt, and she felt it, too. Words couldn't remedy their terror as the Dodge Charger pulled over to the right curb, and Frank threw the car up into park.

"So, change of plans?" Penny nervously smiled. "I thought we were going to The Trolley Car Café first."

"Yeah, well, we both know Lennie doesn't work during the day," said Frank, looking to his left, focusing his eyes on the house at 3211 West Coulter Street. "To be honest, I would've preferred to go there instead of here."

"Yeah, me, too," confessed Penny, squinting to get a look through the driver-side window.

"Penny, did you ever see the movie *Amityville Horror*, with James Brolin and Margot Kidder?" asked Frank. "The original one from the seventies, not one of the knockoffs?"

"Is that the movie where the house was haunted because some kid killed his family there?" asked Penny.

"That's the one," said Frank.

"Yeah, I saw the one with Ryan Reynolds but not the original," said Penny.

"Yeah, well, I went there once to see it," Frank said as he stared at the house that sat across the street from where he, Penny, and the Charger idled. "That visit still haunts me to this day."

"Where?" Penny was confused. "Long Island?"

"Yeah," Frank looked over at Penny. "I sat right across the street from it with my cousin Kenny and his girlfriend. Just like we are now," he said. "It was getting dark, and it was wintertime, just like it is now." Frank's face looked hollow as he was transported back in time. "We just sat in that car forever, Penny. We just stared at the evil that lived in that place." *Just like we are now*, Frank thought to himself.

"Why are you telling me this?" asked Penny with a blank stare.

"Because you see the way the house is positioned?" Frank pointed. "Its side facing the street instead of the front?" Frank just stared up at the house that was slightly elevated from street level and to his left.

"Yeah, so what?" asked Penny, beginning to get a little freaked out.

"It looks exactly like the Amityville Horror House at 112 Ocean Avenue," said Frank, turning to look at Penny.

"They actually changed the house number to 110 because people kept driving there to see it. Like changing the house number would make it harder to find." Frank was dismissive of the notion.

Looking back at the house, he looked up at the small half-arched windows that bookended the chimney at the very top. "Those creepy-ass windows at the top of the house are exactly like the ones on the old DeFeo House. They've changed those, too," said Frank.

Penny squinted again through the window and the burgeoning darkness to see what Frank was staring at. "Who's DeFeo?"

"The family that lived there back in the day."

"What were you doing in Long Island, and what really happened at that house?" asked Penny.

"Well, the movies are all bullshit, but back in November of 1974, a twenty-three-year-old kid named Ronald DeFeo, Jr. killed his mother, father, two sisters, and two brothers with a .35 caliber rifle while they slept in their beds."

"Jesus!" Penny grimaced. "Yeah, I remember that story now. I think the guy is still alive, wasting away in prison somewhere."

"Yeah, somewhere in upstate New York." Frank just stared at the house.

"What were you doing there?" asked Penny.

"I was visiting my cousin who was getting ready to join the New York City Police Department. He wanted me to join up with him, so he invited me up," Frank explained. "He lived in Suffolk County but had an aunt in Queens that he said we could live with. I wasn't so sure about living on an island, though. I'm a little claustrophobic, and even though Long Island is big, I just couldn't get comfortable living on an island. Anyway, I read the book when I was twelve and asked him to take me to it."

"Wait a second! You're claustrophobic?" Penny looked both surprised and amused.

"Where have you been?" Frank looked over at her. "Why do you think I never go up to the third floor of the 39th? That staircase is way too narrow. That shit fucks with me." Frank turned back to face his fear, his gaze now fixed on the house on the corner.

"Huh." Penny shook her head and pursed her lips. "I had no idea."

After a moment of silence, Penny spoke up. "Frank, are we going in there, or what?"

"What? Yeah." Frank was snapped out of his trance. "Yeah, we're going in. I was just thinking about....." he paused, "the evil that lives there," he mumbled under his breath.

After a deep breath and the summoning of his courage, Frank said, "Let's go!"

Standing in the middle of the street, both Frank and Penny affixed their shields on the outside of their coats. Frank wore a black Philly P.D. jacket over a white button-up shirt and black slacks, while Penny wore gray slacks and a grey trench. Her brown hair was pulled back into a ponytail, with gun holstered on her hip. Frank carried his gun in a shoulder holster under his left arm.

"So, how's it gonna go?" asked Penny.

"I don't know," said Frank. "Let's go knock on the door and see what happens." Frank's nervous smile worked hard to conceal his apprehension.

The two followed the street around the corner, staring at the house every step of the way. The white Cape Cod-styled home was adorned with black shutters and a red door with the gold number 3212, but Frank saw the number 112, thinking of the DeFeo house in Amityville, Long Island. The red door did little to calm his fears of what might lie inside.

As the two detectives walked up the driveway, Frank looked into the driver's side window of a single car parked haphazardly in the driveway. It was as if someone pulled in abruptly and got out without looking back or simply didn't care. Frank noticed that the seat was positioned as far back as it could go, indicating to him that someone very tall last drove the vehicle. Frank identified the dirty black car as a late model Lincoln Continental. "2010, ya think?" he asked Penny.

"Thereabouts," she responded, placing her palm on the trunk of the car to leave proof that she had been there. When she did, she got salt and slag on her hand. Walking to the door, she wiped her hand on the side of her jacket, leaving a smudge.

"Well, somebody's home because all the lights are on." Frank used his left bicep to squeeze his 9mm Smith & Wesson M&P, reassuring himself that it was still there.

Penny, too, ran her hand across her sidearm, ensuring it was at the ready.

Their hearts raced only mildly as they climbed the three front stairs up onto the stoop, salt crunching under their shoes with each step.

Frank rang the doorbell, but no muffled ring could be heard coming from inside the house. He looked at Penny and rang it again. Still nothing.

"Okay," he said. "Let's do it the old-fashioned way." Frank pulled open the screen door and knocked heavy-handedly three times, making it clear to anyone in the house that they had visitors.

Through the living room window to their left, they could see a silhouette rise from a chair and make their way over to the door.

"You think they'll have us over for dinner?" Penny joked while holding the screen door open for her partner.

"Or, have us for dinner," Frank joked back, hoping to ease his own fear.

The door opened, and a tall, older woman stood before Frank and Penny. The woman was mostly gray-haired and wore a navy blue sweater with her right arm in a cast and sling.

"Yes, can I help you?" said the woman, looking curiously at Frank and Penny, her eyes fixated on their detective badges.

"Yes, Ma'am, we're with the Philadelphia Police Department and were wondering if this was the Clark household?"

The woman clutched the top of her sweater and leaned out to look both ways. "Where is your car? And what is all this about?" The woman looked curiously skeptical.

"Our car is parked over there," Frank pointed to his left, "on West Coulter. Is this the Clark house, Ma'am?" he asked again.

"Yes, it is," the woman's tone changed from curious to concerned. "What is all this about?"

"We were wondering if Willard Clark lived here?" asked Penny, flashing a disarming smile.

"Yes, he does," said the frail-looking sixty-something-year-old woman. "Is this about my arm?" she asked nervously.

The statement piqued Frank's curiosity. He looked at her cast, then over to Penny, and then back to the woman and said, "No, but may we come in? It's starting to rain again."

"Why, I suppose." The woman hesitated and then backed out of the doorway, allowing Frank and Penny to enter the tiny home. "I still don't know what this is all about, though." She closed the door behind the two detectives.

"Honey!" she yelled into the kitchen. "There's someone here to see us!"

"You must be Mrs. Clark," said Frank. "I'm Detective Frank Collazo, and this is my partner, Penelope Bristow."

"Yes, very good to meet the both of you, but...." Skeptical of a visit by police, the woman anxiously waited for her husband to enter the room, nervously looking back at the kitchen.

"What's all this?!" said a tall, heavyset older gentleman, alarmed to see two police detectives standing in his living room.

"Yes," said Penny. "We were wondering if we might speak to Willard Clark?" Penny's eyes flashed back to the cast on the right arm of the slender woman.

"We already told the doctor at the hospital that that was an accident. Willard didn't mean anything by it," the older male barked back.

"Yes, Sir," Frank interjected. "As we told your wife a moment ago, this is not about her arm. We're with the Philadelphia Police Department and would like to ask your son some questions regarding a missing persons case that we're investigating."

The old woman took a half step back, and her left hand rose to cover her mouth. "Oh, dear. Is this about Mr. Carpenter from down the street?" she asked the detectives.

"Yes. In part," said Frank.

"Is your son home?" asked Penny, again flashing a pleasant smile.

"In part?" said the old man abruptly. "What in the hell does that mean?"

"Mr. Clark," Frank was stern, hoping to regain control of the conversation. "Is Willard Clark home, or not?"

The old man immediately changed his tone. Now calmer, he replied, "Detectives, please sit down, won't you?"

"I'll stand," said Frank.

"I would love to," said Penny with a smile, hoping to persuade her partner to do the same. She could sense that the old couple was ready to cooperate.

"That'd be fine," said Frank, looking to the old woman for an indicator of where he should sit.

The man and woman sat down onto a couch backed up against the interior wall and motioned to Frank and Penny to sit in matching floral upholstered armchairs that backed up to the house's front windows.

Frank was as comfortable with the seating arrangement as Penny, and he had a view of the two doorways entering the room from the back of the house. He unzipped his jacket and took a seat. Penny, too, unbuttoned her coat so that in the worst-case scenario, she'd have easy access to her sidearm.

Frank again used his left bicep to press his gun against his rib cage before saying, "Mr. and Mrs. Clark, our visit here today is not to alarm you, but we're investigating multiple crime scenes, and your home is near one while Willard's place of work is near two others."

The old couple looked at each other as if they had reason to be worried.

Penny's eyes flashed to a newspaper sitting on the small wooden coffee table separating the old couple, she, and Frank. The newspaper headline read, *Schuylkiller on the Loose*.

The old woman saw Penny's eyes make contact with the headline and immediately said, "Are you suggesting our Willard had something to do with the recent disappearances?"

Her husband added, "Just what is it that you want from our son?"

"Mrs. Clark, how exactly did you break your arm?" asked Frank. His eyes toggled between the old woman's arm cast and then back to her and her husband. He made sure he looked both directly in the eyes.

The older couple looked at each other for several uncomfortable seconds, not knowing how or if they should answer the question.

The two simultaneously answered with Mrs. Clark saying, "It was just an accident." While her husband barked, "That's none of your business!" sneering at the detectives.

"Very well, so may we speak with Willard then?" asked Penny.

"Willard is sleeping downstairs in the basement. He works in the evenings, so he usually goes to sleep at around noon, wakes up at nine o'clock sharp, and eats something before heading in at eleven.

"Is that his car out front?" asked Frank.

"What's it to you?" asked the old man.

"Mr. Clark, have I done something to offend you, Sir?" asked Frank. "You seem uncomfortable with me being here. Is there anything you'd like to share with us while we're here?" Frank was again trying to regain control of the conversation.

Penny jumped back into the discussion, showing empathy for the old couple. "Mr. and Mrs. Clark," she paused. "While I know that it may be unsettling to have two police detectives make an unannounced visit to your home, we feel that Willard might be able to assist us with information about both the abduction of Mr. Keith Carpenter and the two homicides down near the Twins....."

"How's that?!" the senior Clark interrupted Penny.

Frank jumped in to answer the old man's question. "Sir, we've seen Willard's timecards from this past Saturday morning, and the timestamp coincides with the disappearance of Mr. Carpenter's abduction," Frank lied. "We timed the car ride over here, and if Willard got off work when his timecard suggests he did, then he would've ended up on Coulter street right around the time Mr. Carpenter went missing."

"You see, Mr. Clark," Penny smiled politely. "We just want to ask Willard if perhaps he saw anything unusual. A car? A strange man that doesn't live around here? Anything that might be considered suspicious." Penny nodded, hoping to gain cooperation from the old man.

Before the senior Clark could answer, Frank thought he'd heard someone in the hallway just off the kitchen and living room, and his eyes went to an area behind the old couple. He instinctively thought to grab his gun but quickly reconsidered. He didn't want to show his fear of who might be standing just out of sight.

Penny detected Frank's concern, and her eyes, too, went to the doorway to her right, just over the old woman's left shoulder.

"Is someone there?" Frank asked Mr. and Mrs. Clark, motioning with his chin, lifting it in the direction of the hallway.

Both of the older Clark's looked over their shoulders and chorused, "No, that's just the furnace clicking on."

"Yes, just the furnace," repeated the old woman, placing her left hand onto the small portion of her right hand that was protruding from the cast.

Frank's eyes stayed fixed on the doorway as he asked his next question. "Would it be possible to speak to Willard now? Might you wake him up for us?"

"I'm sorry," said the old man. "That won't be possible. Willard is a deep sleeper, and it's very difficult to wake him before nine."

Frank was certain that Willard was very much awake and standing just around the corner listening to the entire conversation, and he sensed that Penny thought it, too.

"Fine then, Mr. Clark," Frank changed his approach. "Can you tell us when your son had his accident at Temple?"

The old man was caught off guard by the question. "Why....I....," he stuttered. "Of what relevance is that?" he replied to Frank.

"I understand that your son was a phenomenal swimmer," said Penny, directing her comments to Mrs. Clark. "Is that right? You must've been very proud of him. Walking on and making the swim team at Temple." Penny feigned admiration.

Frank jumped back in, knowing Penny was onboard with his tactics. "Mrs. Clark, can you tell us when the civil lawsuit you filed against Temple University on behalf of your son came to an end?"

"Well, I....," Mrs. Clark's voice faltered.

"Now, you wait just a minute!" The old man stood from the couch, raised his finger, and pointed it at Frank. "I see what you're trying to do here!"

At that moment, Mrs. Clark blurted out with tears, "Is this about the Schuylkiller!" she cried. "Is my Willard the Schuylkiller?" she sank back into the couch.

"Helen!" the old man shouted. "Stop talking!" he demanded of his wife.

"Richard!" the old woman sobbed. "Tell them!" she cried. "Tell them!"

"Get out!" screamed the old man. "Get out of my house right now!" he ordered.

At that moment, a hulking, lurching figure appeared in the doorway where Frank's eyes had gone earlier. In Frank's estimation, the man looked to be six foot six and three hundred pounds.

The two detectives stood abruptly and discretely inventoried their sidearms. The behemoth entered the room and placed his lunchbox-sized hand on the shoulder of his crying mother. "Are you okay, Mom?" asked the giant as she grimaced at his touch.

"Get out of here, now," shouted Richard Clark as his wife sobbed.

"Willard, get back downstairs," the older Clark ordered his son.

"I heard shouting and crying," said the deep, raspy voice coming from the leviathan.

Penny couldn't conceal her fear and had her right hand planted firmly on her Glock, unclicking the leather strap that held it in place. Frank's left fist was filled with the lower front portion of his jacket, ready to pull it back to reveal his ready Smith & Wesson.

The giant Willard Clark politely said, "Leave my mother alone."

"Please leave!" cried Richard Clark. "Just leave my family alone!"

Helen Clark stood, rubbed her eyes, and tried to look brave. "It's okay, Richard. It's okay, Willard. I'm fine," she sniffled, wiping her runny nose onto the sleeve of her sweater. "The detectives were just leaving." Her eyes pleaded with the two detectives.

Helen Clark gently pushed her husband and son into the kitchen and walked the two detectives to the door. Putting on her slippers, she escorted them out onto the front porch.

"We're so sorry, Mrs. Clark." Penny was heart-sick. "We just wanted to ask your son some questions." In her mind, Penny thought that the entire visit to the home was a complete disaster and regretted she and Frank being there. She wasn't sure how a future conversation might be had.

The old woman choked back her tears and said, " He broke my arm because I forgot to iron his work shirt three weeks ago. I don't think he understands how strong he is. I want to believe he didn't mean to hurt me, but sometimes I just don't know." A tear ran from her eye. "I love my son, but ever since the accident, he's...." she paused. "Something's not right with him. I don't know what caused his breakdown at the end of last month. I think he may have stopped taking his medication." Helen Clark wiped another tear from her cheek as Frank reached for a handkerchief that wasn't there.

"Mrs. Clark, when did the swimming pool accident happen?" asked Frank.

The old woman struggled for the answer before saying, "New Year's Eve, 1996."

"Mrs. Clark," said Penny, "I think you should come with us. At least for the night," she offered.

"It might be for the best," said Frank.

Just then, the door opened, and the massive, younger Clark filled the doorway. "Come on, Mother. It's raining and cold," he smiled politely.

Frank studied the man and thought that he looked every bit like Lennie from *Of Mice and Men*. A gentle giant that could squash a person's head like a grape all while wearing a smile.

"Lennie, I mean, Willard, I think you should come with us down to the 39th District Headquarters," Frank suggested. Anything he could do to get him away from his mother for a while.

"I don't think so, Officer," said Willard. "Now, come on, Mother. Let's get you back inside."

Before turning to go back inside, Helen Clark looked at Penny. Her eyes were crying out to the female detective. Penny felt helpless.

Frank and Penny wanted to remove the old woman from the volatile situation but had no probable cause to arrest the younger Clark. Nothing was linking him to any of the victims directly. No physical evidence, no eyewitness testimony, no interview of their person of interest. All they had was speculation and a pit of fear in their bellies.

Chapter 16 – St. Pete

Tuesday Morning, January 24, 12:17 am – Seven hours after Frank and Penny's visit to the Clark residence.

Frank skidded to a stop in front of *Fabrics*, his dashboard flashers on. Penny quickly ran from the stairwell door and got into the Dodge.

"Whatta we know so far?" Penny looked petrified and guilt-ridden.

Frank's knuckles were white as he tightly gripped the steering wheel. "Well, CSU is on the scene, so we know there's been a killing."

"Jesus Christ, Frank!" Penny's eyes were glassy and wide. "What have we done?" She just sat there slowly shaking her head side to side.

"We did our jobs, Penny. That's all," said Frank. "We were following up on a lead."

"Frank, we pushed that couple too far. Our questions may have crossed the line. They weren't suspects, and we pushed them as if they were." Penny was frightened.

"Penny, we did nothing out of the ordinary. Our questions could have all been answered through public records." Frank reasoned with his partner, but he, like her, knew they'd gone too far.

"Yeah, but Frank, you saw that woman." Penny was shaking. "She was terrified of something. Someone."

"No shit!" Frank was defensive as he picked up speed. "She had a monster living in her basement."

The radio crackled, and Frank and Penny listened in. *"Two dead, one male, one female,"* the voice said. *"One male is in custody."*

"Oh my God!" said Penny. "I'm going to be sick. Pull over! Pull over!" she demanded.

Frank stopped the car. Penny jumped out and lurched over, and began vomiting. Frank got out to tend to his partner.

"Penny, it's okay," said Frank, rubbing her back as she finished heaving. "We did our job," he reassured his partner.

Penny looked up, crying, and fell into Frank's arms. "We killed those people!" she cried. "We killed them, Frank!"

Frank embraced his partner and again reassured her that they'd done their jobs.

"Penny, they gave birth to a monster, and that monster consumed them, along with five others." Frank spoke softly. "They have him in custody now. It's over. It's all over, Penny," he whispered into her ear as he held her tightly.

After several minutes Penny regained her composure, and the two got back in the car.

"I just can't believe it," said Penny, shaking her head again in horror, staring blankly out into the darkness.

As the Dodge turned right onto Fox Street from Midvale and then left onto West Coulter, the two saw the entire northside of McMichael Park washed over with a red glow from the units on scene.

"This is bad, Penny."

Penny cringed as she saw a coroner van slowly taking a right onto West Coulter off Netherfield Road, the tiny side street in front of the Clark residence. Coming to a stop, the two detectives counted no less than seven police units and CSU vehicles still on site.

Before exiting the vehicle, Frank looked up at the house at 3211 West Coulter and felt like he was back at 112 Ocean Avenue in Amityville, Long Island. Frank suddenly wasn't sure he wanted to get out of the car.

Penny looked at her partner and asked, "Do I look okay? Can you tell I've been crying?"

"It's okay to cry, Penny." Frank reached over and gently tucked a misplaced strand of hair behind her left ear. "It's okay, Penny." He reassured her again, "It's okay."

The two got out and walked upon the scene where they saw a uniformed supervisor talking on his cell phone. The supervisor lifted his chin to acknowledge the approaching detectives and ended his call to greet them.

"Hey guys," said Steven Di Silva. "It's a bad one," he said.

"We were here earlier today, questioning the parents about their adult son," offered Frank. "He was a person of interest, and we were following up on a lead."

"Yeah, I heard about that," said Di Silva. "Wade and McCurdy are in the house now. They've already mapped the scene."

Di Silva paused, "So, one of the victims worked at Trolley's, huh? I just had dinner there earlier this evening. Guess I won't be eating there anymore." Di Silva's eyes displayed his resignation.

"Victim?!" Frank was confused as he looked over at Penny.

Penny came out of the shadows and asked, "Victim?! The son was the victim?" She was confused. "Don't you mean the son was the assailant?"

"No, the father shot and killed the son after the son allegedly killed his mother with his bare hands," explained Di Silva.

"Self-defense?" Frank was surprised.

Penny looked sick again when her memory flashed to the old woman on the porch just before they'd left. The woman's eyes told Penny that she'd never see the light of day again.

"If it was self-defense, then why is he in custody?" asked Frank, as he looked at Penny and then back to Di Silva.

"Yeah, well, that's the thing," said Di Silva. "It wasn't exactly self-defense. He said that he'd killed his grown son to save him from himself." Di Silva threw his hands up and added, "His words, not mine. He's over there, in Unit 88. Ask him yourself."

"Euthanasia?" Frank whispered while shaking his head. He struggled to make sense of it all as he and Penny looked at each other. Their baffled looks mirrored one another's.

"What in the hell happened here?" Frank shook his head.

"Apparently, the adult son broke his mother's neck in a rage, and his father stepped in," Di Silva explained what the old man told he and the other officers on the scene. "The older Clark told us he put his son down in a show of mercy."

"We kept him here until you guys arrived." Di Silva again motioned to Unit 88. "Go talk to him yourself, or we can take him down to Headquarters, and you can talk to him there. Just tell me what you want us to do, Frank."

Without another word, Frank and Penny turned toward the Police Unit sitting at the bottom of the Clark driveway.

As they got closer, Frank could see the flashers illuminating the older Clark's gray hair through the back window of the police unit. The man's head was slumped.

Frank opened the back driver's side door and found a sobbing Richard Clark.

Clark looked up and immediately recognized Frank and Penny. He wailed in anguish. "My Helen is gone! My Willard is gone!" he moaned.

"Mr. Clark," Frank knelt next to the opened door. "What happened in there?"

Penny stood back, hand over her mouth, and just cried.

"What happened in there, Sir?" Frank asked again.

"After you left, everything was calm. We just sat and talked, the three of us," Richard Clark said through his tears.

He paused and continued. "Then Helen kept asking Willard if he'd done those terrible things. If he'd hurt all those people." Clark shook his head, still in shock. "Willard kept saying, no, but Helen didn't believe him. She kept pushing him. She was terrified of our son. He broke her arm earlier this month without even trying to. He was just so angry that he shook her and hurt my Helen," explained Clark.

"He wasn't right in the head, you see. The accident changed him. He's been different for twenty years. He wasn't born that way," pleaded Clark. "My son was normal. He was a good kid. He loved his mother." Clark hunched over again, crying in agony.

After a minute, Frank leaned back in, rubbing the old man's back, consoling him. "How did Willard die, Mr. Clark?"

"I killed him!" howled Clark. "I shot him. I told him to look away. I told him that we could all be together again if he'd only look away. I asked him to stare at a picture of the three of us on the wall. Just stare, I said to my son."

Frank began to tear up. Penny stood nearby inconsolable.

Clark cried and continued. "Willard started to cry. He knew what was about to happen, and he let it. He could have taken that gun from me. He could have taken my life after taking his mother's, but Willard loved me. He loved his mother," the old man whimpered.

"I cried with my son, and I told him to stare at the picture of the three of us. It was a picture of us in Florida after he'd graduated High School. He was named Valedictorian of his class, and we were proud. We took him down to St. Pete, and we were a family. That was the last time we were a normal family."

"Then, what happened?" asked Frank.

"We cried together, and I told him that I loved him, and he cried that he loved me."

Richard Clark looked lost. A ghost in the backseat of a police car in front of the house he'd shared with his wife of almost fifty years."

"Then, what happened, Mr. Clark?" Frank hated that he needed to ask the grieving man, but it was his job.

"He looked at the picture of the three of us in St. Pete," said the grieving father. "He looked at it and cried, "It's okay, Papa. I love you. I just want to be normal again. I will see you in Heaven soon." The old man wept. "Willard said he would take care of his mother when he got there and that he would never hurt her again."

"I cocked the gun, and he heard it, but Willard never looked back. Such a good boy," cried Clark. "He said he was sorry, and then I pulled the trigger. I killed my son."

Frank stopped and thought of what the old man said. Clark stated that he'd cocked the gun before firing.

Frank inhaled fully before asking, "Mr. Clark, what type of gun was it?"

"It was an old .38 revolver. I never fired that gun in my life before tonight," Clark was inconsolable.

So, not a .22, then? Frank thought to himself.

"Mr. Clark, did Willard own a gun?"

"No!" the old man screamed. "I killed my son! I killed my son!"

Frank reached in and helped the heartbroken man out of the car and to his feet. Turning him around, Frank removed the cuffs from Richard Clark's hands, and he hugged the man. Frank thought of his son, Conner. He thought of his dead father, and he cried. Frank cried for Helen Clark, and he cried for the old man. He now understood that Willard Clark was broken. A sick, broken man, and now the monster he became back in 1996 was dead.

The next thing Frank heard was Penny screaming, "NO!"

As Frank pulled back from the old man, he spotted the barrel of his city-issued Smith & Wesson M&P in the hand of Richard Clark.

During their embrace, without Frank being aware, Richard Clark's hand found Frank's gun, and then and there, chose to join his wife and son in Heaven.

Frank, now fully aware of the situation, lunged for the gun as a thunderous clap exploded into the night. Richard Clark had placed the gun's barrel into his mouth and pulled the trigger, and then fell into a heap onto the ground. A stunned Frank turned to Penny in shock by what'd just happened. Blood splatter on his face, hands, and jacket. He fell to his knees in front of the old man and went into shock.

Frank couldn't hear the commotion around him. He couldn't hear Penny's voice or feel her touch. He didn't see the uniformed officers rushing to the scene. He couldn't hear Di Silva's radio crackle calling for Wade and McCurdy.

Frank just sat frozen on the wet ground, reflections of the red flashers melting into his tears.

All Frank Collazo could see were holes in a wooden fence in the backyard of his childhood home. And all he could hear was his father saying to him, "I'm so sorry, Son."

Chapter 17 – Dominos

Municipal Services Building – Easter Sunday, April 16, 2017 – Three months later.

Frank and Penny stood side by side at the unveiling of the Penny Bryce Statue at the Women's Rights Ceremony being held in downtown Philadelphia.

Former Philadelphia Police Detective Penelope Bryce finally received the recognition she'd deserved for more than forty years. A bronze statue in her likeness would stand on the steps of the famous Municipal Services building. The sculpture would replace the statue of disgraced former Philadelphia Mayor Frank Rizzo.

Frank leaned over and whispered to his partner. "Penny, when we're done here, I want you to run an errand with me up to the Twins," said Frank.

"Geez, Frank. Let it go, already," Penny encouraged her guilt-ridden partner. "It was awful, everything that happened, but, you have to let it go," she said. "Case closed, Brother."

"I get it, Penny," said Frank. "but I need personal closure. I want to go to The Trolley Car Café and apologize to the manager there. Bender was his name. The tall kid, remember?"

"What am I, hard of remembering, or something?" Penny was dismissive. "Of course I remember the guy. It was less than three months ago. He led us to Lennie, REMEMBER?!" Penny busted Frank's balls.

Frank and Penny turned when they'd heard the ceremony begin. Standing with them was Penny's mother, Bonnie Ross. Ross was a close friend to fellow women's rights activist Penny Bryce back in the seventies before Bryce vanished without a trace.

As the trio looked on, along with several hundred others, they saw Mayor Donovan Taylor, who was flanked by Police Commissioner William Holden and Chief Inspector Jonathan Caffey. Standing just behind them were the twenty-one District Captains; only three were women. The obvious lack of female leadership didn't go unnoticed by anyone in attendance that day.

Penny chuckled. "We've still got a long way to go, apparently," she said to her partner.

The microphone let out a high-pitched squeal before the Mayor gave it three loud taps. Clearing his throat, Donovan Taylor began to speak. "While Penelope Bryce lived a life that was far too short, her legacy has lived long and will continue to do so, in part by today's dedication. The life of Penelope Denise Bryce is one of a hero. Her legend will endure for many generations to come. Sadly, Penny left us far too many years ago, and her husband Joe passed away just last year. However, her two children and eight grandchildren are here today to witness this historic event."

Donovan Taylor looked over to his right at the veiled bronze statue to acknowledge the legacy Penny Bryce had left behind.

"When Penny Bryce chose not to lay down, not to sit back, but instead demand equal rights for her and all women, she could finally take her rightful place as a detective in the Philadelphia Police Department. By doing so, she followed in the footsteps of her father and brothers before her. When Penny became the first-ever female Police Detective for the City of Philadelphia, she changed the lives of thousands of little girls. Penny changed the course of how this city works, how we conduct ourselves, and how we treat women."

Taylor continued to evangelize Bryce. "Her story of standing up for herself and all women led to a permanent change in discriminatory hiring and promotion practices, not only in the City of Philadelphia but around the country."

"Far too few of us know Penny's story, but after today, my hope is that the world will take notice of her example and open up the very history books that Penny helped to write." Taylor preached loudly from his pulpit.

"I am honored to shine a light on Penelope Bryce's life, legend, and legacy. I am equally proud to bring her story and legal case back into today's conversation about gender equality in the workplace," he said.

"Today, as we pull back the curtain on the gift that was Penelope Bryce, we must also pierce the veil on the failure to advance women's rights, even today, well into the twenty-first century. Here today, I formally and publicly commit to bringing a change to our modern-day practices of promoting officers based on their merits, not their gender."

The Mayor paused, "But I am not blind," said Taylor. "Looking at the fine group behind me, I see far too few women leading our District Headquarters around this great city."

Only mild applause came from the onlookers.

"With the help of our City Council and Police Leadership Council, I commit to promoting one female per year to the rank of District Captain until we see as many women standing behind me as there are men!" Donovan stepped back from the podium as the crowd erupted in cheer. He then turned to look behind him and joked, "I guess that means some of you will need to retire at some point." The crowd laughed and cheered while some of the male Captains clapped and uncomfortably nodded in agreement.

Taylor himself began to clap as he walked over to the veiled statue of Penny Bryce. Pulling back the thin layer separating a legend from her place in history, Mayor Donovan Taylor pulled down years of oppression and misogyny. And shared Penelope Denise Bryce's story and legend with the world.

Walking back to the podium, clapping along the way, Taylor yelled out. "We're not there yet, but we soon will be thanks to Penny Bryce, then and now. Penny will stand out here on these hallowed steps for generations to come. Now, as she did then, Penny will inspire men, women, little boys, and little girls just as she had when she turned the City of Brotherly Love into the City of Inclusiveness and Gender Equality!" He barked into the microphone. "Thank you for coming today, and thank you, Penelope Bryce, for standing watch over these hallowed steps and inspiring us still."

And just like that, the presentation ended. The Mayor then did what all Mayors do; he shook hands and kissed babies in front of every camera he could see. All in attendance hoped his words were true, but few knew how hard it would be to forward the march for women's rights and gender equality across all walks of life and all fields of endeavor. Penny Bristow and her mother Bonnie were two of those women, and they'd continue to be skeptical.

Frank and Penny hugged Bonnie and then got back to work.

"So whattaya say, Penny, the Twins?"

Penny shook her head and reluctantly said, "Fine. But we're getting some lunch while we're there. They have great cheesy bread."

"Deal," said Frank. "You buyin'?" he joked.

On 76 North, Penny asked Frank, "So, what was it like being on leave for the last sixty days?"

"You mean what was it like being suspended for two months?" Frank corrected his partner."

"It was paid time off, so I call it 'Leave,'" said Penny.

"Listen, Penny. It wasn't the demotion. It wasn't the suspension. It was the time away that killed me." Frank was contrite when repeating himself. "It was the time away. Not going into the 39th every day killed me. I mean, that place is a dump, and I know we all hate being there, but man," he paused and shook his head. "When someone snatches that out from underneath you, it hurts."

"How's it going with Captain Head Doctor anyway?" Penny tried to joke but empathized with her friend and partner. "Is it helping?"

Frank looked in the rearview mirror, changed lanes, and said, "It must be. She gave me the 'all clear' to go back to work."

"So, what about you?" asked Penny. "Do you give yourself the 'all clear' to come back?"

Frank looked over at his partner and said, "I did, and I do. I've come to grips with what happened, Penny. I mean, I could've lost my job and even gone to jail for manslaughter or negligent homicide. I feel lucky to still be carrying a gun and a badge."

Penny dismissed Frank's comments. "Horse shit! It was a freak thing. Something like that only happens once in a million times. The man wanted to die, and that's that."

Frank pushed back harshly. "Yeah! Well I gave a suicidal man a gun! I'd say that makes me culpable, don't you?"

"Frank, I was there. You can't tell me that's how it went down," said Penny. "You gave a grieving father and husband a hug. I would've too if our roles were reversed that night." Penny softened her tone and added, "That act of compassion impacted me more than anything I've ever seen or even heard about. That night will stay with me forever, Partner."

Frank mumbled, "I relive it every day."

"So, how'd you stay busy?"

"Outside of the mandated visits to Dr. Bixby twice a week, I spent a ton of time with Conner and Joanne. It was actually really nice."

"Yeah?" Penny asked with a tinge of jealousy in her voice. "You guys gettin' back together, or something?"

"God no!" said Frank, but he wasn't sure. "I mean, she's great and everything, but there's someone else in the picture."

Penny shoved Frank's shoulder and said, "No shit?! She met a guy?"

Frank's eyes narrowed and teeth clenched. "Not actually," he said.

"I don't get it," said Penny looking confused.

Frank looked at his partner and raised his brow.

A look of amazement came over Penny's face, and her eyes went wide. "Holy shit! Joanne's gay?!"

"I don't know," said Frank. "Hell, she doesn't know either. She just knows that she finds peace with this woman."

"So, who is it?" asked Penny, dying to know.

"It's Conner's teacher, believe it or not," revealed Frank. "Her name is Polly, and she's nice. She's great with Conner, too."

"I'm sure she is but isn't that a little unethical?" asked Penny.

"She's dating Joanne. She's not dating Conner, you idiot!" Frank laughed. "Now, unethical is me sleeping on your couch."

Penny's head went back as she smirked, "Wouldn't have been any sleeping that night, I can tell ya that right now," she whispered under her breath.

"What's that?" said Frank. "I didn't hear ya," he lied as he smiled.

"Nothing," said Penny. "Not a goddamn thing."

"It's like I told you, Penny. The Ritz Carlton, downtown."

"Yeah, you're full of some serious shit, man."

Minutes later, the Dodge pulled into The Trolley Car Café parking lot. The two detectives got out, and Penny began walking toward the door. Halfway there, she turned to see Frank staring apprehensively at the building.

"You coming, or what?" asked Penny.

"Yeah, yeah," said Frank. "Just thinking about the last time we were here, that's all."

Standing in the parking lot, Frank replayed the night of January 23. He knew that The Trolley Car Café started a domino effect that ended with the last domino, Richard Clark, falling onto the ground, dead at his feet. He'd never forget that night, and he'd always remember the old man.

Shaking off the memory only temporarily, Frank overcame his fear and joined his partner inside. Standing near the hostess station, the first face they saw was Kyle Bender.

The manager saw the two detectives and immediately turned away.

"Kyle, wait!" yelled Frank. "We just want to talk for a moment."

"What do you want from me?" said Bender.

"To apologize," said Frank, in a moment of sincere contrition. He was sorry, and he selfishly wished he'd never gone to the café that Saturday back in January. The last time he was there was a fishing expedition, and he never thought for a moment that their meeting would result in anything, let alone two precious old people dying because of his actions. Frank never did reason that those two old people dying rid the streets of a menace to society, forever. Frank thought Willard Clark was neither a domino nor the Schuylkiller. After that night, he only thought of him as Lennie.

Frank stopped Kyle Bender in his tracks with his words. Bender didn't expect an apology from the detectives but rather accusations, judgment, and blame by the police. But not, an 'I'm sorry.'

"Oh," said Kyle. "That was unexpected. I'm actually not sure why you would be sorry," said Kyle, trying to reason who owed who the apology.

"Listen, Kyle. The last time we were here, the place was packed, but now it's slow. Can we sit down for a few minutes and talk?" asked Frank. "This time at a table and not your office."

"Are you allowed to talk police business out in the open?" Bender asked the detectives.

"This isn't police business," said Frank. "I, I mean we, just want to talk," Frank corrected himself, looking over at Penny. "We wanted to see how you and your co-workers were holding up. After that, Penny, over here, wants some of that cheesy bread you guys have."

Bender cracked a smile. He would've liked the two to think he didn't have much time, but it was only 10:30 am, and the Easter crowd wouldn't start arriving until noon. "Sure, I can spare fifteen minutes for you guys."

Frank returned his smile and said, "Great!"

The three sat and talked, and Kyle Bender apologized to both Frank and Penny. He even had some cheesy bread, and two glasses of Coke brought to the table.

Since the events of January 23, Kyle and his staff wondered if they should have seen or observed something in their co-worker that would have tipped them off. They were also relieved that having a serial killer in their midst didn't result in one or more of them being killed.

"It's weird coming to work knowing that he worked here and that we were all around him." The restaurant manager pondered for a moment. "I mean, we were all at risk at one time or another," he said.

"Kyle, don't blame yourself," said Penny. "Every serial killer that ever lived had a friend, family member, co-worker, or neighbor that would swear the person wasn't capable of hurting anyone." Penny tried to reassure Kyle that no one expected him to be able to sniff out a maniac in his midst.

Kyle Bender shook his head in frustration. "You see, that's just it. I could see him hurting someone, but not intentionally. Like I told you back in January, he was Lennie. If he held a mouse in his hand and crushed it, it was out of love, not anger."

Penny and Frank saw that Kyle Bender was both frustrated and confused.

Frank, too, thought the same thing. His doubts grew every day since that fateful night. *"Willard was Lennie, and Lennie couldn't possibly be the Schuylkiller,"* he'd been telling himself for weeks.

"Listen, like I said a moment ago, the signs are hard to see," said Penny. "It's hard to tell sometimes who the man or woman standing, lying, or working next to you is." Deep down inside, Penny was also trying to convince herself of Willard's guilt.

Since the murder-suicide back on January 23, Frank had always doubted Lennie's involvement, but he pointed out the obvious to Kyle. "Whether we choose to believe in Lennie's innocence, or not, one thing is clear. No one has come up missing since Lennie died. No bodies have turned up down by the river. No nothing. The end of Lennie and the end of another horrible winter has brought a sudden calm over North Philly. It's kinda weird, actually," said Frank.

Penny agreed, and Kyle's eyes widened in acknowledgment. "Yeah, but I'll tell you what's really weird," he said. "There was a big guy that used to work next door at the daycare. He befriended Lennie back in the day. That dickhead would always squirt us with the hose to get a reaction from us," revealed Kyle. "That big ass motherfucker always gave me the creeps. A guy like that....I could see killing someone, but like Lennie, he also disappeared at the end of January."

Frank swallowed hard with Kyle's recollection. Frank always felt weird about the man with the hose since he ran into him the

Saturday before the Clark deaths. There was something in his eyes that bothered Frank. He agreed with Kyle, though he'd only ever seen the man one time.

"It was strange," added Kyle. "That lunatic was there all the time, even on the weekends. I mean, aren't daycares closed on the weekends? I never see anyone else there on Saturdays or Sundays. He was always out there cleaning that bus. Gave me the creeps every time I saw him."

"Okay, boys, it's been fun, as always," Penny joked. "But seriously, Frank and I have to get back."

The three rose from the table, and Frank said, "You still have my card?"

"I do," said an emphatic Kyle. "I still have Penny's, too," he winked at the female detective.

Penny's eyes flew open wide in disbelief that the twenty-something restaurant manager with zero facial hair just hit on her. "Give Frank a call should you need a Philly Detective," smiled Penny.

As the door closed behind the two detectives, Frank chuckled and asked his partner, "Seriously, Penny, when was the last time you were asked out on a date, anyway?"

"Still waiting on you to ask me," Penny zinged her partner.

"No, really, how long?" asked Frank.

"Years," said Penny.

"More like ninety seconds, Partner." Franked laughed as he walked right past their car and headed north up the sidewalk toward Ridge.

Penny was confused. "Where in the hell are you going?"

"Be right back, Sister."

"Sister?" mumbled Penny. "Yeah, in an Alabama sort of way, maybe," she joked to herself.

Two minutes later, Frank got in the car and said, "Guess what? The kid was right."

"About what?" asked Penny.

"The daycare lists their hours as closed on Saturday and Sunday."

Penny shook her head and said, "Come on, Frank! Give me a break! That's some hefty bullshit right there. Are you that gullible to fall for a comment like that?"

"We came here on a Saturday, Penny." Frank looked his partner square in the eyes." His gut was talking to him, and it had been since that night up on West Coulter.

"What exactly are you saying, Frank?" Penny felt a little worried about her partner's psychological state for a second. "Did you ever think that like Lennie, he worked odd hours when the place was closed, and he did cleaning and repairs, and.... Oh, I don't know," said a facetious Penny, "washed the fucking bus at the end of each week?!"

"Okay, okay,!" Frank threw up his hands to calm his partner's anxiety level. But his gut was talking to him, and it would continue to do so.

Chapter 18 – 2Close

As the two headed back up north to Penn Knox, so that Frank could drop off Penny at her Mom's place, Penny asked, "So, whatta you doing for Easter dinner, going up to Joanne's?"

"Nope, her folks are over, and she invited Polly and her son over for the holiday. We've agreed to alternate holiday visitation to every other. So, I get Conner next Easter," responded Frank. "Besides, I was there this morning for an Easter egg hunt. Conner had his friends over, and I put a fifty-dollar bill into a golden egg. I pretty much told him where to find it." Frank smiled with the memory.

Penny laughed. "Could you imagine if one of the neighbor kids found that egg before Conner?" she howled. "Word would get out fast! You'd have a hundred kids over there every year for that Easter egg hunt."

"Yep, that's why I made sure he found it."

"So, where'd you hide it, anyway?" asked Penny.

"Look in the glovebox," Frank motioned with his eyes.

Penny looked aghast. "You did not!" she said, looking at the glove compartment. Opening it, she saw the golden egg, picked it up, and laughed until she cried.

"You're such a goofball, Frank Collazo!" Penny playfully shoved Frank's shoulder in a show of affection. "Of course none of the other kids would've found the egg. They could've ended up being arrested for rummaging through a cop car," she joked.

"Go ahead, open it up," said Frank with a straight face.

Penny noticed his expression change and looked down at the egg. Jokingly she said, "There better be a fifty in here."

She looked at Frank again, and he motioned for her to open the egg. Looking back down at the egg, Penny slowly cracked it open and immediately saw the words, *Ritz Carlton.* Penny was shocked.

Speechless and confused, she looked at Frank and said, "Are you serious?"

"I missed you, Penny." Frank looked at his partner and threw the car up into park. "I thought we could celebrate my return to work tomorrow. I thought we could celebrate us."

Penny's dream had come true. She was in love with Frank and had been for years.

"Well, whattaya say, Partner?" asked Frank. "Is Easter Sunday a good enough day to consummate the relationship?"

Penny was flustered and red-faced, holding the Ritz Carlton room key firmly in her hand. "Okay, let me call my mom first."

Frank laughed as Penny fumbled for her purse.

"What's so funny?" she asked.

"Penny, look over there." Frank motioned with his head out Penny's window.

Penny looked out her window and was completely embarrassed when she saw the *Fabrics* storefront staring back at her.

"All right," said a flustered Penny. "Let me run up and get a change of clothes. I'll tell my mom we're going out for dinner instead of eating at home. By the way, she asked me to invite you over if you weren't doing anything tonight."

"Hmmm," Frank rubbed his chin and asked himself aloud, "Dinner at Bonnie Ross's apartment, or with Bonnie Ross's hot daughter downtown?" Frank feigned uncertainty.

"Whatever!" said Penny. "I'll be right back!" As she turned to go, she ran back to the car, opened the door, and said, "Don't you drive off, now."

"I'll be right here, Penny Bristow," he smiled. "Don't you worry."

Twenty minutes later, Penny emerged from the stairwell door dressed like she was going out on a first date. After throwing an overnight bag into the backseat, she got in the front and said, "Sorry it took so long! I had to rinse off real quick."

Frank's nostrils flared. "Penny Bristow, is that perfume you're wearing?" His smile revealed his approval. "I'm pretty sure I've never detected perfume on you before."

"Don't push it, Frankie Boy."

As Frank pulled away, Penny got a text notification. She looked at her phone in her purse and quickly looked back up. The text seemed to change her demeanor.

"Who was that? Your mom?" asked Frank. "Is she excited, or nervous about our first date?"

"Yeah," Penny nervously smiled. "She just said, 'Have fun.'"

Frank detected Penny's nerves getting to her. "Penny, are you sure you're up for this?"

"One hundred percent!" Penny tried her best to look truthful.

"Okay," said Frank. "Just know that I'm nervous, too."

Penny reached across the seat, keeping her eyes focused out the front window. Taking Frank's hand into hers, she closed her eyes and took a deep breath, then exhaled. Her nerves were shot.

After the fifteen-minute drive into downtown without much conversation, Penny and Frank exited the car, and Frank tossed the keys to the valet.

"We won't need it back until midnight," Frank informed the valet.

"Right, Sir. Can I get a name and a cellphone number?" asked the college-aged valet.

"You bet, it's Frank Collazo. 267-808-2248."

"Hey, aren't you the guy that caught the Schuylkiller?" asked the valet as he handed Frank a business card.

"Nope! That's not me," replied Frank, sneaking a look in Penny's direction, smiling.

Penny smiled back and rolled her eyes.

"But I saw you on the news. I'm sure that was you. No?"

"Must be a good-lookin' guy, but it wasn't me." Frank threw his hands up.

"Hmm. Oh well," the young man shrugged. "My name's Matt. Call me at this number fifteen minutes before you're ready to leave."

"Will do!" said Frank.

As the valet got into the vehicle, Frank said, "Penny, don't forget your bag."

"Oh yeah." Penny was startled as she finished and then hit send on a text. She again looked flustered.

Sixty minutes later, and halfway through dinner, Frank asked, "Penny, what gives? I can see that you're uncomfortable? We don't have to do this."

Penny looked mortified. Starting to cry, she said, "Frank, I need to tell you something."

"Penny, it's okay. I get it. You're nervous. I am, too."

"Yes, I'm very nervous, but that's not it." Penny looked away.

"Just say it, Penny." Frank was supportive. "It's okay, whatever it is."

"It's just that," she paused, "while you were away, I missed you so much. I was lonely, and I really needed you in my life...."

"I missed you, too." Frank cut her off.

"Let me finish, Frank," she paused. "I started seeing Dan again."

Frank's face went white with embarrassment and then red in anger. "What?! Penny, he abused you! Dozens of times." The volume in Frank's voice rose, and the other patrons in the restaurant all stopped and stared at him and Penny.

"Mind your own business!" Frank snapped at an older couple sitting nearby.

"Frank, you're embarrassing me," Penny cried in a low whisper.

"You're embarrassed?" Frank felt like a jilted lover. "Good ole Danny boy swoops in and rescues the lonely girl. Three weeks later, she's back at the hospital wondering how she fell for him again."

"Frank, he's changed. He really has." Penny attempted to reason with her partner.

"Whatever!" Frank carefully covered his half-eaten, hundred-dollar filet mignon and said, "We're out of here!" Checking his pockets for the valet's card, he stood up and tossed Penny the room key. "You go get your bag, and I'll go get the car."

Tossing two crisp one hundred dollar bills onto the table, he added, "I'll meet you out front."

"Frank, wait! We can at least finish our dinner." Penny reached for his arm as he brushed by her.

"I don't think so!" he said. His words dripping with disdain.

Penny sat and cried, and the people around her stared.

Frank grumbled, "Let's go, Matt!" as he texted the valet from the street curb in front of the hotel for the third time. A minute later, another valet arrived at the podium and asked Frank if she could help him.

"Yeah, where's Matt, and where's my fucking car?!" Frank was humiliated.

"Good question," said the female valet. "Haven't seen him in an hour."

"Yeah, well, I need my car. And I need it now!" Frank ordered the girl, flashing his badge.

The young woman was taken aback. "Ah, yes, Sir!" she said. "I'm gonna need a few minutes as we use two underground parking levels, and I have no idea where Matt parked your car."

"It's a black 2015 Dodge Charger with city plates. Find it fast, and I'll give you twenty bucks."

"You got it, Mister! I'll just need the stub."

Frank reached into his pocket and produced the ticket stub Matt had given him.

After the valet disappeared, Penny came out of the front entrance of the Ritz, wiping her tears. She walked over to Frank and said nothing. For ten agonizing minutes, both wrestled with their feelings and what to say.

"I'm sorry," said Frank, speaking first. "This is all my fault," he said, looking shellshocked. I saw something that wasn't there, that's all."

Penny said, "Stop it, Frank. You're wrong! I do care for you."

Frank shook his head. "My bad, Penny. I'm sorry."

Penny suddenly grabbed Frank, threw her arms around him, and kissed him passionately in a moment of inglorious weakness. At first, Frank tried to resist his partner but quickly melted into her arms. The two kissed until they were one. Only the horn sounding from the approaching Dodge Charger could pull them from that moment.

Both were speechless as the valet exited the vehicle, walked up to Frank, and held out her hand. "That'll be twenty bucks, please?"

Frank drew a twenty from his right pocket and handed it to the smiling girl.

As he and Penny got into the car, the young valet shouted, "By the way, your trunk was partially opened. I closed it for you."

Frank could barely understand a word she said, lost in the euphoria of Penny's kiss.

A minute later, sitting at a red light, Penny noticed something under the windshield wiper blade. "What's that?" she asked. "Is that a valet ticket, or something?"

"I don't know," said Frank. The light turned green, and he accelerated to the next intersection where the light was red. Throwing the car up into park, Frank got out and reached beneath the wiper blade and removed a white envelope.

With the light still red, Frank turned to see the writing on the front of the envelope. The single number and letters read, '*2CLOSE.*' Frank looked at Penny, baffled by the text. He could see that she, too, was at a loss.

Penny's phone alerted her of incoming text messages, but she ignored them, thinking it was her ex-husband, Dan.

"Open it up," said a curious Penny.

Frank shoved his thumb under the seal and anxiously pulled away. Reaching in, he removed a single page. Starting to read the letter, the scream of a horn came from a car behind the Dodge. Frank looked up to see the signal had turned green.

Frank handed the letter to Penny and pulled over in front of a fire hydrant, and asked Penny to reveal what was written on the page. Penny again ignored text messages that were now coming fast and furious. Opening the letter, she was baffled by what it said.

"It says, *'Getting too close for comfort. Sorry about the fancy dinner. Should have stuck to tinder. Nice Car. Your tenacity, eye couldn't take! Come visit when you can. Be two seeing you soon in the papers tomorrow, big shot!'*"

Penny handed Frank the letter and said, "Look how it's written." she was baffled.

Frank turned on the dome light to get a better look. He studied the writing, examined the text, and read the letter again.

getting 2Close for comfort. sorry About the Fancy dinner. shouLd have stuck to tinder. nice car. your teNacity, eye CouLdn't take!"
COme visit When you can. be 2C'ing u in the pApers tomorrow, big shot!

"What the fuck is this shit?!" he looked at Penny. Looking back at the letter, he mumbled its contents, and his face went white.

"Penny, what's your mom's apartment number?!" Frank felt sick.

"2C. Why?" Penny was frightened by the look of horror on Frank's face.

"Penny, 2C appears twice in this message!" Frank reached up and turned on the dashboard flashers.

"Oh my God!" Penny trembled as she pulled her cell phone from her purse. Swiping up the black screen revealed five missed calls and eight text messages. All the calls and texts were from her ex-husband and firefighter Dan Bristow. The last message read: *'FABRICS is on fire! CALL ME!'*

Penny screamed. "Fabrics is on fire! Frank! Hurry!" her face, enveloped with fear.

Penny frantically called her mother over and over, each time it went straight to voicemail. "She's not answering, Frank!" Penny screamed.

"Call Dan!" Frank's panic was purposely subdued.

Penny fumbled with the phone and frantically tried to reach her ex, but he didn't answer either.

The Dodge Charger barreled through the streets of East Falls now and roared past the 39th District, racing to get back up to Penn Knox. From twenty blocks south of Germantown Avenue, the two could see an orange glow lighting up the night sky.

Penny grimaced and quietly moaned in horror seeing the horizon painted orange. The two could now smell the burning ash ten blocks away as it fell like snow onto the windshield.

Two minutes later, Frank slammed on his brakes in front of St. Luke's, and the two jumped out. While Penny ran toward the fire units spraying the blaze, Frank stopped and stared in awe. The heat rained down on him and held him captive for a moment.

The bullhorn crackled as a Fire Captain called for Ladder 18 to redirect its ladder pipe nozzle to the northwest corner of the building, near where Frank had pulled over. The three-alarm fire had attracted three departments that included Dan Bristow's Engine 59. They witnessed flames rising more than one hundred feet from street level as they approached.

The Fabrics linen store and neighboring dress shop were filled with linen and fabrics that had been on-site for years and were primed for the flames as they'd become more brittle over time.

The intersection of Germantown Avenue and West and East Coulter looked like Armageddon, illuminated by a pulsating titian inferno. The flames could be seen for miles.

In addition to *Fabrics,* and the dress shop next to it, being consumed by the flames, the four apartments above the stores, two on the street side and two in the rear of the building, had been completely devoured by the still-raging fire. The flames were so hot that when the winds shifted southwest and across the street from *Fabrics,* they melted the windows on the second floor of the Germantown Friends School.

Penny ran crying and screaming toward the blaze but was intercepted by two firefighters before getting too close.

"Dan! Dan!" Penny screamed, and within moments she was pounding on the chest of her ex-husband. "Get her out of there, Dan! Save my mother!"

"Penny!" yelled Dan, over the roar of the blaze and the copious sirens. "She's gone, Penny! They're all gone!"

"No!" screamed Penny as she wailed. "Save her, Danny!"

"Penny, we can't get up there!" yelled Dan. "The stairwell is collapsed! She's gone, Penny. I'm so sorry, Baby!"

Penny crumbled into a heap at Dan's feet and sobbed.

Now snapped out of his trance, Frank did everything he could do to help. When he'd noticed a car and tree in front of St. Luke's catch on fire, he ran back to the Charger to get a fire extinguisher, popping the trunk while en route. As he reached the back of the vehicle, he opened the trunk fully and, through darkened skies and Dante's Inferno, saw Matt's severed head and tattered body, the young valet from the Ritz Carlton.

Frank recoiled in terror, hit the ground, knees first, and heaved up his half-eaten dinner.

Wiping his mouth, he spider-crawled backward, trying desperately to put distance between him and the Dodge.

Everything went quiet for Frank when he looked up and saw Ladder 18 stretched as far as it could go, dumping its watery avalanche on top of what was left of Penny's life, and mother.

The tinderbox Frank had always warned Penny about had ignited into a netherworld. Bonnie Ross was gone, and whatever remaining chance Frank and Penny had of a normal life was gone with her.

As Frank lay on the sidewalk, the colors around him faded to black. Gone, like the sound of death had done moments before.

Frank just stared at the sky, and all he could see was the scarred wooden fence in the backyard of his childhood home, which was now on fire. He could feel the heat on his face as his father dragged him away. The only sound he could hear now was his father's voice saying, "I'm sorry, Son."

Chapter 19 – The Day After

39th District Headquarters – Office of Captain Rosalyn Sumner – April 17, 2017. The Day After.

Frank backed the Charger into his usual spot against the station house on Schuyler street and just sat there for a while. The sound of the intermittent wiper blades wiping away the drizzle helped to clear his mind.

Frank knew very well he'd be calling someone for a ride as his days with the Philadelphia P.D. were over. Frank had a lot to answer for, and the questions would be many as he had a mandatory debriefing with his captain and her lieutenants.

Frank pulled out his Smith & Wesson and dropped the magazine out of its handle. Pulling the slide back, a single bullet from the gun's chamber shot upward, with Frank snatching it from the air just before gravity took over.

Frank pulled the slide again to ensure no bullets remained in the gun and then placed the single bullet into his interior, left-chest pocket. In Frank's mind, that bullet had a date with a killer, a serial killer. Frank would be the one to pull the trigger and end the terror that was the Schuylkiller. The maniac's days were numbered, and the countdown would start the minute Frank Collazo walked out of the 39th, no longer a cop.

On this, his final day, Frank would enter the building through the front entrance instead of the back. He wanted to take it all in one last time. The sights, the sounds, and the smells. And because, in his mind, he was no longer a cop.

Frank was buzzed in, and as he walked through the Operations Room, passing his long-time friends, none of them made eye contact with him.

Without looking up, ORS Sergeant McLaughlin said, "She's expecting you."

The walk was similar to the one that Penny Bryce took her first day on the job after finally earning her Detective Badge back in 1974. The temperature inside was as cold as it was outside, and the lowered stares of his colleagues meant that he was now a pariah, a leper, persona non grata, and he could care less. Frank was on a mission. *Kill or be killed* was his new motto, and he was up for the task. Like he and Penny always said, *Get all the bad guys off the street,* he thought. Well, there was one more on his list, and whether he killed or whether he be killed, he was fine either way.

Now upstairs, instead of turning right to go into the Detective Room, Frank took a left and headed to see Captain 'Roz' Sumner, a no-nonsense cop that got the job done but not at any cost. She did things the right way, and her way got her to the rank of District Captain.

Frank walked in without knocking because he didn't care. There would be no repercussions that could stymie his new goal, kill the Schuylkiller.

"Well, nice knock there, Detective." Sumner downplayed her displeasure at the disrespect shown by her subordinate. "Where in the hell have you been? It's after two o'clock."

Frank stood tall and sarcastically said, "I had a rough night last night in case you hadn't heard."

"Sit down, Collazo!" she barked from her maple throne.

"I'll stand," replied Frank. "I don't plan on being here for very long." Frank placed his shield and service weapon on Sumner's desk.

"What's this? Your resignation?" Sumner wasn't expecting that but played a little chess with Frank as she needed answers. Without him being under her supervision, he was under no obligation to speak to her, and she would instead treat him like her subordinate.

"If you don't sit down, you won't be here for very long!" Sumner had already lost control of her city-ordained power over Frank.

Frank was defiant. "Like I said, I'll stand."

"Sit your goddamn ass down, or I'll have you arrested for.....! Ah, hell! I don't know what I'll have you arrested for!" Roz Sumner was flustered.

"Where's your Knight and your Rook, Captain?"

Sumner rose to her feet and walked from behind her desk. Walking over to Frank, she stood six inches in front of him and was nearly a foot shorter. Looking up at her former Detective Sergeant, she said, "You've got a lot of balls walking in here with an attitude. You have a lot to answer for, and I want only straight answers from you. If I don't get the truth, legal counsel for the Philadelphia Police will be on scene in an hour, and you can answer theirs." Sumner regained control, if only for a moment.

"Now sit down, you arrogant son of a bitch!"

Turning her back on Frank and returning to her desk, she turned to sit, but Frank was still standing.

"That's fine, Collazo. Stand if you want," she said. "But everything you say to me from this moment on will determine whether I ever see you in this building again."

"Please proceed with your questions, Captain." Frank was stoic. "But before you do, know this. I only care about one thing from this moment on, and that is killing the sick motherfucker that killed that kid last night, Penny's mother, Mereby, Jacks, and all the others. That motherfucker dies at my hand whether you like it, or not."

Frank sat down and said, "One more thing, I will answer every single one of your questions, first, with an 'I don't give a shit,' and second, with the truth."

"Good for you!" said Sumner, rolling her eyes and flipping through the notes in front of her.

"I asked my Rook and Knight, as you so poignantly described my Lieutenants, not to be here. This portion of the legal Q&A is between us and stays in this room. What you say to anyone else is your business, but I demand the truth right now."

"Like I said," Frank was dismissive, "you'll get your truth."

"Let's start with the Ritz Carlton, then," said Sumner. "Why exactly were you out to dinner with your female partner. And why in the hell did you have a room booked there?"

"I was there having dinner with my partner."

"And?"

"After that, I was planning on taking her up to the room I reserved, and we were going to have sex."

Frank could see the discouragement on Sumner's face as she shook her head in disappointment. "Jesus Christ, Frank, you were willing to throw it all away for sex?"

"No," he said. "I was willing to throw it all away for Penny."

"Really?" Sumner rolled her eyes again and fell back into her chair in disgust.

Frank leaned forward in his chair. "Like I said at the top of this meeting. I don't give a shit what you think. I'm telling you the truth whether you want to hear it or not."

A calm furor lived in Frank's eyes, and Sumner could almost taste his acrimony for the proceeding.

"Okay, tell me about the kid in your trunk. What do you suppose happened there?"

"I take back what I said earlier. I do care about that one. That poor kid parked the wrong car last night. It's because of me and my desire for my partner that he's dead. I will take that one to the grave with me."

"So, you think the Schuylkiller did the deed?"

"Of course," Frank's eyes went dim. "He left me an invitation on the windshield. He killed them all, and he's gonna die."

"So, vigilante justice, then, Cowboy?" Sumner sat back in her chair. She was warming to the cool fire burning in front of her. She'd made a career out of controlled aggression. She'd just realized that Frank was the perfect weapon to turn loose on the Schuylkiller.

"You have my badge and my weapon, Captain. Call it whatever you want. But he dies at my hand. I will be the one that ends that fucker's life."

"All right, I got it!" Sumner leaned forward, interlocking her fingers. "You're going to kill the son of a bitch. Could we possibly put that part of the conversation aside until I get the rest of my questions answered?"

"Fine. Continue, Captain."

"How long have you and Penny been involved?"

"We've never been involved. We've only ever been partners. And damn good ones, too!"

Sumner smiled. "You see, you just blew it, Detective. You told me that you would be truthful, and now you're lying right to my face."

"First of all, it's former Detective, and second of all, save the bullshit for someone who'll actually fall for it. You're getting the truth out of me, and then I'm leaving. The next time you see me after that, I'll be in handcuffs for murder."

"My family's safety and protection are priority one, and that means the Schuylkiller dies."

Sumner concealed her shock at Frank's words. She still knew, though, that he was her best chance of taking down the most prolific serial killer in the history of the City of Philadelphia since Joseph and Michael Kallinger back in the mid-1970s.

Rosalyn Sumner knew that revenge was a powerful motivator. She also factored that Frank was now in full 'protect my family mode' and that that alone would ensure his senses were keen and sharp. Sumner knew that he was a sharpened blade and that he would be blind-sided by nothing. She also knew that Frank's singular focus was on killing the Schuylkiller, and short of putting her best detective behind bars, there was nothing she could do. And she certainly had no legal right to lock him up.

"Okay, fine. Let's talk about the Clark's...."

Frank sighed. "We've been over the Clark family killings ad nauseam. You want me to give you a transcript of the internal affairs report?"

"No, that's not what I'm asking you, Frank," said Sumner. "I want to know if you think the Schuylkiller had a hand in the way it all went down. Do you?"

"Yes, I do. You'll want to send the two detectives that reopen the Mereby and Jacks case down to the daycare under the Twins, next to The Trolley Car Café. I think our suspect worked there for a period of time and became friends with Willard Clark. It's also possible that he and Clark attended Temple University during the same time back in the nineties and may have even crossed paths there."

Sumner wrote down Frank's comments. "You think Clark had anything to do with Mereby?"

"Not a chance in hell," he said. "He might have killed mice, but he would never kill men."

"You forgetting about his mother's broken neck, Frank?"

"You won't understand this, Captain, but she was a mouse. Willard saw her as a sweet little animal he loved with everything he had. He simply loved that woman too much, and it was at that moment that her neck snapped."

Frank's words sent shivers down Sumner's spine. She paused for a moment before speaking again.

"So, I have your word you and Penny were not romantically involved?"

"You must be hard of hearing the truth, Captain. I will not repeat myself again."

Frank stood up and was ready to leave when he uttered, "The truth never lies, Captain. The truth never changes. No matter how much time goes by, no matter how much the world, things, or people around us change, the truth never does. The truth unifies the righteous and fractures the corrupt."

Frank paused. "I have one truth going forward, Captain."

Sumner looked impressed with Frank and said, "Let me guess, you're going to kill the Schuylkiller?"

Without a word, Frank turned to leave.

"Oh, and Frank," said Sumner. "You might want to take these with you?" She handed him his gun and shield. "You can retire anytime you want after that son of a bitch is dead and off the streets of East Falls. But when you kill him, I want it to be on the job so that I don't have to see you in handcuffs the next time we meet," she smiled.

"You giving me a license to kill, Sheriff?"

"This conversation never happened, Cowboy. And this ain't no wild, wild, West, so don't go shootin' up the place," said Sumner. "To be clear, though, when you find him, I want you to aim straight."

"Will do." Frank almost acknowledged his Captain with a smile.

"Captain, listen," said Frank. "Any chance you put a word in with the Cheltenham Township Police Chief regarding keeping an eye on my house?" he asked. "I can't be there 24/7, and I'm sure this guy knows where I live by now."

"Sure, Frank," said Sumner. "Have you told Joanne yet?"

"Yeah, she's at her father's retreat for now. It's up in Wrightstown. No way our killer finds that place. I've only been there once, and I can't even remember how to get there."

"Another thing," Frank said, "You won't see me around this place for a while. I'm going hunting for a killer."

"Frank, I wanted to let you know....," Sumner paused, "I'm promoting Penny to Lead Detective when she comes back from her leave. If she comes back, that is." Sumner had her doubts. Anyway, I'll be placing Ali Ashfaq under her wing."

"How's she doing, Captain? Have you heard anything?"

"She's now lost both of her parents in the line of duty," Sumner raised her brow. "No one should ever have to pay that price."

"I have her on leave for as long as she needs. I just hope she comes back. She's one of the best I've got."

"She is the best you've got," said Frank.

"I beg to differ, Detective Sergeant."

Frank smirked. "You throw around that title like it's a football, Captain." He then paused and said, "Well, I never cared much for the sport, so you can keep that title."

"Oh, and Captain," Frank paused again. "Ash is a good man. He'll be in good hands with Penny."

Frank turned to go, and just before the door closed, he heard Sumner say one last thing.

"Frank, the letter that bastard left for you and Penny last night. What does it all mean?" asked Sumner.

Frank turned and said, "2C. It was Bonnie Ross's apartment number above *Fabrics*."

"And the other stuff?"

"You got me." Frank threw up his brow and shrugged.

"I thought we were speaking the truth, Frank." Sumner wasn't convinced Frank was being forthright. "You had me hanging on that 'unifies the righteous and fractures the corrupt' stuff," she said, wanting to make sure that Frank knew she thought there was a hidden message in the note.

"Captain, I'll put it this way. The Devil himself has invited me to his Den. Just as he had my father back in 1992. He may be wearing a different skin, but he's the Devil, and he's gonna burn."

Frank paused. "Now, if you'll excuse me, I have to go kill a psychopath."

Sumner shouted one last order at Frank before he left. "Hey, Frank!"

"Yeah?"

"Take some Kevlar with you but leave the bodycam behind. No one should ever see the carnage that you're going to leave."

"Sure, Cap." Frank turned to go.

After Frank closed the door, Rosalyn Sumner held a copy of the letter the Schuylkiller left on the windshield of Frank's car. With it laid out on her desk, she looked closer and circled the ten capital letters in the message with a red pen.

In order, they were listed as A-F-L-N-C-L-C-O-W-A. Listed alphabetically, they read A-A-C-C-F-L-L-N-O-W.

Captain Rosalyn Sumner couldn't make any sense of it but was sure that Frank did.

Chapter 20 – Old Man Winter

Location: Old Germantown – 888 Bedford Street – The FalconClaw Mansion – An hour later.

For almost a week, it hadn't rained, and then suddenly, the North Philly landscape was deluged. Frank sat in his car down on Bedford Street, looking up at the sleeping giant on the hill.

FalconClaw had been abandoned since 1998, and the city was still wondering what to do with it. Each time someone had a bid for the land, a demolition date would be set, and when the deal fell through, so would the date of its demise.

Back in the day, local gangs, thugs, and junkies did business there, but the place was so dilapidated now that even the criminals deemed it unsafe to enter. However, that didn't stop the homeless when the temperatures made their way down into the teens during the winter months. It was now mid-April, and it'd been a mild spring to date, but the temperature seemed to be dropping rapidly.

Frank looked up the hill and could almost see his father traversing the expanse between the old wrought iron gates and the once magnificent main entrance of FalconClaw.

Detective Frank Collazo hesitated before exiting the Dodge as the rain began to fall heavier. It wasn't the rain that had him second-guessing climbing the hill, but rather the ghost of a dead father who never came home. A father that stood waiting for his son at the top of that hill. Frank could almost see him waving him up.

"Come on, Son!" Frank heard the echoes of his father's voice as they rolled down off of the hill in an avalanche of pain.

Frank reached over and grabbed the .40 caliber Smith & Wesson from the passenger seat and pulled back the slide just far enough to see a bullet in the chamber. He then hit the mag release button, and the clip dropped out into his left hand. Frank then added an extra bullet in the mag vacated by the one in the chamber. He then reinserted the clip into the mag well and holstered his sidearm.

Cocking his neck to the left and right, Frank donned his Philly P.D. ball cap and jacket and stepped out of the vehicle. Though it was only 5:30 in the afternoon, the sun was setting behind the gray skies over North Philly just as it was on Frank's life. He looked forward to seeing his father again, but not until he'd seen the Schuylkiller first.

Frank jogged across a street that was both cold and barren. It was rush hour, but strangely no cars could be seen or heard. Now standing at the rusted, black iron fence, Frank imagined that his father had stood in the same spot before pushing through the heavy gate.

Inspecting the gates and their massive pillars, Frank could see the cement domes that once crowned them were gone. Vandalism, the elements, and a lack of nostalgia for a simpler time had eroded away the history of the place and the memory of its occupants.

He lowered his shoulder and leaned into the gate. A metal, 'No Trespassing' sign fell to the ground face-first when he did. Frank half-smiled and said aloud, "I guess it's okay then."

Now on the other side of the gate, Frank could hear his calling from the top of the hill. As it tumbled down upon him, he embraced it. Closing his eyes and breathing in the oxygen-rich air helped release Frank's anxiety and took him to another place and another time.

Looking to his immediate left, he could hear and see Penny Bryce saying to Frank Bruno, who was standing near the Tudor-style outbuilding, "I see you found the gatehouse!" Looking over at the long-abandoned outpost at the bottom of the driveway, he could see a smiling Bruno reply, "It's kind of quaint." And then, without warning, a gust of wind blew away the ghosts of 1974.

Frank Collazo climbed the hill in the same footsteps as his predecessors. Now at the top, he stared at the massive front doors, one pushed in slightly, both crowned with a broken out stain-glass window of the archway that hung overhead.

Now at the top of the steps, the smell of urine crept from the mansion, invading both Frank's nostrils, and porous psyche.

The little boy stood there, a baseball glove in one hand and a ball in the other, and wondered what his dad would say when he saw him. He wondered if it was all right to go in. Looking back down the hill, he looked for every reason to turn around and go home. Suddenly, a massive gust of frigid wind blew up the hill, the rain swirling in its wake. The gust seemed to push Frank forward toward the opening. It was as if a hand were at his back.

In the wind, a fourteen-year-old Frank Collazo heard his father say, "It's okay, Son. Go ahead."

Frank looked back down at his thirty-eight-year-old hand, and instead of a baseball glove was a .40 caliber Smith & Wesson, and he went in. Holding a flashlight in his left hand at eye-level, he readied his trigger finger and stepped forward.

The dark, dank, and moldy hallways seem to narrow with each step. Wincing at the rancid odor, Frank could smell death in the air. The further he walked, the more his claustrophobia scratched away at his sanity. Looking left and then right, he saw broken furniture, the kind no one had claimed when the house was finally vacated for good.

He could see the outline on the walls where massive portraits and murals once hung. Now empty, just like the soul of the long-dead estate.

The floor groaned with each of his heavy steps, and Frank couldn't help but think that the next one might send him to the lower level in a heap. Staying close to the walls, he feared what might be around the next corner.

As Frank reached the end of a long foyer, one built to inspire its guests, he was faced with going right, or left.

As he looked left through a massive arched doorway, his flashlight's beam found its way to a massive pillar, and then another, and another. As he panned upward, his breath was taken away. The massive, arched cathedral ceiling, with decadent crown molding, was painted with brilliant colors that not even time could fade. Down the length of the room, Frank could see three dangling cables where chandeliers once hung.

Continuing forward, gun and flashlight in hand, Frank could feel a presence in the room with him. He began to hear the treble of jazz trumpets, the squeal of a sliding trombone, and the moan of an upright bass. Startled by the sound of muffled voices laughing and socializing all around him, Frank frantically turned and looked in every direction. As quickly as the music came, it disappeared into the now frigid air.

His frozen breath preceding him, he looked straight. Reaching up with his gun hand, he zipped his jacket. Looking forward, he stared into a solarium some twenty feet away and saw two immaculate armchairs, untouched by time and sitting alone. The chairs, pointing away from his position, book-ended a backgammon table that sat benignly, two dice ready to roll. As he got closer, his flashlight revealed an old man wearing a long-sleeve flannel shirt and leaning forward in his chair. The man smiled and said, "I believe you're looking for Mr. St. John."

Frank gasped and dropped his flashlight, causing it to shut off. No longer alone in the darkness, he could hear the sound of dice tumbling and rolling to a stop on a velvet board. "Snake eyes!" lauded the old man, cheering in delight.

Frank, now terrified, frantically searched for the flashlight, dragging an empty hand along the floor in every direction.

Finding his flashlight and flicking it on, he fell backward. Looking up at a glass ceiling, he saw Dante's Inferno burning the night sky and heard the sound of Bonnie Ross screaming for help.

Frank shook his head to clear the disturbing sights and sounds that terrorized him. Looking down, his flashlight picked up depressions in the old, faded carpeting where two chairs and a backgammon table once sat. The old man was gone, and with it, Frank's courage.

Frank immediately ran for the arched doorway leading back to the foyer. Once there, he turned right, intending to go back to the main entrance and into the rain-soaked, eight-acre courtyard. But instead, Frank stopped. Something or someone was pulling him down another long hallway. In the distance, he could see a light emanating up from what looked like a long-retired elevator shaft. His fear had subsided just long enough for him to take five steps down the hall. His flashlight flickered, causing him to stop, and then went completely out.

Frank's fear returned as the tired gears of a broken elevator screamed reluctantly back to life and began to raise the elevator from its forgotten depths. Frank turned to run, but the elevator stood in front of him when he did. No matter his direction, the elevator was directly in his path.

Frank heard the crack of a baseball followed by the cheers of a crowd. He then heard a man crying, followed by the words, "I'm coming, Jeanie! Don't leave! Wait for me!" the voice wailed.

And just as suddenly as it started, it all stopped. Frank's flashlight again illuminated the walls and floor, and a welcoming presence appeared at the end of the hallway. His father, Salvatore Collazo, waved him on and then disappeared left into a doorway at the end of the long hallway.

Frank teared up and cried out, "Dad!"

Holstering his gun, he hastily walked toward the doorway. As he got closer, he heard his father say, "Come on, Son! Hurry! He's in here!"

Frank again cried for his father, and as he rounded the bend into and through the doorway, he saw his father standing next to a locked door. Terrified but determined, Frank moved closer to his father. When he did, his father's voice got shallower until he heard his dad's final whisper. "He's down there, Son. He's in The Sleep Room."

Frank reached for the empty void occupied by his father just moments before and then fell to his knees and cried. "Dad!" he screamed. "Dad!"

Frank was suddenly cold, again. Another sobering gust of wintry air awakened him from his nightmare. As he shined his light toward the whistling air, he saw a partially opened door at the end of the hallway, and he could hear the rain falling.

Frank rose to his feet and slowly walked toward his emancipation. As he passed a massive arched doorway to his right, he could hear two men and a woman speaking politely to one another.

Listening closely, Frank heard the voice of a distinguished sounding man say, "I'm not sure if you're aware, but from 1949 to 1965, these facilities were used for psychiatric care for only the most mentally disturbed patients."

The voice suddenly faded into the sound of falling rain, and Frank's attention went back to the slightly ajar door at the end of the hallway.

Now outside, the April rain washed away his insanity and momentarily steadied his nerves. Frank then turned toward the southwest corner of the house, where he saw open exterior basement doors. Looking over the scene, he observed a lock sitting passively on the ground nearby.

Frank's sanity was washed away again when he saw his father standing before the doors looking back at his son. Frank cried out to his father but was too afraid to get closer, in fear he would disappear again.

"I know you're upset, Frankie. But I have to work tonight," said his father.

As his father waved goodbye to his son, he took three steps forward into the basement's entrance.

In a muffled scream, with his teeth clenched, spewing saliva, Frank yelled, "Don't go down there, Dad! Don't go!" he cried louder.

Salvatore Collazo just smiled and waved to his son and slowly disappeared down into the depths of hell. Frank continued to plead with his father, but he was gone. Again.

Chapter 21 – St. John

Parking Lot behind the Mad River Bar & Grill – Front seat of the Dodge Charger – Tuesday, April 18, 2017, 7:14 am.

Frank woke to the sound of a locomotive as it roared across the Schuylkill River. The Mad River bar sat between Main Street and the banks of the Schuylkill, just southeast of the Locke Street Pump Station. It was an interchange where the railroad tracks crossed the river heading south past the Twin Bridges, following Interstate 76 until it crossed back over the Schuylkill into Fairmount Park, just south of Strawberry Mansion.

After the train passed, the steady hum of rush hour traffic on I-76 wouldn't allow him to close his eyes again. Frank got out of the Dodge and walked through the rear entrance of his building and up to his third-floor claustrophobic prison. He hated it there, but for now, it was home. Frank rummaged through week-old leftovers, spoiled milk, and condiments. For breakfast, he'd settle for coffee and a stale bagel.

After his shower, Frank wiped the fog off the bathroom mirror and saw a man he didn't recognize. He was starting to resemble his father, a middle-aged cop who was getting ready to die at the hands of a serial killer. Frank pulled a rusty razor from behind the mirror, looked it over, and threw it away. After getting dressed, he headed up to his old house in Melrose Park. He tried calling Penny again along the way, but like the eight previous attempts, it went straight to voicemail.

Twenty minutes later, Frank took a right off Valley Road on to 12th and then an immediate left into the rear driveway behind his old house. Frank sat in the car for a moment surveying the south side of the residence and its detached garage, looking for any sign that the Schuylkiller might have been there. He saw none.

After exiting the vehicle, he walked around the perimeter of the stack-stoned home, inspecting basement and first-floor windows for evidence of tampering.

After entering the side door into the mudroom, Frank turned off the ADT Alarm, took off his muddy shoes, and hung his coat. Walking into the kitchen, the cold house felt abandoned to him. Conner's toys were strewn about, and it had the appearance that Joanne and his son fled in a hurry, which they had.

After only fifteen minutes in the house, the back door chimed, and Frank reached for his sidearm. A man's voice rang out from the mudroom. It was Joanne's father, Vance Conroy.

"Frank!" the voice rang out, almost echoing through the empty halls.

"Up here!" yelled Frank back to his father-in-law.

Frank made his way down the steps and saw the old man standing in the kitchen with a shotgun.

"Damn," Frank's eyes got big. "You brought the double-barreled cavalry with you, I see."

"You're goddamn right I did. Thanks to you, my daughter and grandson are hidden away up in Tyler State Park."

"Thanks to me?!" Frank was incensed. "You mean thanks to a homicidal maniac wreaking havoc on all of North Philly!" he yelled. "I'm the one out there protecting people, putting my life on the line!"

"Yeah, and because of your profession now, my daughter and grandson's lives are in danger." The seventy-year-old Vance Conroy had veins erupting from his forehead.

"Well, it looks like we have something in common then. Protect our family!" said Frank.

The statement struck a chord with Conroy, and he pulled a chair from the kitchen table and sat down, resting his shotgun on its buttstock and up against the table.

"So, whatta we do now?" said Conroy. "We can't keep them at the cabin forever. Conner's got school."

"Conner's on Easter Break. It's just for this week," said Frank. "I'll be staying here, and when I'm not, you should be here with the street howitzer." Frank lifted his chin and motioned to the shotgun.

"That's good and fine, but to what end?" asked Conroy. "What good is a week going to do?"

"I've got a lead on the whereabouts of the guy and hope to end this whole ordeal soon." Frank sat down at the table across from the old man.

"I'm sorry to hear what happened to your partner's mother. Did you know the woman?"

"I'd only met her twice," said Frank. "Her name is, (was), Bonnie, and she was such a sweet woman and didn't deserve what she got."

"Nobody deserves to go out like that." Conroy shook his head.

Frank was frustrated. "I always told Penny that she and her mom needed to get out of that place. A one-bedroom apartment above an old linen store....," he paused, "it was a powder keg, Vance. One match and POOF!" Frank threw open his hands in the air.

"Frank, if he were gonna get to Penny's mom, it wouldn't have mattered where she lived," reasoned Conroy, leaning forward and interlocking his fingers on the table.

Conroy then furrowed his brow, and before he could speak, Frank said, "I know what you're thinking, and I don't know if he knows where this place is."

"He found Penny's mom," said Conroy. "That means he can find Joanne and Conner."

"He found Penny, Vance," said Frank. "Penny lived there, too. We don't know if Bonnie was his intended target, or not."

"Lucky for her, she wasn't home when it happened, then." Conroy pursed his lips and pondered.

Frank knew very well that Bonnie Ross was the intended target because the Schuylkiller knew that he and Penny were at the Ritz.

"Could he have followed you here today?"

Frank shook his head. "I took the long way here and didn't see anyone tailing me."

"Did you check your car for a tracking device?" asked Conroy.

"The car is a former State Patrol Special Ops vehicle. It has software installed that makes it impossible to track," explained Frank. "It would scramble any signal emanating from the vehicle."

Vance Conroy looked impressed.

"Shit! Joanne's car?!" Frank looked terrified.

"It's in the garage." Conroy motioned over his left shoulder. "I drove them up there after you called yesterday. We fled in a hurry. That's why I'm here."

Frank sighed in relief.

"I also let the Park Police know to check in on them regularly."

"Good thinking, Vance."

"Frank, so what's the plan?" asked Conroy again. "As I said, Conner's got school, and Joanne's got a life."

"Yes, she does." Frank looked resigned. "So, you met Polly, then?"

"Yep," Conroy raised his brows and nodded his head. He still wasn't sure how he felt about his daughter's new relationship or how it might impact Conner. "She seems really nice. Smart, too. She brought her son along. The boys seemed to get along nicely."

Suddenly there was a commotion outside, and the two instinctively reached for their guns. Looking out the kitchen window, Frank saw the neighbor pulling his boat out of an oversized shed.

Frank looked relieved and re-holstered his weapon.

"So, again, Frank, what's the plan?"

Frank sat back down and said, "I reached out to a retired FBI profiler named Douglas Cantrell. I'm waiting for a callback."

"That name sounds familiar," said Conroy.

Frank nodded emphatically. "It should! He made quite a name for himself after he and another guy started up the Behavioral Science Unit for the FBI back in the early seventies. He helped Frank Bruno solve the Gary Michael Heidnik case back in the late eighties."

"Is that the guy who kidnapped and killed all those women in his basement?" asked Conroy.

"Yeah, and after he killed them, he fed their remains to his other prisoners in the basement."

"God, I remember that case. Joanne was just a little girl back then." Conroy shook his head in disgust.

"There's a show coming out on Netflix later this year called *Mindhunter.* It's about how he and this other guy founded the Behavioral Sciences Unit in Quantico back in 1972."

"Anyway, I'm gonna ask him to lend an ear to the investigation and see what he has to say," said Frank. "I'm hoping he can help me piece it all together."

"You said earlier that you had a lead on the killer's whereabouts. What's all that about?"

"FalconClaw." Frank's memory went back to his visit there the night before, and his face went pale.

"You okay, Frank? You look like you're going to be sick." Conroy looked concerned, getting up and walking to the refrigerator to get his son-in-law a bottle of water.

Frank said, "Yeah, I was there last night but didn't see much going on. It's in pretty bad shape."

"When's that thing coming down, anyway? It's an ugly eyesore on the side of that hill."

"Not sure," replied Frank. "They keep talking about it, but it's still there."

"What was it like in there?" Conroy was curious. "That place has quite a history."

Frank's mind again went back to the night before, and he'd recalled hearing the voices of the people that'd occupied the once-fabled halls and again looked terrified.

"Here, drink this." Conroy handed Frank the bottle of water.

"Thanks, Vance." Frank took the water and twisted off the cap. "You should get out of here and go see Joanne and Conner."

"That's why I'm here. I need to get a few things as we left here in quite a hurry yesterday."

"Vance, listen. The only way the Schuylkiller finds that cabin is if he follows you there. Take the Dodge and take the long way there, if you know what I mean?" Frank's brow rose. "Keep your eyes in the rearview mirror, and don't go there if you suspect you're being followed. Call me if you do," suggested Frank. "Just come back later and drop off the car. I'll be here for the rest of the day. There's no hurry to get back."

"Okay, Frank. If you say so." Conroy seemed to agree.

"Listen, Frank." Conroy looked concerned. "About what happened back in January. You know, with the Clark family. That must've been rough. Joanne never said too much about it to me, and the newspapers only give you so much information," he paused. "I just wanted to say that I'm sorry you had to experience something like that."

"Thanks, Vance. I'll be okay. I didn't talk much to Joanne about it. She gets freaked out about that stuff. You know, after the bullet through my back window last year."

"Well, you can't really blame her, can you?" Vance Conroy stood before Frank, placed his right hand on Frank's left shoulder, and squeezed. "I might not like your politics or your career choice, but you're Conner's father, and that makes you family. Be safe out there, Frank."

"Will do, Vance." Frank nodded his head in appreciation.

As Conroy exited the kitchen, he turned and said, "The offer is still on the table. New house nearby if you agree to the terms," said Conroy. "Give it some more thought, would ya?"

"Yeah, Sure, Vance. I'll let you know," Frank said half-heartedly. What he really wanted to say to his father-in-law was 'Fuck you!'. He had no intentions of living under his father-in-law's thumb as he had his entire marriage to Joanne.

After Conroy gathered some items for Conner and Joanne, he left.

Frank then called fellow detective, Robert Brooks, who'd been texting him while he was talking to his father-in-law. Brooks had informed him in the text that he and John Cole were handed the Mereby case and wanted to debrief on what more Frank could offer.

"Brooksie! Hey, it's Frank. Sorry I missed your call."

"Frank, how ya doing? Man, sorry to hear about what went down on Easter. The Captain told me you'd be in the field and off the grid for a while. I wanted to make sure that we got everything we need to pick up the Mereby/Jacks case."

"Well, your case is gonna get bigger after the arson investigation. All of this is going to be tied back to the Schuylkiller, no doubt."

"Yeah," Brooksie said. "Cap told us about the letter found on your car. That's some sinister shit right there. I look forward to collaring this guy!"

Frank thought to himself that if he had his way, the Schuylkiller would never see the inside of a squad car, let alone a jail cell. Frank had a bullet with the killer's name on it, and he intended to use it.

"Brooks, listen. You need to visit the Creative Minds Daycare on the corner of Ridge and South Ferry Road under the Twins." Frank's tone told Robert Brooks he was on to something.

"Whatta we looking for over there, Frank?" asked Brooks.

"They had a guy working there recently, a big guy," said Frank. "As recently as January. He may or may not still be there."

"Okay?"

"The guy's big. I think his name is St. John," explained Frank.

"What's his story?" asked Brooks.

"I got an anonymous tip. I can't explain right now. But listen, Brooksie, if they give you a different name than St. John, you run a background check on the guy. He may be using an alias."

"So, St. John?" Brooks paused, "I got it. So, what do you want us to do with the info we gather?"

"Get an address for the guy. My guess is that he lives within five miles of East Falls. Get employment dates and work schedules if they'll hand them over to you. If they don't comply, threaten a warrant for information on him and all of their other employees," said Frank. "But don't tell them it's regarding the Schuylkiller case. If you do, they might clam up and not want to get involved."

"So, what's the deal with this guy, anyway?"

"I only met him once, but the manager of The Trolley Car Café thinks he's suspicious, and I agree. He put off a bad vibe when I first encountered him, and it's my understanding that he worked at night, unsupervised, or at least had access to the place during off-hours. That would have allowed him to commit the crimes. He also fits the description of the chauffeur who picked up Mereby from Strawberry Mansion and the person pushing the car into the Schuylkill. He may have also been an acquaintance of Willard Clark. I think it's all connected."

Brooks wrote down everything Frank told him and said, "Okay, I think I got it, Frank. But to be clear, you think this guy may be dangerous."

Frank went silent for a moment. "I think this guy's the Schuylkiller. If his name comes back St. John, proceed with caution," he said.

"If we interview him do you want to be there?" asked Brooks.

"Yes, but don't interview him in his house if you determine where he lives. It might be too dangerous. Ask him to come into Headquarters instead.

"All right, Frank," said Brooks. "I'll reach out when we learn more."

"Hey, Brooksie, one more thing," said Frank. "In the background check, find out if he has any connection to Temple University, too."

"Will do, Frank."

"Okay, Brother. Stay alert and keep me posted."

After Frank hung up the phone, he spent twenty minutes online Googling FalconClaw. He was freaked out by his experience the night before and needed to learn more. He needed to make sense of the random hallucinations he'd had while there. What was simply his imagination, and what was real? Was he going mad, or was something else at play?

Just as he'd ended his search, his cell phone rang. It was Conner.

"Hey, Con Man! You having fun at the Lake House?"

"Yeah, Dad. Grandpa just got here. Thanks for the fifty-bucks!" Conner yelled through the phone.

"Fifty bucks?" Frank was puzzled. He was also pissed that Vance Conroy hadn't taken the long way to the cabin.

"Yeah, Grandpa gave me the fifty bucks you told him to give to me. Thanks a lot, Pop!"

Frank rolled his eyes and shook his head. Grandpa Conroy was always throwing money at Conner, but this time he did it in Frank's name. Frank thought that perhaps he and Joanne's father made a little breakthrough in their years-long head-to-head battle.

"So, what do you guys have planned for tomorrow?"

"There's not much to do, Dad. I can't spend my money out here." Conner sounded bummed.

"Well, Grandpa's got my car. Tell him I said you can sit behind the wheel and pretend you're a copper."

Suddenly Joanne's voice came through the earpiece and said, "Frank, what's going on? Are we in danger?"

Frank was blunt. "Yes, you are. Your father's going to stay with you when I can't be there. That's why you're at the cabin, Joanne."

"I know. He just told me." Joanne paused and said, "I told you something like this could happen!"

Frank got upset with his ex-wife. "Joanne, Penny's mom is dead, and there is a serial killer on the loose, and no one knows what's going to happen next! No one is safe," said Frank. "There will be plenty of time later to assign blame. For right now, you and Conner need to lay low."

"What about you, Frank? Are you laying low, too?" Joanne was sarcastic.

"They've handed the case over to Brooks and Cole, but the killer doesn't know that!" said Frank. "I'm not waiting for him to strike first."

Frank hadn't shared everything with Joanne about the letter he'd received and how it pertained to FalconClaw.

"Wrap your head around being at the cabin at least until the Easter break is over. Let's talk every couple of hours," said Frank. "Joanne, listen. Call me if you feel unsafe, and make sure your father stays with you. I'll be staying here at the house while you're gone."

"Frank, I'm really scared. Do you think this guy would actually come to our house?" Joanne sounded frantic.

"Joanne, I didn't have your father rush you out of the house yesterday for nothing. I'm working with the Cheltenham Township Police Chief now to see if we can have regular patrols up and down Valley Road, but I need more time."

"Okay, I get it," said Joanne. "I'll just have Polly bring her son out here so that Conner doesn't get bored."

"Joanne, no! Please. No visitors to the cabin, just your parents, that's all. It's just until Monday for now."

"Fine. Okay, Frank. I trust you."

At that moment, Frank's Caller I.D. flashed an incoming call from an Unknown Number. He told Joanne he had to take the call.

"I'll check in later. I've got to take this call. Tell Conner I love him. Bye."

Frank clicked over and heard nothing. He'd hoped it was Douglas Cantrell. "Hello? Hello?" Frank said into the phone. He was just about to hang up when he'd heard a voice come over the line.

"Hello, Frank," said the caller. "Nice to speak to you again." The man's voice was deep and throaty.

"Come again?" Frank was puzzled. "Who is this?" His eyes narrowed as he asked the questions.

"It must be nice being home for a change. This little apartment on Main must be driving you crazy. It's so tiny in here. Good thing you're not claustrophobic."

Frank swallowed hard. "Who is this?" he asked again. "Where are you?"

"So, you have a nice view of the river out your back window, I see?" said the caller. "The train's a little annoying, I bet. But the view of the river is wonderful. Oh, how I love the water."

Frank could hear a train in the distance.

"I bet the crowd downstairs at Mad River must be maddening." The man chuckled. "Please forgive the pun."

"Is this St. John?"

The caller paused for a moment.

"Cat got your tongue?" asked Frank.

"Well, I must say," said the caller. "I don't know anyone named St. John, but I'm sure he's a fine man. I know you, though. I know where you live, where your wife lives, where your son goes to school. All of it," said the dark voice.

The voice went quiet. Frank heard someone rummaging around.

"Oh my, you really must do some grocery shopping. The fridge is completely bare."

"Well, you can have it," said Frank. "I don't spend much time there these days."

"I know," said the Schuylkiller. "Sleeping in your car is bad for your back. I'm so tempted to wake you up every time I see your seat reclined all the way back."

Frank was terrified. "Why are you calling me?"

"Ahhh," the caller exhaled. "I wanted to tell you that you and your little slut were getting way too close and that you needed to back off."

"Couldn't you have told us that before you killed her mother and the others that were in that building?" asked Frank, as his anger stirred.

"I could've, but what's the fun in that?" the caller sounded nonchalant. "Everyone enjoys a good bonfire."

"I'm off the case," said Frank. "In fact, I've been suspended indefinitely."

"Oh, really?" The caller was skeptical. "I take you for a man that doesn't take time off. A diligent worker, to be sure. I bet you don't stop until you get your man. Does that sound about right, Frankie Boy?"

Frank was convinced the man would attempt to kill him and his family, so he had a message for the killer.

"Listen here, you fucking psycho! I'm going to kill you. I don't care if I die in the process. But I will kill you. So watch your back. I've got your name, and soon I'll have an address. Circle this day on the calendar, you cock-sucker. I'm coming for you. Let's see who gets to who first."

"I was there, you know?" said the caller.

"Where?" asked Frank.

"At the bonfire," said the Schuylkiller. "I saw you. You were on your hands and knees, crying like a baby. I saw your girlfriend, too. Sobbing like a little bitch."

Frank was seething.

"I have her cellphone, you know. I took it off the front seat of your race car when you were puking your guts out all over Germantown Ave."

Frank screamed. "I'll kill you motherfucker!"

"Yeah, we'll see about that." The voice was calm. "Hopefully, you'll catch me before I'm done with my list. I have taken and killed three of the five on my list but still have two more who are proving quite elusive. They always seem to be traveling. Perhaps they're on to me."

"If I finish off my list before I kill you, I just may spare you and your family. But," said the madman, "if you continue to be a nuisance to me, then you and your family will all die. Your wife and child first, of course."

"You said five? Is that right?" asked Frank. "At last count, I have ten," said Frank.

"James Loftin, Belinda Mereby, Warren Jacks, Daniel Oliver, and Keith Carpenter. And the five that died on Easter." Frank listed out the victims as he knew them.

"So, it was five at *Fabrics* the other night?" The Schuylkiller seemed pleasantly surprised. "I thought maybe three or four at the most."

"Why kill the others if you only have five on your list?"

"Collateral damage," said the killer. "All of you need to get out of my way and let me finish what I started."

"Why are you doing this? Why the list?"

The madman chuckled. "I promise to tell you just before I kill you, Detective Frank Collazo."

"Well, I'll tell you about my list then," said Frank. "It only has one name on it, and that name is St. John. Soon I'll have your full name and address, and then you'll be on the run for the rest of your very short life."

"Oh, Detective. You do so humor me."

In Frank's mind, the caller seemed to be enjoying the conversation.

"I might just have to kill your son even after I complete my list. You know," he paused, "just for shits and giggles," the lunatic added.

"Or," said the Schuylkiller, "should I kill you and let him live? Have him grow up without a father just like you?" He paused. "It seems we have that in common, no father in our lives. I can relate. I bet it drives you every day the way it drives me. Oh, what we won't do to get back at those who stole away our childhood. An endless search for a closure that we'll never find."

"To be clear," said Frank. "I will have closure when you're laying at my feet in a fetal position, a bullet in your head and piss soaking your pants." Frank was now calm. "I will describe to the press how you went out like a coward. Didn't even put up a fight." Frank ended with a final comment. "I will be seeing you soon, motherfucker, and I will find you before you find me!"

Frank hung up on the Schuylkiller before he could respond. Seconds later, a call from an Unknown Caller lit up Frank's phone again. He looked at the screen and swiped left, dismissing the call. He would never take another call from the monster. He would have the last word.

He was in St. John's crosshairs, and St. John was in his.

Frank immediately called his Captain to notify her that the Schuylkiller had Penny's phone and all of her contacts.

"Captain, he knows where Penny and Joanne live. He's at my apartment in Manayunk right now! Get a couple of units over there fast! Main and Shurs Lane," said Frank. "Unit 3, above the Mad River Bar!"

Frank's heart was exploding out of his chest. "Make sure you send back-up. Get Brooks and Cole there, too. And have CSU sweep the place for prints and DNA."

"Got it, Frank!" said Sumner. "Where are you now?"

"I'm at Joanne's. I'll be laying low here for a while," said Frank. "Get a car over to Penny's old place. She's back with her ex-husband. Check her file for the address."

"All right, Frank."

"Call my cell if you need me. Let me know what you find at my place," said Frank. "I'm waiting on a call from a former FBI profiler. I'll let you know what comes out of it."

"Oh? Who is it?" asked a curious Sumner.

"It's Douglas Cantrell. He's retired but may be able to help out."

"Cantrell?" Sumner was impressed. "Isn't that the guy who helped Frank Bruno catch Gary Michael Heidnik back in 86?"

"Yeah, and a lot of other bad guys, too," said Frank. "Just get a car over to Penny's, would you? She's in the Schuylkiller's sights."

"Will do," said Sumner. "Oh, and Frank...."

"Yeah, Cap?"

"Watch your six, Frank!"

"Got it!"

Minutes later, Frank was still trying to calm down. His confident tone while talking with the Schuylkiller was an act. He was scared. Scared for Penny, Joanne, and Conner. Frank, however, was not scared for himself.

Suddenly the phone rang out and startled Frank. He went to swipe left but saw the call was coming from New Hampshire. He got excited as he knew that Douglas Cantrell lived there.

Chapter 22 – Cantrell

Frank took a deep breath in an effort to collect himself before answering the phone. "Hello?"

"Yes, is this Detective Frank Collazo?" asked the caller.

"Yes, it is. Who's calling?"

"Frank, this is Douglas Cantrell. You had emailed me yesterday regarding a case that you're working on. I was wondering how I might be of assistance?"

"Wow!" Frank was surprised. "Thanks for getting back to me so quickly!" He felt like he was no longer alone in his quest to understand the Schuylkiller.

"As you might've heard, we've got a madman on the loose here in Philadelphia."

"Another one?" Cantrell sounded surprised.

"No, the same one from January," said Frank. "The Schuylkiller."

Cantrell was confused. "But I was under the impression he was dead. The Clark guy, right?"

"Did you hear about the Easter fire here in North Philly that killed five people?" asked Frank.

"Yes, of course, it's been all over the news."

"Well, give it another day or two, and you're gonna hear that Willard Clark was not the Schuylkiller."

"Wait a second, Frank," said Cantrell. "Your guy's still on the loose? How did you guys get that one wrong?" Cantrell was perplexed.

"We thought we had our guy, and the killing and disappearances stopped after the elder Clark killed his son," explained Frank. "It was the press that jumped the gun on that and started the rumors. We never actually closed the case," revealed Frank.

"But your Mayor and Police Chief went on the news and said, 'Case Closed.' What was all that about?"

"Ill-advised, that's what." Frank exhaled in frustration. "The one person closest to the case never believed that Willard Clark was the guy. That person was me," revealed Frank.

"The higher-ups, the Mayor, and Police Commissioner desperately wanted the reign of terror to be over. I never signed off on Willard Clark being the guy," explained Frank. "I did initially. That's why we went down that rabbit hole, because of me. I'm the reason the Clark family is dead," he added.

"Yeah, that was rough. I'm so sorry, Frank," said Cantrell. "I'm also sorry about what happened with the suicide that you had to witness. That must have been hard. I, too, witnessed a suicide early on in my career. It was horrible." Douglas Cantrell paused and said, "How are you handling the guilt associated with such an event?"

"Well, I had two months to think about it after I got suspended."

"Oh, so it wasn't a self-imposed hiatus, then?"

"Oh God, no." Frank expelled his frustration. "I almost lost my job after an internal investigation ruled that I was negligent for removing the handcuffs off of a man that was emotionally distraught and likely suicidal."

"So they suspended you, then?"

"Yeah, sixty days," said Frank. "It almost killed me being away that long. Especially when I knew in my heart that our guy was still out there."

"So, you're sure he's still on the loose?"

"Yes. And he's coming for me and my partner and our families," Frank also revealed. "I was due to return to work yesterday, and he struck on Easter. The fire was arson. The investigation hasn't wrapped up yet, but you can bet it'll come back arson. The Schuylkiller left his calling card that night. We're sure that it was him."

"The timing of your return likely isn't a coincidence, Frank," reasoned Cantrell. "To be clear, you were the lead detective on the case, is that correct?"

"Yes."

"And all the killing ceased while you were off the case, correct?"

"Yes."

As Frank listened to Cantrell, his mind began to wander. *Could there be a connection between the killing stopping and his absence?* Frank wondered.

"Frank, your face was on the news a lot. The case was mentioned on CNN almost every night back in January. I saw you in several clips on Anderson Cooper's 360° during that month and a few times since. Your killer may have associated you with the investigation."

"I was following the case closely from my home here in Portsmouth," said Cantrell. "I even thought to reach out to your guys. I'm going a little stir crazy in retirement. I must tell you that it's much more exciting helping the good guys chase down the bad guys."

"Well, this isn't very exciting, Doug. My partner's mother was killed in that fire." Frank sounded remorseful. "Her name was Bonnie Ross, and she was an amazing woman."

Frank sighed before continuing. "Mr. Cantrell...."

"Please, call me Doug," offered Cantrell.

"Okay, Doug." Frank was a little nervous. "Just ten minutes ago, I was on the phone with the Schuylkiller," he paused.

"Holy shit!" said Cantrell, immediately perking up with the disclosure. "He has your number?"

"Yes." Frank collected his thoughts. "He's in possession of my partner's cellphone, and I'm sure he's making the rounds right now."

"Jesus Christ! Is your partner in danger?" Cantrell was afraid for all involved.

"Well, her mother was intentionally murdered, so, yes. She is in danger. Her name is Penny Bristow, and they're sending a unit over to her house now."

"Frank, listen. I want to assist in any way that I can." Cantrell was genuine. "What more can you tell me about the case? And more importantly, what more can you tell me about your call with him?"

Frank exhaled fully. "I'm not sure where to start...."

"Start at the beginning," suggested Cantrell. "Why did he call? Was he calm? Was he threatening?"

"Well, first, he acted as if he knew me," said Frank.

"How so?"

"He told me it was, 'Nice to speak to you again.' He said it like we'd met before. Like he knew me."

"Okay, and?"

"He was calling from my apartment...."

"Your apartment?" Cantrell was disturbed by the fact.

"Yeah, and here's the thing," said Frank. "My apartment is small, and he mentioned being claustrophobic."

"Was he referring to him, or you?" asked Cantrell.

"Well, I am a little claustrophobic, and I got the feeling he knew that about me."

"Frank, who all knows that you're claustrophobic? It's important."

"My partner, Penny, and my soon-to-be ex-wife. That's it. My mom knew, but she died last year."

"You sure he was actually in your apartment? If he could see it from the street, he could likely ascertain its size. Narcissistic sociopaths are cunning and like to be in control. They'll convince you that they know things about you that they don't. All in an effort to control you. They'll steer the conversation and try to manipulate you," explained Cantrell.

"No, I could hear the train in the background as it passed behind my apartment. He also described the contents of my refrigerator," said Frank. "I'm sure he was there."

"Wow, that takes gumption," thought Cantrell aloud. "It's not surprising, though. Sociopaths feel like they have nothing to lose. They live in a world of invincibility, and that's what makes them so dangerous. They'll do what a sane person will not. They'll take more chances and risks...."

"Like kidnapping someone in broad daylight just steps from their home?" Frank referenced the Carpenter abduction.

"Yes. Most of them whom I've met secretly wanted to get caught. They want to share their story with everyone, but they can't until they've been apprehended," Cantrell explained.

"Well, that makes sense," said Frank.

"Why is that?"

"Because he was too chatty," revealed Frank. "It was like he didn't want to get off of the phone with me."

"They do love to talk," said Cantrell.

"I asked him why he was calling me, and he told me that me and my partner were getting 'too close.' His words, not mine."

"So, two things I see here, Frank. One. He's worried that you'll stop him from finishing what he's set out to do. He might not be after you or your partner. He's just worried that you'll stop him before he can fulfill his fantasy," surmised Cantrell.

"What's the other?"

"Well, this may disturb you, Frank...."

"Tell me," said Frank. "I'm a big boy. I can handle it."

"Frank, he may have become fascinated with you."

Frank was confused. "Come again?"

"You may have become his counterpart," explained Cantrell. "His adversary. His nemesis. His muse."

"Muse?" Frank sounded puzzled as a chill ran up his spine.

"In many cases, for a bad guy to legitimize his own status, he needs a good guy out there pushing him. The whole 'good versus evil,' cliché." Cantrell explained further, "You may have given him a new sense of purpose, which is terribly frightening."

"Why's that?" Frank was concerned.

"Because he may stretch his killing out far beyond his narrative or purpose."

Frank was mortified. "That's terrifying, Doug!"

"Frank, did he tell you that he had a goal or plan that needed to be executed or finished?"

"Yes! That's what's so terrifying. He said he had a list of five people he wanted dead and that there were two left!" Frank was shocked that Doug Cantrell knew that.

"It's very common in serial killers that they start killing for a reason and will continue to kill until they've satisfied their reason for killing." Cantrell educated Frank.

"An example would be that a person's mother was a prostitute, and he hated his mother for whatever reason. He would kill a prostitute because she reminded him of her. The only problem with a prostitute being a target is that the killer would never run out of targets and ultimately, never satisfy their initial need or fantasy."

"How many victims do you associate with the killer so far?

"Ten," replied Frank.

"Okay, in the case of your guy then, he said five were on his list, is that right?" Cantrell asked for clarification.

"Yeah, five, and he said he's killed three of them so far."

"If your killer becomes fixated on the dynamic that he believes the two of you share, then he may continue killing even after he's achieved his initial goal of five," reasoned Cantrell.

"Do the victims have anything in common that you know of thus far?" added Cantrell.

"We know that all three of the targeted victims are connected with law firms back in the seventies and eighties. All of their fathers are still alive, and they worked or were partners in various law firms," said Frank. "We believe that of the ten, either dead or missing, that seven of them are collateral damage, as the Schuylkiller put it."

"Did he actually say the word 'Collateral?' His words?" Cantrell asked for clarification.

"Basically, yes."

"Ten?!" Cantrell was astonished. "And only three were targeted?"

"There you go," said Cantrell. "He may have killed more just to get your attention or to get you back into the game."

Frank was again terrified by the thought. He was already guilt-ridden about Bonnie's death, and now he had reason to believe that she was killed because of him directly.

"Our evidence, so far, indicates that only three were targeted, and that's backed up by what the killer told me moments ago," said Frank. "Any chance that he's boasting?"

"I doubt it." Cantrell relied on forty years of experience personally dealing with more than one hundred serial killers. "If he said he had five targets and the rest were 'collateral damage,' then he's either telling the truth, or he killed to raise your interest in him."

"What else, Frank?" Cantrell was attempting to get into the mind of the Schuylkiller. "What else did he say?"

"He did say that the remaining two people on his list were proving to be elusive. He said, and I quote, 'they always seem to be traveling.' It made me sick just to hear the sound of his voice."

"Okay, so here's what may be happening, Frank...." Cantrell jotted some notes. "What makes a serial killer a serial, as opposed to a spree killer, is that they'll kill and then take a period of time to cool off."

"Cool off?" asked Frank.

"Yes, cool off," said Cantrell. "They will take time to reflect on what they've done. Sometimes they bask in their own repugnant glory while other times they are sickened by what they've done," he explained. "If they celebrate or can internally justify what they've done, they will start killing again at some point after they've come down from their euphoric high. Once the high fades away, they need it back. Much like a drug addict."

"We need him to call you back and tell us more."

"I'm sorry, Doug. I'm not taking that call if it comes in." Frank was adamant.

"Why, Frank? You need this guy to keep talking." Cantrell understood that no one would want to talk to a serial killer about their victims but needed to if they wanted to uncover means, motive, method of killing, and the victim selection process.

"Frank, if you're going to catch this guy, you'll need to get into his head. The reason the Behavioral Science Unit was so successful is that we studied these killers by interviewing them for hundreds of hours," explained Cantrell. "You can't get answers if you don't ask the questions."

"Doug, with all due respect, I just watched my partner witness her mother being burned alive, along with four other victims. I'm in no mood to talk to the lunatic that did that." Frank was candid.

"Frank, I understand, but if he calls again, I strongly encourage you to take the call. People like your killer want to talk, and when they do, they'll reveal information that you don't currently have. Just keep him talking."

Frank hesitated before saying, "He may not call back after what I said to him."

"I hope you didn't threaten him or call him crazy." Cantrell was concerned that Frank poured fuel onto an already burning fire.

"Sorry to say, but I went off on the guy."

Cantrell winced. "Well, you can't change history, but you can make sure not to do that again if he calls you back."

Frank went silent for a moment, lost in thought.

"Frank, what else can you tell me about the call?"

"He's smart," he said. "Like college-educated smart. I have a hunch that he's somehow connected to Temple University."

"What makes you think that?" asked Cantrell.

Frank said, "Three of our victims are associated with the university. All three graduated there, and two were professors at one time."

"Hmm. Interesting. You may want to follow that path until you rule out any connections. Like the timing of your return and the Easter killings, which can't be a coincidence," suggested Cantrell.

"Revenge is almost always the reason people murder, even if the victim is someone they've never met before. However, I believe that the killer either knew or knew of his victims in this case. I think they're all connected, Frank."

"This may be a situation where your suspect was passed over for a promotion, or was dismissed due to the actions of one or more of the victims," added Cantrell. "The timeframes that your victims either studied or worked there may be relevant."

"That's what I think, too. We also have a peripheral connection of the killer to Willard Clark."

"How so?"

"Clark went to Temple back in the nineties. For all we know, they knew each other while there. Nearly all of our non-collateral victims were in their mid to late forties. That put them at Temple in the mid-nineteen-nineties. That includes Clark, who wasn't a victim of the Schuylkiller but may have been associated with him."

"Where's the connection with Willard?" Cantrell thought the answer would help give Frank something to go on.

"Willard worked at a restaurant next to a daycare where I suspect our killer worked," said Frank.

"You think the Schuylkiller worked at a daycare?" Cantrell found that interesting.

"Yes, I ran into him while visiting the place where Willard worked."

"What makes you think the guy was the Schuylkiller?"

"I can't put my finger on it. It's just a hunch, that's all," said Frank.

"Okay," said Cantrell. "When you talk to the daycare, find out why they hired him," he suggested. "See if he has a degree in child psychology, childcare, early childhood education? You name it."

Cantrell continued his initial profile of the Schuylkiller. "Perhaps this guy's father was into psychology or psychiatry, and his mother was a schoolteacher. That may sound sexist, but based on his age, it would have been common for his mother to either be a nurse, an educator or schoolteacher, secretary, or a homemaker."

"How in the world did you come to that conclusion?" Frank wanted to learn.

"Frank, just two generations ago, women had very few choices. With few exceptions, young women were steered to find a suitable husband and have children, or were steered to education or nursing," explained Cantrell.

"That's crazy how far we've come, huh?" asked Frank.

"Still got a long way to go, I'm afraid."

Frank thought about Cantrell's early profile when Cantrell spoke back up.

"Frank, something's missing here." Cantrell thought there was more that Frank hadn't divulged. "Did he say anything else? Anything that the two of you might have in common?"

Frank racked his brain. "Wait a second. He said his father was dead and that we had that in common!" he remembered.

"So, your father's dead, then?" asked Cantrell.

"Yes. He was killed by a notorious serial killer here in Philadelphia back in 1992," revealed Frank.

"Oh, my God, Frank. Your father was Salvatore Collazo?" Cantrell was stunned.

"Yes," replied Frank. "He was killed by...."

Cantrell finished his sentence. "Vincent Charmaine Walker."

"Yes." Frank paused. "You do know your stuff, Doug."

"Yeah. I've been at this a long time. I actually interviewed Walker when he was in prison. He wasn't very forthcoming, though. I did, however, study your father's case. I'm so sorry, Frank."

Both men went silent for a moment before Cantrell spoke back up. "Frank, this changes everything."

"How so?"

"You may be one of the people on his list."

Frank swallowed hard. "How do you figure?"

"He may have a fantasy about killing you the way your father was killed," suggested Cantrell. "Was there anything else he said that might connect either you and him or the circumstances of your father's death? Serial killers like to mimic other serial killers."

Frank froze. Saying nothing, he remembered what he saw in the steamed-up mirror after his shower that morning. He saw a man that resembled his father. A middle-aged cop about to be murdered by a serial killer.

After several more moments of silence, Cantrell spoke. "Frank, are you still there? Frank?"

"Yeah, I'm still here." Frank almost stuttered. "It's just that...." Frank couldn't articulate his thoughts.

"What is it, Frank?"

"The letter he left on my windshield the night of the fire...."

"Frank, what did it say?"

"It had a hidden message in it. It was an invitation."

"What do you mean, an invitation?"

"The letter read, *'Getting too close for comfort. Sorry about the fancy dinner. Should have stuck to tinder. Nice Car. Your tenacity, eye couldn't take! Come visit when you can. Be two seeing you soon in the papers tomorrow, big shot!'*"

He used the word 'eye' in place of the letter, and ten of the letters were capitalized," revealed Frank. "Also, instead of writing 'too close,' he wrote out the number two followed by a capital C."

"What did that mean to you, Frank?"

"Bonnie Ross's apartment number above the fabric store was 2C."

"What letters were capitalized?" asked Cantrell.

A-F-L-N-C-L-C-O-W-A.

Cantrell scribbled the letters onto his notepad, trying to unscramble them to form a word that might connect Frank to the killer.

"It spells FALCONCLAW," Frank exclaimed.

"Good grief, Frank. He's made a connection with you. He's trying to lure you to FalconClaw to kill you just as your father was lured to and killed there in 1992."

"Yeah, I figured that out already."

"Frank, have you told your supervisor or any of the other detectives on the case yet?"

"No, and I may not do that." Frank was determined to kill the Schuylkiller and didn't want anyone else to get to him before he did.

"Frank, don't make this about your father or your pride," said Cantrell. "You have a target on your back, and you're in danger. This guy is a professional killer. He's likely been practicing for years and is more adept than you might think."

"I don't want to die, Doug. But if I do while ending that man's life, I surely will."

"Frank, you listen to me, now. You get a goddamn army together, and you go to FalconClaw, and you take that son of a bitch down."

"I'll have an army with me, all right," he said. *An army of one,* Frank thought to himself.

"Okay, don't do anything foolish. You have a family, Frank." Cantrell now feared for Frank's life.

"Frank, listen. In the words of Abraham Lincoln, just months before he was assassinated, he said, 'If a man is willing to give his life to take yours, then there is little you can do to stop him.'"

Frank responded by saying, "That goes both ways, then."

"Come on, Frank. Don't die a hero."

"I'm just dreaming out loud, Doug." Frank lied to Cantrell. "I'll get a team of special operators together, and we'll sweep FalconClaw and get this guy."

"Good, Frank. That's what I want to hear." Cantrell was momentarily relieved but wasn't convinced Frank would follow through.

"So, I can call on you moving forward when I know more?"

"You're damn right you can," said Cantrell. "I am officially invested in the outcome of this case."

"That's great!" Frank was relieved.

"By the way, Frank, I see they finally honored Penelope Bryce. I saw it on television on Sunday. It's about time. I met her once, and she was an inspiration."

"Wait a second! You knew Penny Bryce?!" Frank was shocked.

"Indeed," said Cantrell. "In the early days of the BSU, she and Frank Bruno visited me and my late partner, Richard Kessler."

"It was the early years of criminal profiling when she and Frank came down looking for insight of a serial they were chasing. Some old guy named Garrison O'Donnell, aka Old Man Winter. It was shocking the way she went missing, just like the other victims of their killer."

Frank just sat back and listened to the remarkable story of how all of these great criminal minds were somehow interconnected.

"Did you know that Frank Bruno and I joined forces to track down some very violent killers in Philadelphia back in the eighties?"

Frank shook his head and said, "I was aware that you worked with Frank Bruno, but I can't believe you knew Penny Bryce, too. My partner's mother knew Penny Bryce back before she went missing."

"We tried to recruit both she and Frank to come and work with us down in Quantico, but they were all about Philly and staying put," said Cantrell. "You know, Frank. it almost feels as if I'm talking to a young Frank Bruno, right now."

"I could never fill his shoes." Frank was humble.

"If you catch the Schuylkiller, you'll be well on your way."

Cantrell's smile made it through to Frank.

"Who knows," Frank wished out loud, "Maybe you can join forces with me, and we can take down this guy."

Cantrell chuckled modestly and said, "Frank, I'm seventy-one years old. A little long in the tooth for your line of work. Plus, I was always a mind hunter and not a killer catcher. I wanted to know what made them tick. I usually got involved after they were neutered by prison bars. I only helped Frank Bruno understand the people he was chasing. I never kicked up any dirt with him."

"Well, then," said Frank. "You asked me how you could help."

"Yes, I did."

"Well then, might you also help me understand my suspect?"

"I would be thrilled to assist, but that means you have to take his phone call if he decides to reach out to you again," said Cantrell. "I will need to know everything he tells you. Just keep him talking, Frank."

"That's a deal," said Frank. On the inside, though, he wasn't sure he could hold up his end of the bargain with the legendary criminal profiler. Frank wanted to kill the Schuylkiller. And that's precisely what he would do.

"Okay, Frank. Contact me the next time you hear from your suspect, and we'll attempt to break down what he says and what clues he might unintentionally provide you with."

"Do you really believe he'll call again?" Frank was unconvinced.

"I'll bet money on it," said Cantrell. "Frank, you may not know it yet, but you may be this guy's only friend. Meaning, someone he can talk to."

"Friends is a term I would not use to describe how I feel about him."

"It's more about how he feels about you," explained Cantrell. "He may not have another person in the entire world to talk to," he said. "You may be what's driving him. You may have very well become his muse."

Frank shivered again at the notion.

"Frank, when he found your partner's phone, it was like Christmas for him. He found a conduit between himself and his nemesis. Frank, you are his nemesis."

"He feels connected to you, Frank. If he ever tries to kill you, it will be tough for him to complete the act because if you die, then a little piece of him dies. However......," Cantrell paused.

"However, what?" asked Frank.

"Well, many of the serial killers I've interviewed....killed their muse last."

"That's some sick twisted shit, right there," said Frank, feeling a little sick inside. "To be clear, Doug. I won't have any trouble killing him when it comes that time."

"Now you understand the advantage you have over your suspect, Frank," explained Cantrell.

"Interesting," said Frank.

"Oh, and Frank." Douglas Cantrell wanted to ensure Frank understood with whom he was dealing.

"Yeah, Doug."

"Listen, this guy may have trouble killing you, but he'll have no trouble killing everyone around you, including your partner and your family. The only thing he may have trouble with, if I was right about his education or his mother's career choice, is that he'll have trouble killing a child," surmised Cantrell. "But to be clear, he's a sociopath and is likely erratic and prone to rage. My guess is that he's a psychopath, and something triggered a switch to flip. Likely an anniversary, the death of a loved one that kept him from crossing over. Something happened recently that caused your guy to go to the dark side."

"Look for something like that if you talk again," suggested Cantrell. "Ask him point-blank, what caused him to kill now?"

"Okay, Doug. I will," said Frank.

"Okay, you call me if you hear from this guy again." Cantrell felt invigorated. "Hell, call me with updates either way."

"Will do, Doug." Frank felt like he had a partner in crime. Doug Cantrell would help to fill the void left by Penny.

Frank would take the Schuylkiller's next call, but he dreaded the day that it would come.

Chapter 23 – Penny

Penny's house, the next day – April 19, 2017, 8:15 am.

Penny sipped on a cup of coffee as she made her way to the front of the house to open the living room blinds. When she did, she saw a black Dodge Charger parked out on the street. A smile formed on her face but was quickly replaced with a dubious glare. Her initial reaction was heartfelt, but she wasn't sure how she felt about him being there.

Penny knew that if Frank hadn't invited her to the Ritz Carlton, she would have had dinner at her mother's on the night of Easter and would've been there and likely saved her mother from the fire.

In her heart, though, it gave her peace to see Frank outside, protecting her in his own way. She loved the man but just didn't know how to fulfill that love.

Ten minutes later, her sidearm in place, she tapped on the driver's side window.

Hearing the tap on the glass, Frank was alarmed into consciousness and immediately reached for the gun in the center cupholder. After seeing Penny standing outside the door, he sighed in relief.

Penny smiled at her former partner and yelled, "Roll down the window, asshole!"

Frank lowered the window but wasn't sure if he should smile or not. He felt the guilt of the moment and didn't want to make light of it. All he knew was that he was happy to see his friend and former partner. And he was happy and relieved that she was safe.

"Hey, Penny. How are you?" His monotone voice conveyed his reservation of being there.

"I've seen better days," she said. "I've called my mom at least ten times in the last few days just to hear her voice on her voicemail," revealed Penny. "It's awful. I miss her so much."

Frank looked up at his partner. "I'm here for you, Penny."

Always the quick wit, Penny's eyes surveyed the dirty car and said, "Yeah, I can see that," she smirked.

Frank, still not knowing what to say, said, "Listen, what I really want to do is to give my grieving friend a hug right now."

In a gesture of modesty and acknowledgment, Penny took two steps back. "Then get out of the car and hug me already."

As Frank opened the door, a deluge of tears began to flow from Penny's eyes. "She's gone, Frank!" Penny cried as she threw her arms around her friend. "She's gone!"

"I know. I'm so sorry, Penny." Frank was glassy-eyed. "It's all my fault," he said.

"Frank, I should've been there with her. I should have stayed with her that night."

"I know, Penny. It's all my fault. We should've stayed with her. I was wrong."

Penny recoiled in anger and insufferable heartbreak and slapped her former partner across the face.

Frank, in shock, cradled his jaw but understood Penny's anguish.

Looking her straight in the eyes, he said, "I'm so sorry, Penny."

Penny then lunged at Frank and kissed him passionately.

Frank didn't resist and held onto his last hope for salvation for as long as he could. When the kiss was over, the two held onto each other up against the Dodge for as long as their arms would allow. For Frank, it was more than he could have ever dreamt the Ritz Carlton could ever be. For Penny, it was a coronation. The love she had always felt was her birthright was now crowned.

As the two hugged in the street, the rain began to fall, and they kissed again. As the skies opened up, they ran into the house, shedding their wet clothes along the way to the bedroom.

Standing next to the unmade bed, Frank said, "Wait! What about Dan?"

"He's working his twenty-four on shift!"

"Penny, that's not what I meant." Frank looked Penny in the eyes. "What about you and Dan?"

Penny said, "There is no me and Dan. There never was," she added. "When I kiss Dan, I'm really kissing you. When I look into his eyes, I see yours."

"I love you, Penny! I always have."

"I love you, too, Frank."

Frank's cellphone rang as they fell back onto the bed, barely dressed. At first, he chose to ignore it, but then he remembered what Cantrell said. If the Schuylkiller called back, he had to take it.

Frank looked at his phone and just before the missed call notification popped up, he saw UNKNOWN CALLER on his screen. When the phone went silent, he looked at Penny and said, "That was the Schuylkiller." His eyes went to the floor.

"What?!" Penny looked frightened.

"Penny, he has your phone." Frank's tone was serious.

"Whattaya mean?! I lost it at the fire." Penny's face went pale. "I must've dropped it in the street."

"No, you didn't. You left it in the car, and the Schuylkiller took it. He was there, Penny, walking amongst the crowd. He watched us suffer."

Penny, couldn't wrap her head around what Frank was saying. Shaking her head, she said, "What are you talking about?! The Schuylkiller?! My phone?! Took it?!" Nothing made sense to Penny as her memory went back to that night.

At that moment, Frank's phone rang again. The screen flashed UNKNOWN CALLER.

Frank looked at Penny and said, "It's him. I'm putting the phone on speaker. Don't say a word." Frank motioned by putting his index finger to his mouth.

He then swiped right and said, "Hello?"

"Well, did I catch you two before you consummated the relationship?" The caller let out a subdued sinister laugh.

"Who is this?" asked Frank, knowing full well it was the Schuylkiller.

"Frank, are we really going to play this game every time I call you? It's your old friend. Remember?"

"What do you want?"

"I didn't mean to interrupt the little love affair, but when I passed your car earlier, I saw you sleeping, and when I passed it again a few minutes ago, the car was empty," said the Schuylkiller. "I thought I better call now before things went too far between you and Penny."

Frank looked at Penny, and she looked mortified. Penny knew the man on the other side of the phone was likely right outside and that he was the man who took her mother's life. Penny looked ill and then ran from the room, taking her t-shirt with her.

Frank reached for Penny as she ran but was unable to grab her arm.

Frank begrudgingly held back what he really wanted to say and instead appeased the sociopath on the other end of the phone.

"I wasn't sure you would call back after what I said to you yesterday. I may have been a little out of line." It was difficult for Frank to say those words.

From the bedroom, Frank could hear Penny vomiting in the kitchen. He'd hoped the Schuylkiller couldn't hear her.

"Not to worry, Frank. We're old friends," said the caller, "and sometimes friends have harsh words for one another, but in the end are still friends."

"So, where are you right now?" Frank walked over to the window and pulled back the curtain slightly to reveal a sliver of the front yard and driveway.

"Oh, you know. Here and there," he said. "Don't worry. I'm not planning on dropping in to see you, or anything like that. I wouldn't want to catch you two doing it or anything," he paused and added, "Or, maybe I would."

"Nothing to see here," said Frank. "Just two cops, polishing their bullets before we hunt down and kill a madman." Frank winced and instantly regretted his words, again recounting what Cantrell had told him.

"Now, Frank. Is that any way to talk to an old friend?"

"Well, we've never met, so it's hard for me to consider you an old friend." Frank was baiting the killer, hoping to extract information on when and where the two may have met before.

"Well, that's fair," said the Schuylkiller. "While we haven't known each other for long, we definitely know each other, and the last time we saw each other, the conversation went quite well. You were very well-behaved and restrained."

"And where was that, exactly?"

"You know the answer to that question, Frank. But since you seem to have forgotten, I'll keep it a secret, for now."

"But friends don't have secrets, do they?"

"Oh, don't be naïve, Frank. Everyone has secrets. Just ask your little girlfriend how many men she's already kissed so far today. That was quite a lip lock she laid on her ex-husband, Dan, this morning as he was leaving."

The Schuylkiller tried to get under Frank's skin, and it worked. Frank clenched his teeth and asked, "What is it that I can do for you, Mr. St. John?"

"Again with this 'St. John' business," said the killer. "I know of no one named St. John, but if you insist on calling me that, then so be it. It seems a sufficient surname. If I was ever going to change my name, that might be befitting enough."

"You can go ahead and call me St. John if you'd like, Frank," conceded the madman. "But, oh, how I do like the name *Schuylkiller*. Befitting of someone who likes the water."

Frank detected two reveals in the words of the madman. He had just realized that St. John was not the killer's birth name and that he liked the water. Perhaps he was a swimmer, as Frank had originally thought of the killer.

"So, what is it that I can do for you, Mr. St. John?" Frank was matter of fact as he asked the question for the second time.

"I was wondering why you didn't stop in to see me the other night when you came by?"

"I was pacing myself." Frank clenched his teeth. "It's a big house."

"Well, in due time, I hope that you will visit again," said St. John.

"Listen," said Frank, "I was hoping to chat with you about some other items. Since you clearly know that my father is dead, and you likely know how he died. I was wondering how your father died?" he asked.

"My father took his own life, but he had no choice in the matter."

"Anyone who takes their own life has a choice, no?" asked Frank.

"I disagree," said St. John. "When your name and life are stolen, there's no reason to carry on."

"Well, now I'm the one disagreeing," said Frank. "If a father loves his son, then he would never leave him alone in this wicked world, would he? If he did, perhaps he never loved his son at all." Frank tried to push the killer's buttons to coax an honest response.

St. John went silent for a moment. Frank could hear breathing but said nothing. He waited patiently for the madman to speak up. He knew he'd struck a nerve. Frank now deduced that St. John's motivation for killing was his father's death.

"So, I guess your father didn't love you after all, then." The Schuylkiller tried to turn the tables on Frank.

Frank took a moment to shake off the comment before speaking again. "I was talking about your father, St. John."

St. John countered, "I'd rather talk about yours, Detective."

"Why is that?" asked Frank. "Do you think about my father often? Do you think about the way he died?"

"Oh, yes," said the killer. "And where he died, too. FalconClaw is such a fabled place. It encompasses time, body, and spirit."

Frank knew he was in the head of a killer and wanted to stay there for as long as he could.

"Well, if I were going to die, I wouldn't want to die there," said Frank. "What happened there, back in the day before you and I were born....," he paused. "That whole Canadian mad scientist thing, brainwashing people who couldn't fight back. A rather cowardly thing to do. Don't you think?" asked Frank.

"You must be referring to MK Ultra and the government work that was done there. As I see it, the good doctors were patriots, fulfilling the duty of supporting their governments."

"Mr. St. John, why is it that you are so fascinated with the decaying monstrosity on the side of that hill overlooking Bedford Street?" Frank poked the bear.

"I find that place to be glorious. You will, too, once you lay there dying in it, Detective."

"Were you or a family member ever a patient or resident there, Mr. St. John?" asked Frank.

"A patient? Please!" St. John seemed offended. "That question might infer that I was mad. A simpleton whose mind was corrupted by chemicals and governmental lies."

"So, then, one of your family members was a resident, then?" Frank was narrowing down how the Schuylkiller was associated with the old mansion.

"Wrong again, Detective," said St. John. "Did it ever occur to you that I'm a historian and love the place for its glorious history?"

"Inglorious, don't you mean?" Frank poked the monster again.

St. John again went silent, and by his breathing, Frank could tell that he'd struck another nerve.

"Well, enjoy it now, Mr. St. John, because it might not be there much longer. The city has a new bidder for the property," Frank lied. "If you're going to kill me, you might want to do it soon, as high-rise condos will fill that land by the end of next year. I hear demolition begins in July."

"Hmm." St. John seemed surprised. "I hadn't heard that."

"Well, you know, I work for the city, and we city workers get that kind of information before the public," Frank lied again. "My guess is that if you knew what I knew, I'd be dead already."

"Perhaps you would be, Detective Collazo."

"Well, listen, old friend, "I've got breakfast waiting for me, so I'll need to drop off now."

"Yes, you do that, Frank. "We'll see each other very soon, my friend."

"Until next time, Mr. St. John."

Frank hung up on the Schuylkiller while he was still talking, trying to get in the last word. He hoped that cutting him off had irked the sociopath a little, prompting a future call.

After hanging up, Frank immediately called his Captain.

The desk phone of Captain Rosalyn Sumner rang out, and she answered on the second ring.

"Sumner, here."

"Captain, this is Frank Collazo. I need you to get a tactical squad geared up and ready to converge on the basement of FalconClaw. The Schuylkiller has contacted me personally, for the second time in two days, and has invited me to FalconClaw to die there." Frank's adrenaline was pumping.

"Frank, what in the hell are you talking about?" Sumner wasn't quite ready to move on Frank's request. "A level one emergency has to be confirmed before I can organize a tactical squad. You got a hostage situation on your hands?"

"No, it's just a hunch. The Schuylkiller may be hiding out in the basement of FalconClaw, and we may find Mereby and the others down there if we act fast!"

"Detective, I just heard you say 'hunch,' and 'may,' in the same sentence," Sumner was pragmatic. "That's not how the Philadelphia P.D. operates. I need a verified emergency in which lives are at stake. Unless you got a bank robbery with hostages, I'm not assembling a special operations unit to go anywhere."

"But Captain! The calling card he left before the fire. The capital letters spell out FALCONCLAW!"

"Frank, I like a word scramble as much as the next person," said Sumner. "And I've unscrambled those letters, too." Sumner referenced the scratchpad in the top drawer of her desk. "Do you know how many words I've been able to make so far?"

"No, Captain." Frank was perturbed.

"Twenty-one, twenty-two, twenty-three," she counted aloud. "Twenty-three words and FalconClaw is only one of them," said Sumner. "Now, can you verify that the person who called you is the actual Schuylkiller? Did you ever consider that it's a prank caller?"

"Captain, listen to me. The Schuylkiller is in that basement, and our missing victims may be down there, too. I need a team of officers, detectives, or whoever you can spare," Frank pleaded his case.

"Frank, I trust your instincts," said Sumner, looking at her scratchpad again. As she spoke with Frank, she, too, could make out FALCONCLAW with the capital letters on the note left on Frank's police unit. She saw it for the first time and couldn't believe that she hadn't seen it before.

"All right, listen," she said. "I'll give you Ashfaq, Cole, Brooks, and four uniformed officers. That makes eight of you."

"I'm with Penny," said Frank, "so now we've got nine."

"What are you doing with Bristow? She's on leave!"

"It's a long story, Captain. I'll fill you in later. Get Brooks and Cole to round up the guys and have them meet me at the front gates of FalconClaw in thirty minutes."

Frank hung up the phone and walked into the kitchen to find Penny sitting at the table.

"I'm not going with you, Frank." Penny looked forlorn.

"But Penny...."

"Frank, I'm not ready. And I'm not ready to lose you," she said. "That maniac wants us all dead. I'm not ready for that."

Penny had lost her nerve and was unwilling to enter harm's way. Frank could see it in her eyes, and he understood.

"Frank, I'm sorry about before. The kiss, and all of it." Penny looked ashamed. "Let's just call it another moment of weakness. Too many of those lately, and the one on Easter got my mother killed. It won't happen again, I promise."

"But, Penny." Frank knelt next to her at the table. "I'm not sorry for the kiss, but I understand."

Penny took Frank's hand and said, "Take the shotgun from the trunk when you go in there."

Frank leaned in to kiss Penny goodbye, but she turned away.

Penny was conflicted. She wasn't sure if she still wanted to be a cop. The mean streets of North Philly had now claimed her mother and father and seemed to be on track to claim the only man she'd ever really loved.

Chapter 24 – The Smell of Death

FalconClaw – Forty minutes later.

By the time Frank had arrived, it'd started to rain again. The skies were gray and air humid. It felt as if another storm was on the way. The seven men who were ordered to meet Frank were all on the sidewalk of 888 Bedford Street, standing near the huge vehicle gate, which was flanked by two pedestrian gates.

Frank parked and exited his vehicle and popped the trunk on the Dodge. After donning his Kevlar vest, he grabbed a crowbar and a shotgun that was mounted in the trunk. Slamming the trunk, he approached the men.

"Frank, whatta we looking at here?" said Robert Brooks, as the other men listened in.

"I got a tip that the Schuylkiller may be in the basement of FalconClaw or may have been there recently." Frank's exterior showed the men that he was calm and cool. Inside, however, he was terrified.

"It's also possible that if our killer was here, then we may find clues as to the whereabouts of the three missing victims, which include Belinda Mereby, Keith Carpenter, and Daniel Oliver," he added.

"So, did you go to the daycare yet?" Frank asked Robert Brooks.

"No, they're closed all week for the Easter break. We'll be heading over there on Monday."

"My bad, I knew that." Frank was scatterbrained. "Let me know what they say. That place may hold the answers to this mystery."

"We'll do, Frank."

Frank instructed the seven men to grab their flashlights, shotguns, and at least two more crowbars. After reconvening at the gate, Frank said, "All right, let's lay out our plan down here before we climb that hill."

Frank tossed his shotgun to Ashfaq and tucked the crowbar into his belt. He then inventoried his sidearm, dropping its clip into his hand. He then inventoried his bullets.

Taking back the shotgun, he said, "Ash, you're with me along with Sullivan and Kemper," Frank gave Penny's new partner a nod. Looking over to Robert Brooks, he said, "Brooksie, you and Cole take Farhad and Nowak."

"When we get up there, we're going to divide and conquer. The reporting I have suggests the basement is where he's hiding with his victims," said Frank.

"Okay, Frank. Where is your intel coming from? And shouldn't we have a tactical squad if the Schuylkiller is in there?" Robert Brooks looked through the wrought iron gates and up to the colossal mansion on the hill. "I mean, what if this is a set-up?"

Frank's mind immediately went to his father and that Halloween night when Salvatore Collazo entered hell through the Devil's door without back-up, never to return.

Frank replied, "First of all, you guys are my backup, and" Frank looked around at all of the men and said, "The Schuylkiller is the one who told me."

The seven men had a visceral reaction. Some looked eager to get up the hill, while others seemed to take their personal safety into consideration. However, all would follow their Detective Sergeant, some willingly, some unwillingly.

"Okay, so listen up. Once at the top of the hill, the four of us," Frank motioned to the three men behind him, will enter the mansion and access the basement from the inside, while you four will head around the back and access the basement from an exterior entrance on the property's southwest corner," explained Frank.

"Frank, have you been here before?" asked Detective John Cole. "It sounds like you know your way around the place."

"Yes. Two days ago." Frank's face was deadpan. "Now, let's move!"

As the men traversed the hundred-plus feet up the hill, some had trouble with their footing as the grass and soil were still wet from the rain that had fallen earlier in the day and falling heavier now.

Now at the top, the eight men stood in front of the steps leading up to the dilapidated mansion. Their faces said it all. While some were impressed with its size, others surveying the estate's condition looked decidedly unimpressed. Facing the house, Frank pointed to his right and directed Brooks, Cole, and two of the officers to make their way around back from the mansion's northside.

"Bob," Frank addressed Brooks. "Once you get in there, clear every room you encounter until we all meet up in the middle of the basement."

"Frank, hold on a second. If we're going to meet in the middle, and whatever's waiting for us stands between us, what happens if shots ring out. We'll all be firing in each other's direction." Brooks wore a look of concern. "Does that make any sense to you? Because that sounds like a bad idea to me."

"Bob, listen. We can't take the chance of all going in one side together, just to have the Schuylkiller escape out the other side," Frank reasoned.

"Everybody, listen up," said Frank as he addressed the group. "A flashlight means friendly, so don't fire in the direction of one. Additionally, yell out the word 'Friendly' if you see the other group approaching your position. Got it?"

"And what if the killer has a flashlight, too?" asked Officer Tom Nowak.

"Smart thinking, Tommy!" Frank acknowledged the eighth-year uniformed officer. "Brooksie, your team will flash their lights three times when you see our flashlights. In return," said Frank, "we'll flash ours back at you twice."

Robert Brooks and the men behind him nodded in agreement as if they understood. "Got that, guys?" asked Brooks. "We look for two flashes. If you see two flashes, we're looking at friendlies."

"Guys," Frank addressed the three men behind him, "we're looking for three flashes."

The three nodded and chorused, "Got it, Sarge!"

"Listen," said Frank. "Go in quietly. If he's down there, we don't need him hearing us before we get through the door."

"Okay, let's go!" said Frank.

Splitting up in front of the mansion, the two groups divided up with Frank and his men entering the partially opened front door, while Brooks and his guys disappeared around the northeast corner of the house.

Now inside, Frank said, "Guys, stay close to the walls as the floor is rotted out in some places. I don't want any of you falling through." He paused and added, "Ash, you're with me to the right, you two, walk down the left side."

"We'll cover your eleven o'clock, and you cover our one," said Frank.

Everyone except Frank was impressed with the mansion's former opulence. While it was moldy and decrepit, it was obvious to all the men that the place was built for royalty.

The deeper into the mansion the four got, Frank's breathing became shallower. His claustrophobia was kicking in, and the others could hear his labored breathing.

"You okay, Frank?" asked Ali Ashfaq.

"I'm good," said Frank. "I was here recently, and the mold spores got to me." Frank tried to hide his affliction.

"Gotcha," said the recently promoted detective. "It smells like shit in here." His mouth gaped; Ali Ashfaq tried to avoid breathing through his nose.

The smell of urine and feces was rampant, and it pervaded the nostrils of the men as they shined their flashlights downward, hoping to avoid stepping in some homeless guy's excrement.

Officer Billy Kemper whispered to the group, "You guys know what this place smells like?" he asked jokingly.

Brian Sullivan chuckled and said, "Yeah, the front hallway of the 39th!"

Kemper busted out laughing and said, "That's exactly what I was thinking!"

"Guys, tone it down over there. We're trying to sneak up on a serial killer, and you two are fucking around." Frank wasn't happy.

"Whew! That's awful!" Ashfaq said under his breath while brushing his forearm across his mouth and nose. "I can't take the smell!"

"Suck it up, Ash. It's about to get worse." Frank had smelled death before, and what they were experiencing on the main level would be nothing compared to what they would likely encounter in the bowels of the mansion.

At the end of the foyer, the four men took a right and headed down the long hall where Frank had come across the elevator that had frightened him two days earlier. He'd hoped he didn't hear the crying voice of a man pleading to someone named Jeanie again.

As the three men behind him crept along the walls, Frank could've sworn he'd heard the elevator crank up again. Startled for a moment, he stopped the men with an arm motion and said, "Did you guys hear that?"

The three men all looked at each other and shook their heads, and chorused a muted, "No."

Frank tried to control his emotions. He thought having backup would give him more peace of mind, but FalconClaw unnerved him, and it wasn't because of the Schuylkiller. But rather the ghost of his dead father.

As they passed the elevator, Frank looked away while the others focused in on it.

With four flashlight beams and shotgun barrels leading the way, Frank turned the corner at the end of the long hall and focused his eyes on a faded plaque above a door that looked decades old. The locked door was labeled *Basement*.

Frank grabbed the handle and turned it, but as he'd suspected, it was locked. "Here, hold this light, Ash," said Frank, as he set his shotgun down and pulled the crowbar from his back belt.

Frank wedged the crowbar in the seam between the door and frame and proceeded to rip it open.

FalconClaw had been his father's home for twenty-four years. When pieces of the fabled home went flying, Frank felt strangely sad and guilty. Not in body but in spirit. Frank felt his father all around him, and now he stared down into the abyss and was terrified to proceed.

Detective Frank Collazo took a deep breath and said, "Stay alert, fellas. And nobody shoots me in the back of the head. Don't forget. If you see flashlights, then look for three flashes and return two." Adding, "Nobody from the Philadelphia P.D. gets hurt today. Got it?"

"Roger that," said Ashfaq. "I'm all about going home tonight."

The officers nodded in agreement. Their facial expressions told Frank they counted on him to guide them through whatever awaited them in the basement.

As the men entered the stairwell, there was a wicked odor that became stronger with each step.

At the bottom of the first flight of stairs, Frank heard the sound of squealing rats down below. Making the turn on the landing to the second flight of stairs, Frank's flashlight hit the bottom of the stairwell, and he saw the filthy white tiles of yesteryear and an occasional rat looking up, investigating the strange visitors.

Now at the bottom, Frank saw a scene that likely hadn't changed since the fifties or sixties, by his calculations. Old gurneys with brown leather straps dangling from their sides littered the hallway for as far as his flashlight could see.

Billy Kemper started to dry heave. "What the fuck is that smell?"

All the men covered their mouths with the sound of Kemper gagging and the smell of rotting flesh in the air.

"That's the smell of death, gentlemen." Frank's mind went to Belinda Mereby. He knew she was in the bowels of FalconClaw, and after three and a half months, he could only imagine the condition of her body. *"And what of Carpenter and Oliver?"* He asked himself. Frank quickly realized that they were likely dead, too.

"Everyone, turn off your flashlights for a second," Frank whispered?"

Billy Kemper could be heard whispering, "Why?"

"Just do it," said Frank.

Now, in total darkness, Frank pointed his stare down the long corridor, hoping to see any form of light coming from the south end of the basement. He saw none.

"Okay, guys, light it back up and be 'shotgun ready,'" he said. "And remember, no friendlies get killed tonight. Stay alert."

"Ash," Frank turned to look back. "Take Kemper and clear those two rooms on the left." Frank aimed his light down the left side of the hall, indicating to Ashfaq two doors that stood roughly fifteen feet apart in his estimation."

"Brian, come with me," Frank ordered Officer Brian Sullivan.

As Frank looked in the first door down the right side of the hall, just behind the staircase, he noticed Ashfaq, and Kemper separate and attempt to enter each room alone.

"Ash!" Frank whispered loudly. "Stick together. Do not separate for any reason. Understood?"

"Roger that, Frank." Ashfaq rejoined his partner, and they entered the first room on the left.

Now standing in the room behind the stairwell, Frank and Brian Sullivan saw a long row of desks and metal-backed rolling chairs sitting like relics behind them. The row of desks went as far back as their flashlights would reach. As Frank peered into the darkness, his claustrophobia began to affect his perception of the room's size.

Down the right side, tall filing cabinets, some with drawers open and papers half-tucked into their files, gave the two men the feeling that the people that worked there decades prior left in a hurry. It was as if a dark plague had washed over the floors, walls, and ceiling, leaving the carnage of bad memories and failed human experiments behind.

"What is this place, Frank?" asked Brian Sullivan.

Frank's neck twitched, and he tried loosening it by stretching it out. "Did you ever hear about what happened down here, Brian?"

"No. I only know that it's been closed down since the nineteen nineties and that it was some old mental hospital."

"They did mind control experiments here back in the fifties and sixties," said Frank. "The CIA backed the whole thing."

Frank sifted through desk drawers, leaving each one the exact way he'd found it. Not wanting to disturb the past as if the woman that once sat in the chair behind the desk was coming back soon.

"What are we looking for, Frank?" Brian Sullivan was skittish. "It feels like we're not supposed to be in here."

With his shotgun barrel and flashlight beam leading the way, Frank turned slowly back toward the door and said, "You're right." He then imagined a red-headed woman entering the room in a white blouse and long plaid skirt with high heels and a bob cut. Gum cracking in her cheek, with fake eyelashes fluttering as she glided, not walked. Frank shook the vision from his head and added, "We're not supposed to be here. No one is."

A second later, Frank saw the woman again as she sat down at a nearby desk. She looked him up and down and smiled. As he looked closer, he saw Belinda Mereby smiling at him. With a wink from her black eyes, Frank again shook the image from his mind.

"Nothing to see here," he said to Sullivan. "Let's go clear another room." As Frank re-entered the hallway, he heard one of the other two men, Ashfaq, or Kemper, vomiting just down the hall.

Frank then saw Ali Ashfaq run out of the second room, dry heaving in the hallway. His flashlight captured strings of saliva dangling from Ashfaq's mouth. Seconds later, Billy Kemper emerged with vomit dripping from his chin. The beam of Frank's flashlight caught the glassy eyes of Kemper as he hunched over and threw up the remaining contents of his stomach.

"Ash! What is it? What did you find?" Frank quickly closed the distance between him and Ali, and when he did, the smell of decomposition stopped him in his tracks.

Ashfaq spit on the floor, trying to rid his mouth of the stench and odor. "Frank, there're are like five or six dead dogs in that room. They're covered in maggots, and the rats are running through their decomposing bodies." Ashfaq then turned away and vomited, too.

Frank walked into the room to inspect the gruesome sight and immediately wished he hadn't. As he stared down at the rotting carcasses, he spotted a rat that looked up at him, and in Frank's deluded mind, almost seemed to smile. Frank shook off the vision and tried to clear his head.

He thought that the only way dogs would be piled up dead in the locked basement was if someone put them there. *"Why dogs?"* He asked himself.

"Okay, get it together, Frank." He said to himself. *"We've got to clear these other rooms."*

Back in the hall and looking south, Frank was relieved when he'd spotted four flashlights in the dark distance. He'd calculated them to be more than one hundred feet away. He aimed his light down the long black hall and clicked it off and on twice. Waiting for a second, he saw three flashes come back.

"Okay, guys. We got friendlies at our twelve o'clock," said Frank. "Let's keep clearing these rooms. Remember, stay alert."

Thirty minutes later, the eight men met at what they perceived was the halfway point between the north and south sides of the mansion.

"Frank, we've cleared every room from here south, and we see no signs of life. "We found two decomposing deer and several rabbits back near the entrance where we first entered, but no signs of human remains," said Robert Brooks.

"No shots fired today, huh?" Frank mumbled. "Not sure if that's a good or a bad thing."

"What's that, Frank?" asked Brooks.

"Nothing." Frank was torn. Shots fired meant they would have encountered the Schuylkiller and hopefully stopped him. With no shots fired, the lunatic would live to kill another day.

"Brooks, why all the dead animals?" asked Frank. "We've got a half dozen dead dogs about fifty feet back. Some recently killed."

"Someone's hiding something, Frank." Robert Brooks looked suspicious. "My guess is that it's human decomposition."

"I agree," Frank nodded, keeping his flashlight beam on the lookout. "Animal and human decomposition are hard to differentiate."

"This whole place feels like death," said Brooks.

Frank looked hopeless, his eyes drifting in thought.

"You okay, Frankie?" asked Brooks.

Frank looked off into the darkness and reluctantly said, "My father was murdered down here, Bob."

"What?!" Brooks was flabbergasted. "Frank! I didn't know. I'm so sorry." Brooks placed his hand on Frank's shoulder. "When was it?" He hesitated when asking the question.

"I was just a kid. It was back in 1992," revealed Frank. "He was killed by a serial killer named Walker."

Brooks flashed a look of astonishment. "Vincent Charmaine Walker?"

"Salvatore Collazo was your father?! Holy shit!" Brooks paused. "I'd heard about that but never knew that he was your father." Brooks shook his head in stunned silence. "I never made the connection," he said.

"I never told anyone except for Penny." Frank felt relieved to tell someone other than his former partner.

"Man, I'm so sorry, Frank. No one deserves to die in a place like this."

"Bob, do you get the feeling this place is a morgue?" asked Frank.

Looking over his shoulder and then back at Frank, Brooks said, "Yeah, and a cemetery, too."

"Let's get everybody out of here," said Frank. "If the Schuylkiller was here, he isn't here now."

"This is a big place, Frank, and it's dark," said Brooks as the other men approached. "We might've missed something down here. And what about the upper floors?" he added.

"There's nothing up there but ghosts," said Frank. "Let's get out of here."

Looking around, Frank said, "I can feel Mereby and the others down here, Brooksie." Looking off into the darkness again, he whispered, "My father, too."

"Something evil is at play, that's for sure," said Brooks.

Seeing beams of light flash off the walls, and in some nearby rooms, Robert Brooks yelled to the others, "Let's go, fellas! We're done here!"

As the men headed for the distant thread of sunlight near the south entrance, Frank felt the walls begin to close in on him. He looked down at his feet and wondered if it was the spot where his father had met his end.

When Frank Collazo turned to go, he heard his father say, "I'm sorry, Son."

Minutes later, after everyone had gone, a large man stepped out of one of the previously searched rooms. He then preceded to pull on a false wall that concealed a door leading into The Sleep Room. The Schuylkiller was wearing night-vision goggles and ointment under his nose. He smiled and said, "Poor little Frankie. He'll die right here, just as his father did. Once I complete my list, Detective Frank Collazo will join his father right here in hell."

The Schuylkiller then walked away, whistling into the darkness.

.

Chapter 25 – St. Croix

Joanne's House – Later that evening.

Frank sat at the kitchen table feeling defeated. He needed a pep talk, so he called Douglas Cantrell to update him on the day's events.

As the phone rang, Frank thought about Conner. He didn't have to imagine what life for Conner would be like if the Schuylkiller got to him before he could kill the sociopath. He knew that his son would wander through life, sometimes aimlessly, looking for purpose and looking for revenge.

"Hello." A voice rang out in Frank's ear. "Is that you, Frank?"

"Yeah, Doug. You got time for me?"

"Of course, just flicking the channels," said Cantrell. "I was just thinking about you. What's the latest?"

"Yeah, he called again this morning."

"Okay, and?"

"I took your advice, and I kept him talking for as long as I could."

"That's good, Frank. So break down the entire conversation for me." Cantrell reached for a pen and legal pad.

"This guy thinks we're friends, Doug," said Frank. "And I found out something very important about his mindset."

"Oh, and what's that?" Cantrell listened closely.

"His father committed suicide, and he blames those who drove him to it," said Frank.

"Good. This is good, Frank."

Frank could hear Cantrell's pen clawing at the legal pad.

"So, now that we've established that revenge is his motive, we're one step closer to identifying him," said Cantrell.

Frank was pessimistic. "It feels like little progress has been made since Belinda Mereby was abducted."

"Frank, you got motive out of your second call with the man. And because in his own delusional mind he's befriended you, he'll keep divulging more information. This is good news for your case. What else did he say?" asked Cantrell.

"You mentioned that serial killers like to mimic other serial killers...." said Frank.

"Yes?"

"Well, he seems fascinated that my father was killed at FalconClaw. But when I tried to link him to the place by asking if he, or anyone he knew, was a patient there, he seemed offended."

"What else did he say?"

"He almost seemed defensive about the place," said Frank. "It was as if he was somehow fond of FalconClaw and its sordid past."

"This is good," said Cantrell. "If your instincts are correct, then he might be connected to the place beyond the fact that your father was killed there."

"In fact, Frank, he may have become even more obsessed with you because he might also be connected to the place. When he discovered that you also have a deep connection to FalconClaw, it may have triggered a delusional bond between you and him. A deadly bond, at that," suggested Cantrell.

"But, how would he even know about my father?" asked Frank.

"Frank, listen. After you told me about your father being killed there, I Googled your name and your father's name, too," revealed Cantrell. "I needed to see everything online that anyone searching might find. It's all right there," he said. "Frank, we know that no one has disappeared in more than two months. You said the killer told you his fourth and fifth victims have proven to be elusive, right?"

"Yeah."

"Well, he's had some downtime, then," said Cantrell. "During the last two months, he's had time to learn more about you. Things like where you live and where your partner lives...." Cantrell was benign. "Frank, not to alarm you, but, the Schuylkiller may have been following you for weeks. He knows where your family lives, works, goes to school. He likely knows your habits, too, like where you eat, when you're home, and when you're not. You said yesterday that he was at your apartment. Did that prove to be true?"

"Yes, someone was there," said Frank. "The door was jimmied, and the place was in disarray, I've been told."

"Have you been back there?" asked Cantrell.

"No, and I may never go back." Frank sounded adamant.

"Well, wherever you sleep at night, Frank. Do it with one eye open," cautioned Cantrell. "He likely won't attempt to kill you until after his fifth victim has been claimed," he surmised. "Unless, of course, you are the fifth victim."

"Well, that's all very comforting," Frank chuckled, trying to mask his uneasiness.

"Frank, you need to do what I told you and get an army over to FalconClaw."

"I did. I went there this morning after I got the psycho's call."

"Oh my goodness!" Cantrell was surprised. "Who went with you, and what did you find there?"

"Not the Schuylkiller," revealed Frank. "There were eight of us armed with shotguns and flashlights."

"Was there anything there that would lead you to believe that anyone had been there recently?" asked Douglas Cantrell."

"Oh, yeah!"

"What did you find, Frank?" Cantrell was solicitous.

"We found the carcasses of no less than twenty animals," revealed Frank. "The smell was atrocious!"

"No human remains, though?"

"No, just deer, dogs, and rabbits from what we could see," said Frank.

"Were they fresh, or had they been there for a while? You mentioned the odor, so that implies some were killed within days or weeks. Is that your assessment, Frank?"

"Yes, I think they were put there...."

Cantrell cut Frank off. "By the killer in an effort to mask human decomposition." Cantrell finished Frank's sentence.

"That's what I'm thinking, too."

"So when are you going back?" Cantrell thought the place should be searched again.

"Likely won't be going back unless I can convince my Captain there's a reason to," said Frank. "She barely approved the seven men that went with me today. When I debriefed her on what we'd found there, she wasn't convinced that there was any reason to send a larger contingent of police."

"That's too bad, Frank," said Cantrell. "Murderers commonly disguise the odor of human decomposition in many ways. My guess is that those animals died at the hands of a person as opposed to another animal."

"You'd be right, as the place was sealed shut before we got there," revealed Frank. "We found no way for animals to get inside."

"And that wasn't enough to convince your C.O.?"

"Nope."

"Okay, Frank. I'm giving you a little homework."

"Oh yeah, what's that?" asked Frank.

"This might be difficult, but you need to google yourself and your father. Specifically, your father's death," suggested Cantrell. "You need to fully understand what the killer knows about you."

"You're probably not in immediate danger as he needs to complete his list. I'm beginning to think that his list of five might not include you. But there will likely be an attempt on your life and those you know and love after that. Stay vigilant, my friend."

"Why do you think I'm not on the list of five as you had mentioned earlier?" asked Frank.

"He's going to stretch this out, I feel. If you were on the list of five, he wouldn't tell you that. He's likely fascinated with you and wants to believe that you and he are friends. That fascination, however, will turn deadly at some point, I'm afraid," said Cantrell.

He added, "Before he comes after you, he'll have to build up some anger toward you. When you talk to him again, look for signs of that."

"You seem sure that he'll call again."

"Frank, he will call again," Cantrell was certain. "This guy wants to go out in a blaze of glory. Either by killing you or by being killed by you. That's his fantasy."

"Listen, Frank. Your guy will try to create an epic showdown of good versus evil. To do that, he'll need to provoke you in some way. You may not be in immediate danger, but your family and your partner surely are. Keep them close, Son."

Frank's only reprieve from the void left by his father's murder was Douglas Cantrell. When he'd heard Cantrell call him 'Son,' his heart yearned for his father. Frank needed his father to guide him and counsel him. He again felt like he wasn't completely alone in what felt like his final days before he'd join his father again in the backyard. He'd dreamt that he and his father could patch the holes in the fence together.

Frank sat in his Dodge Charger on Old Bridge Road early the following morning, which separated the daycare and The Trolley Car Café. There, he waited for Detectives Robert Brooks and John Cole to arrive. It was Monday, April 24, 8:46 am, and Frank was physically and emotionally exhausted.

Frank had asked Brooks if he could join them when they'd visited the daycare to learn more of the man that'd splashed water on him three months earlier.

As Frank sat there, he thought of Penny and hoped she was okay. He couldn't call as he didn't have a number for her. He'd hoped that she would contact him soon.

Frank scrolled through his text messages, and Joanne had confirmed that a Cheltenham Township Police car escorted her and Conner to school while her father remained at the house. She texted Frank that her father would remain with her until he got home. The previous Friday, the Police Chief of Cheltenham Township had agreed to help out when and where he could.

Minutes later, a Ford Crown Victoria pulled up behind Frank, and Brooks and Cole got out. Frank joined them in the rear parking lot of the daycare, and the three discussed how the meeting would go.

"Do they know we're coming?" asked Frank.

"No," said Brooks. "When I called over the Easter break, I didn't leave a message. I figured it'd be better if they didn't see the meeting coming."

"I agree," said Frank. "Listen, I don't want to step on your toes in there. I just want to hear everything firsthand."

"Frank, listen. John and I talked it over." Brooks nodded at his partner, who nodded in agreement. "We think you should lead the conversation."

"Yeah, Frank," said John Cole. "You led the case up until your suspension, and not much happened while you were gone. And, you may have had a run-in with him behind this building back in January."

"All right, fellas," Frank smiled in appreciation. "Chime in as we go, though."

Minutes later, the three stood in the daycare's lobby and were immediately greeted by a woman who looked at them suspiciously.

Walking out from behind a counter, the woman greeted and smiled at the arriving parents dropping off their children.

"Gentlemen, how may I help you?" In her late thirties, the petite woman wearing blue slacks and a sweater glanced down at the badges worn on each detective's belt. She flashed a look of concern that the three men were wearing sidearms near small children. She'd hoped that no one other than she was alarmed.

"Ma'am," Frank flashed his badge, "my name is Detective Frank Collazo, and these are Detectives John Cole and Robert Brooks. We're out of the 39th District, and we'd like to speak with the owner if they're in."

With a look of concern, she studied Frank's face longer than she had the other two detectives. Looking the men up and down, she said, "I'm the owner. My name is Cindy Stafford. What is it that I can do for you, gentlemen?"

"Mrs. Stafford...." Frank addressed the woman whose name sounded familiar to him.

"It's Miss, but call me Cindy."

"Fine. Cindy, is there a place where we can sit down and talk with you about an ongoing investigation?" asked Frank.

Stafford looked flustered. Unable to articulate an answer, she looked around for one of her employees. After she flagged down a young woman, she nervously smiled and said, "Right this way, gentlemen."

Passing by the young woman, Stafford said, "Karen, watch the front for a few minutes, please."

"Sure, no problem, Cindy."

The daycare owner led the three men to a back-office down a long hall lined with classrooms for children of varying ages. As Frank looked through the glass windows of each room, he began to doubt that the Schuylkiller could have been employed in a place that cared for innocent children. However, when he'd remembered back to January and the man who likely purposefully squirted him with the hose while washing the bus, he quickly reconsidered his doubt.

The daycare owner and the three detectives squeezed into a tiny office, and Cindy Stafford said, "I'm sorry, but this will have to do. Now, please, what is this all about? I'm a bit nervous, I must confess." Stafford was too agitated to sit down.

Frank nodded in acknowledgment of Stafford's apprehension and proceeded to speak.

"Ma'am, by now, I'm sure you've heard of the Schuylkiller case."

"Why yes, how could I have not? The killer worked right behind us, and we had no idea."

"Yes, well," Frank paused. "What you may not know is that the case has been reopened as it appears that Willard Clark was not the Schuylkiller after all."

"So, the killer didn't work at The Trolley Car Café?" Stafford looked relieved but needed to confirm what she'd just heard.

Frank began to speak but was interrupted by the owner.

"We lost a lot of business due to the proximity of where the killer worked. This news will help us get our customers back," she said.

"Miss Stafford, I'm going to need you to take a seat, please." Frank motioned to her chair behind a tiny, cluttered desk.

Stafford again looked concerned. "Well, all right."

Once she was sitting, Frank said, "Ma'am, do you currently have any male employees working here?"

"No, we don't," said Stafford.

"How about in the last ninety days?" asked Frank, as Cole and Brooks looked on.

Stafford responded by saying, "Yes, we had a gentleman who worked here for about three months but then abruptly quit at the end of January." Stafford shook her head and rolled her eyes. "I was glad to see him go as he wasn't a very good fit."

The three detectives almost simultaneously took their small notepads from their pockets to take contemporaneous notes of the conversation.

Stafford noticed it and again looked alarmed.

"What is happening here?" she said.

"Miss Stafford," Frank spoke in a calming voice ahead of his next set of questions. He knew the daycare owner would be terrified by the outcome of the meeting. "What was the man's name that worked here in January?"

Now trembling, Stafford said, "George St. Croix."

Frank's eyes went wide. "Did you say, Saint Croix?"

All three men looked at each other and jotted the information down.

Stafford again noticed the men's reaction and looked deflated, sinking back into her chair.

"Why was Mr. St. Croix not a good fit, Miss Stafford?"

"Well," she hesitated, "he was very intimidating and was short-tempered. He was a very large man, and he didn't like being told what to do. During his interview, he seemed quite nice, and his credentials were very impressive."

"Miss Stafford," Frank readied his pen, "do you conduct background checks on each of your employees during the hiring process? And if so, do you have those results in their employee files?"

Stafford seemed offended. "Well, of course, I do, Detective. Parents place their children into our care. What exactly is going on here?" she demanded.

"Miss Stafford, you said I can call you Cindy, correct?" Frank was trying to calm the woman's now agitated state.

"Not anymore," Stafford was almost defiant. "I demand you tell me what's going on here?"

"Of course, Ma'am." Frank decided to be a little more forceful. "Miss Stafford, please remind me, are you a franchisee, part of a larger chain, or are you the actual business owner?" asked Frank, knowing full well that she'd told him she was the owner.

"I'm the owner." Stafford again sank back into her chair with Frank's change in demeanor.

"I'll need to see the background check for Mr. St. Croix, please." Frank all but demanded of the woman.

"Umm, I'm not sure I have to show you that information," said Stafford. "That's confidential, and employees, either former or current, have the right to their privacy." Stafford looked at the three men with skepticism. "You can't just come in here without telling me what's going on and demand that I show you employee files."

"You're correct," said Frank, "I'm not demanding anything. I am asking you to provide the information. If you'd like, we can get a court to issue a warrant, and we can take a look at all of your files when we come back in and shut down the place. Your choice." Frank put his notepad away.

"Well, I," Stafford paused as she rose and turned toward a filing cabinet in the back of the room.

When she turned, the three detectives all looked at each other to communicate that the 'tough cop' tactic worked better than the 'nice guy' routine.

"Is Mr. St. Croix in some kind of trouble?" asked Stafford as she sorted through hanging file folders.

"For now, he is a person of interest, and we simply need to know more about him," said Robert Brooks.

"Has he been in touch with you since you terminated his employment?" inquired Frank.

"No, no. As I mentioned to you before, Mr. St. Croix quit. I didn't fire him." Stafford now stood facing the three men with a singular file folder in hand.

"Hmmm," Frank pondered aloud as his eyes went to the folder. For a moment, Frank thought the secret to the Schuylkiller's identity was just inches away from where he stood. "If he wasn't a good fit and he intimidated you, then why didn't you fire him?" he asked.

"Well, I, umm." Stafford was tongue-tied. "As I said, he intimidated me. I'm sure I would have eventually let him go."

"Cindy. May I call you Cindy?" Frank tested the waters to see if she was now more receptive.

"Yes, Detective, you can call me Cindy."

"Would you feel more comfortable if fewer Philadelphia Police Detectives were standing over you in such a tiny office?" Frank read the signs that Stafford was intimidated by her former employee and was likely intimidated by the three of them.

"Yes, I would be much more receptive if there were only one of you present." Stafford looked timid and welcomed the offer to speak with only one detective.

"Would you boys mind if I spoke to Cindy here for a few minutes outside of your presence?" Frank directed his question to Brooks and Cole.

"Not at all," said Brooks as John Cole nodded in agreement. "We'll wait outside for you," he added. "Ma'am," said Brooks as he tipped his head in appreciation of her time.

After the men left, Frank sat down in the only other chair in the tiny office. It sat opposite Stafford's desk.

"Thank you for your time, Cindy." Frank was warm and sincere. "I promise not to be too much longer."

"That'll be fine," she replied.

"I was in the rear parking lot of your establishment on the morning of Saturday, January 21, when I encountered a man hosing off one of your buses," recounted Frank. "Would that man have been your employee, George St. Croix?"

"Yes, it must've been if he was washing our bus."

In Frank's observation, Stafford was still very nervous by his presence.

"Why was he here on a Saturday if you're closed on the weekends?" Frank pulled his notepad out again.

"Well, I hired him to work with the children as his background suggested that he was qualified to do so...." she paused.

Frank's curiosity was piqued, now sitting fully erect in his chair.

Stafford continued, "But he soon lost interest in having any interaction with both the children and the other people working here."

"Cindy, when you say 'qualified' to work with the children, what do you mean?" Frank could feel her answer before she responded based on the profile Douglas Cantrell had come up with. Cantrell told Frank to determine whether the Schuylkiller had a degree in child psychology, childcare, or early childhood education.

"Well, his work history was impressive, and I couldn't understand why he'd applied for the position of Pre-K teacher. He had worked with children in both school and clinical settings and had a degree in Child Psychology from Temple University."

Frank nearly fell out of his chair. He found it hard to contain the rush of adrenaline pulsating through his veins.

"Temple, you say?" asked Frank.

Stafford confirmed with a nod.

"Cindy," Frank tried to be calm. "let me ask you the obvious question. And please, don't be offended." Frank again readied his pencil. "Why would a candidate of St. Croix's considerable qualifications be applying to a small, locally-owned daycare? Again, no offense meant by the question."

"No offense taken, Detective."

"Please, call me Frank."

"Sure, Frank," the woman gingerly nodded. "That was just it. I asked him the same question, and he said that he wanted to get back to working with young children prior to entering the public school system." Stafford was now working off of her notes from the interview. "It says here that his career had taken him to a place he didn't want to be. Working with children after it was too late to help them. He said he worked as a teacher, a social-services counselor for child welfare services, and the Department of Family and Children Services."

"And you said that he quickly lost interest in caring for the children shortly after he started his employment? Is that right?"

Stafford nodded and said, "I didn't want to give up on him right away, so I kept him busy doing odd jobs. Children can be messy, as you can imagine. And we do a good deep clean every weekend, getting the business ready for Monday. He also became our regular bus driver when we took the Pre-K kids on field trips."

"And that includes washing the bus out back?" asked Frank.

"Yes, both inside and out."

Frank jotted more notes as Cindy Stafford sat looking more and more haggard.

"Frank, please tell me what's going on? I'm frightened right now, and I need you to be forthright."

"Cindy, there's no easy way to put this," Frank winced, "we have a lead that suggests your former employee, George St. Croix, might somehow be involved in the murders and disappearances that occurred back in January. It's still very early in our investigation of St. Croix, though."

Stafford gasped, raising her hand to her mouth as she began to tear up. "Are the children in danger?" she cried. "Am I in danger, Detective?"

Frank tried to calm Stafford's fears but was challenged when doing so. "We have little evidence to support that anyone here is in danger," Frank spoke calmly. "But again, it's early in our investigation of your former employee. As I mentioned earlier, he is a person of interest in the case and not a suspect."

Frank was simmering on the inside. He knew in his heart that St. Croix was really St. John. His only fear was that the name St. John first came to him during a conscious nightmare while first visiting FalconClaw.

St. John, or St. Croix, Frank was certain that the Schuylkiller was the man who'd recently quit working for Cindy Stafford.

Looking again at Stafford, Frank could see that she was terrified.

"What should I do?" Stafford was beside herself. "Should I close the place temporarily?"

"Miss Stafford, please calm down." Frank leaned forward in his chair. "How about if I stop by daily to check in on you and your employees? I'll even come by on the weekends to make sure the place is secure. How does that sound?"

Now crying, Stafford nodded frantically and said, "Please, would you?"

Frank stood and walked to the side of the desk. Stafford shot from her chair and fell into his arms when he did. Frank held the woman uncomfortably, hoping that no one witnessed the embrace.

"Cindy, how about we exchange cellphone numbers, and you call me if you see or hear from St. Croix."

Stafford nodded, quickly wrote down her number on a post-it note, and stuffed it into Frank's hand.

"I'll text you shortly so that you'll have all of my information," said Frank. "Will that be okay?"

She nodded, yes, wiping her tears.

As Frank was about to request the man's home address from his employment file, Cindy Stafford handed Frank the entire folder and the entirety of its contents without a word. Frank looked surprised and relieved and gladly accepted the file.

Before Frank turned to leave, he suddenly placed the name of the daycare owner. "Excuse me, Cindy...."

"Yes," replied Stafford.

"Did you attend Germantown High School in the mid-nineties?"

"Yes." Stafford was perplexed by the question. She had no idea how the detective would know that about her.

"I graduated there in 1996," revealed Frank. "I think you were a year ahead of me if I'm not mistaken."

Stafford smiled, slightly embarrassed by the recognition. Rubbing her eyes again, she asked, "Big city, small world, huh?"

"I'll say," said Frank. "I'll be in touch with you very soon." He held up the crumpled post-it note, pursed his lips, and then turned to leave.

Minutes later, as Frank was walking out the front door, He was quickly approached by John Cole, as Robert Brooks stood on the corner talking on his cellphone.

"Frank, there's been another disappearance," said Cole. "A middle-aged lawyer from Chestnut Hill. And get this? The guy's father worked with Clinton Mereby back in the seventies and eighties."

"Holy shit!" said Frank. "He's number four."

Chapter 26 – Puzzle Pieces

Two days later, on Wednesday, April 26, Frank was back at the 39th, and the Detective Room was buzzing. A massive storyboard was assembled, and detectives from the 5th and the 39th were present, along with Captain Rosalyn Sumner and CSU Supervisor Daanesh Patel.

Frank was the last one in the room after finalizing his presentation. When he'd entered the room from the rear, he did a quick inventory of those in attendance. Some he recognized, some he did not.

Frank's breath was momentarily taken away when he thought he saw Penny sitting near the front of the room. As he walked around the group, his hopes were dashed when he saw Cindy McCurdy instead, sitting next to her partner, Kyle Wade. As his eyes made contact with Cindy's, he nodded in recognition. His empty face and gesture told Cindy that he thought she was Penny. Like everyone else in the 39th, McCurdy knew that Frank cared deeply for his partner, and most were sure they were secretly a couple.

Penny still hadn't returned from her leave, and Frank, glancing at the door from time to time, kept waiting for her to walk in.

"All right, all right! For the first order of business," Sumner yelled over the chatter of the more than a dozen in attendance, "we're going to chronologically lay out the facts of our case to date, as we must ensure everyone in attendance is brought up to speed. Additionally, by reviewing the facts in all of the murders and disappearances, we're hoping somebody in the room can make a connection that we haven't made yet."

"Frank Collazo's going to walk us through everything, and if anyone has anything else they want to add, by all means, speak up. The Schuylkiller case is back open for business, and we need the smart people in this room to catch that son of a bitch before he finds another victim," said Sumner. "Frank, come on up!"

Frank made his way up to the front of the room. Looking around, he had a captive audience, as everyone had skin in the game. Either they'd worked the case personally, were brought in for their special expertise in the crimes, or worked in areas where the crimes occurred. All had families and wanted nothing more than to take a homicidal sociopath off the streets.

Frank lit up a seventy-inch flatscreen television positioned on the Schuyler Street side of the Detective Room, and he tapped away on a laptop until a set of images popped up on the display. The images that filled the screen included Belinda Mereby smiling with bright orange hair, a grainy secondary image of Mereby getting into the back of a limousine outside of Strawberry Mansion, and an image of Strawberry Mansion from the front. Additionally, there was a close-up of the suspect in the case holding the limo door open for his victim.

Frank addressed the room. "While many of you have seen these images before, along with dozens more that we'll focus in on today, it is critical that we review each one again. The more context we give to each image, event timeline, and forensic detail, the easier it will be to determine who our killer and or killers are."

"Frank, are you suggesting there may be more than one killer?" asked Detective John Reigns from the back of the room.

"No, but what I think isn't relevant for this part of the conversation. Rather, if we're going to take a fresh look at the case, it's best if I don't disclose what I think until the end of our discussion today," said Frank.

"Which he will be doing, People!" yelled Sumner from the front row, looking over her shoulder.

"Okay, so, the timeline of events for our first victim." Frank looked over his notes. "Belinda Mereby, a well-known socialite, and philanthropist, was invited to a New Year's Eve party at Strawberry Mansion by her then-lover, Warren Jacks. Jacks was a prominent defense attorney and former U.S. Attorney for Philadelphia's Eastern District. He was also a former Professor at his alma mater, Temple University's Beasley School of Law."

"Jacks and Mereby had been involved in an affair since their days as students at Temple University back in the late eighties and early nineties," said Frank. "We know that sometime around 11:30 that evening, the two rendezvoused in the mansion wine cellar in the basement and had what appeared to be consensual sex. After they'd finished, a verbal altercation resulted in her spitting in the face of Jacks and him grabbing her and pushing her against a wine rack."

"The altercation resulted in Mereby's dress being torn and several wine bottles hitting the floor. It was at that moment, Mereby unknowingly dropped her cellphone and subsequently left the mansion roughly two hours later, intoxicated and without her phone."

Frank continued, "Without her phone, Mereby would have been unable to call for help from the backseat of the limo as it drove her to an unknown destination."

"Frank, what more do we know about Mereby's family ties?" asked Detective Nate Jackson from the 5th District.

"Belinda Mereby's father is Clinton Mereby. You've likely all heard that name before," said Frank. "Many of us have seen him doing his thing in court."

Frank went on, "Mereby was a long-time partner in the Mereby, Godfrey & Faulkner law firm that handled many famous cases spanning the nineties and two-thousands." He further explained, "Mereby had made a name for himself as a junior partner in the Johnson, Gholston, and Sayers law firm that represented victims and their families in the MK Ultra case back in 1970 and '71. Mereby was the lead for the defense, and he buried all those involved in the experiments and got a huge settlement for his firm's clients. It made him a household name from that point on."

Frank added, "We'll be talking more about MK Ultra later. For now, you each have a packet that outlines what MK Ultra was, so reserve your questions regarding that until later."

"Now, let's get back to Jacks," said Frank. "While we have no evidence that suggests Jacks was part of Mereby's disappearance, we should not rule out his involvement simply because he turned up dead less than a week later on January 5."

"We also know that Mereby's purse was found on the southbound side of Route 1 near Fernhill Park," said Frank. "Unless someone was trying to throw us off by disposing of the purse there, the assailant would have been in Germantown within hours of the abduction." Frank added, "This will be the first of many times today you hear the name Germantown."

"What do we know about the limo driver that dropped Mereby off at the party that night?" asked Detective Constantine Lykaios from the 5th.

"Victim number one, and ground zero in the case." Frank clicked the controller in his hand, and the slide changed to show a black male on the screen. "James Loftin, forty-two years old, of Glenwood. Our lack of evidence regarding Mr. Loftin indicates that he was simply collateral damage. It could have been anyone who was driving that particular limo that night. We suspect that Mereby was followed after being picked up from her apartment complex at the Chamounix Condominiums on West Ford Road."

"We also suspect, through Loftin's cellphone records, that the killer approached him as he waited to pick up Mereby at a B&M Grocery Store at the intersection of West Dauphin and 21st Street, just east of the Strawberry Mansion neighborhood. Witnesses have gone on record to say that a tall, white male, with a stocky build, somewhere in the mid to late forties, got into the back of the limo before it drove off. It's conceivable that the killer offered our victim cash for a ride, and Loftin, earning only nine bucks an hour, likely wouldn't have turned it down."

"From there, we think he was murdered in the Mount Peace Cemetery near the intersection of West Indiana and West Hunting Park. It was the last place his phone pinged a cell tower before being smashed on the ground near some tombstones."

"Loftin was shot behind the right ear, beheaded, and left in the limo under the Twin Bridges in the early morning hours of January 1. His body in the trunk, his head in the backseat."

Frank sighed and shook his head as he pressed the clicker in his hand. "Now displayed on the screen, for all in attendance, is the decapitated head of James Loftin sitting in the wet grass just off the River Trail that day."

Audible gasps could be heard from the group just before the Detective Room door flew open. It was Penny Bristow, and she said, "It was a lot worse in person!"

Frank smiled when he saw Penny. He was thrilled to see his friend and former partner. He'd missed her, and he loved her.

"Hey, Partner!" yelled Ali Ashfaq.

Penny raised her chin to acknowledge Ashfaq and took a seat in the back of the room.

Frank continued to smile on the inside as Penny's presence buoyed his confidence. Captain Rosalyn Sumner could see a sparkle in Frank's eyes, and selfishly, she was glad Penny was there even though she thought it was too soon for her to be back at work.

"All right, any more questions about victims one or two?" asked Frank.

No hands went up, so Frank clicked the slide to an image of Warren Jacks.

On the screen was an image of a dark-haired, handsome Caucasian male, with jet-black hair threaded with strands of gray. At six-foot, two, thinly built, people and the press had often compared him to Pierce Brosnan, the Irish actor who'd portrayed James Bond back in the late nineties and early two-thousands. Warren Jacks had been dubbed '007' on more than one occasion by the press.

In the photo, Jacks could be seen at a black-tie affair, wearing a tuxedo, and shaking hands with Mayor Donovan Taylor at an undetermined function the year before.

"Okay," said Frank, "we suspect that Warren Jacks is victim number three. Again, while we can't exclude him as a suspect in the disappearance of Mereby, we have zero evidence to suggest that he had anything to do with her going missing."

"Not even the fight in the basement?" asked a female detective from the 5th who Frank didn't recognize. "Wasn't there a text message?" she added.

"Yes," replied Frank. "There was a text from Jacks to Mereby that night that stated, *'You've threatened me for the last time!'* Additionally, Jacks also threatened Mereby at the party. A witness heard him say: *'If you decide to make that call, then you will pay an awful price.'"*

"So he can't be ruled out then?" clarified the detective.

"That's correct. As I stated earlier, Jacks has not been ruled out as a suspect, and we're about to cover him at length right now."

Sumner turned to the group behind her and said, "Girls and Boys, keep the questions coming and be taking notes."

"Okay, so let's talk about Jacks in more detail." Frank resumed his presentation.

"As I mentioned earlier, Jacks was a prominent defense attorney and former U.S. Attorney for Philadelphia's Eastern District, and a Law Professor at Temple," Frank reminded everyone.

"We were scheduled to meet with Jacks and his lawyers downtown on January 9, but as you already know, he was murdered in the early morning hours of January 5."

"And we're sure he was murdered?" asked Carol Loggins, another female detective from the 5th.

"To answer that, I'd like Daanesh Patel to come up and explain why we think he was murdered as opposed to committed suicide." Frank waived the CSU Supervisor up to the front of the room.

"Okay, so," Patel grabbed the clicker from Frank's hand, "since we're here to discuss the Schuylkiller, I can add some context as to how we've determined Jacks' cause of death. We can prove forensically that Warren Jacks' death was not a suicide. If he was murdered, then it's likely his killer is also responsible for Mereby's disappearance. We feel the death was staged to make it look like a guilt-ridden suicide after having his lover killed."

As Patel detailed the forensics in the case, Frank quietly walked to the back of the room to greet his former partner.

"Penny, I'm so glad you're here," Frank whispered. His subdued smile couldn't hide his happiness.

"Hey, Frankie." Penny's joy was more subdued.

"I wasn't sure when I would see you again. I don't have your new number. What if I need to contact you? What happens if you're in danger and I can't get ahold of you?"

"Frank, calm down," said Penny. "I texted you half an hour ago with my new number. Where do we stand in the case? What more do we know?"

"Well, I'm just getting started up there, and you're going to hear it all in a minute." Frank looked at Penny with eyes that longed for her. Not physically, but emotionally. Penny was Frank's best friend, and he felt incomplete without her.

"Okay, so I didn't miss anything that I need to know?" she asked.

"No, you walked in during the part when the limo driver was discovered."

Frank turned as he heard Patel wrapping up his part. "There's a lot you don't know. Let's talk after the meeting."

Frank walked back up to the head of the room and held out his hand to Patel to regain access to the slide clicker.

Patel finished by saying, "So, as you can see. This was a murder and not a suicide. If Jacks was murdered, then why? And by whom?"

"Thanks, Denny." Frank used the mouse to locate the next image in the presentation. After double-clicking, a picture of Daniel Oliver appeared on the screen.

"You've all seen this picture in the newspapers. It's Daniel Oliver. Oliver is the Grandson of Quinten Oliver, the newspaper magnate that broke the story about several big cases back in the seventies and eighties, but none were bigger than MK Ultra. Oliver is the

Senior Editor at the Philadelphia Inquirer," said Frank. "We believe he is the fourth victim in the case."

"Many of you already know that Daniel Oliver was out jogging near his home on the westside, just blocks from the UPenn campus, yet his wallet was found up in Germantown," Frank disclosed to the group.

After a brief pause, Frank said, "What in the hell is going on up in Germantown?"

Clicking to change the slide, Frank revealed a picture of Keith Carpenter. "Here, you see a picture of Keith Carpenter, a man we believe is the fifth victim of the Schuylkiller."

Frank changed the slide to reveal a snow-covered McMichael Park. Clicking again, he showed images of footprints and blood in the snow.

"We can confirm that a violent abduction occurred here, but we cannot confirm that Carpenter is dead. The CSU believes with the amount of blood loss at the location of the violent attack, that Carpenter was shot in the gut area, and if so," said Frank raising his brow, "Carpenter may very well be dead by now, more than three months later."

"Like Oliver, many of you know the details of the Carpenter case," said Frank. "He is, or was, a Temple University Professor."

Chatter came from the group, all of which were engrossed in the commentary.

"That's right," said Frank after hearing mumbles of 'Attorney,' 'Lawyer,' 'Temple,' and 'Professor.' "We have a lot of circumstantial evidence that link our victims," said Frank. "Hell, we can even connect the Schuylkiller to Willard Clark, the mentally challenged man that killed his mother with his bare hands, to then be killed by his father in what has been deemed a 'mercy killing.' But we have much more that you have not been made aware of, and I'm going to share it with you today."

Frank reached into a manila envelope and pulled copies of the note the Schuylkiller left the night of the Easter fire and passed them around the room. Handing copies to those in front, and those in front handing copies to those in the back.

Frank then put the letter up on the screen, and the group, most of whom were seeing the letter for the first time, were introduced to details that were the catalyst for re-opening the case.

"Many of you thought that Willard Clark was the Schuylkiller, as did the Commissioner, the Mayor, and most of the city of Philadelphia. But those who know me, and have access to my testimony from the internal investigation of the elder Clark suicide, know that I never believed Willard Clark was the Schuylkiller."

Penny and Sumner nodded.

"Before I go into the details of this letter, I want all of you to understand something. Penny Bristow and I have been partners for more than three years, and all of you know that you become close with the person you go to work with every day, the person you'd take a bullet for, the person who would take a bullet for you."

Frank needed to clear the air regarding his and Penny's relationship once and for all before continuing the discussion of the case details.

"As some small minds will tell you, Penny and I are more than partners. We must be sleeping together simply because we're of the opposite sex, and we work strange hours and drive around in a car all day." Frank was sarcastic. "Oh, yeah, and our marriages crumbled right around the same time. Hell, we must be lovers," said Frank. "Well, we're not!" he yelled. "Sorry to disappoint anyone who thought we were."

"Now, with all that being said, Penny and I, as friends and partners, were having dinner at the Ritz Carlton, downtown. During that dinner, the valet that parked our city-issued Dodge Charger was murdered by the Schuylkiller. After killing the valet, the killer then drove north and killed Penny's mother and four other innocent people in the Fabrics Easter Fire. That brought the killer's victim total to ten."

Frank pointed to the screen and held a copy of the letter in his hand above his head, and said, "Now, let's dissect this letter."

Frank again pointed to the seventy-inch monitor and broke down several aspects of the letter that would help make a case for the Schuylkiller's motives.

"If you look closely, everyone. I have emboldened all the capital letters, excluding the number 2 and the letter C, when they appear side by side in the letter. The number 2 and the letter C that you see are clear references to Penny's late mother's apartment, 2C."

Visible on the screen for the group was the contents of the letter verbatim:

"getting 2Close for comfort. sorry About the Fancy dinner. shouLd have stuck to tinder. nice car. your teNacity, eye CouLdn't take! COme visit When you can. be 2C'ing u in the pApers tomorrow, big shot!"

"The capital letters, when laid out in order, are as follows," said Frank.

"A-F-L-N-C-L-C-O-W-A"

"When you unscramble these letters and use every letter to form a word, you can only come up with....."

Frank clicked to advance the slide. The word revealed to the group was F-A-L-C-O-N-C-L-A-W.

"Where is FalconClaw located? In Germantown!" Frank was animated. "The killer has been leading us there since he purposely dumped Belinda Mereby's purse and Daniel Oliver's wallet just south of Old Germantown. His letter, left on my windshield, was an invitation to me."

Except for Captain Sumner, everyone in the room gasped, including Penny. Even Brooks and Cole, who'd breached the basement of FalconClaw with Frank just seven days earlier, weren't aware of the contents in the letter that was left for Frank and Penny.

"Now, to be clear," said Frank. "I'm unable to translate the entire letter for you, but it's clear that the place where Penny and her mother lived was apartment 2C. And the word FalconClaw is clearly spelled out," he added.

"I can tell you now that I believe the Schuylkiller has a list of five people that he intends to kill. His motive?" Frank raised his brow and said, "Revenge."

Subdued chatter could be heard as the detective group processed the information.

"I believe our killer has a second list that includes two more people." Frank purposely paused to ensure he made eye contact with everyone in the room before revealing the names on the second list.

"Detective Frank Collazo and Detective Penny Bristow," Frank revealed the name of he and Penny on a new slide.

Audible gasps could be heard as the room exploded in commentary and, for some, doubt.

"Come on, that's a little over the top!" Someone in the group yelled over the other voices. Others perceived it as vain of Frank to arrive at such a conclusion.

Captain Sumner stood up and yelled, "Calm down, everyone! I'm presuming that Frank has a perfectly good reason for his claim. And I, for one, would like to hear it, myself."

Sumner looked back at Frank and raised her brow. Her expression told Frank that what he had to say better be good.

"To everyone in attendance here, except for two or three of you, I would like to disclose two things that you may not have known." Frank was riddled with nerves, but his exterior didn't show it. "One, in nineteen ninety-two, my father Salvatore Collazo was murdered by a serial killer named Vincent Charmaine Walker in the basement of FalconClaw."

With Frank's admission, the room went quiet, and stunned silence filled the faces of those in attendance. Many were shocked and quickly tried to piece together the letter from the Schuylkiller and the murder of Frank's father. After another moment, someone else yelled out, "Why Penny, then?"

Frank raised his hand again and said, "In 1974, the first-ever female detective in the history of the Philadelphia Police Department went missing from FalconClaw. Some think at the hands of a notorious serial killer named Garrison O'Donnell, and Penny Bristow was named after Penelope Bryce."

While the chatter died down a little, there were still several skeptics in the room. Frank made eye contact with Penny and saw that her mouth was agape.

"I have more information to share with you that will assist you in connecting the dots," said Frank. "I have been in touch with the Schuylkiller personally, and he has validated some of the assertions that I have made here today."

The detectives in the crowd were shocked. Sitting more quietly now and shaking their heads in disbelief, they looked up when Frank continued sharing information of which many were unaware of.

"I went to FalconClaw alone on Monday the 17th," revealed Frank. "And then again, on the 19th, with seven other men. Two of those men included Robert Brooks and John Cole, both sitting in the front, here to my left," Frank motioned.

"We breached the basement and found the rotting carcasses of recently killed animals. Dogs, deer, and rabbits. I believe some of our victims may have been killed there, and the smell of the human decomposition was masked by the dead animals that were likely placed there purposely."

"On Monday," Frank continued, "another person was abducted. We believe it was the work of the Schuylkiller. An image of a man with his name spelled out appeared on the screen behind Frank. The victim's name? Martin Stanbey. That's pronounced STAN-BEE."

"Stanbey is a lawyer whose father, Colten Stanbey, worked as co-counsel with Clinton Mereby for the plaintiffs in the case brought about in the, you guessed it, the MK Ultra scandal."

"Stanbey was out walking his dog just days after an extended European vacation when he was abducted near his house in guess where?" Frank asked the group. "Valley View Road up in Chestnut Hill, just two miles from FalconClaw."

"While I'm not an expert in criminal profiling, I know someone who is, and he's willing to help us find our killer," said Frank. "Would everyone please welcome the legendary founder of the FBI's Behavioral Science Unit, Douglas Cantrell!" Frank looked to the back of the room and acknowledged his special guest.

Cantrell had slipped into the room unnoticed just minutes earlier.

Frank began to clap as everyone turned toward the back of the room to see the seventy-one-year-old legendary criminal psychologist and serial killer hunter.

"Doug has interviewed more than one hundred serial killers and worked closely with the legendary 39th District Detective Frank Bruno! Together, they solved several of the most notorious cases in the City of Philadelphia's history."

"Doug, the room is yours!"

Cantrell, dressed in a tweed jacket and carrying a leather satchel, walked to the front of the room, shaking hands with those along the way.

Chapter 27 – School's Out

It was June 2, 2017, the last day of school for Conner, and Frank would be there to see him get on the bus in the morning and then off again in the afternoon. After school, Frank, Joanne, Conner, and Joanne's parents would spend the weekend at the cabin in Tyler State Park.

It'd been thirty-nine days since Martin Stanbey vanished without a trace, and things seemed eerily quiet in North Philly. Street crime was down as people laid low with the serial killer on the loose. Even the bad guys were in fear for their safety.

There was no sign of the Schuylkiller, no ominous messages left on car windshields, and no random phone calls. Nothing. The Schuylkiller had gone dark again.

Frank hadn't slept in his apartment above the Mad River Bar & Grill since the Schuylkiller had been there more than six weeks earlier. Most nights, he stayed at Joanne's and slept on the floor next to Conner's bed.

Frank's cellphone alarm went off at 4:45 am. After getting up, he'd get a shower and then head up to Joanne's and be there in plenty of time to help get Conner ready and then onto the bus at 7:15 am. The bus stop was located directly in front of the neighbor's house just east of Joanne's.

Before Frank could sit up in bed, he had to gently remove two cats that were lying on top of him. It was now 4:49 am, and he wanted nothing more than to hit the snooze button and sleep for another eight minutes. This day, however, was a big day. Conner had completed the fifth grade after struggling mightily with ADHD, and it was his last day of elementary school. In the fall, he'd be going into middle school.

As Frank's feet hit the floor, his elbows met his knees, and he just sat there and rubbed his eyes. After his eyes adjusted to the dark room, Frank pulled the sheet back and saw that he was naked but didn't remember going to bed that way.

Just then, a hand found Frank's back in the darkness and stroked it from his shoulder down to his bottom.

"You're not leaving this early, are you?"

"Yeah," said Frank. "Remember, I told you it's Conner's last day of school today."

"Oh, yeah. Can't miss that one."

Frank stood, and his chiseled glutes were on display, and a sultry voice behind him said, "You sure you don't have a quick ten minutes for me?"

Frank ignored the question and looked around for his underwear. "Where are my damn boxers?" he asked, checking the floor at his feet and then under the bed behind him.

Pulling back the blankets and smiling seductively, Cindy Stafford said, "I stole them from you last night. How do you not remember that?" she smiled flirtatiously.

Frank looked at Cindy, who was wearing nothing but his underwear, and said, "Those look a lot better on you than they do me."

"I like them best when they're lying on the floor at the foot of my bed," she smiled.

"Me, too." Frank launched a reluctant smile and said, "But I gotta go."

After a quick shower and getting dressed, Frank went to Cindy's side of the bed and kissed her goodbye.

"Don't open that door for anyone. Got it?" asked Frank.

"Call the super and have him walk you out to the street."

"Yeah-yeah," said a sleepy Stafford.

"I'll stop by the daycare later this morning."

"Okay, Frankie," said Stafford. "I love you, Babe."

Frank shook his head as he headed for the door. Opening it, he whispered to himself, "I love you? Jesus Christ, we hardly know each other."

The time was 5:25, and the sun was on the rise in the East Falls section of North Philly, and Frank was excited to see his little man and wanted to be there before he woke up. When Frank couldn't be there, Vance Conroy stayed overnight and kept his shotgun nearby.

Sitting at the Dobson Mills Apartments' entrance, Penny's old place, ready to turn left onto Ridge, Frank stared across the street to his right at the front of the Creative Minds Daycare. His memory flashed back to January and its rear parking lot.

In his head, Frank could see the sinister smile of the Schuylkiller standing there, holding a hose. He recalled the man's words. 'Sorry about that, Detective. I was just washing the bus. I didn't know anyone was over there.'

Frank thought to himself, *"That son of a bitch knew I was a detective. He must've been on my tail since the beginning of the investigation."*

Snapping out of his funk, Frank took a left on Ridge heading down to Scotts and then another left heading north. Minutes later, while on Abbotsford Avenue passing the Queen Lane Reservoir, Frank let the Dodge Interceptor fly. The roar of its engine made the sound of someone running scared. That, someone, was Frank Collazo, and he didn't know if he was running toward something, or running from someone.

Twenty minutes later, Frank turned off York and onto his old street. Seconds later, he pulled into the driveway behind Joanne's house and then conducted his normal inspection of the house's perimeter to ensure nothing was amiss.

He entered the house and turned off the alarm, and took off his shoes in the mudroom, just off the kitchen. At that moment, a light went on, and his ex-wife, wearing only a robe, entered the kitchen to investigate who'd come in.

"Oh, God! You scared me, Frank!" Joanne was startled when seeing her ex-husband.

"Joanne," Frank smiled. "If you hear the alarm being turned off, then you know it's your dad, or me."

"I know, but I'm afraid of my own shadow these days. I just can't wait for things to get back to normal."

"So, when are you guys heading up to Michigan, anyways?" asked Frank.

"Next Wednesday," said Joanne. "I figured two days back from the cabin, and then Mom, Dad, Conner, and I will hit the road."

"Is Sue excited you're coming?"

"You know, my smart-ass sister," Joanne smirked. "She said I could only come as long as no mass murderers tagged along."

"That shit's not even funny." Frank shook his head as he opened the refrigerator door.

"So," Joanne shot Frank a curious look. "Stayed at Cindy's place again, huh? Things must be getting serious between you two?" she raised a curious brow.

Frank pulled out a quart of orange juice and said, "No!"

"That's like the third time in the last week you spent the night there." Joanne smiled. She was happy for Frank. She knew he needed a distraction from his tumultuous year. But she also felt a little jealous.

Frank poured a glass of OJ and sat at the kitchen table. Looking over to his ex, he said, "Yeah, well, I may have gotten myself in too deep. That girl actually told me she loved me before I left this morning." Frank nervously chuckled. "Can you believe that?"

"Cindy's got it bad for old Frankie Boy!" Joanne busted Frank's chops, but inside she was envious. Her new relationship with Conner's teacher was fizzling out. "I remember those days," she said. "I don't think you and I saw the outside of your bedroom for the first month we dated."

"It's only been six weeks since I met the woman, and she's already saying I love you?" Frank shook his head in disbelief.

"You guys are like Whitney Houston and Kevin Costner," Joanne giggled. "She's got her own little personal bodyguard."

"You're in rare form today, Jo. So what's up with you and Polly anyways?"

"Things are good between us, but I'll tell you this right now, I'm not gay." Joanne shook her head with the admission. "I thought I was, for about five seconds, but....nope. Not gay."

"Oh, yeah?" said Frank. "To be honest with you, I never did wrap my head around it. It just didn't seem like you."

"Well, listen. My engine could use a little tune-up, so when you get a minute away from your little high school sweetheart over there, throw me a little sympathy sex, would you?"

Frank shook his head in astonishment and smiled. "For the love of God, Joanne, you're in rare form this morning. What's gotten into you?"

"Certainly not you. At least not lately." Joanne chuckled and winked at her ex.

"What in the hell is up with you?" Frank again shook his head and blushed a little.

"Where's Vance, anyway? Frank asked. "You better hope he's not right around the corner."

Joanne smiled back, flashed Frank a boob, and then laughed it off.

"Joanne! What the fuck?!" Frank whispered.

"I'm just saying," said Joanne. "I'm not asking for a ring, or anything. Just a little somethin-somethin before I hit the road." She laughed again while putting on a pot of coffee.

Frank didn't know whether she was serious or not. He again shook his head in disbelief.

"You want me to go get Conner up for you?" he asked.

Looking at the kitchen clock above the sink, she said, "Would you? That'd be great. It's almost 6:15, and I'm gonna make chocolate chip pancakes for him. He finished the year so strong," she said. "I'm so proud of him!"

"Me, too. And he got his grades up despite everything that's been going on," said Frank. "No little kid should have to go through what I've put him through this year."

For the first time in years, Joanne was empathetic toward Frank and his job. "Frank, go easy on yourself. Life's fucked up, and you're trying to make it better."

"Jo, our family is in danger because of me. Because I took the case. Because I'm a detective." Frank finally put himself in Joanne's shoes and realized that everything was his fault.

Joanne walked over to Frank and softly said, "Frank, we'll get through this. Together. Just keep yourself alive," she said. "Conner doesn't need to go through life without his father like you have."

Frank looked distraught and shook his head in defeat. Joanne recognized his pain, put her arms around her ex-husband, and squeezed. After the mutual hug, the two pulled back slightly and stared into each other's eyes. At that moment, they were together again, back to a time before life stepped in and messed everything up. Joanne closed her eyes and kissed Frank, and he kissed her back.

During that kiss, the two were taken to a place where serial killers and mortgages didn't exist, where every day was a blessing and not a curse. A time when they ran toward the future instead of running from their past.

"Ahem!" Vance Conroy cleared his throat loudly as he walked into the room.

Embarrassed, the two quickly separated like they did the first time Joanne's father caught them kissing many years ago. Both blushed, smiled, and said nothing.

"What's the matter? Cat got your tongues?" said Conroy.

"Oh, dad." Joanne sighed. "We were just having a moment together."

"Yeah, well, your gonna confuse that little boy upstairs," her father rolled his eyes and went for the coffee pot.

"That's the kind of confusion that would make him smile, though. Right?" Frank jabbed at his ex-father-in-law.

"Frank, I probably never told you this before but, the secret to life is...."

"The successful management of people's expectations!" Joanne and Frank chorused together loudly. They finished his sentence and rolled their eyes at the comment they'd heard dozens of times before.

"Yeah, Dad. We got it." Joanne smiled as her father handed her ex-husband a cup of coffee.

"Is Conner up yet?" asked Joanne.

"Yeah," said Conroy. "He's getting dressed. He's pretty excited about today. That little guy didn't need us waking him up this morning, that's for sure."

"I'll go up and check on him," said Frank.

A few minutes later, Frank walked into the upstairs bathroom and saw his son combing his hair. Conner ran his comb under the running water and then stroked it against his scalp, trying to get his cowlick to go in the right direction.

"Hey, Buddy," Frank said in a soft voice. "Big day, today, huh?"

Conner was frustrated. "Dad, I can't get my dang hair to go the right way."

"Here, let me help." Frank studied his son's hair and then took the comb and knelt in front of him.

"Why does my hair do that, anyway?"

"They call that a cowlick, Son." Frank wet the comb and parted Conner's hair.

"A what?"

"A cowlick."

"Why?" asked Conner.

"Because it looks like a cow walked right up to you and licked your forehead. That's why." Frank smiled.

Conner looked confused. "That's disgusting, Dad!"

"You're hair looks great, Son!" Frank gently wiped a drop of water off of Conner's forehead and left cheek. "You ready for your big day today?"

"Yeah!" Conner now seemed excited. "We're gonna do lots of things, and we won't even have homework! Polly said we get to play games outside and that there's even gonna be Cotton Candy for everyone!"

"Wow! Cotton Candy, huh?!" Frank shared in his son's enthusiasm.

"Yeah, Polly's great!"

"Conner, you make sure you call her Miss Gray and not Polly while you're at school. You got that?"

"Dad, everyone knows that her and mom are together." Conner rolled his eyes.

"Conner, it's Miss Gray when you're at school. Do you understand me?"

"Yes, Dad, I got it." Conner rolled his eyes again.

Frank stood and said, "Where's your backpack?"

"Mudroom," Conner replied as he ran into his bedroom.

Frank followed and witnessed Conner jotting a note on a scratchpad in his nightstand. Frank said nothing as his son ran back past him out the door, yelling, "I'll be downstairs!"

Curious, Frank walked over to the nightstand and opened the drawer. Seeing the notepad, he pulled it out and inspected the pages, wondering what his son had written.

Turning to a page that was earmarked, Frank's heart was broken. The page was titled, 'Days Since Daddy Left Home.'

Frank didn't need to add the tallies. He knew that it'd almost been a year since he'd moved out the prior July. Tearing up, he flipped the page and saw the heading, 'Days Until Daddy Comes Back.'

Holding back his tears, he counted the days. It was thirty-eight. Frank was now reminded of the anniversary that he'd moved out. It was July 10, 2016.

As Frank closed the notepad, a tear fell from his eye and left a watermark on the date. He panicked for a moment, thinking that Conner would know he'd been in his drawer. Then a sense of calm came over him as he'd promised himself that when Conner discovered the tear stain that he would be there to explain it to him.

Seconds later, Frank heard Joanne call for him. "Frank, it's almost time!"

Frank rejoined his family downstairs and said, "Ready to go, Son?"

"Ready, Dad!" Conner wiped his mouth and jumped up from his chair at the table.

Joanne smiled and shook her head in Frank's direction. That indicated to Frank that Conner didn't want anyone walking him to the bus.

Frank pretended that he wasn't tipped off and knelt down next to Conner as his son tied his shoes. Okay, Con-man. It's time for me to walk you to the bus, just like the first and last day of every other school year."

"Daaaad!" Conner threw his head and hands into the air. "I'm going into middle school. It's embarrassing when you do that."

Frank pleaded his case and tried hard to look sad. "Conner, come on! Just this one last time."

"No, Dad! I'm too old for that." Conner was adamant.

"All right, fine," said Frank. "Can I at least walk you out and stand on the front porch?"

"Fine," said Conner, holding up his index finger, pointing it at his father. "But you're not allowed off of the porch."

"Deal!" said Frank.

"Now, let's go," Conner demanded. "I want to be first in line getting on the bus."

"Okie-dokie," said Frank.

Frank looked at Joanne and then the clock thinking it was a few minutes too early to walk outside. Joanne just smiled and shrugged her shoulders.

It was now 7:05, and Conner gave his mom and grandfather a kiss goodbye, and he and his dad walked out the front door.

Frank knelt to face his son and said, "Conner, I want you to know that I'm proud of you and that I'm always going to be here for you. I love you, Son."

Conner said, "I love you, too, Dad. I can't wait until you and Mom get back together."

Frank said nothing, not wanting to lie to Conner, and instead gave his son a long hug.

Just then, at 7:10 am, a bus rolled to a stop in front of the neighbor's house, and Conner went running for it.

Joanne and her father stood just inside the door and joined Frank in witnessing Conner get on the bus.

Conner slowed to a stop as the bus door opened. His head strangely tilted to one side as he looked up at the driver. He paused for a moment before eventually looking back at his father. Smiling, he waved goodbye and stepped up onto the bus. The bus door closed, and it roared down the road out of sight.

Frank followed the bus down the street with his eyes until it'd gone. Normally he'd expect to see little heads bopping around inside the bus, but from his vantage point, the bus looked strangely empty.

Behind him, the screened door opened, and Joanne walked out and handed her ex-husband a cup of coffee.

Frank grabbed the cup and remarked, "God, the years go by so fast!"

"He's getting so big, Frank." Joanne shook her head in disbelief and wrapped her arm around Frank's lower back, with her head coming to a rest on his left shoulder.

The two stood on the porch and took in their surroundings, taking a deep breath between each sip of coffee. Just before walking back inside, the two witnessed a neighbor boy, named Frankie Markham, run toward the bus stop from his house across the street. Before Joanne could remark that the little boy missed the bus, Tiffani Mackie, another neighborhood child, ran from her house, just three doors down, and joined Frankie at the bus stop.

Frank looked at Joanne, both exchanging a confused look.

"What's going on?" said Joanne, shaking her head.

"I'm confused." Frank wasn't sure what was happening.

Frank and Joanne's trepidation grew with the roar of an approaching bus.

As the bus stopped and the now three children boarded it, Joanne looked at the bus number, and it was 8, Conner's bus.

Frank's face went white as his mind flashed back to when he'd interviewed Cindy Stafford about the Schuylkiller. Cindy told him that George St. Croix became the daycare's regular bus driver when the Pre-K kids went on field trips.

Frank went into slow motion as his head grew heavy and his sight grew dim. Standing frozen, he lost control of his senses, and his coffee cup fell to the ground.

At that moment, Frank was standing in front of the scarred fence in the backyard of 454 E. Locust Avenue, his childhood home. Behind him, his house was ablaze, and he could hear Bonnie Ross screaming for help. Looking to his left, Frank could see Penny sobbing uncontrollably, pleading for him to help. Turning to his right, he saw his father, Salvatore Collazo, who was also weeping. Through his father's tears, Frank heard him say, "I'm sorry, Son."

Frank could feel his heart being squeezed by his chest. As he looked back at the scarred fence, it too was now on fire. As he stared through the flames, he could see the silhouette of the Schuylkiller. And he was laughing.

Chapter 28 – Sins of the Father

FalconClaw – The Sleep Room – April 24, 2017, 11:46 pm – Six weeks earlier.

St. John carried a body bag containing an unconscious and badly beaten Martin Stanbey over his shoulder and dropped it at the exterior basement door to FalconClaw. When the bag hit the ground, Stanbey could be heard moaning inside.

Just minutes prior, St. John removed Stanbey from the trunk of his car, which was parked on Old Olmsted Trail, a retired jogging path that was now mostly grown over with weeds and homeless people.

The walk between the path and the rear of the old mansion was roughly one hundred yards. It was a walk St. John had taken many times before, hundreds of times, in fact, dating back to the mid-1980s when he was a small child. St. John would accompany his father Gregory on morning walks before the elder St. John would go to work at the Heavenly Gates Retirement Home. Gregory St. John served as an on-site physician and was charged with caring for the elderly from 1985 to the spring of 1990, when he was unceremoniously terminated after it was determined who his father and grandfather were.

On August 8, 1990, his son's sixteenth birthday, Gregory St. John, died by hanging. Still alive, squirming at the end of his rope, his only son was unable to save him.

St. John unlocked the cellar door and threw the body bag, with Martin Stanbey still in it, down the brick stairs leading into the bowels of FalconClaw. Stanbey grunted and groaned with each tumble until no more muffled sounds could be heard.

At the bottom of the steps, St. John pulled a set of night-vision goggles from behind a loose cinder block that would never be noticed or found unless someone knew it was there.

Donning his goggles, St. John closed the double doors behind him and lifted the body bag of the now-deceased Martin Stanbey, then placed it onto an old gurney. In the pitch-black basement that reeked of both human and animal decomposition, St. John wheeled the relic from the 1950s roughly fifty feet to the false wall that concealed the door to The Sleep Room.

Opening the door fully, St. John wheeled Stanbey's dead body to the center of the room. There, hanging from three large meat hooks, were three body bags containing the bodies of Belinda Mereby, Daniel Oliver, and Keith Carpenter. After using a metal hand crank to lower the bar containing the five meat hooks, St. John hung the fourth body bag on the fourth hook and then hoisted the four corpses back up to the ceiling.

Looking up and admiring his work, St. John whispered to himself, "The last of the five will join you four in good time."

After sealing the door with the false wall, St. John recited a phrase he'd been reciting since he was eighteen years old. "Patience is a virtue to man, and patients are a virtue to doctors. When my father lost his patients to men, I lost my patience for man."

"I will no longer carry the burden of the sins of my father's, father's, father."

After concealing his night-vision goggles back into place and locking the cellar door at the rear of FalconClaw behind him, St. John again spoke to himself. Turning to walk back toward Old Olmsted Trail, he said, "I will have my revenge with the first five, and I will then have my glory with the final two."

As the Schuylkiller walked away from the mansion, the large cinder block, concealing his goggles, slid away from its housing as if pushed by an unseen force, revealing itself to the next visitor to hell. As St. John cut across the western grounds of the estate, a chilling wind blew up from behind him and stopped him in his tracks. Looking back to the mansion, he could almost swear he'd heard two old men talking to each other.

It was now Tuesday, April 25, and Frank was preparing for his presentation to detectives of the 39th and 5th the following day. Working in the Detective Room, he was approached by Kyle Wade and Cindy McCurdy.

"Frank, Cindy and I are at your full disposal," said Kyle Wade.

"The Captain has officially shelved the Frank Bruno disappearance until the Schuylkiller has been either apprehended or killed." Cindy McCurdy was matter of fact. "As Kyle said, we're all yours."

"What?" Frank wasn't thrilled. "So the greatest detective in the history of the 39th just gets cast aside like any other cold case?" Frank was disgusted.

"Frank, listen," said Wade. "We've been on it for months. He's a ghost. He just disappeared into thin air. There's no place for us to look," reasoned Kyle Wade.

"Fine, follow me then."

Frank walked back to his desk and said, "Listen, I got a lead on a guy named St. John. I think he's the Schuylkiller. This is an employee file for a guy named George St. Croix." Frank handed the file to Kyle.

Kyle Wade handed the file to McCurdy, and she flipped through the contents.

"So, what's the deal with this St. Croix?" asked Wade.

"I think St. Croix is an alias. I think St. John and St. Croix are the same man, the Schuylkiller." Frank looked confident with his assertion.

"So, we run down the alias and see if we can link him to some guy named St. John, right?" asked McCurdy.

"Yeah, and I need you to link St. John to FalconClaw. Go as far back as the seventies and eighties when it was also known as Heavenly Gates. I think our killer is somehow connected to the place," said Frank.

"You think?" asked Wade.

Frank looked Wade and McCurdy in the eye and said, "I know it! Now you two find the connection while I go find and kill that motherfucker."

Cindy McCurdy recoiled and took a step back, allowing Frank to pass by her. "Whoa! That man is on a mission," she said.

Kyle Wade said, "You heard the man. Let's get busy."

As Frank walked out of the Detective Room, he yelled back to Wade and McCurdy. "Hey, Kyle! Hey Cindy! Don't bother me with anything less than a St. John FalconClaw connection, or if you find Detective Frank Bruno!"

"Okay, then." Cindy McCurdy raised her brows. "Let's get to work."

What Frank Collazo didn't know is that he would soon discover both.

Chapter 29 – Panic

June 2, 2017 – Where's Conner?

Her heart racing, Joanne ran into the house to get her cellphone. Before she could dial the school's number, she saw a text alert on her phone from the school. The message read: *Issue with our buses – DO NOT place your child on a Cheltenham Township School Bus until you have been notified that the issue is resolved. All buses have been recalled from their morning route. Please call the school for more details OR if your child boarded a bus this morning.*

Joanne frantically dialed the school's number, but all lines were busy. She immediately ran out the front door to tell Frank about the text with her father in tow. When she got to the front porch, Frank was gone. Seconds later, she heard the engine of the Dodge Charger roar as it turned off of 12th Street onto Valley Road, tires spinning and car fishtailing, as it zoomed past the house in the direction of the bus.

Frank's heart was pounding. He knew Conner was in jeopardy, and he'd known that the Schuylkiller had driven buses before. It was his fault, again, he thought.

An incoming call flashed on his phone screen. It was Joanne. Frank ignored the call and instead called the Cheltenham Township Police Chief, whose cellphone number he'd saved from their previous conversation.

After three rings, Chief Darren McMichael answered and said, "McMichael, here!"

"Chief! This is Frank Collazo, and I'm on Valley Road heading southeast. My son just boarded a bus that he wasn't supposed to be on, and I suspect foul play."

"Frank, it's early, but I just got a call to come in to the station. The school has notified us that one of their buses was stolen early this morning. They're recalling all of their buses now. Why do you suspect that your son is in danger?" asked the Chief.

"Chief, you're forgetting that my family is the target of a madman! I believe the bus my son boarded was empty. His actual bus pulled up just minutes after the bus he boarded pulled away. I think it's the Schuylkiller!"

"Now hold on a second, Frank. We don't know that, and it's best not to panic in this situation."

"Chief, I'm thinking very clearly right now, and I need you to get every police and city vehicle on the road and stop every single bus they see! I'm not in a panic!"

"Well, dammit, Frank." The Chief exhaled fully, weighing his options before continuing.

"Chief, I see a bus! I'll call you right back! Get the cars on the road!"

Chief McMichael tried to speak, but the call ended.

Frank turned on his dashboard flashers and floored it. Zooming by the bus, he pulled in front of it and slammed on his brakes, causing it to swerve off of the road, hitting a mailbox before it came to rest.

Frank jumped out of his car, weapon in right hand, badge in the other, and ordered the driver to open the door.

The bus door opened and revealed a woman with both hands extended in the air, wearing a look of terror. As Frank leaped up the three steps to the top of the bus, he looked back to see more than a dozen children crying and holding each other. Conner wasn't one of them.

"Dammit!" Frank screamed. "I'm sorry!" He then jumped back down off the bus, got back into his car, and sped away.

Over the next ten minutes, Frank had crossed paths with more than five buses and noticed that they all seemed to be filled with children. He knew the bus he was looking for would only have one passenger, Conner.

Frank called the Chief back, and he answered on the first ring.

"Chief! Whatta we know?!" Frank was distraught.

"Frank, all but six of the buses in service today have returned to the school. The other buses are being stopped by our people where possible," said the Chief. "We're doing everything we can. I believe you, Frank. I've put out an APB on the bus to every county in eastern PA. That includes the Staties. We know the stolen bus is a Cheltenham Township bus, and the number on the bus is 16. That should make it easy to identify."

"Okay, Chief, listen," Frank tried to remain calm, "tell your folks to go slow once they spot that bus. This guy has killed or kidnapped eleven people, and now my son."

"Frank, you be careful, too. I know you're out looking for that bus right now. You call for backup if you find it before we do," cautioned McMichael. "I'll call you hourly with updates. If you try to get me, I may not answer for obvious reasons."

"Thanks, Chief!"

Frank hung up and called Joanne back.

Joanne picked up the phone on the first ring and was hysterical. Crying, she screamed into the phone, "Frank, a bus was stolen! Frank! He's got our son, Frank! What do we do?!" she screamed into the phone.

"Joanne, listen." Frank tried to be calm. "I'm out looking for Conner right now. The Cheltenham Police are stopping every bus on the road, and there is an All-Points Bulletin in place right now. Everyone in Pennsylvania and New Jersey is looking for that bus, Joanne. Stay calm, and I'll call you with more information as soon as I get it. I love you, Joanne. I'm going to find our son."

Through her tears and anguish, Joanne yelled, "This is your fault, Frank! You bring my baby home to me!"

Frank felt sick. His wife was right. It was his fault, and he had to find his son and bring him home safely.

"Joanne, I'll find Conner, I promise."

"Frank, this is Vance." Conroy had taken the phone from Joanne. "What in the hell is going on?" Frank's father-in-law was livid but calm. He didn't want to lose control in front of his daughter.

"Vance, listen to me. Conner boarded a stolen bus. It was bus number16. The locals and state authorities are looking for it now," said Frank. "I believe it's the Schuylkiller, Vance. I'm not coming home until Conner is safe with me."

"You're damned right you're not." Conroy was tempered in his delivery. "You bring my grandson home to his mother. And you make sure he's in good health when you do."

Frank said, "I'll call every thirty minutes with updates...."

The call was abruptly disconnected.

Frank knew that it was him versus the Schuylkiller. Nothing else mattered. The Schuylkiller would die at the hands of Frank Collazo.

Frank immediately thought to call Douglas Cantrell, who answered the phone after only one ring.

"Frank, it's early. Are you calling about the missing bus?!" Cantrell was tuned into CNN.

"Doug, he's got my son."

"What? Who?" Cantrell paused to process Frank's words. "Oh my God! Conner was on that bus? They didn't say it was a child abduction on the news." Cantrell was shocked. "Frank, they've got helicopters in the air. You can't hide a school bus for very long. They'll find him, Frank!"

"Where's he taking my boy, Doug?" Frank was calm but determined.

"Frank, I don't know. Hmm, let me think here." Douglas Cantrell didn't have an answer for Frank. He was still processing the fact that Conner had been abducted.

Frank suddenly exploded into the phone. "Where's my son?! You're the expert! Tell me where he took him!"

Cantrell understood Frank's emotional state. He didn't take the harsh words personally.

"Frank, let me think for a second." Cantrell racked his brain. "He likely ditched the bus and transferred Conner into another vehicle. He won't take him down to FalconClaw, though. He's reserving that for his list of five, and you." Cantrell paused again. "Frank, he's going to take Conner to a safehouse. I don't think he'll hurt him. I think he's trying to show you that he can get to you and your family. He needs you, Frank. He needs to control you. Having your son is his way of doing that."

"Are you sure?" Frank was calmer.

"No, I can't be sure. I'm applying human psychology and forty years of studying the minds of sociopaths," said Cantrell. "My gut is telling me that Conner won't be harmed, at least not in the short-term."

"So, where then? Where is he taking him?"

"I don't know, Frank." Cantrell was at a loss. "I only know it won't be FalconClaw or any of the other crime scenes. Conner is different. He'll change his Modus Operandi for this situation."

"I don't know what to do, Doug. I'm lost." Frank teared up. "He's got my son."

"Frank, let me get on the phone and see if we can get more resources thrown at this," said Cantrell. "I'm going to put a call into the Bureau. Let me call you back in a little while."

"Okay. I'll call you if I hear anything." Frank was despondent.

As Cantrell hung up the phone, he could see a 'Breaking News' alert on his television. The caption stated: *BUS FOUND in nearby Lorimer Park.*

Cantrell watched as helicopters hovered over a densely wooded area, and through the trees, the unmistakable yellow color of a school bus could be seen peeking through. Cantrell knew they'd found the bus but was Conner in it? That question had Cantrell fear-stricken.

Sitting in his car, Frank called Penny, and she picked up on the first ring.

"He's got him, Penny. He's got Conner." Frank was dejected. He was resigned to the fact that he'd never see his son alive again.

"Frank, what are you talking about?" It took Penny a moment before she realized that Conner was involved in the stolen bus incident that had occurred just sixty minutes earlier. The news was still breaking, and it hadn't been announced yet that a child had been abducted.

"I watched it happen, Penny. I watched Conner get on that bus. That son of a bitch watched me stand there as he took my child."

"Frank, what's going on?" said Penny. "Where are you, right now?"

The call ended abruptly as Penny asked the question.

It was now 8:15 am, and Conner had been missing for sixty-five minutes, and Frank answered his call-waiting.

"Hello?" Frank answered the call when he saw that it was the Cheltenham Police Chief.

"Frank, it's Chief McMichael. Listen, we found the bus."

Frank lost his breath. His heart felt frozen, and he was unable to respond. He couldn't fathom that the bus would be found so quickly, and he wasn't sure he wanted to hear what the Chief was about to say next.

"Conner wasn't in the bus, Frank. There are no signs of where he might have taken your son, but we're working hard to figure it all out."

"How? Working hard, how?" Frank demanded to know.

"Frank, you've got friends in high places. The FBI just contacted us and asked if they could assist with the search," explained McMichael. "I accepted their offer. They'll be on-site within the hour."

"Thanks, Chief."

"Frank, go to your wife. There's nothing you can do at this moment. We've got guys on the ground and in the air. I'll keep you posted."

"Where was the bus found? I need to be there. I need to be part of the search." Frank was at his wit's end. He didn't know what to do.

"Campers were alarmed when they saw a school bus ditched in the park. When they saw helicopters overhead, they called it in," McMichael explained.

"Where?! Where was it found?!"

"Lorimer Park, near the Pennyback Pavilion, just off Pine Road, near the old Fox Chase Farm. I'll radio my guys manning the roadblock. They'll let you through."

"That's just a few miles from me. I'm on my way, Chief." Frank had hope that Conner was still alive. "Thanks for everything you're doing."

"Frank."

"Yeah?"

"Do you know who Walter Scott is?"

"Yeah, he's the dog breeder, right?"

"Yeah, he's committed his hounds to the search. It's early in the day, but people are coming out of the woodwork to help out. We're going to find Conner, Frank. We're going to find your boy."

"Thanks, Chief." Frank's excitement was subdued.

Frank called Penny back before pulling off the narrow shoulder near Cedar Road and Shelmire Street.

"Penny, sorry about that. I had to take that call. They found the bus, but Conner wasn't on it. I don't know where he took my son."

"Frank!" Penny couldn't control her excitement. "We got a name! Frank, we got a name!"

Frank didn't know what to say. "Whaaa-aaat? What do you mean? Who? What?" he was confused.

"Frank, Wade and McCurdy made a connection between St. John and FalconClaw early this morning. They worked on it overnight. Check your texts!" Penny's voice was animated.

Frank didn't know what to do. He had to join the ground search for his son, but the Schuylkiller's true identity might reveal his whereabouts.

"We've got an address, too. Units are on the way," said Penny. "He owns a home between Penn Knox and Germantown. It's on the corner of Schoolhouse Lane and Wayne Avenue, right across the street from the Germantown House. House number 5446!"

"Jesus Christ, Penny!" Frank was stunned. "That's just a half-mile from McMichael Park and only two blocks from Fabrics!"

"I know, Frank. I'm gonna be sick."

Frank's phone pinged in his ear. It was an incoming call. He looked at his phone, and the screen flashed *Unknown Caller.*

"Penny, I gotta go! Someone is beeping in. It could be information about Conner."

"Okay, Frank. Call me back!"

Frank swiped right and took the call. "This is Frank Collazo."

"Hello, old friend." The voice was deep and rich. It was a voice that was familiar to Frank.

Frank recognized the Schuylkiller's voice immediately and was careful not to offend him or make overt demands. Frank first needed to know if Conner was alive. He also wouldn't disclose that he was in possession of the killer's street address.

"Do you have my son?"

"As a matter of fact, I do." The voice was robotic and mundane.

"Where are you?"

"Well, I can't tell you that, Frankie Boy. But I will say that the view from my window is absolutely lovely," said the killer. "Listen, Frank. I was hoping to make a little trade with you."

"How do I know he's alive?" Frank tried to remain calm.

"Just a moment, and I'll put him on the phone."

"Conner, it's your father. He would like to speak with you."

Frank could hear the killer's words though his phone was held away from his mouth.

The next thing Frank heard was the heartbreaking whimper of a child sobbing, unable to speak due to being in shock. Frank recognized the danger Conner was in as shock can be fatal if not treated.

"Conner, this is Dad. Listen, Son. You don't have to speak. I want to tell you that I'm coming for you, and you'll be home soon with me, mommy, and grandpa."

Frank could hear shallow, rapid breathing and tried to stay calm for his son. "Are you hurt anywhere?"

Conner couldn't speak. He just audibly conveyed a trembling moan. Frank knew he was in trouble and said, "Conner, I love you. Now let me talk to the man who's with you, Son."

The Schuylkiller got back on the line and said, "You see? I told you. Your son is alive and unharmed."

"How do I know he's unharmed?"

"Because I told you he was. Now listen to me. I have a deal for you."

"Please listen to me," Frank pleaded. "My son is in shock, and we need to make sure his condition improves, or he may die."

"The only way he dies is if you don't comply with my request...."

Frank cut off the killer. "Lay him down on his back and elevate his feet roughly twelve inches. If you have a blanket, please place it over him and keep him warm."

"Anything else I can do for you, Detective?" The Schuylkiller was dismissive and condescending.

"Listen to me," Frank again implored the killer. "Give him water. As much as he'll drink."

The Schuylkiller chuckled. "Perhaps I'll sprinkle some on him, just as I did to you back in January."

At that moment, Frank heard what he always knew to be true. The killer himself had confirmed that he was the man Frank saw in the rear parking lot of the Creative Minds Daycare. The man holding the hose was indeed the Schuylkiller. The only thing Frank didn't know now was his real name. He knew Penny and Kyle Wade held that key. He needed to buy time.

"Listen, If my son dies, then we don't have a deal." Frank was now in control of his wits. He knew that Conner was alive, and he would agree to anything the sociopath on the other end of the line asked him to do.

"I guess I'll render some aid to the little fella. He is looking a little pale," said the killer. I'm sure I can find a blanket somewhere around here. "I'll call you back in ten minutes," he paused. "Don't miss that call, Frankie Boy, or it's lights out for little Conner over here."

"Ten minutes," said Frank. "I'll be waiting."

Chapter 30 – The Connection

It killed Frank to hang up with the person who held his son's fragile life in his hands, but he needed to ensure Conner was cared for properly.

Frank Immediately called Penny back. He would seek any information that could give him leverage over the madman that held his son captive.

"Penny, you have ten minutes to tell me everything you know. After that, we'll figure it out. Start talking," said Frank.

"Okay, Frank," said Penny. "Listen, I'm going to put you on speaker. I'm in Captain Sumner's office, and Kyle and Cindy are with us. I'll have them break down what they've learned.

"Frank, it's Sumner. I'm sorry about your son. We're sending Search and Rescue's K-9 Unit up to assist the Cheltenham Police with the search. I've also got a marine unit on standby should the township, or the Staties need further assistance with any water searches up there."

"What about his house, Cap?"

"I've got a tactical unit surrounding the house now."

"They won't find Conner there." Frank could feel it in his gut. "I just spoke to the maniac, and he seemed unfamiliar with his surroundings."

"Well, we're gonna find out in a few short minutes."

"Thanks, Captain, but we're running out of time. I spoke with the Schuylkiller moments ago, and he's calling back in now less than eight minutes." Frank was in distress. "Kyle, give me what you've got and make it fast."

"Frank, it's Kyle. I'll have Cindy brief you as she's the one who made the connection."

"Hey Frank, it's Cindy. I'm going to rapid-fire here, as we don't have time for a Q&A. Stop me whenever you want."

"In 1985, a doctor named Gregory St. John began working at FalconClaw after it reopened as a retirement home, named Heavenly Gates, its former namesake twice before," explained McCurdy.

"St. John worked there from 1985 to 1990 until he was fired after it was determined that his father and grandfather had both worked at FalconClaw during the MK Ultra years."

"Okay," said Frank. "But I've seen the Schuylkiller, and he's not that old."

"Stay with me, Frank," said McCurdy.

"The reason St. John was terminated was because his father and grandfather were found guilty in the civil case against all those involved in the human experiments done at FalconClaw. The place was known as the Allan Institute during the years the experiments were conducted. They were the doctors who actually conducted the brainwashing and psychological torture," revealed Cindy.

Frank wasn't following. "But, I thought the guy running the show back then was a guy named Cameron."

"It was, Frank." Kyle Wade interjected. "Gregory St. John changed his name in the summer of 1975 after he'd lost his job as a medical resident at Temple University Hospital. Apparently, no organization wanted to employ someone associated with what happened at FalconClaw, and he became a pariah in the medical field."

"He changed his name to escape the stigma of his father's and grandfather's name. His birth name was Cameron. Gregory Ewen Cameron," Wade explained. "His father was John Ewen Cameron, and his grandfather was Donald Ewen Cameron. Both were contracted by the CIA and brought down from Montreal to conduct the experiments on marginalized patients."

Cindy McCurdy spoke back up. "Gregory Cameron, or Gregory St. John, earned his M.D. from Temple, and as Kyle said, served his residency at Temple University Hospital. Inside of a year, he was let go. He knew he wouldn't find work again with the last name of Cameron, so he legally changed it to St. John. And," McCurdy paused, "he changed his son's name, too," she said. "After that, he bounced around from job to job before ending up at Heavenly Gates in 1985."

Frank began to tremble. He knew the next thing Cindy McCurdy would reveal was the name of the Schuylkiller.

"His son's birth name, Getty Ewen Cameron, was changed when he was only one year old."

"What was it changed to, Cindy?" Frank needed a name.

"His name was changed to Cameron Ewen St. John in 1975, and he still holds that name today," revealed McCurdy.

"Son of a bitch!" Frank couldn't believe it.

The ghost at FalconClaw, the old man wearing the brown flannel shirt, told him the man he was looking for was named St. John. Who was the old man sitting in the armchair playing backgammon alone? It seemed to Frank that it may have been his guardian angel.

"Frank, this guy's a genius, earning his Ph.D. in 1997 at the age of only twenty-two. He got his M.D. in Clinical Psychology from Temple's Lewis Katz School of Medicine in 2000. He was only twenty-five years old."

"So, what happened to his father after he was fired from Heavenly Gates in 1990?" asked Frank.

"He hung himself, Frank," said McCurdy. "And guess who found his father dangling from the end of the rope, still alive?"

"The Schuylkiller." Frank's stomach turned with the revelation. He knew the monster that held his son captive was seeking justice for what his father had done to him. A justice that the sociopath would try to find by killing until his vengeful appetite was satisfied.

"Frank, he was only sixteen when he found his father. He couldn't save him. His father died on that rope with his son trying to hold him up," said McCurdy.

"Jesus Christ!" Frank was disgusted. "But why start killing today?" he wondered aloud.

"Frank, New Year's Eve was the anniversary of the verdict in the civil case from 1971. Part of the settlement was that Donald Ewen Cameron, and his son, would lose their licenses to practice medicine in both the United States and Canada. Then, on August 8, 1972, less than eight months later, while living in Sweden, the Schuylkiller's great-grandfather, Donald Ewen Cameron, hung himself at the age of 70. His son, John Ewen Cameron, also committed suicide by hanging, on the same date, 8/8, in 1974.

"Let me guess, the Schuylkiller's father hung himself on 8/8 of 1990?" asked Frank.

"Frank," said Kyle Wade. "Getty Ewen Cameron, the Schuylkiller, found his father hanging thirty minutes after his family sang Happy Birthday to him. His father killed himself on his son's sixteenth birthday."

"Jesus!" Frank groaned. "Happy Birthday, Son."

"So, our killer's birthday is also the anniversary of the suicide deaths of his three-generational paternal fathers?"

McCurdy spoke up and said, "Frank, there's one more thing we found out about our guy."

"What's that?" asked Frank.

"He had a twin brother who died at birth," revealed McCurdy.

"Jesus Christ!" Frank was shocked. "So that's four male family members who died on 8/8?" he said rhetorically.

"Now we know why he chose The Twins, Frank," Penny said, finally answering the lingering question of why the Schuylkiller chose the location under the twin bridges just off of MLK.

"So, this guy was an only son, living with the guilt of losing his twin and now his father." Frank was thinking aloud. "He's got a death wish, people. We'll never take him alive."

Frank never intended to take the maniac alive, though. He would instead grant the killer his wish of death.

"So 8/8 is a significant date for our killer, then?" Frank wanted to ensure that everyone on the call understood the significance of August 8."

"Not just the date," said Penny. "The numbers. Eight plus eight is sixteen. A suicidal birthday gift on his only son's sixteenth birthday."

"My God," said Sumner. "If this were fiction, you wouldn't believe it. But it's true."

"So, then," Frank exhaled heavily. "Are we all in agreement that the killings have to do with the death of his father, grandfather, and great-grandfather? And that the number eight and sixteen are meaningful to him?"

The group all chimed in and choroused, "Yes."

Frank remembered back to something Douglas Cantrell said about the killer's mother when profiling him. Cantrell thought the killer's mother may have been a teacher, or educator.

"All right, Guys, this is important," said Frank. "What do we know about the Schuylkiller's mother? Anything?"

Kyle responded, "Our records indicate that Josephine St. John was a teacher at the St. James School up in Alleghany West."

"Cantrell called it." Frank thought to himself. "That's an Episcopalian School. It's private," said Frank. "What else do we know about her?"

"Nothing more at this point other than the fact that she died of natural causes in December of last year," said Cindy McCurdy.

"So, he loved his mother, then?" Frank was again rhetorical.

"Where're you going with this, Frank?" asked Sumner.

"Think about it. He didn't start killing until after she died. He didn't want her to know that he was a monster," said Frank. He thought he could use the information when dealing with his son's captor.

He added, "Do we have any more on the victims and how they might be connected to St. John?" Frank wanted as much ammunition as possible for his imminent call with the monster.

"Oh, yeah," said Penny. "Tell him, Kyle."

"Frank, we're still doing our homework, but we have linked all of our victims so far to the *MK Ultra – Sleep Room* case."

Just then, Operation Room Supervisor McLaughlin barged in and said, "They cleared the house on Wayne Avenue! It's empty, Cap!"

"Frank, did you get that?" asked Sumner, unsure if Frank had heard the news.

"Yeah, I got it, Cap." Frank added, "He's way too smart. We're not going to find this guy before he finds us first."

At that moment, the call waiting beeped in Frank's ear. The words *Unknown Caller* appeared on the screen of his cellphone.

"I gotta go! It's him!" Frank swiped right as fast as he could, not wanting to miss the call.

"Hello." Frank's heart raced, but his voice was calm and steady.

"Detective Frank, is that you?"

"It's me. May I please speak to my son."

"In due time, Detective. In due time."

"I need to know that my son is okay," Frank softly demanded.

"My, my, aren't we pushy?" said the Schuylkiller.

Frank, fearing he'd agitated the Schuylkiller, caught himself and tried to defuse the tension.

"Listen, I just want to know that my son is okay," Frank explained. "Is he covered up? Is he drinking the water you gave him? Please, I'm his father. I need to know."

"Such a lucky young boy to have such a caring father." The Schuylkiller purposely tried to sound sarcastic. "If my father were still alive, he'd applaud you. If your father were still alive, I'm sure he'd give you an 'attaboy.'"

"What would your father say about you right now, Mr. St. John?" Frank's stomach sank. He had just thrown a lit match onto a powder keg, and he had to suppress the flames before the monster exploded in anger.

"He'd tell me to kill them all. He'd tell me to kill your son."

Frank was calculated. "What would your mother say about what you're doing?" He tried to restrain the inclinations of a killer void of conscience. "My mom taught Sunday School at an Episcopalian Church." Frank lied and hoped he could calm the killer. "She once believed in God's love for every human being. When my father died, her faith was challenged forever, but she would have never hurt anyone."

"Episcopalian, huh?" The Schuylkiller surmised that Frank was lying and knew more about him than previously thought. He was educated in child psychology and psychiatry and could tell Frank was deceitful. "And what church would that have been, Frank?" he challenged the gritty detective.

"St. Gabriel's up in Olney." Frank didn't flinch. His best friend's mother taught there, but Frank would borrow the story. Anything to save his son.

Frank remembered going there on several occasions and would use his memory to fool a man that couldn't be fooled. He could tell the lunatic was onto his lie, but he was ready to continue it.

"And when was that, Frank?" The killer's question dripped with skepticism that was now on full display.

"From 1983 to 1992. My mother quit after my father was murdered. She never fully believed in God after that."

"I've been to that Church, Frank, but I seemed to have forgotten the address. Could you remind me of it, please?"

Frank searched his memory. "I don't know the number, but it's on East Roosevelt Boulevard. Right there on the corner, across from the Dunkin Donuts."

Frank was convincing in his charade. He was in the head of the monster, and he thought that St. John may have been Episcopalian and also gave up on God after his father's suicide. Frank held his breath until the killer spoke again.

The Schuylkiller was beginning to believe that Frank could be his brother. The twin brother he was cheated out of. A brother that perhaps could have altered his path. Someone to lean on when his life was stripped away, along with his sanity.

"Just one more question, Detective. Who was the Priest back then?"

"You mean Reverend?" Frank knew St. John was trying to trip him up. "It was Reverend Doctor Michael Gianpollo. He died a few years ago, I'd heard."

Frank was sick to his stomach. He was playing a game of Russian Roulette with a lunatic, and the gun was pointed directly at his son's head.

"Well, Detective Frank Collazo, it does seem that we have even more in common than I had initially thought." The killer's tone relaxed. "Now, back to what I was saying earlier about a trade."

Frank could breathe again and thought that he'd bought his son more time. If St. John were thinking of a trade, then he wouldn't kill Conner, Frank had hoped.

"Your son's life, for the lives of you and your little slut."

"So, you'll spare my son if I let you kill me and my former partner?" Frank tried to diminish Penny's role in the investigation, hoping that St. John would ween himself from his fascination with killing her.

"You do impress me, Detective! So smart, you are."

Frank could feel the sinister smile worn by the Schuylkiller through the phone.

"But don't you have some more killing to do?" Frank knew the killer had one more victim on his list of five and had hoped that that person wasn't already dead.

"If you're talking about unfinished business with regards to my list of five, then you would be correct."

"So, how will the trade work, then?" Frank was apprehensive.

"The honor system, Detective."

"The honor system?" Frank was confused. He didn't trust the man holding his son captive.

"Yes, Frank."

"I'm listening." Frank was spooked.

"You must agree, right now, to meet me at a place and date of my choosing. And you must absolutely bring your little girlfriend, or your son dies now. If you agree, your son will live."

"But if I agree, how will you know I'm being truthful?" Frank thought the Schuylkiller's offer was too good to be true.

"Believe it or not, Frank, I trust you. I believe you're a good man. A man stripped of his lineage and legacy as I have been. I seek the goodness in you in hopes of drowning the evil in me."

"Like a baptism?" asked Frank.

"Yes, of sorts. However, after I kill you and your little 'pretty,' I will kill myself as my fathers did before me. I will then take my place next to them. A place that I have been deprived of since I was only a year old."

Frank noticed that St. John didn't mention his twin brother. He was astonished, though. Kyle and Cindy's research seemed to be accurate, all the way down to the killer's name change from Cameron to St. John when he was only one.

"And if I don't hold up my end of the bargain after getting my son back, what then?"

"Then you will all die, Detective Frank," said St. John. "You, your ex-wife, your son, your wife's parents, your little girlfriend, even the little whore from Creative Minds. The murdering spree I will go on will make the last six months seem like a day at the beach."

"Okay, I'll do it," Frank agreed. "But you can't tip-off Penny. If she finds out that I'm leading her to her death, she'll never agree to come with me. You can't let her know. Is that okay with you?"

"Yes, Frank. That'll work for me."

Frank treaded lightly with his next question. "Can you please tell me where I can find my son? I'm certain he needs medical attention."

"Detective Frank, your son is lying comfortably in bed with his feet elevated. Oh, he does seem bored here. The sound of the river outside has helped slightly to relax him, but it is a pity your father-in-law never got internet installed."

Frank's face went white. He was unable to breathe at that moment. As he pulled the phone away from his face in shock, the screen showed the words, *CALL ENDED.*

Frank caught his breath and frantically dialed Chief McMichael. He put the phone to his ear and prayed he would answer.

"McMichael here." The Chief answered immediately.

"Chief, it's Frank Collazo. My son is in a cabin in Tyler State Park! Get a helicopter to Fox Chase Farm. I'm less than a mile away. I'll meet you there."

Frank hung up the phone and peeled out, narrowly missing a passing car. He would test the limits of his Dodge Charger Interceptor en route to Fox Chase Farm.

A minute later, Chief Darren McMichael met Frank at the entrance of the farm on Pine Road. A helicopter was approaching from a mile out. Frank jumped from his car to meet the Chief, and as the helicopter prepared to land, the sound of the propeller worked hard to drown out the trembling voice of Frank Collazo.

"Chief, let's go get my son!" he yelled.

"Frank, where's the cabin?"

Frank hollered, "We'll find it from the air!"

"Let's move out!" The chief roared, spinning his right hand over his head in a circular motion to alert the pilot they were boarding the chopper and to prepare to liftoff.

While en route to the park, Chief McMichael contacted his FBI and State Police contacts and told them to get to Tyler State Park, look for a hovering helicopter, and move cautiously on their location. He then called the park police, informed them of what was happening, and instructed them to get an ambulance to the Conroy Cabin.

After five minutes of searching the park, Frank spotted the cabin near the Neshaminy River Falls, right on the river's curve.

"Set it down there, Chief!" Frank yelled while pointing to the boathouse parking lot. "It's the cabin with the orange roof!"

The Chief informed the pilot where to land, and two minutes later, they were on the ground. Frank never considered calling Joanne as he feared the worst for Conner.

The Chief then instructed Frank to wait until their backup arrived before approaching the cabin. Frank nodded in the affirmative. But seconds after the chopper touched down he ran the hundred-plus yards to the cabin, which was hidden, nestled in an alcove amongst giant Oaks and Pines, up against the riverbank.

The Chief yelled for Frank to stop, but Frank would not be denied another second without his son.

Park Police were on scene and jogged in Frank's wake but would not enter the cabin until back-up arrived.

The Chief and Park Police watched Frank disappear into the cabin's front door.

Now inside, Frank found his son lying on the bed, hyper-ventilating, panting in fear. Conner, too incoherent to recognize his father, feared the Schuylkiller had returned.

Frank ran to the bed and held his son. "I'm so sorry, Conner! I'm so sorry!" he wailed.

With the ambulance set back from the cabin, the Park and State Police surrounded the cabin with guns drawn.

After two agonizing minutes, the cabin's front door flew open, and the police troopers readied their aim. Walking out the door was a father carrying a child in arms that provided shelter and solace. Conner's little arms were wrapped loosely around his father's neck; he was still in shock. Frank ran from the cabin as if he was running from death itself.

The nearby EMTs spotted Frank and yanked the wheeled stretcher from the back of the medical transport.

Minutes later, the sirens rang through the trees. It'd been only four hours since the ordeal started, but it was a lifetime in hell for Frank.

Back at 1108 Valley Road, Joanne, her father, and Polly Gray waited for word from anyone. Joanne sat almost catatonic on the couch between her father and Polly.

Suddenly, their greatest wish and worst collective fear rang out. It was Joanne's phone, and the caller I.D. said, 'Frank.'

Joanne was too afraid to answer her phone and, with trembling hands, handed it to her father.

"Frank, it's Vance!"

Vance listened to Frank's words and began to weep. Joanne again wailed as Polly gasped, both thinking the worst.

Vance Conroy said into the phone, "Okay, Frank. Okay." Conroy sobbed.

Joanne and Polly both looked terrified but hopeful, not knowing what Frank had said to his father-in-law.

Conroy ended the call. Crying and nodding his head, he looked at his firstborn and said, "Conner's alive! He's alive, Joanne!"

Chapter 31 – This Little Piggy

It was Wednesday, June 7, and Conner had been released and taken home after spending three days in the hospital recovering from the shock. While there, he was given 24-hour police protection. After two additional days of bedrest at home, Conner, his mother, grandparents, Polly, and her son were all preparing to leave for Michigan. The Cheltenham Police Department stationed an officer in front of the home around the clock until they'd left for their trip.

The six of them would fly instead of drive so that they couldn't be followed by car. They would stay with Joanne's sister, Rachel, and her husband for an indeterminant amount of time. Joanne had vowed not to return to Philadelphia until the Schuylkiller had been caught or killed. Frank would stay at the house on Valley Road to ensure its safe keeping, but both Joanne and her father told him not to be there when the family returned home.

Conner hadn't said a word since being kidnapped by the madman, but doctors had ensured the family that he would recover fully as no damage to his internal organs occurred due to the shock.

Frank stood in the backyard, waiting for his ex-wife and son to emerge from the house so he could say goodbye to his boy. A few minutes later, Vance Conroy walked out the side door holding Conner's hand. The old man gave Frank a look that conveyed his contempt for his son-in-law.

Frank couldn't have cared less what the old man thought of him, but how Conner felt, he cared deeply.

Frank knelt in front of Conner as both stood next to a Cheltenham police car that would escort the family to the Philadelphia airport. There, he embraced his son.

Frank held onto Conner tightly, imagining his father, Salvatore, holding on to him. He whispered to his son that he loved him and hoped Conner would return those words to him. Frank Collazo would be disappointed, as Conner remained silent.

Frank stood by and assisted the family in loading luggage into the rear of the Range Rover, which was gifted to Joanne by her father several years before.

Joanne avoided eye contact with Frank, but Polly managed to say, "Good luck, Frank. Please be safe. Conner needs his father."

"I will, Polly. Thank you." Frank was grateful that somebody actually spoke to him.

After all the bags were packed, everyone except Conroy got into the vehicle. Frank stood back and made sure he was clear of the cars.

Frank's mind wandered to an uncertain future. Lost for a moment, he was unaware that Vance Conroy had approached him.

Standing in front of his son-in-law, Conroy begrudgingly held out his hand to shake Frank's. Caught off guard, Frank didn't immediately extend his hand.

"Oh, I'm sorry, Vance. I was lost in thought for a moment." He then reciprocated.

Conroy shook Frank's hand firmly and said, "Thank you for returning Conner to his mother. For that, I am grateful." Vance paused and added, "Take care of this house, but make sure you're not here when we get back."

Frank wasn't surprised by the self-centered old man. He blew off the insensitive remarks and recoiled his hand.

"I never liked you, Frank," said Conroy. "I only ever tolerated you."

"You take care, Vance. Please call if you need me." Frank took the high road as he had so many times before.

"Tell Joanne that I'll be in regular contact with Rachel and that I'll be hoping to speak to Conner every couple of days."

Vance Conroy turned away, got behind the SUV's wheel, and closed the door. Vance rolled down the window, looked Frank up and down, and said, "You kill that son of a bitch. And as he's taking his final breath, put another bullet in him for me." Frank could see Joanne holding onto Conner in the back seat, crying.

Again, Frank stood back, clear of the vehicles, and watched as they backed down the driveway, the police car first. As the Discovery made it to the end of the driveway, it stopped. The back driver side door opened abruptly, and Conner stepped out. Without closing the door, he raced to his father and jumped into his arms, crying. Conner cried in his father's arms and, for the first time in five days, said, "I love you, Dad!" The connection between the two was deep. They would miss each other dearly and would worry for the other's safety.

Frank fell apart and cried with his son. "I love you, Conner! I love you, big man!"

Conner sniffled. "When will I see you again, Daddy?"

"After I get the bad guy off the street."

"Get him, Dad!"

"I will, Son. I promise"

"Protect your mom and your grandparents up at Aunt Rachel's house, Son." Frank smiled and kissed Conner on the forehead.

"I will, Dad." Conner wiped his last tear and half-smiled. "Call me every day, okay?"

"I promise I will, Con-man."

Frank choked back his tears as he realized that his son might never see him again. His mind reverted to the back porch of the house at 454 East Locust Street. He remembered storming off after his father said, 'I know, Son. It's just that we're getting close to catching a real bad guy, and I have to work tonight.' That was the last time he'd ever see his father, and those were the final words he'd ever hear him say.

Frank prayed that the moment he shared with Conner in the driveway would not be the last time his little boy saw his father.

The following day, Thursday, on June 8, Frank sat at a large conference table with Penny, Kyle Wade, Cindy McCurdy, Ali Ashfaq, and Captain Rosalyn Sumner.

"Okay, everyone, Frank's back." Sumner shot a welcoming look in Frank's direction and said, "We're gonna lay out all the facts and make sure everyone is on the same page."

"I'm looking for cohesion, people," said Sumner. "Our guy has proven to be elusive, but now we know who the son of a bitch is."

"Kyle, walk me through the connection St. John has to each of the victims. I still haven't had that laid out for me," requested Frank.

"Okay, let's start at the beginning, with Belinda Mereby." Kyle Wade handed Frank a packet that covered in detail everything he was about to discuss.

"Belinda Mereby's father, Clinton Mereby was a junior partner in the Johnson, Gholston, and Sayers law firm that represented victims and their families in the MK Ultra case back in 1970," explained Wade.

"Mereby was a rising star for the firm and was assigned lead counsel for the plaintiffs."

Frank interjected, "Okay, so he was a hotshot on the rise, but why would they have a junior partner take the lead in a lawsuit against two governments? I mean, there was a good chance they'd lose that case, right?"

Wade nodded. "That's just it. The firm thought they would easily lose a case in which they went up against the Allan Institute, the U.S. and Canadian Governments with all of their unlimited resources. That's why they'd assigned junior partners instead of one of the big three."

"And they won, anyways." Frank shook his head. "So, that's what propelled him into instant stardom in the legal community, then?"

"Yep," said Wade. "It also likely got his daughter killed, some forty-six years later."

"We believe that Cameron Ewen St. John sought revenge against those who helped to destroy his family's reputation. Ultimately leading to the suicide of his father, grandfather, and great-grandfather."

"Clinton Mereby didn't know it," said Kyle, "but his rising star put a target on the back of his then two-year-old daughter. And three years later, in 1974, spawned the birth of a madman serial killer named Getty Ewen Cameron, then Cameron Ewen St, John, and then the Schuylkiller."

"So why not just kill Clinton Mereby, then?" asked Frank.

Cindy McCurdy chimed in. "We can only rationalize that the junior St. John thought he could inflict greater suffering to the elder Mereby by killing his only daughter."

"So my theory that the Jacks' murder was simply death by association holds water then?" asked Frank.

"Everyone here agrees with that hypothesis," nodded McCurdy. Others around the table also nodded in agreement.

"Same for the limo driver, James Loftin, too. The right place at the wrong time," said Frank.

All agreed.

"It all seems to match up with everything the Schuylkiller told me directly. He said he had a list of five and that there was one more victim still to come. If that's the case, the four missing victims, Mereby, Oliver, Carpenter, and Stanbey, are four of the five on his list. Suggesting that everyone else was collateral damage, or killed simply to create mayhem."

Penny rose from her chair and said, "I think I'm gonna be sick." She then stormed out of the room.

Realizing that his words were insensitive, Frank rose from his chair and said, "Penny, I'm sorry. I didn't mean....."

Cindy McCurdy also rose from her chair to go after her friend. With a stern look, Captain Sumner told McCurdy to sit back down.

It was too late. Penny was gone.

"Don't worry about it, Frank," said Sumner. "I told her she didn't have to attend this meeting if she wasn't ready."

"Penny will be fine. All of us need to keep plugging away." Sumner was anxious to get all of the facts on the table.

"I just referred to her mother as 'Collateral Damage,' though." Frank was upset with himself.

"She'll be okay, Frank," said Ashfaq.

Frank shook it off and directed another question at Wade and McCurdy, both sitting to his left, Wade closest, followed by McCurdy, then Sumner.

"So, how then is Daniel Oliver a victim of St. John's ire?" Frank rifled through the contents of the envelope that Wade had provided him.

"Same thing, we think," McCurdy answered. "Like Mereby, Daniel Oliver's grandfather is still alive and would be deeply troubled by the death of his only grandchild."

"Quinton Oliver sold a lot of newspapers when the paper he owned, the Philadelphia Inquirer, broke the exclusive story of MK-Ultra in 1969. It was the reporting of his investigative journalists that led to the breaking of the story. It was his publication that informed the world just how morally corrupt Donald Ewen Cameron and his son, John were." Kyle paused.

"So, you're suggesting that if the eighty-something-year-old Quinton Oliver were dead, his grandson would never have been a target, then?" asked Frank.

"That's the only connection we can make. So, yes," replied Wade.

Frank looked over a page in the manila envelope and handed it to Kyle. "And what about this guy?"

Kyle looked at the document's header and saw the name Keith Carpenter. "Ahh, yes. Cindy made that connection, so I'll let her tell you what she came up with."

"You guys have been busy over the last seven weeks, huh?" Frank smiled at Cindy and Kyle. "Great job!"

Cindy nodded and blushed with the recognition. She admired Frank Collazo, and his words meant a lot to her. She and Kyle had worked hundreds of hours on the case, and it felt good to be appreciated.

"Thanks, Frank," said Kyle. "Lots of late-nights, huh, Cindy?" Wade looked over his shoulder.

Cindy nodded and looked back at Frank. "We knew that our killer, Cameron St. John, attended Temple back in the early to late nineties, so all we had to do is cross-check if anyone named Carpenter worked at Temple during that period," said Cindy.

"It was a stretch, but we had to start somewhere," she said. "So we just started cross-referencing names. We pulled employment records from Temple for anyone named Carpenter." McCurdy's eyebrows went up. "As it turned out, there were more than a dozen administrators and faculty over the years with that last name."

"Okay, so what did you find?" Frank seemed a little impatient.

"Well," said Cindy. "While we couldn't link anyone named Carpenter to Cameron Ewen St. John, we did discover that a medical professor named James Carpenter was there," Cindy paused. "And you're not gonna believe this," she said, "it was during the eighties and nineties."

Carpenter's father, James, was on the medical staff at Temple University Hospital from 1974 to 1978, before joining the faculty at Temple University."

"So, this James Carpenter, Keith Carpenter's father, would have known the Schuylkiller's father while working there, prior to his termination and the changing of his name?" Is that what you're contending?" asked Frank.

"Correct," said McCurdy.

"Yeah, well, that's a stretch to suggest that Gregory Ewen Cameron, the Schuylkiller's father, was outed by Keith Carpenter's father back in 1974 or 75."

"Yes, I agree. But," McCurdy smiled, looked at Kyle Wade, and then back at Frank and said, "In Cameron St. John's school records, there was a report that he'd vandalized a professor's car in 1995. Care to guess who the car belonged to?" asked Cindy of Frank.

Frank's eyes slowly opened wide. "You've got to be kidding me!" he said. "So, Cameron St. John, our killer, while a student at Temple University, vandalized a car that belonged to a man that once worked with his father. And he worked there during the time he was outed for being related to the monsters that ran the mind-control experiments at the Allan Institute?" Frank was astounded. "Why else would he have vandalized the guy's car? He clearly had a grudge against him."

"Yep," said Kyle Wade as Cindy McCurdy sat proudly between her partner and her captain.

Frank looked like he was lost in thought for a moment.

"Did you guys happen to make any connection between St. John and Willard Clark, by the way? They were both at Temple at the same time." Lennie was never far from Frank's mind. His guilt regarding the killings of the Clark family was crippling.

Wade nodded his head in the affirmative and looked over at his partner. "Tell him, Cindy."

"Cameron St. John was on the swim team for at least one season with Clark. We can't confirm that they were friends, but they had to have known each other as teammates.

Frank went quiet for a moment while collecting his thoughts.

"Okay, back to James Carpenter." Frank shook his head. "It's a connection, but not a definitive one," he wasn't convinced.

"Frank," said Sumner. "James Carpenter is still alive. He's seventy-seven years old. Like all the other victims in the Schuylkiller case, their father or grandfather, that had a connection to our killer, is still alive and made to suffer through the loss of their child, or grandchild."

"Well, if he's still alive," said Frank, "why don't you just ask him?"

Kyle Wade and Captain Sumner both looked at Cindy McCurdy and smiled.

Cindy again felt the recognition as she looked at Frank and said, "I did."

"Did what?" Frank leaned forward in his chair. Astonished by what he thought he'd heard.

"I asked the old man, Frank." Cindy smiled. "He did, in fact, out Cameron St. John's father."

"Holy shit!" Frank sunk back into his chair. Hands behind his head. "He told you that?" Frank was amazed. "He kept the dominos falling."

"Think about this for a second." Frank leaned forward. "Suppose Keith Carpenter's father never outed the father of Getty Cameron. In that scenario, Gregory Ewen Cameron doesn't lose his job at Temple University Medical Center, doesn't have to change his name, and doesn't kill himself on his only son's sixteenth birthday. Jesus Christ! James Carpenter was the catalyst. He was the first domino."

The others at the table all nodded with the revelation.

"The twisted Camerons that ran the mind control experiments at FalconClaw were responsible for making the Cameron name poison," reasoned Frank. "But James Carpenter's actions in 1975 is what really gave birth to our killer." Frank was amazed.

"And Martin Stanbey?" Frank asked rhetorically. "If I remember correctly, didn't he work for the plaintiffs in the MK-Ultra case, too?"

Wade nodded. "Yes, Sir. In the MK-Ultra case, Colten Stanbey was Clinton Mereby's co-counsel, and they won big."

"Jesus Christ!" said Frank. "Who the fuck is next?"

At that moment, Penny stormed back into the room and shouted, "We've got another disappearance, and this time there was a note left behind." Penny raised a piece of paper in the air and walked it over to Frank. Slapping it down on the table in front of her old partner, she said, "It's the fifth victim on the Schuylkiller's list."

Everyone sat fully erect in their chairs and waited for Frank to read the note.

Leaning forward, both elbows on the table, Frank read the note that Penny had given him.

My first little piggy went to a party before she died.

My second little piggy went for a run before he died.

My third little piggy walked his dog before he died.

My fourth little piggy had just returned from vacation before he died.

And finally! My fifth little piggy went fishing in Lake Luxembourg before he died.

Frank stopped reading and looked up at Penny and asked, "I guess they're all dead then. Who's the fifth victim?"

"Clinton Mereby!" she said.

"Oh my God!" said Frank as he sunk into his chair. "His list of five started and ended with a Mereby. Jesus Christ!"

The others at the table all just looked at each other in shock.

Frank exhaled fully and said, "Guys, he's not done yet."

Sumner looked puzzled. "But you said his list was only five people."

"You're forgetting the other list." Frank wore a look of bemused resignation.

"Penny, sit down." Frank directed his former partner with a sobering stare. "Penny and I are next."

Frank Collazo knew that the clock had run out. He was certain that Cameron Ewen St. John would call upon him and Penny in just hours or days and that FalconClaw would be the stage in the Schuylkiller's final act.

Frank was not about to put Penny in harm's way, though.

"All right." Frank was stoic. "All cards on the table." He took a deep breath and exhaled slowly. "When the Schuylkiller called me to tell me that he had my son, he offered me a trade."

"A trade?" Sumner shook her head.

"Yes. St. John promised to release my son unharmed if I offered myself up to be killed at a time and place of his choosing. He never said when or where, but I'm convinced the location will be FalconClaw, and I'm now more certain than ever the date will be the 8th of August."

"And...." Frank paused. "There's one more thing," he looked over to Penny.

Everyone glanced at Penny and then back at Frank when he added, "St. John demanded that Penny be there, too, and I agreed."

"You agreed?!" Sumner slammed her open hand down on the table. "I'll be goddamn if you...."

Penny looked as if she'd been victimized again. Not by Frank but by the Schuylkiller.

Frank cut Sumner off. "Captain, I only told him what he wanted to hear. I would've said anything to get my son back, and that's exactly what I did."

"It's all right, Captain," said Penny, who was now more in control of her emotions.

"I wonder what his fascination is with you and Penny," asked McCurdy, looking at Frank and then over to her friend.

"I'm his muse," offered Frank, using Douglas Cantrell's words. "Penny, too, for that matter."

"His muse?" Sumner was confused again. "What am I missing here?"

"Captain, Douglas Cantrell touched on this back in April with all of us." Frank reminded his Captain.

"In my conversations with him, I learned a lot about how serial killers think. Serial killers are not very original, and they like to copy or mimic sociopaths like themselves. They feel that if another lunatic made headlines by doing things a certain way, then maybe they could be famous, too, by copying those that came before them.

Think of Richard Speck and Ted Bundy. They both went after female coeds in their student housing while they slept."

Frank went on to say, "In the end, they're all looking for recognition. When they get caught, they usually want to talk about their crimes in hopes of getting an 'Attaboy' from another serial killer, or by impressing the authorities with their accomplishments, or the fact that they got away with it for so long."

"Cantrell thinks that when I became the face of the investigation, our killer needed a muse. When creating his profile of St. John, he thought that the Schuylkiller did some research on me and discovered that my father was killed by a serial killer at FalconClaw back in 1992," revealed Frank. "Cantrell also suggests that our killer knew of Penny Bryce coming up missing at FalconClaw back in 1974 at the hands of Old Man Winter, the custodian that was thought to have kidnapped and killed several older people."

"Furthermore, I think I reinforced whatever twisted bond he thinks there is between him and I by addressing him as Mr. St. John during one of our conversations. I wasn't certain that that was his real name until he paused after I'd said it," revealed Frank. "While he blew it off and pretended to know of no one by that name, it was at that moment he realized I knew his name. I believe that that sick bastard felt like he knew me and that I knew him. Like brothers from a past life, or something."

Wade immediately spoke up. "Okay, you see, that's what I still haven't been privy to. Frank, you told Cindy and me back on April 24 that you had a lead on a guy named St. John." Kyle referred to his notes. "But as far as we knew, we were working with the name St. Croix, the guy you saw at the daycare. You said you thought that name was an alias."

Sumner, Penny, and Cindy McCurdy all looked on.

"Okay?" It was the moment of truth for Frank. He knew where Kyle was going.

"Well, who tipped you off to the name of St. John?" Kyle's eyes narrowed. "I mean, without that name, Cindy and I don't have a starting point in our research. Cross-referencing the name St. John with FalconClaw and Temple is what broke the case. How did you know his name was St. John?"

Penny never questioned her partner, but Ashfaq, Wade, McCurdy, and Sumner all looked at Frank, wanting the answer to the mystery of how he knew and who his source was.

Frank raised his brow and modestly said, "It came to me in a dream."

"Now that's bullshit, Frank!" Sumner raised her voice. "All cards are on the table. What we're dealing with here is life and death, and you're messing around. "Who is your source? I demand to know right now!"

"It was more of a nightmare," said Frank. "An old man in my dream told me you must be looking for Mr. St. John." Frank was trying to be honest, but to those around the table, he was being disingenuous. He lied about it being a dream because he didn't want to admit it was a fear-stricken hallucination.

"So that's it, Frank? A dream?" asked Sumner. "Listen here, Detective Collazo, you may not want to disclose your source to the people around this table, but you'll damn sure be telling me with a smaller audience later."

"It was a dream, Cap." Frank threw up his hands and shrugged his shoulders. "I dreamt it. The name came to me in a dream." He just shook his head.

"But why did he wait so long to exact his revenge, I wonder?" Cindy McCurdy floated the question.

Frank said, "I think I know the answer to that one, too."

"Let me guess," said Sumner sarcastically. "An old man told you in a dream?"

"Nope," said Frank. "Without saying the actual words, the Schuylkiller told me the last time we talked. He waited until his mother was dead. He couldn't let her see the monster that she'd birthed."

"Cameron Ewen St. John's mind and his paternal family's mental disease were the malevolent dominos that rained down over North Philly for all of these decades, dating back to 1957."

Frank shook his head. Focusing on no one at the table, he said, "I can promise you this, though. The Cameron reign of terror ends in 2017. Sixty years of this bullshit ends on 8/8.

Frank was sure it would all come to an end at FalconClaw.

Chapter 32 – The Ghost

Billy Murphy's Irish Saloon – Sunday, August 6, 2017, 11:49 am.

Right before Penny walked in, Frank was sure that she wouldn't show. Though they'd met for daily briefings in the Detective Room, they hadn't been out socially since April 16, Easter Sunday. The night of Easter changed both of their lives forever and put them on a collision course with the Schuylkiller on August 8 at FalconClaw.

When Penny walked in, Frank was at their regular table talking with Mike Murphy. When he saw Penny, he couldn't contain his excitement in seeing his best friend in a setting that would set both at ease.

Mike Murphy immediately noticed Frank's demeanor change and knew that Penny was right behind him.

"Hey, Penny," said Mike. "It's been way too long. I'm so sorry about what happened to your mom."

Mike and Penny shared an awkward embrace, and Mike asked her what she was having.

"Coffee for me, Murph."

"Just a coffee? You sure?"

"Yeah, that's all."

"Okay, coming right up."

"Hey, Pen. Thanks for meeting me out." Frank was uncomfortable. In his mind, it felt like meeting a blind date. It was as if he had to reintroduce himself to a woman he'd known for years.

"Hey, Frankie." Penny's enthusiasm was tempered.

"Thanks for meeting me out on a Sunday."

"So, what's up?" Penny was matter of fact.

"Listen, you know how to read a calendar as good as anyone, and you know what Tuesday is."

Penny flashed a look of concern. "Have you heard from him?"

"No, it's been quiet," said Frank. "I'm worried that he'll change his mind and renege on his offer."

"He'll call. He wants us both dead," said Penny. "And 8/8 only comes around once a year."

Frank changed the subject wanting to know how things were going with Penny. "So, how are things with you and Dan?"

Penny rolled her eyes. "I moved out three weeks ago. That guy's an asshole," she vented. "You would think that with everything that's gone on this year that he would've changed or at least been empathetic to my situation. He's a real prick!"

Frank concealed his excitement as best he could, instead trying to seem more compassionate. "Damn, I'm sorry to hear that, Penny."

Penny cracked a smile and threw a sugar packet at her former partner. "You're so full of shit, Frank! You're celebrating on the inside right now."

"No, I'm serious." His smile grew. "There's nothing I want more in life than to see the two of you happy together."

"You're an ass," she chuckled while shaking three sugar packets in her hand. "Boy, whattaya got to do to get a fucking cup of coffee around here. Geez, they're not even busy."

Just then, Mike Murphy walked over to the table with a coffee in one hand and a paper bag in the other. After he set the coffee on the table, Mike looked like he was going to propose to Penny, or something. Whatever he had to say, it would be awkward for all three of them.

"Hey, um. Yeah, Penny, so listen. When we heard your mom passed away, we put a couple of donation jars out on the bar, and people gave. Sorry it took so long to bring out the coffee, but I had to get it all out of the safe. It took a minute."

Penny blushed. "Ah, Mike, you didn't have to do that."

"Yeah, I did, Penny." Mike handed Penny a brown paper bag that looked crumpled and used, its contents bulging.

Penny was curious and grateful as she gladly accepted the bag. "Whoa, it's kinda heavy, isn't it?" She supported the bag from the bottom and could feel and hear coins rattling around inside. "Wow! There's loose change in here, huh?"

Penny smiled as Frank just sat back and took in the kind gesture. Frank knew that Mike Murphy, like his mother and his late father, all had hearts of gold and would give you the coat off their back if you were cold.

Mike said, "Yeah, people gave what they could. And they gave a lot." He flashed a look of approval and appreciation.

Penny blushed again and said, "Can I look inside?"

"Yeah, yeah, yeah! Go ahead, Penny." Mike Murphy was eager for her to see what his patrons had done for her.

Penny opened the bag and was stunned. There were hundreds of bills, ranging from ones, fives, tens, and twenties. She even spotted some fifties and a one-hundred-dollar bill. Tearing up, Penny set the bag down and stood to hug Mike. Looking over Mike's shoulder to the bar, she spotted Dane Mandato and smiled at him.

"Here's to you, Penny!" Dane yelled out as he raised an empty glass he'd been cleaning. His salute was meant to convey that she was family and had many friends.

"Thanks, Mike. I don't even know what to say." Penny wiped a tear that was welling in her eye.

"Don't say nothin', Penny. Just go and buy some new clothes or somethin.' It's tough when you lose everything in a fire," Mike showed compassion. "It's tough when you lose a parent."

Mike Murphy knew because he'd lost his father, Billy, several years earlier.

"Well, thank you, anyway." Penny was humbled by the gesture.

Frank said, "You got friends, Penny. People love you. We're all here for you. Take your time coming back from the hell you're in, but we're all here for you."

"Thanks, Frankie." Penny rolled up the paper bag and set it aside. "Did you know about this?"

"Yeah. I must've put two or three bucks in there, myself. Most of the coins are from me. Sorry about that." Frank smiled at his friend.

Penny threw another packet of sugar at Frank.

"So, where are you staying these days?" Frank wasn't sure what Penny's options were.

"I'm staying with Cindy."

Frank's eyes went wide. He was surprised. "No shit, you'd never know by the way you guys act around each other at work."

"We don't want anyone to know our business, so we keep it professional while at Headquarters," explained Penny.

"Makes sense." Frank nodded.

"She's been awesome! We wear the same size, so she's been letting me wear some of her clothes. I lost everything I had in the fire." Penny felt sad thinking that she'd lost her mother in the fire, too.

"Listen, it's already tough to tell you guys apart. Wearing each other's clothes is gonna make it harder. I'll need to look twice before leaning in for a kiss next time." Frank chuckled, but his humor fell flat.

Penny pursed her lips and nodded. "You still up at Joanne's?"

The wrinkles on Frank's forehead gathered, and he said, "Yep."

"So, do you feel safe over there, Pen?"

"Yeah, we got two cops under one roof packing heat. Surprisingly, I sleep pretty good at night."

"Well, that's good."

"She's been staying at her boyfriend's house a lot lately, so we don't see each other as much as you might think."

"Again, do you feel safe there at night? Because you can always stay up at Joanne's with me if you want."

"Frank, stop." Penny shook her head. "That won't work for me. I told you."

"I got it, Penny," said Frank. "That's not where I was going, but I got it."

"So, what did you want to talk to me about?"

"I have some news regarding what's about to happen on Tuesday."

"Whattaya mean?" Penny leaned forward in her chair.

"I've been working with the IT guys up in Manayunk, and I have a plan for when our psychopath calls me again."

Penny now sat up straight, curious about what Frank had to tell her. "Oh?"

"Penny, go into your phone settings, and then select *Call Settings,* and check the *Hide Number* box and then call me."

Penny adjusted her phone settings and then dialed Frank's number.

When Frank's phone began to ring, he turned it towards Penny and said, "Look."

Penny looked and saw her number appear on the screen, paused in confusion for a second, and said, "Wait a second! How did you do that?"

"It's an app that only law enforcement uses. It's still being developed and only works on Android phones so far. It lets you see blocked numbers."

"Okay, and? Um, I'm not really following." Penny cocked her head to one side, looking puzzled.

"Penny, when that motherfucker calls me, I'll be able to see his number!"

"That's great!" Her eyes flew open. "We can track him then."

"He's smart, Penny. He may have burner phones. A new one every time he calls. I'm not sure we'll be tracking the bastard. But if he calls me and doesn't dump that phone, yes, we'll be able to track him."

"Why are you telling me this?" Penny had a 'what gives?' look on her face.

"I have a plan." Frank leaned in and said, "You can't tell anyone! Do you understand?" Frank wore a grim look.

"Of course," said Penny.

"Penny, I'm going to FalconClaw tonight."

Penny had a visceral reaction. "The hell you are!" she was abrupt. "I'll fucking kill you if you go up there without backup."

"Penny, that son of a bitch doesn't live there. He only goes there to kill or torture. It's been more than two months since Clinton Mereby went missing. He's dead by now. The only reason that psycho will show up there again is to kill you and me."

"What are you talking about?"

"Penny, I'm going to beat him there. I'm going to take away his element of surprise. I'll hear the motherfucker come in, and I'll ambush him the way he plans on ambushing me."

Penny looked terrified. "Frank! Don't!" she began to cry. "I can't lose you, too."

"Penny, the only way Conner can be safe is if either I'm dead, he's dead, or we're both dead."

"That's not true!" Penny wiped her tears. "If you die, then I have to die, too. That was the deal you made with him. Frank, if something happens to you up there, I'm not sure I can keep Conner safe."

"Penny, if I die, then Joanne will never return from Michigan. Her sister's husband is a tactical specialist for the Michigan State Police. He'll keep them safe should that maniac venture up to Saginaw after killing me," explained Frank. "It's you I'm worried about. Get with Denny up at CSU and get the app on your phone, too."

"Okay, I will." Penny tried to be strong, but the tears kept coming. "How can I talk you out of this?"

"You can't, Penny. There's a reckoning coming his way, and he's gonna get all I have. I promise to let you know when he contacts me. If I know anything about him, he'll call the night before he wants to meet. I'll agree to his time. We already know the date. I'll call you," promised Frank. "If you decide to come, don't come alone. Bring the whole 39th Calvary with you."

"Okay, Frank. But what am I supposed to do for now?"

Frank shook his head. "Nothing. Just wait for my call. Only one of us is walking out of FalconClaw alive, and I intend on seeing my son again. If it's him that walks out of there, then you'll have the place surrounded."

"Frank, come on!" Penny implored her friend. "That cowboy shit is going to get you killed!"

"Penny, I no longer have a death wish. There are people in this world that I love, and I plan on showing them how much. My plan is for me to live and for Cameron St. John to die." Frank stood up from his chair and threw ten bucks on the table. "You look for my call, and get that app on your phone. Got it?"

"I got it." Penny just sat there and cried.

"Tell no one anything about me going there tonight. And don't call me. Only text until I tell you otherwise."

Penny acknowledged Frank with tears, unable to form words.

Frank said, "I love you, and I always have. No matter the outcome of Tuesday, nothing will ever change that." Frank turned to walk away.

Penny was frozen, unable to go after him. She sat for another moment until the blood rushed back to her legs, and then she ran. She ran after the man she loved.

Outside, standing at the intersection, she looked up Indian Queen and in both directions on Conrad, but she couldn't see Frank. He was a ghost, she thought. Standing alone on that empty street, she'd hoped he'd be invisible like a ghost when he entered hell up in Old Germantown.

Half a block away, a rusted-out 1988 Chevy Nova idled. Behind the wheel? A madman. As Penny looked up and down the street, Cameron St. John vacated his parking space and drove right past her. She never saw his face.

Chapter 33 – The Devil's Den

Later, just before midnight. Frank exited an Uber near the front gates of 888 Bedford Street.

Wearing a backpack, black jeans, a black jacket, and black boots, Frank carried a black gym bag, too.

He pushed his way through the heavy wrought iron gates. Rubbing his hands together to get the rust off, he accidentally rubbed one hand on his left chest, leaving an orange stain there.

Before leaving Joanne's an hour earlier, Frank had inventoried his backpack and gym bag. Inside his backpack were two flashbangs, metal wire, four flares, two flashlights, and a Ruger LCP, equipped with three extra clips, all filled with .38 caliber hollow-tipped bullets. The Ruger was there to supplement his Smith & Wesson .40 caliber M&P and his Glock 9mm.

For health and nourishment, his gym bag was full of breakfast bars, six bottles of water, four Red Bulls, toilet paper, and a first aid kit. Frank made sure that the gym bag had also contained a set of night-vision goggles.

Once at the top of the hill, Frank donned his goggles and entered the front of FalconClaw through its broken-out glass and steel double doors. He then walked the hallowed halls of what was once the pride of the gilded age. One minute in, and the foul stench of death hit his nose. He was no longer back in yesteryear. Frank quickly reached into his jacket pocket and pulled out a small can of Vick's VapoRub Ointment, and applied a generous portion under his nose.

Perhaps the VapoRub affected his senses, but Frank was surprised that his claustrophobia hadn't kicked in yet.

Passing the elevator this time, he looked down into the shaft, overcoming his fear. Frank stopped to take in the darkness and the terror of FalconClaw, strangely feeling as if he were welcomed. It was as if he were now a part of the mansion's infamous legacy. He feared for himself no more. He would kill the Schuylkiller, or he would die trying.

After reaching the old administrative hallway that he'd seen three times before, he examined the door that led to the basement. Still covered in yellow police tape, it appeared the door hadn't been disturbed since the last time he, the CSU, and the tactical squad searched the basement back in June, looking for signs of Clinton Mereby; there were none. Though the cadaver dogs were alerted to human decomposition, no human remains were found. After that, Captain Rosalyn Sumner determined that FalconClaw was not the scene of multiple homicides as Frank had originally suspected.

Frank then traveled back to the main hallway and traversed the stairs to the second floor. The stairs were located halfway between the old elevator and the foyer that led to the massive dining hall. As he passed the elevator again, he looked his fear head-on. Eyes wide open, he almost welcomed the sound of tired gears cranking to life once again, but there was nothing.

Now positioned on the western side of the estate, or the rear of FalconClaw, Frank could see above the courtyard that led back to a wooded area. The tree line helped to conceal the Old Olmsted Trail, where Frank had suspected the Schuylkiller used to secretly access the mansion's basement.

Frank could see that the area was clear and went back down to the admin hall and out the rear of the building.

After surveilling the grounds in the back of the estate, Frank opened the unlocked cellar doors on the southeast corner of the mansion and slowly descended the stairs into the bowels of the Devil's Den, gun in hand, flashlight off. Under no circumstances would he use his flashlight unless it was to inspect the dead body of Cameron Ewen St. John. Using a flashlight in the pitch-black basement would give away his location to the killer.

With each step, Frank's mind played tricks on him. He was suddenly wearing his father's clothes and began breathing heavily. At the bottom of the steps, Frank tripped on a loose cinder block. When attempting to put it back into place, Frank discovered a set of night vision goggles hiding behind the block. He knew they belonged to the Schuylkiller. The fact that they were hidden told Frank that the maniac was not there. He'd suspected the basement was empty but wasn't sure until that moment.

Frank smiled and put the goggles in his gym bag. He left the cinder block out of place so the killer would think a kid or homeless person had found and taken the goggles. If he had taken them and placed the stone neatly back into place, the killer might think someone was waiting for him on the inside.

Two hours later, after inspecting every room, an emotionally exhausted Frank found a nest in an old archives room that somehow had cellphone coverage and a sightline to the door and hallway. Frank installed a tripwire twenty feet away from each side of the room he was holed up in.

Frank had rigged the perimeter around the archives room so that if anyone tripped the wire, it would result in a bottle crashing to the floor. If someone tripped either wire, they wouldn't immediately know what room Frank was in, but instead, would have to follow the wire to its origin. Because the wire would've been pulled from its place of origin, the person tripping it would only have a general idea of where it came from, giving Frank even more time to assess the threat. On the ends of each wire were old bottles that looked like they'd been around since the nineteen-sixties.

If a bottle broke, the element of surprise would be gone, and a battle of good versus evil would ensue.

The room Frank had chosen to hunker down in had files and old black and white photos strewn about the floor.

Frank assessed the area and could see several boxes had been tipped over, and their contents spilled onto the floor. He could also see old photos and hand-written documents lying scattered as if there'd been a struggle.

Knowing that he was alone in the basement, Frank broke his rule of not using his flashlight unless it was to flee or identify the menace that wanted to kill him. But the photos in his hand were calling out to him, and he felt compelled to look at them.

After removing his goggles, Frank clicked on his flashlight, going against his better judgment, and viewed the old photographs. The black and white images included many black men, and white and black women, who all seemed to be dressed in staff uniforms. The women wore long gray dresses and white aprons, while the men wore long-sleeve white shirts buttoned to the top and what looked to be gray wool pants.

As Frank continued sorting the contents, he came across a series of photographs that appeared to be of the home's residents. He'd determined this by how they were dressed. The old men wore three-piece suits while the gray-haired women were almost all wearing what appeared to Frank as ball gowns, with many wearing bonnets and ribbons in their hair.

As Frank thumbed through another stack of photos, he saw an old man who looked familiar to him. He shined his flashlight on the image, and though grainy and in bad condition, Frank was able to make out a man sitting in a familiar armchair. The man was wearing a brown flannel shirt, and he realized it was the old man from his hallucination. Suddenly Frank felt as if he wasn't alone in the basement. Looking around in fear, he felt the temperature drop and could now see his frozen breath. Turning the image over, Frank saw faded letters that read, Garrison Winter, 1920.

Studying the man's face, Frank felt drawn to him, as if the two were somehow connected. His fear had suddenly evaporated along with his frozen breath. Frank felt alone again in the basement and put the photograph in his backpack for later inspection.

Frank settled in for the night and checked his texts. All sounds, including vibrate mode, were disabled. If the Schuylkiller had contacted him while he was already in the basement, he wouldn't hear any sounds coming from Frank's phone.

Frank also dimmed the backlight on his phone screen to its lowest possible level. He was now stealth, armed, locked, and loaded. He would ride it out until his unwelcome guest arrived.

Later, checking emails and texts, Frank saw several messages from Penny. She told him that she missed him and that she was worried.

In another message, she had asked him to call her. Frank instead texted Penny to let her know he was okay.

Frank also asked if Cindy was with her, as he was worried for her safety, too. She replied that Cindy was staying at her boyfriend's house again.

Frank also responded to a text from Rachel's phone. Conner had typed it out, and it read, *I LOVE U DAD. Call me tomorrow.*

It was now 3 am, and Frank dozed off. Before he did, though, he'd eaten an energy bar hoping it would prevent him from entering into a deep sleep.

It was now 6:45 on Monday morning, and Frank was awakened by a rat the size of his boot. As it nibbled on his left boot, he crushed its skull with the heel of his right foot and then pushed it away.

Now fully awake, Frank again inventoried his three pistols. On his left ribcage was his .40 caliber Smith & Wesson. On his right belt was the Glock, and hidden on the inside of his left pantleg was the compact Ruger.

After a breakfast consisting of two protein bars, a Red Bull, and a water, Frank relieved himself in the far corner of the storage room. After that, he'd wait. Frank sat with his phone and gun at the ready. Because the ringer and vibrate function was turned off, he'd have to keep it in his line of sight. His infrared, night vision goggles easily picked up the dim backlight of the phone, with the minimal light radiating brightly on the inside of his goggles. Frank continuously adjusted the goggles trying to get comfortable wearing them.

After checking in with Penny through texts, he tried to call Conner, but the phone kept going straight to voicemail.

As Frank was about to look away from the screen, it illuminated. The incoming call was recognized as coming from a 267 area code. It could have been many different people, but he had to answer in case it was the Schuylkiller.

"Hello?" he whispered.

"Why, Frank, did I wake you?" said the Schuylkiller.

Frank played along. "Yes, you did. Is this Mr. St. John?" he asked.

"Now, Frank, are we really going to play that game again? St. John? St. Croix?" asked the killer. "I'm no saint. That's for sure."

To the best of his recollection, Frank had never referred to the killer as St. Croix. The slip on the killer's part now confirmed to Frank that Cameron Ewen St. John and George St. Croix, from the Creative Minds Daycare, were one and the same. Frank looked forward to meeting him again.

"I don't know what else to call you. You haven't given me your name yet," said Frank. "I was hoping that you'd forgotten all about me."

"Frank, how could I ever forget you," he said. "Soon, we'll meet face to face, and I will answer all of your questions right before I kill you." When the sun rises on the 9th, you and I will be connected forever. They'll be talking about us until the end of recorded history."

Frank thought that Cameron St. John's elevated self-perception was his weakness. He knew that the sociopath would like nothing more than to go down in history and would ensure that he did. No matter the outcome of their meeting, though, the Schuylkiller would live in infamy for many years to come.

"When might that be?" Frank was terrified but purposely acted impatient. "If I'm being honest with you, I'd really like to get the whole thing over with."

"It will be very soon. I can assure you."

"So, where would you like to meet, and when?"

"This will be the last call before then, so listen carefully," said St. John. "Meet me at FalconClaw at 6 am tomorrow. If you're late, your whole family dies. No matter where they call home these days, I will find them."

"FalconClaw is a big place," Frank's eyes wandered. "A man could get lost in a place like....," he paused, almost saying the word 'this,' instead of 'that.' Doing so would have indicated to the Schuylkiller that he was already at FalconClaw.

"Come in through the back of the home, through the cellar doors, on the southwest corner," St. John directed Frank. "They'll be unlocked, just as they were when your father visited back in '92. You should bring a flashlight, Frank. It'll be very dark upon your arrival and will get darker and darker with each step you take."

"No chance of that," Frank thought to himself. He knew that a flashlight would give away his position. "Anything else I need to know?" Frank asked the Schuylkiller.

"Yes, don't forget your little slut, Penny. I want to see if she squeals like her old lady did when taking her last breath."

Frank ground his teeth, listening to the psychopath. "Okay, 6 am it is."

"Oh, and Frank, if you bring an army with you, I'll know. I have a friend on standby to kill your family. You break our deal, your family dies. Got it?"

"I got it, Mr. St. John."

Frank noticed the screen illuminate his palm and looked to see the *Call Ended* prompt. He then saved the number in his phone and had it on standby, ready to call back at a moment's notice.

Frank now knew that Cameron Ewen St. John would arrive later in the day to ensure that he was there long before he expected Penny and he to arrive. Once Frank detected anyone entering the basement, he would shoot first and ask questions later.

Later that evening, around 9 pm, Frank texted Penny. Penny told him she was getting ready for bed and asked if he'd been notified by the Schuylkiller, yet.

Frank told her that he had and that she should have an army assembled inside the gates of FalconClaw at exactly 5:45 pm the following afternoon. Frank lied to his partner because he wanted her out of harm's way. He quietly hoped that he would see her when she arrived. Any other outcome would include Frank and the Schuylkiller being dead, likely laying side by side.

Penny told Frank through texts that she worried for him but would have the whole 39th there to take down the madman. She then signed off for the night by informing Frank that he shouldn't worry about her because fellow detective and friend Cindy McCurdy planned to be home that evening.

Frank signed off on the text by sending the Schuylkiller's number. He directed her to run it in the morning as soon as she got in.

After interacting with Penny, Frank texted Conner. After telling his little man he loved him, he told him that he'd call, not text, the same time the following night. To Frank, everything seemed fine up in Michigan, and he didn't believe the Schuylkiller's claim to have someone standing by in case he didn't uphold his end of the bargain. It didn't matter, though, Frank would hold up his end of the deal, and he would either kill St. John, or be killed by him. He was now of the mindset that nothing else would matter to him until the sun rose on August 9.

An hour later, Penny, unable to sleep, could feel her skin crawl. She looked at the text Frank had sent her with the killer's phone number on it. She needed to find the Schuylkiller before he found Frank, so she called Denny Patel.

"Denny, it's Penny. I've got a cellphone number we need to trace. I need to know the name associated with it and an address. After that, we need to see what tower's it's pinging off of."

"Wait, who is this?" It was 10:15 pm, and Patel wasn't sure who was calling so late.

"It's Bristow. I think I have the Schuylkiller's cellphone number, and we need a name and address." There was urgency in Penny's voice.

"Frank's in danger, and I need you to do this now."

Denny Patel understood and said, "Give me thirty minutes!"

"Negative," said Penny. "You've got fifteen."

Penny got dressed and would risk anything to help Frank. Her fear stemmed from never having gone to FalconClaw before, and she certainly didn't know the layout of the basement. She'd hoped that Frank didn't mistake her for the Schuylkiller in the process.

It was now after 2 am, and Frank had nodded off. After thirty minutes, he was awakened by another rat gnawing at his feet. After his eyes fully opened, he saw a middle-aged man standing over him.

Terrified, he instinctively pulled the trigger on the Smith & Wesson, but it failed to fire. The man in front of him smiled, and it was then that Frank noticed he wasn't wearing his goggles. They had fallen off while he was asleep.

"Frank, you must wake up now. Frank, come on, Son." The man tapped Frank's boot with his foot.

No longer afraid, Frank thought he was dreaming. For a moment, he thought it was his father visiting him. As he looked closer, he saw that the man looked nothing like his father, yet looked very familiar. The style of the stranger's gray threaded, raven black hair and dated clothing told Frank the man was from another time. Perhaps a part of FalconClaw's past, a part of its history, a part of its fabric, he thought.

Frank thought he was dreaming again and wished he'd wake up. He felt a sense of wonderment. Even without his goggles, Frank could see the man in front of him because of a strange white glow lighting up the room. As Frank studied the stranger's face, he felt somehow connected. Much like the old man in the images from 1920, he felt as if he knew him. And then it hit him. It was Frank Bruno standing before him. Frank shook his head, trying to wake himself from his dream.

Just then, a voice came from the doorway at the front of the room. An old man was calling for Frank to join him.

Frank thought the old man, dressed in a long-sleeved brown flannel shirt, was speaking to him until the man hovering over him replied, "I'm on my way. My work here is done."

Frank Bruno looked down at Frank, kicking his boot again, and said, "You need to get up and go to work now."

Frank was again paralyzed by fear as he watched Frank Bruno join the old man at the door. Suddenly, all of his apprehension was lifted when he recognized the old man in the doorway as Garrison

Winter, the man in the photo from 1920. The same man sitting in the Solarium in front of the backgammon table.

After the two men from another time disappeared into the darkness, the subtle glow that had just moments ago washed over the room was gone. With it, the trepidation Frank had for what awaited him. Detective Frank Collazo rose to his feet and stepped forward. He no longer feared the darkness, and he no longer feared the man that all of North Philadelphia called the Schuylkiller.

In total darkness now, Frank felt the familiar tug on his boot. Was it the man that felt so familiar to him, or was it something else?

Frank closed his eyes and wiped away the ointment under his nose. He wanted to take in the foul and retched odor through his nose, the musty air through his pores, and the darkness through his eyes. Now fully aware of the time and his surroundings, he threw the backpack over his shoulder and moved toward the door.

Before donning his goggles and his weapon, Frank reached up and cradled his head between both hands and cracked his neck. The sound of bursting sacs in his brainstem freed him from the tension that no longer filled his heart. It was now time to go to work.

As he drew his weapon, Frank heard a commotion from the southern side of the basement. The side with the exterior basement door.

His heart began to pound when he'd heard the sound of a woman's cries. Peeking around the door frame, Frank could see his nemesis dragging a woman who had a pillowcase over her head and a belt around her neck. Her muffled screams told Frank she had been gagged. But he knew who the woman was. The terror in her sighs, and her familiar clothes, told Frank that it was Penny.

Studying St. John through the infrared, Frank tried to identify if he'd had any weapons on him or accomplices, but he saw none. He then compared the size of the man to his female victim and was reminded of just how big St. John was. At six foot two, and two hundred and thirty pounds, Frank could handle himself in a scuffle, but looking at St. John now, he knew he'd be challenged.

Frank saw that the killer wasn't wearing goggles and instantly knew he had the upper hand, as he possessed the power of sight and surprise. Looking again at the monster, he noticed that St. John was moving in a way that told him the madman's familiarity with the basement would benefit him greatly during a game of hide and go seek.

Frank aimed but didn't fire in fear he might hit Penny. He watched as St. John threw his captive to the ground and stomped on her. Through the pillowcase, Frank heard an agonizing moan.

Frank lined up the killer in his sights, his aim hindered by the infrared goggles. He would have to get closer. He again declined to discharge his weapon from the roughly fifty feet away.

Frank desperately wanted to save the woman he loved but would have to be calculated in his approach, or both he and Penny could be killed.

Choosing not to act, Frank watched as St. John pulled out a small penlight and placed it between his teeth, freeing his hands. He then watched the Schuylkiller reach up and grab hold of a nearly imperceptible latch, roughly eight feet high on the wall. Pulling one latch and then another, a false wall gave way and swung open, revealing a door that led to a room that had gone undiscovered in Frank's two previous trips to the basement.

The Sleep Room was now revealed, and the devil himself took his victim, now unconscious, by the feet and dragged her into the room.

Frank looked in all directions, surveying every square inch of wall, floor, and ceiling between he and St. John. Reaching for his backpack, his Smith & Wesson in his right hand, he pulled out a flashbang with his left.

He slowly crept down the hall toward the Sleep Room, careful not to drag his feet. As he got closer, he heard the monster begin to whistle. The next thing Frank heard was the sound of breaking glass.

Frank had inadvertently tripped the wire he laid out for St. John. The element of surprise was gone, and the homicidal maniac held the life of Penny in his hands, and there was a door between Frank and Penny's life.

The whistling stopped and was followed by complete silence. Frank could hear his own heartbeat and tried frantically to move, but fear had taken control of his legs, and they wouldn't budge. Standing frozen, he contemplated what to do next.

In near surrender, he exhaled fully and, with all his might, moved one leg and then the other. Now, free of his fear, instincts took over, and Frank dipped into a nearby room.

As he moved deeper into the room, he could feel the walls begin to close in. Claustrophobia now gripped him, and he'd realized the only way out was through the door in which he'd entered. Putting shelter between him and the next person to come through the door, Frank hid behind an old desk and plotted his next move.

"Well, well, well." St. John's deep cryptic voice echoed through the musty halls of the torture chamber.

Like several times before, Frank could detect St. John's smile as he exited the Sleep Room looking for his prey.

"So, Detective Frank kept his word. Sort of," said St. John. "I'm the one who brought your little whore with me."

Frank's fear and claustrophobic state made him dizzy as he surveyed the room, looking for anything that could help him. He crept to within several feet of the door and waited.

"Come out, come out wherever you are." The sinister voice of the madman got closer.

"I know everything. I know who you are. You're Getty Ewen Cameron." Frank's heart raced as he tried to buy time for his partner. "5446 Wayne Avenue!" Frank yelled. "Happy Birthday, Brother!"

"You know nothing about me." St. John's voice was calm.

"The Allan Institute, Heavenly Gates, Temple, August 8, 1990." Frank looked down at the flashbang and pulled its pin. Squeezing its trigger, he knew that it would explode in roughly 1.5 seconds after releasing it. He knew he'd have to get closer to the door and wait until he saw his target.

"The year I remember most is 1992," said St. John. "You're just feet away from where your father died. Just feet away from where you'll die, too."

After sixty seconds of silence, Frank had realized that St. John had turned the tables on him. Instead of looking for his victim in near-total darkness, St. John would hang back and make Frank seek him out. The very game of *Hide and go Seek* that Frank feared had begun. And Frank knew that Cameron St. John was far more familiar with the hell that he was in. A calculated approach was not an option as Penny was hurt and in grave danger. Frank had to act now.

Holding the flashbang, Frank's hand was beginning to perspire, and his grip on the device's trigger was weakening. He knew he'd have to let it fly soon.

Whistling again, St. John called out to Frank. "Yoo-hoo, Little Frankie, I just sunk a knife into your girlfriend's belly. I think she's hurt. You might want to come in here and help her. She's bleeding a lot, I'm afraid." The killer was merciless.

Frank heard a gurgling moan, and his heart sunk. Penny was dying, and he had to move, and he had to move fast.

Frank leaned several inches out into the hallway and looked south. Seeing nothing and no one, his M&P led the way. Now just feet from the Sleep Room, Frank yelled out, "Hey, Getty! Catch this!" He then let the flashbang fly. Banking it off the doorframe of the concealed room, he closed his eyes so the flash wouldn't blind him.

Frank then stormed the Sleep Room, his goggles painting the landscape green. Now inside, he could see the floating gases from the explosion and five body bags hanging from hooks, all sagging from the bottom and dripping the last of their bodily fluid onto the dirty white tiled floor. Frantically looking for the madman, his eyes raced around the room but didn't see the target of his ire.

Frank quickly surveyed the room looking for St. John but saw nothing except for two more hooks; Penny dangling from one of them, bleeding profusely from her gut.

In anguish, Frank cried out as her motionless body dangled above the red puddle that once gave her life.

Enraged, Frank turned to leave the room and, when he did, saw a blinding flash and then felt the searing heat of a bullet hit him in the chest. Frank never heard the blast. As he lay on the floor, his blood painting the filthy white tiles, he looked up at the ceiling and saw paint-chipped wood slats, all scarred by nail holes.

Smiling, his goggles lying to his left, Frank could see his father hovering over him.

Salvatore Collazo stood over his son, holding a penlight; he drew his city-issued, 9mm Glock and pointed it at his son's head.

As Frank looked up at his father, he smiled and said, "I'm sorry, Dad."

The voice of Cameron St. John regurgitated from the mouth of Salvatore Collazo and said, "I'm not sorry, Son."

Just before Cameron St. John pulled the trigger and cemented his legacy, his cellphone rang.

Puzzled and caught off guard, he pulled the phone from his pocket, inadvertently lighting up the room around him. He then slowly looked back at the door of The Sleep Room.

The light of her cell phone captured Penny Bristow's smile as she held it out for the madman to see.

The next thing the Schuylkiller saw was a muzzle flash. The homicidal sociopath was dead before he hit the ground.

Penny ran to her partner and found him bleeding from the right chest near his armpit, the area not protected by his Kevlar vest.

Penny dialed 911 and screamed for help.

Looking down to Frank's left, Penny saw the dead monster, his head lying in a growing pool of blood. His pants, soaking in urine.

Penny thought of her mom, Bonnie, and she thought of her love. Crying, she pleaded with Frank to hold on as she squeezed the wound to his right chest.

Epilogue – Home

Three months later.

Frank, Penny, and Conner stood in front of 454 East Locust Avenue.

"I can't believe it!" said Frank. His right arm, in a sling, still recovering from his wounds. "It looks amazing, Penny!" He stared in awe at his childhood home.

"Well, it should. The remodel took two months to complete." Penny smiled.

"But why? How?" Frank stood in astonishment.

"Frank, this is your home. It's always been your home, and you need to be here."

"Whattaya think, Conner?" Frank rustled his son's hair. "You want to stay here with Dad every other weekend?"

"More like every weekend, Pop!" Conner was elated.

"Conner," Penny addressed Frank's son. "I left a package for you and your dad up there on the porch. Why don't you go find it and tell me what you think."

Penny and Frank watched as Conner ran to the porch and found a small package. Clawing at the box, he opened it and yelled, "Oh, Boy!"

Inside was two baseball gloves and a ball. "Thanks, Aunt Penny!" Conner put the glove on and started playing catch with himself.

Frank looked at Penny with a tear in his eye and said, "Thank you."

"You need to play catch with your son when your arm gets better," said Penny.

"You're something else. You know that?"

Penny winked and smiled.

Just days after Cameron St. John, the Schuylkiller was silenced, The Mereby Estate awarded Penny the one million dollar reward. Penny took the money, bought Frank's dilapidated childhood home, had it remodeled, and would now give him the deed. Joanne's parents contributed money for the interior decorations, but Penny made sure she was in charge of the décor as she knew Frank wouldn't like anything the Conroy's picked out for him.

Penny also gave the family of Cindy McCurdy one hundred thousand dollars and paid for her burial plot in the Ivy Creek Cemetery, near where she grew up. Cindy McCurdy was the thirteenth and final victim of the Schuylkiller. And because of Penny, just as in the case of her mother, Bonnie Ross, Cindy was dead because of her choice of where to stay. Penny would have to live with that for the rest of her life.

The Schuylkiller had kidnapped McCurdy as she returned home from her boyfriend's house late in the evening of August 7. Penny was just inside on the phone with Denny Patel and was unaware of the abduction.

Cameron Ewen St. John mistook Cindy for Penny. A mistake that ended his reign of terror in North Philadelphia.

The front door opened to Frank's house, and Joanne and Polly yelled for Conner, Penny, and Frank to come in.

Frank looked at Penny and said, "You're just full of surprises, aren't you?"

"There's a few more waiting for you inside." Penny smiled.

After Conner ran in, Penny grabbed Frank's hand and kissed him. "I love you, Frank Collazo."

Penny smiled and said, "Come on! Let's check out our new house."

Frank shook his head and mouthed the word, "Our?"

When Frank walked through the door, Vance and Debbie Conroy were crowded next to Joanne, Conner, Polly, and Polly's son. On the other side of the room stood Captain Rosalyn Sumner, Robert Brooks, Ali Ashfaq, and Kyle Wade. All raised their beer bottles and congratulated Frank and Penny on their early retirement from the police force.

Frank just shook his head and smiled. At that moment, something caught his eye from across the room. He thought he saw the shadow of someone walking up the stairs just off the living room.

As the party guests celebrated, Frank excused himself and curiously made his way to the second floor. Once at the top of the stairs, Frank looked left and saw his mother and father's old bedroom door slowly closing. Unafraid, he walked over to the door, slowly turned the handle, and stepped inside.

Standing at a window that faced the backyard, Salvatore Collazo waved at his son to join him. "Hey, Frankie, come over here. I want you to see something, Son."

Frank walked over and looked out the window to see what his father was pointing at. As he stared deep into the backyard, he saw a mended fence, and he cried. He turned to hug his father, but his father had gone.

Minutes later, Penny walked in and saw Frank sitting on the end of the bed, crying.

Deciding to say nothing, she closed the door behind her and let the love of her life grieve again.

Later that night, after everyone had gone home, Penny walked out of the kitchen and saw Frank sitting on the back stairs, staring at the fence.

She handed him a beer and sat down next to him. "Welcome home, Frankie Boy. I hope you like it."

Frank tapped his beer bottle on Penny's, looked to his left, and said, "Thanks, Partner!"

"Burr, it's getting cold out." Penny nestled up against Frank and placed her head on his shoulder. She paused for a moment and then nervously asked, "Did you see him there?"

Frank knew exactly who Penny was referring to. "No. I always thought I would, though. I thought he was down there, Pen."

"When I was growing up, I always envisioned him in that hell, but now I think he's been here the whole time." Frank stared at the fence.

"I thought that, too," said Penny. "That's why I bought the house for you. I thought you'd feel closer to him here."

"I just miss him, Penny. I've always missed him." Frank sobbed. Turning to hold Penny, he broke down in her arms.

"I know, Frankie. I know." Penny stroked his hair. "I hope my mom meets him up there." Penny cried, too. "I hope he'll approve of me the way my mom approved of you."

"I'm so sorry, Penny. I'm sorry about what happened."

Penny pulled back from Frank and looked him in the eyes. "We got 'em, Frank. We got another bad guy off the street!"

"You saved my life, Penny."

Penny stood and looked down at the man she loved and said, "And you saved ours."

Frank smiled through his tears and nodded. Tilting his head in confusion and looking back at Penny, he said, "Ours?"

"I'm pregnant, Frankie." Penny smiled. Turning to go in, she said, "I'm going to get a shower and hit the sack. Take your time out here. Tell your father I said, hello."

Shaking his head, Frank smiled, looked back at Penny, and said, "If it's a girl, we call her Bonnie."

"That's a deal." Penny and Frank bucked the notion that a child should have their own identity and not be named after someone else. Anything to carry on the name of Penny's mom. Bonnie Ross's only grandchild would keep her memory alive and remind Penny and Frank of the treasure that was lost on Easter Sunday, 2017.

"Penny," Frank said right before she walked into the house.

"Yeah?"

"They're never gonna find Frank Bruno, you know."

Penny seemed to know what Frank was trying to say. "Was he there?"

"Yeah," said Frank.

"So, it was him, then?" Penny looked off in the distance and pondered for a moment.

Frank shook his head in confusion. "Whattaya mean?"

"It was dark," said Penny. "I didn't know where you were in the basement, but I could feel St. John's presence." Penny paused. "But then I heard a voice, and I thought it was your father's."

Frank could hardly speak. "What did he say?"

"He said, 'Call Him.' He was telling me to call the number that you'd given to me. So I did. And there he was, lit up like a Christmas tree. Cameron St. John was impossible to miss." Penny got her revenge on the man who'd killed her mother, and friend.

"Huh." Frank shook his head and said, "I'll be damned. He saved both of us, then."

Frank turned to look at Penny, but she'd gone.

He rose and turned to walk into the house. Finishing the last of his beer, he turned for the door when a cold gust of wind reminded him that it was November in North Philly. Something was pulling him to the fence. When he'd turned, he saw his father.

Standing at the fence, a toolbox at his feet, Salvatore Collazo waved his son on again.

Frank joined his father and said, "It looks great, Dad."

"You think so?"

Penny looked down from the second-floor bedroom window and saw Frank standing near the fence, alone. She loved him, and she knew that he loved her.

"I do, Dad. You did a really good job on it."

"I tried, Son." Salvatore Collazo put his hand on Frank's shoulder and said, "I'm just sorry that it took so long to fix it. That it took so long to mend your broken heart."

"It's okay, Dad."

Turning to see his father walking back toward the house, Frank yelled out, "I love you, Dad!"

"I love you, too, Son."

Salvatore Collazo walked into the house, and Frank smiled. His father finally came home, and he did, too. That would be the last time Frank Collazo would ever see his father. And Frank was okay with that.

Now, back inside, Frank looked around the house before going up to bed. As he turned for the stairs, something on the mantle caught his attention. Standing on the hearth, Frank picked up a picture frame and studied it closely. The picture was faded in black and white, but Frank recognized it from the basement of FalconClaw.

It was the picture that he'd stuffed in his backpack. Penny found it after the shooting and thought that it was important to Frank. It was an old man wearing a brown flannel shirt. Garrison Winter was smiling, and Frank was, too.

Frank's thoughts suddenly flashed to when Penny Bryce had gone missing from FalconClaw early on Christmas morning back in 1974. Frank smiled and knew that Penny was in good hands. He knew that she was safe with Old Man Winter and that she and Frank Bruno would be partners forever.

Six months later, FalconClaw was finally demolished, and Frank was there when it came down. Leaning up against his new Dodge Charger down on 888 Bedford Street, Frank looked up the hill from just outside the rusted gates and watched as the fabled mansion was turned to rubble. The sound of cranes and bulldozers faded for a moment and were replaced with the voices of yesteryear. Penny Bryce, Frank Bruno, Old Man Winter, and his father, Salvatore Collazo, had all moved on. Neither the place nor its memories would haunt Frank any longer.

As he stood to leave, his eyes became focused on the street number placard that had adorned the estate gates for one-hundred and fifty-four years. Frank removed a crowbar from his trunk, walked over to the gate, and ripped the faded white placard off the brick pillar it had always called home. Holding the weathered, oval sign in his hand, he could hear it whisper 8-8-8.

Just before getting back into his car, a cold gust of wind rolled down the hill from the mansion, causing Frank to look back up at the home. Staring in awe, FalconClaw had been restored to its original glory, if only for a brief moment. Frank shook his head when seeing the sight. After rubbing his eyes he looked closer. There, just south of the front entrance, Frank could see four silhouettes disappearing over the hill around the southeast corner of the estate, forever. Frank shook his head again and smiled.

The End

Special thanks to my friend, **Bonnie Ross**, who inspired a portion of my story with her own. Bonnie is and always will be an inspiration to all women and all people. She has spent her life fighting for Women's Rights and for the rights of all women. I honor her story and her fight and am proud to have her appear as a character in my story.

Though the story of Miss Ross's life is fictionalized in my book, her dedication to the advancement of all women is far from fiction. Bonnie Ross, I salute you, and as a father to three daughters, I join you in the cause. Girl power is willpower!

Bonnie, you're my hero and my muse. I will always try to live up to the lofty standards you have abided by your whole life. Thank you for the tour of Philadelphia and the stories of your fight for equality, and your memories of Penny Brace.

Warm Regards,

Michael Cook

A shout-out to my friend and all-around good guy. Philadelphia's finest, **Ali, (Ash) Ashfaq**. Thanks for the tour of the many local sites and scenes featured in my book. I owe you a debt of gratitude and feel lucky to call you a friend.

Stay safe out there on the mean streets of North Philly!

Billy Murphy's Irish Saloon

3335 Conrad Street Philadelphia, PA 19129

(215) 844-9683

Thanks to my buddy, **Mike (Murph) Murphy**, operator of Billy Murphy's Irish Saloon. Thanks for giving my main characters someplace cool to hang out and grab a bite while they hunt down a serial killer. I'd sit down with you for a beer anytime!

A cool look at additional locations used in the book:

Ravenscrag (FalconClaw) Montreal, Canada

https://en.wikipedia.org/wiki/Ravenscrag,_Montreal

The 39th District Headquarters – Schuyler Street side

McMichael Park

The Kelly House

The Historic Strawberry Mansion

https://www.historicstrawberrymansion.org/

The Twin Bridges & The Train Trestle

The Trolley Car Café & Back Parking Lot of the Creative Minds Daycare

The Schuylkiller's House

Fabrics

Frank's Childhood Home

Euthanasia – Understanding the facts.

In this story, I touch on euthanasia, and I want to ensure that you, the reader, understand what it is and what it's not.

Please use the links below to learn more.

https://www.healthline.com/health/what-is-euthanasia

https://bpded.biomedcentral.com/articles/10.1186/s40479-020-00131-9

Mental Health Hotline:

1-800-662-HELP (4357)

https://www.samhsa.gov/find-help/national-helpline

Other titles by this author:

Old Man Winter – Heavenly Gates

Black Earth – How We Got Here

What truths lie in the black void between the stars?

Back to Black Earth

What truths will be revealed?

www.BlackEarthNovel.com

Made in the USA
Columbia, SC
05 August 2022